Romance for All Seasons

WINTER WARMTH

EDITED BY

ANNIE REED AND DAVID H. HENDRICKSON

TVInk
Thunder Valley

Romance for All Seasons
Winter Warmth

ISBN 978-1-954460-08-9

Contents

Introduction

DAVID H. HENDRICKSON

Welcome to *Winter Warmth*, the first issue of *Romance For All Seasons!*

I love writing romance short stories. The problem has all too often been finding a place to publish them. Romance short story magazines don't exist.

And much like the old philosophical question that asked, "If a tree falls in a forest and no one is around to hear it, does it make a sound?" stories without readers... kind of miss the point.

Sure, there can be joy simply in the writing. But from the earliest days of humans gathered around a fire telling stories, the storyteller has needed an audience. It doesn't have to be a big one. Just someone to listen or read and be fascinated or terrified or moved.

Especially *moved*. That's the big one for me. I need someone on the other side of the story, reading or listening, and I need them to be *moved*. Which is why romance fiction is so awesome. It *moves* readers even when they know a happily ever after is coming.

But how can the romance short story writer connect with an audience that doesn't exist beyond the occasional yearly themed anthology? Such was the dilemma until the birth of *Heart's Kiss* magazine in February, 2017.

Heart's Kiss promised to be a game-changer, a major publication filling a gigantic void. When I heard about it, I was euphoric. I was especially pleased that it was edited by Denise Little, who had previously bought two of my stories in other genres for DAW anthologies. This was perfect. Not only a major romance magazine—finally!—but one edited by a woman who appreciated my work!

What could possibly go wrong?

At Denise's suggestion, I sent her two of my stories and waited with eager anticipation.

And waited.

And then waited some more.

As it turned out, Denise had been replaced by Lezli Robyn and Tina Smith, who didn't know me from Adam and who, according to Denise, promised to make *Heart's Kiss* cool and hip. She suggested that I send them one of the two stories but not bother with the other, set in Old Testament Israel. Not exactly cool and hip.

Not exactly cool and hip myself, I sent Lezli and Tina both stories, figuring I had nothing to lose, and waited for at least one rejection and probably two.

To my shock, they bought both! The Old Testament Israel story was actually a "terrific story about female empowerment."

It was a literary marriage made in heaven.

In what felt like the blink of an eye, they then bought my Christmas Eve story "The Boy in the Boxers." And not only bought it, they requested a sequel. What happens the next day? I'd never written a sequel to a short story before. Never even thought about it. But I accepted the challenge and wrote "The Girl in the Glitter," which both they and I loved. I couldn't wait to write the next story for them.

Lezli, Tina, and I were going to, literarily speaking, live happily ever after.

Until, that is, the publisher pulled the plug. *Heart's Kiss* would be no more. So much for the literary marriage made in heaven.

Which put romance short story writers back to square one. No romance magazines.

And so it remains.

Enter Annie Reed, one of the best short story writers alive (and whose novels are also outstanding). She is my writing "accountability partner." Each month, we exchange our goals for the month and our results from the previous month. As part of these exchanges, we recently bemoaned the demise of Kristine Kathryn Rusch's *WMG Holiday Spectacular*, an advent calendar for fiction that provided subscribers with an original story in one of three genres every day from Thanksgiving to New Year's Day. One of those three genres was romance, providing a terrific reason to write romance short stories for the holidays. Arguably, it was the only market for romance short stories you could count on. Now it was gone, too.

Annie, who had edited a Valentine's Day romance anthology (and had the good taste to buy a story of mine), had ruminated for a while about a quarterly romance anthology that would cover all four seasons, not just the winter holidays. It was, I thought, a brilliant idea, but it remained only that for a few more months until she finally popped the question, literarily speaking.

We've been talking about this for months, she wrote in an email. *Let's create* Romance for All Seasons, *starting with* Winter Warmth, *and then* Spring Fling, *and then just keep going. Original romance short stories every three months.*

Since you're reading this now, you can guess my answer. I said, literarily speaking, "I do! I do! I do!"

Now, as I look at the amazing stories we've assembled here, I feel an overwhelming sense of pride and excitement at the release of *Winter Warmth* and the promise of more to come.

Wow! You are going to *love* these stories!

Introduction

ANNIE REED

Welcome to the first issue of *Romance For All Seasons!*

If you read David Hendrickson's introduction (and you really should), you know how this anthology series came about. What you don't know is why I'm involved in the first place.

I'm primarily known as a mystery and crime writer. Or at least that's how I thought of myself when I first started taking this writing gig seriously. Yes, as a friend of mine pointed out at the time, my first few short story sales were science fiction and fantasy. Heck, my first pro sale was to *Strange New Worlds,* a *Star Trek* anthology series that had nothing to do with the current television show. So was my second sale.

Then my third sale was to *Ellery Queen Mystery Magazine.* Back to mystery and crime.

However, I spent a lot of time before those first pro sales writing romance stories. I am, at heart, a romantic. Not the jewelry-and-flowers type of romantic, but one who believes in the power of love that lasts. I *want* the couple who falls in love over the course of a story or a movie or a television series to get their happily-ever-after, and I'm grumpy when that doesn't happen.

Seriously grumpy.

In fact, I have from time to time wanted to knock some sense into showrunners who believed the couples on their highly successful shows had to break up over stupid stuff merely for the sake of "drama." Nope! Not for me. I'm in it for the happy.

That's the thing about romance stories. Even if the story ends with a happy for now, which sometimes is all a writer can fit into a short story, that happy for now implies that the characters will have a much longer happily-ever-after. That's the guarantee a good romance story makes to the reader.

Mysteries make the same kind of guarantee to the reader, only in the case of mysteries the guarantee is that the central mystery will be resolved by the end. Note that I didn't say *solved*, I said *resolved*. There's a difference.

Maybe that's why both genres appeal to me. Mysteries resolve the chaos of the crime. Romances resolve the chaos of the meet-cute (and boy are some meet-cutes chaotic!) and the getting to know each other, back and forth dance couples engage in before they finally get together.

When David and I decided to actually go forward with *Romance for All Seasons*, we weren't sure what kind of reception we'd get from the writers we invited to participate. As David pointed out in his introduction, magazines and anthology series for short romance fiction don't really exist, so we weren't sure how many people besides us were writing short romance stories. Plus, since this series is a project of the heart, we knew we'd have to launch it as a royalty share project, which meant the writers wouldn't be getting paid up front.

Well, we needn't have worried.

We received enough submissions to fill two anthologies this size. Both of us read the stories, and then we had spirited discussions over email trying to figure out how to stick to the word-count limit we'd initially set for these anthologies.

We failed. Miserably.

What you're holding in your hands or reading on your e-reader of choice is a supersized issue because your two co-editors couldn't *not* include each and every one of the stories in this issue.

Like C. S. Stein's "The Baron and the Hanukkah Miracle."

Neither David nor I read or write Regency romance. In fact, we told the writers we invited to participate that a Regency story would be a hard sell. So what did C. S. Stein do? They not only wrote a wonderful Regency romance, they wrote a wonderful Jewish Regency romance that gosh-wowed both of us.

That's just one example.

Johanna Rothman made us laugh at dancing chickens. Karen Abrahamson introduced us to the splendor of Lipizzaner horses. Susan Kroupa made me, a cat person, love dogs. Robert Jeschonek and Dayle Dermatis introduced us to two vastly different types of deer. Ron Collins took us back to the Vietnam era, while Cate Martin took us back even further to the time of Prohibition and backwoods stills. Stephannie Tallent gave us music. Melissa Yi gave us ice skating. Lisa Silverthorne gave us crowded airports and snow, so much snow! Alexandra Brandt and Tina Back gave us holiday celebrations of a different type. And Robert McCarter gave us a nostalgic look back at a perfect childhood day that resonated through the years that followed.

What ties all of these stories together is the romance between the couples that practically radiates off the page. These writers made us fall in love with their characters because they made those characters come alive for us in the best possible way. When you read these stories, I think you'll understand why we couldn't say no to any of them.

David and I each have a story of our own in this issue. David had final approval of mine and I had the final say-so on his. As it turned out, our stories each have a bit of an edge to them before they get to that happy ending. It's another thing we have in common, like our enjoyment of American football—although we do root for opposing teams.

Winter Warmth is the first of four planned seasonal *Romance For All Seasons* anthologies. We'll be back with more stories in the spring, summer, and fall of 2026.

As I said earlier, this is a labor of love. David and I both think the world can use a little more love these days. The writers who contributed to this anthology clearly feel the same way. I hope you enjoy their stories as much as we do.

The Idiot and the Odyssey

RON COLLINS

WHEN MOM SPOKE UP, I WAS READING *THE ODYSSEY*, sprawled over the long, cloth couch in the living room with one bare foot draped over its back and the other pushed under me, knee crooked up to help hold my book. Sure, it was late December, going on Christmas, but even late December in Long Beach can be warm. It was probably seventy that afternoon. I was wearing shorts and my Cal State-ULB sweatshirt—Navy with gold letters.

The shorts were white.

A real tree stood in the corner of the room, smelling of pine and glittering with silver tinsel.

"Bobby Layne gets back on Thursday," Mom said in that casual tone that was anything but.

She was in the living room, too, bent over the ironing board she'd set up earlier, and focused on pressing the hot edge of her iron into the seam of Dad's white shirt. Dad was an accountant. Clearly, his shirt had to be pressed.

"I don't care about Bobby Layne," I replied again, annoyed at having to reread the last sentence. I'd already heard he was coming home, which was good for him. But *The Odyssey* was not light reading.

"He's a good boy," Mom said apologetically, though I could tell she wasn't apologizing for interrupting me. "Madge said he's a full corporal now. Hopefully, he'll be home for good soon."

I bit my lips to keep from snapping.

Bobby Layne may or may not be a full corporal, but as far as I was concerned, he was a Five-Star jerk, and I may or may not be just a college kid, but if there was one thing I already learned when it came to men, it was that once he's an idiot, he's always an idiot. "There's no such thing as a partial corporal, Mom," I finally said.

Mom set the iron on the flat board, and a soft, clicky ping warned against touching it.

The scent of baked linen seeped over the living room, and the tinny sound of the radio filled the room. Frank Sinatra's "Have Yourself a Merry Little Christmas."

Mom loved the Voice, which was annoying. Sure, the guy could sing, but it's 1966 for crying out loud. And Sinatra is no George Harrison. Not even a Paul or John. Or Ringo, for that matter. Ringo may be goofy, but he's a fun kind of goofy. She stood silently until the pressure of her stare made me look up.

"You could do a lot worse than Bobby," she said.

"Seriously, Mom. I need to read this."

The corner of her lips turned down, but to her credit, she didn't say anything else.

Madge was Bobby's mother. She and my mom got together with three other women at least twice a week. *Your mother's Gab Group,* Dad called them, and sexist or not, he wasn't really wrong. The group shared recipes, hairstyles, and vacation plans, mostly. I guessed they still talked about school things. Madge Layne had been president of the PTA at one point, and Mom had been an assistant muckety muck of some sort, but that was back when Bobby and I were both going to Lincoln Elementary. To be fair, Mom's Gab

Group got a lot of things done in their day. She was really kind of amazing.

But now I think they mostly brag about their kids and gossip about neighbors.

The thought made me suddenly angry.

I had no idea what I wanted to do with my life, but spending it raising Bobby Layne's snot-nosed kids and ironing Bobby Layne's crisp white shirts for twenty years and then spending the rest of my life gabbing with a bunch of neighborhood women was not it.

Then, of course, I felt embarrassed.

You do what you can. Mom was a very good mom.

It *was* good that Bobby was coming home, too.

I knew that.

Backward-minded jerk or not, he had been in Viet Nam for over a year now, and we'd been friends before. More than friends for a while.

I couldn't pretend I wasn't worried for him.

But no matter how hard my mom pushed, I had better things to do than darn Bobby Lane's socks for the rest of my life.

And *I* was home for Christmas, too, but that didn't mean the rest of my life had just up and walked away.

I needed to get an essay about the central themes of *The Odyssey* turned in first thing when I got back to campus, or Professor Hilton was going to fail me good. Since Dad was already on the edge about the idea of me going to school rather than earning a secretary's salary while waiting for Mr. Right, this was not on my list of Things I Needed To Have Happen. And the fact was that I hadn't learned how to write an essay while I was in high school.

I know. Bad on me.

But it meant I needed to work both harder and smarter, or I was a dead fish.

And *The Odyssey* wasn't going to read itself.

I had to focus.

After several moments of awkward silence, I turned back to the book.

THE C-124 CARGO TRANSPORT THAT NEWLY MINTED Corporal Bobby Layne was hitching a ride on hit a big bump of air, and a ridge of the hard metal plate that served as his seat stabbed his spine.

"Yee Haw!" one of the other five soldiers strapped in across the way called, then brayed loud enough that Bobby could hear it over the hard grind of the engine noise inside the bay. "Do it to me, Shaky! Do it to me!"

Bobby gasped, clutched the letter from home in his fist, and held tight as the plane settled.

Despite her nickname, "Old Shaky," the 124 was a solid craft, if not known for comfort. In addition to its allotment of six hitch-hiking soldiers, this one was full of equipment destined for places Bobby didn't want to think about. He loved his country, and he wanted to serve, but the war was getting confusing.

He'd probably be bruised for half his time home.

The other soldier's name was Lee Johnson. He was headed to Alabama. Bobby figured this was the only time the two of them would ever be together, but he never knew. That was a thing about the Army. Maybe you see the guys you're with a hundred times, maybe you don't. Best work with him like he's your brother, even when he's not.

"Like a rollercoaster joyride, eh?" Bobby called back.

"Compliments of Uncle Sam!" Johnson grinned.

Bobby wasn't complaining, though. The aircraft would get him and the other guys in the bay home for fourteen days around Christmas, so as far as he was concerned, the 124 was the Cadillac of all rides.

After the ride settled, Bobby folded his mom's letter again and then shoved it into a pocket in his jacket. Olive drab, of course. The height of fashion. The sleeves carried his new stripes. But it still had the earthy smell of Vietnamese grasslands ground into it, a scent that reminded him of the guys back there. He pressed his hand down the jacket, feeling the letter crinkle inside. He could quote it back without looking, but he liked the thin feel of the paper, and he liked running the edge of the fold over his fingertips, so he was constantly pulling it out of his pocket, reading it, and then putting it back.

He rested his head against the metal fuselage and flashed on a single sentence.

Gail is back from school that week.

He grimaced, feeling the foreboding sensation of being lost.

Gail McIntyre was the one thing about coming home he wasn't sure of. She had been his mom's favorite of his ex-girlfriends, and not just because she was the last before he shipped out. She was so much the favorite that every letter from home carried a section that updated him about things going on around her.

But Gail McIntyre had made her opinions of him clear when they broke up.

Nothing to see there.

Not that he blamed her. He'd been an ass, but at the time he didn't think he said anything wrong. I mean, *of course*, Gail would do the cooking. He'd just been poking fun, but facts were also facts. They weren't the commune type, after all. Not hippies at all. She'd shop and she'd make drinks for him like his mom did for his dad.

When she gave him hell, he was so surprised that he got angry and he told her... well, he said things he wished he hadn't said and maybe called her some things he wished he hadn't called her.

The memory made him feel like he'd been gargling acid.

At first he'd just been stupid, but then he'd been a real ass.

He liked reading Mom's letters, though.

Gail was going to school, just like she said she would back when he made so much fun of her. She was studying literature. Mom said she wasn't sure it was going to last, which only proved that Mom didn't know Gail McIntyre like he did.

Ass or not, reading about Gail had helped Bobby get through a lot of the past year. She was beautiful, of course. He would always remember the first time he saw her eyes. Dark and brown. They were comfortable eyes, so easy to look at, set over rounded cheekbones and in a face surrounded by a wild mop of hair that never did what she wanted it to do, but was better for it. That wasn't why he liked reading Mom's letters, though. Thinking about her gave Bobby a connection he couldn't fully explain, even to himself. He liked her gumption, to use an old-fashioned word he figured she'd get mad at him for using. He liked how thinking about her made him feel.

To be sappy, when he'd first understood the mess he'd gotten into, Bobby Layne had decided Gail McIntyre was the person he was there fighting for, and sappy or not, she had been enough to get him through a whole crap ton of jungle.

The engine ground away outside the C-124.

As if on autopilot, Bobby pulled the letter from his jacket, then ran his finger over the crease. As much as he feared her response, Bobby couldn't pretend he wasn't thinking very hard about seeing her again.

"Go help your father," Mom told me. She was anxiously washing the silverware for the party they were throwing tonight.

"I'm kind of busy, Mom."

I was on that same couch again, reading harder than I had ever read before, desperately jotting down every thought the text was giving me into a spiral pad and trying to imagine how they would go into what would certainly be the worst essay ever penned.

The party is Dad's thing. A community dinner on Christmas week.

He picks up huge cuts of beef, a couple of whole chickens, and a turkey, then borrows rotisserie grills from Mr. Baines and Mr. Washington, and spends all day marinating the meat in a super-secret recipe of oils that he promises he'll reveal on his deathbed. Then it's onto the grills for an amazing slow cook. The result is always delicious. Between all that, he spends the entire morning putting up traditional decorations, which consist of strings of lights that run over the hedges along the side of the house, another set that goes along the roof gutters, and then a big Santa with a red bulb for a nose.

Bring your own beer, bring your own dish, but the meat was on my dad. And the neighborhood always came out. It was one of those events of the year.

When I was a kid, it was neat.

All my friends were jealous, anyway. Now it's only mildly embarrassing.

But whatever, right?

It's not Christmas until Dad throws his party. The thin whine of those rotating rotisserie spits is as much of a trigger as Bing Crosby's "White Christmas" will ever be.

He always picked a day that fell a few days before Christmas.

Close enough that everyone's ready to celebrate, but far enough away to recover in time for the real thing!

Naturally, this year he chose the Thursday that Bobby Layne came home.

Even before that tidbit arose, I was truly dreading the party. I still wasn't done reading *The Odyssey*, which meant I wasn't going to finish my report on time, and which meant my scholastic career was officially doomed to go down in flames.

"I don't care if your Titanic is sinking, I need you to go help your father before he falls off the ladder and breaks his neck."

I grumbled.

"Go," Mom said, pointing with a knife.

Closing the book with a *thunk*, I dropped it on the coffee table and went out to save my father from falling to his death before he could pass down his secret recipe.

———

BOUNCY BETTY OF A FLIGHT OR NOT, BOBBY LAYNE landed ahead of schedule.

From the base, he flagged a taxi.

It was a sunny, cloudless day. Warm, but not humid. The breeze buffeting through the taxi's open windows was clean and sharp. So different from the stagnant feel of the jungle. *The world is a big place*, he thought, realizing even then that it was not Long Beach that had changed. The taxi was old but in good repair. It drove a helluva lot better than the jeeps he'd been in for the past year, anyway. The cabbie had a statue of Jesus dangling from the rearview mirror. Christmas music played on the radio between advertisements. Bobby had always liked Dean Martin, but was surprised to find his new version of "I'll Be Home For Christmas" hard to listen to now because he kept thinking about how Dean Martin hadn't gone anywhere at all.

The streets felt different, too.

Smaller, maybe.

The cabbie was probably thirty-five. He wore a flat cap and drove with the crook of his elbow hanging outside his window. He was chatty, and seeing Bobby's jacket, he was full of questions about the war. *Good thing we're there*, he said. *Can't give the Reds an inch, I tell ya. Not an inch.* The cabbie's fervor made him uncomfortable.

"Thank you," Bobby said though, because he appreciated the man's heart.

The Laynes lived around the corner of Kendrick Street and down five houses from the McIntyre house. As the cab turned the corner, Bobby recognized Mr. McIntyre stringing lights in his front yard. Three rotisseries stood side-by-side in the front yard.

It must be tonight, he thought, recalling the annual neighborhood party.

"Stop here, will ya?" Bobby said automatically.

"The address is up there," the cabbie replied, pointing off toward Bobby's place.

He stopped when Bobby pressed him, though, and even declined to take money for the ride as Bobby lugged his duffle out of the taxi. "I'm glad you boys are there," the cabbie said once more as the car drove away with a cloud of exhaust.

Bobby hefted the duffle to his shoulder and went to the house.

"Mr. McIntyre," he said, craning his gaze up the ladder as he approached.

As he spoke, the front door squeaked open.

I FROZE IN PLACE.

Bobby stood there at the edge of the sidewalk, drenched in sunlight. He wore fatigues, a jacket, and a pair of heavy boots. The duffle was obviously heavy across his shoulder. The asphalt under his boots gave a rough scritch as he shifted his weight.

He was as handsome as ever, of course.

Maybe more so now that the army had chiseled him.

He looked stronger. Bigger. But maybe darker, too.

His hair was cut close to his scalp.

His eyes were the same piercing green they had been before, but they seemed deeper now than I remembered them.

When our gazes locked, I felt like I'd been pinned in place.

"Gail," he said as if he'd forgotten I lived here.

Or maybe not forgotten so much as hoped? I didn't know for sure because my brain was apparently on strike right then.

I wasn't prepared for this, and I didn't know what to think.

Bobby had been a year ahead of me in school.

He'd played football and baseball. He made grades that were good enough, but not so good that they made him nerdy. It was fair to say that every girl in my gab group in school thought he was as big of a catch as Mom did, so when we dated, it made me a thing.

Then he made it clear how things would be if we were together, and, thank God I guess, that was the moment I knew I couldn't live like that.

So, no, I did not care about Bobby Layne.

But here he was, fully grown up, and I couldn't stop looking at him.

"Welcome home, Bobby," I said because I needed to say something.

"Thank you," he said.

"Ahem." It was Dad.

"Do you need some help, sir?" Bobby said to my dad, lowering his possessions to the ground and moving to take hold of a string of lights.

"Always open for a hand," Dad replied.

"I can do it," I said in a tone that was too sharp. I wasn't letting Bobby Layne into my family like that.

I stepped off the porch and took the lights from Bobby's grip. He let them go easily.

"I thought you needed to study?" Dad said.

"I'm the one who gets to say when I need to study," I shot back.

"But, your report—"

"I'm sure your mom and dad will want to see you," I said to Bobby, riding a spike of adrenaline that crashed through me.

I pushed the string of lights deeper into the depths of the hedge, feeling the brittle edges leaves against the skin inside my wrists. I always get a rash when I tangle with the hedges, but that was a problem for another time.

I ran that entire string of lights.

When I went to get another, Bobby was gone. My gaze went down the street just in time to see him turning the corner, heavy bag on his shoulder.

"I THINK SHE'S GOING TO FAIL OUT," BOBBY'S MOTHER said an hour later, after he'd surprised them by arriving at the door, and after she had cried on his shoulder for half that time, and then after his dad and his brothers had all given him their firmest handshakes complete with their opposite hands on his shoulder.

His sister, who was only six years old, was shy at first, then broke into tears, too.

It was nice to be home, but he felt strange now, sitting in the quiet of the living room.

"How is it over there?" His youngest brother had asked the question Bobby knew they all wanted to ask.

"It's all right," he replied, mostly because he didn't know what else to say and also because he didn't want to scare Mom. Bobby was her oldest. "I hope this is over before it's your turn," he said to Sammy, his next oldest brother. Sammy would be eighteen in six months.

"Probably over by this spring," Bobby's dad said with enough confidence that Bobby knew he'd have believed him last year. "LBJ's sending the whole damned army over there now. The VC can't last much longer."

Later, though, sitting at the kitchen table made of Formica and sipping the sun tea his mother had been brewing all morning because she knew he was coming, Bobby had asked about Gail.

His mom gave a coy smile and began to talk. *I think she's going to fail out,* she said somewhere in there, explaining that Pat McIntyre, Gail's mom, had been upset that all Gail was doing on her trip home was *reading that damned book.*

Bobby sipped his tea as Mom explained that Gail had to read the whole of *The Odyssey,* which was clearly out of her league, and why any young girl would want to do that, and better yet write about it, was beyond her.

When Mom got around to summarizing all the reasons Gail McIntyre was going to flunk out of college, she said it like it was a good thing.

"I'd say she's going to be looking for a guy any time now," she said, finishing with a wink that Sherlock Holmes might have used to prod Watson. *Come now, man, the game is afoot!*

Bobby sipped the tea. Its grainy flavor was tinged with lemon.

Outside, the sun moved across the sky.

The McIntyres' party would start soon. He could already smell the aroma of basted meat coming to temperature. He recalled the fierceness of Gail's expression as she ripped the line of lights from his hands. She was fighting, he thought then. Angry.

Out the window of his mother's kitchen, Bobby's gaze fell on the old sugar maple, recalling how, when they were younger, all the kids would climb up into it, but how it was always him and Gail who climbed the highest. He had been stronger than her. Bigger than her. He could beat her in almost everything else. But in climbing that tree, her lithe body was a better asset. The branches accommodated her better.

She always climbed higher than he did.

Bobby held onto his smile, feeling it cross his face stronger than it manifested itself physically, and feeling something he'd never really felt before.

Yes, mother, Bobby thought then. *The game is afoot.*

Just not the one you think.

My sister pounded on the bathroom door.

"Come on, Gail! I need to finish getting ready! You've been in there forever!"

"In a minute!" I yelled back.

The rash had come before I was even finished with the hedges. I used the bathroom and cleaned up as best I could, then put on pants and a nice top because my Mom said I couldn't wear my ULB sweatshirt again. Whether I liked that or not, on this matter, she'd made it understood that she was the queen of this castle. Fine. When I was finished, I doused my arms in Calamine lotion, but it could only do so much. Now I was a pink mess, and my arms still itched up and down the back of my shoulders.

Tonight was going to be a Christmas disaster.

I stared into the mirror, feeling stupid, and as mad as I could feel about just about everything in my life, the biggest right now being the fact that I was going to be paraded to the entire neighborhood, and that I'd be pulling an all-nighter no matter what Mom said, and, of course, because I knew Bobby was going to be there and I had no idea what to say to him.

I'd been dumb to react like that. A total ditz. Embarrassing as everything.

Bobby wasn't even doing anything. Just standing there. But I let the idea of him get to me. Or maybe he *was* trying. Maybe he showed up here in his military outfit specifically to wedge himself under my skin. I was certain Mom had spilled all my beans to his mom. He probably knew I was struggling, and after our big blowup, he would probably have a field day watching me melt down.

Idiot.

Only this time it was me who was the idiot.

Even if that's what he wanted to do, I had let the moment get to me.

I could have beaten him at his own game. Let him do the thing with Dad and gone back to work. That would have shown him. Let him get the rash, and use the time to focus on my paper.

Not that it would have mattered.

I was going to fail.

"Dumb," I whispered to myself. "Dumb."

My sister pounded on the door. "Gail!"

"Coming." I grabbed a handful of the tissues I'd been using to spread Calamine lotion and opened the door. We changed positions in a flash, and I saw out the front window that even if it wasn't dinnertime yet, neighbors were already standing in the front yard, talking in a murmur of voices that was going to grow to a strong rumble over the rest of the evening.

I was dead. D. E. A. Double-dead.

Even if I had the time, I was never going to get the quiet I needed here.

I wadded the tissue I'd been using to dab Calamine into my clenched fist and went to the kitchen to throw it into the trash.

That's when I saw Bobby standing at the back door, hand shading his eyes, and peering in.

He was in his dress uniform now. Clean-cut and pressed to so much perfection that I thought perfection itself had used Mom's iron on him.

"What do you want?" I said after I stepped through the panty hall and yanked the door open with enough vigor that he almost tumbled inside.

A blast of the smell of Dad's grilling rolled into the little foyer.

It smelled good, but Bobby smelled better. He was wearing a cologne I'd never experienced, not on him at least.

Bobby gathered himself, then stood taller and held out a firm hand. "Your presence is requested."

"Excuse me?"

"Trust me," he said, then stepped back to give me space and motioned me out of the house. "I'm not going to hurt you."

"I told you before, Bobby. We're finished."

Even as I said the words, though, my chest froze up.

He looked so good. And he stood there with such calm confidence that I thought I might break. And I was going to fail. That much was certain. No grade on this paper, do not pass Go, do not collect $200. His jaw set, and he steeled himself. That *was* something new about him, too. The old Bobby would have flown off the handle when I told him to go pound sand, but this Bobby didn't rise to my rebuke at all. Instead, he simply regrouped.

I didn't know whether to be annoyed or not.

I put my hand on a pantry shelf to make sure I stayed steady.

"What are you up to?" I said, but I wasn't sure it mattered.

Bobby Layne may be a jerk, but I knew he wasn't going to hurt me.

"Please," he put his hand out again. "I have something I want to show you, and it would mean a lot to me if you came along."

My thoughts ran in an infinite number of directions for several beats, but at the end of that infinite process, I still didn't know what to say.

"All right," were the words that came out of my mouth, though I wasn't sure how. "Anything's better than the party, right?"

He laughed then and took another step back to give me even more space.

I closed the door behind me.

We left by the back way, which allowed us to avoid the crowd that was gathering in full force out front—a crowd I could hear included Bobby's mother, and so I assumed also his father.

"You look very good in pink," he said of my Calamine arms.

I rolled my eyes and tried to ignore the fact that I enjoyed the compliment.

Otherwise, the walk—made longways around the block—was

pleasant, if made in somewhat awkward silence broken only by the sharp clip of Bobby's dress shoes on the sidewalk. As we neared his house from opposite my street, I frowned.

"What are we doing, Bobby?"

He put his finger to his lips and let us in the front door.

The layout of his place was familiar in that way of a place you've been to before, but has changed in some subtle ways. The pictures, maybe. Or an arrangement of flowers.

The door shutting behind us felt good because the house was quiet.

"Come on then," he said, pointing me to his room.

"Bobby?" I said.

"I promise," he said. "You'll be fine."

I took him in. Standing in his military uniform, draped in something that felt like calm anticipation. I felt something more than safe in his gaze. Something almost dazzling in the way his lips nearly smiled. It made me think of him standing at the edge of our front yard that afternoon, wanting to help my dad.

We went down the hallway to his room, which was lit only by the fading light that streamed in from a window to my right.

He flipped a switch on the wall.

His bed spanned the wall on that right side, perfectly made, window closed above it.

His closet spanned the left-most wall, sliding door closed.

Across from me, though, was the big table, a piece of furniture that was made of heavy, red-stained wood, that he sat at to do his schoolwork back in our days at school, and that he used to draw the incredibly detailed comic doodles he used to make all the rest of the time.

A thick book lay on the table beside a desk lamp.

A copy of *The Odyssey*.

A notepad and three sharpened pencils lay beside it.

He turned on the lamp, and everything got brighter.

"What is this?" I said.

"Your study hall," he said, unable to restrain the sense of pride that beamed as brightly as the sun. "While I am out running interference for you at the party tonight, you are going to work on your paper."

Heat rose to my cheeks. "What?" I'm sure I stammered.

"Then, tomorrow, if you will have it, I would like to take you to the library."

"You want to take me on a date?" I said, still frozen.

Bobby chuckled and ran his hand, almost sheepishly, across the back of his neck. "I would love it if you thought of it like a date, but mostly, since it seems you need someone to stand guard over your studies, and since I feel imminently qualified for that role, I'm offering my services. The library seems to be a good place for that."

"I don't understand."

Bobby took a deep breath. His eye took me in completely, covering me in ways that I'd never seen from anyone before, but that in some fashion I knew had always been hidden somewhere deep inside him but had now found its way out.

For an instant, he seemed to choke up, and for that same instant, I thought he might cry. But he didn't. Instead, he finished the deep breath and looked at me with such... understanding... I thought I might melt.

"I'm sorry I doubted you, Gail McIntyre. I'm sorry I pretended you were dumb, that you were dumb to have dreams. I was wrong. I was cruel, and I was an idiot. But I understand things better than I did before. And I believe in you. I think you were made to do something big, and if I'm being honest with you—which I promise you I will always be from now until forever—I think I want to do something big, too." He turned his gaze away to collect himself, then came back. "I just don't know what it is."

"I see," I said, feeling power in Bobby Layne, and sensing that power as it mixed with that cologne he was wearing to become a thoroughly dangerous combination.

"If you can forgive me," he said, standing before me and scanning the room in the way of a lost puppy, "and if I can manage to make it back here again, I would love it if we could do whatever those things are together."

"I forgive you," my body said before my brain thought it. That didn't matter, though. My body was right. I could tell. My body understood what that book sitting on the table that Bobby Layne had led me to meant. I was going to succeed. Bobby Layne was going to see to that himself. I was going to pass this class.

My body knew something else, too.

Before those words *I forgive you* were out of my mouth, I had already stepped closer to him, and I had already wrapped my arms around his neck.

Bobby's embrace drew me close, and a new glimmer came to his eyes.

This time, when his chest rose with a breath, I felt it against my own.

"I think it's time you got to work," he said, his lips close enough that I felt the heat of his breath.

"Now, Bobby," I said, my voice feeling suddenly husky. "I'm the one who gets to say when it's time for me to work."

Then I kissed him, and the odyssey began.

RON COLLINS IS A BEST-SELLING SCIENCE FICTION AND Dark Fantasy author who writes across the spectrum of speculative fiction with over 30 books and 200 short stories to his credit. His short fiction has received a Writers of the Future prize and a CompuServe HOMer Award. His short story "The White Game" was nominated for the Short Mystery Fiction Society's 2016 Derringer Award.

He has contributed to Analog, Asimov's, *and several other maga-*

zines and anthologies (including several editions of the Fiction River Anthology Series). Check out his website at https://www.typosphere.com.

About "The Idiot and the Odyssey," Ron says:

"I wanted to set a story in a Christmastime location that wasn't filled with traditional December chill. I also wanted to do something with historical context. A soldier's trip home is always ripe for high emotions, so this one started for me with the image of the idiot on the plane... but it became real when Gail showed up, sprawled out over her family couch, reading."

The Four Dog Night

SUSAN J. KROUPA

BETH SLID INTO BED ON THE LAST NIGHT OF THE YEAR, curling up with her back to the space that had been Mark's, and took stock of the situation. Despite her efforts, which honestly felt heroic, her life had not changed substantially over the last year. Something had to be done.

After Mark had died, sick a year and now dead for three, she'd allowed herself two years of grieving—the first in fierce weeping and chasm-like panicked sobs, the second less intense but with such a profound, bewildering lack of focus that she felt dead herself.

At the beginning of the third year, she'd decided it was time to get her life together. Fortunately, she worked at a library. She had resources: books, magazines, articles brimming with advice for the grieving, and she worked to put it all into action.

She made lists from the recommendations: daily exercise, getting up early, sunlight, reaching out to friends. She went to her doctor and got an antidepressant. Honestly, she was practically a poster child for all the self-care memes on social media.

Every morning, no matter the weather, she got up early to sit outside with her coffee and recount all the reasons she had to be grateful: for having Mark for twenty-six years in the first place—more happiness than many got in a lifetime. And for her children, Andy and Jessie, who had grieved with her, who had held her as she wept and struggled to survive, who were always there for her even if they could occasionally—okay, often—lapse into bossiness. For good friends, neighbors and coworkers, and the fact that she had a comfortable two-story home in Utah Valley, and enough to live on without worry. And, and, and... she could go on with all the things *right* in her life and often did until her coffee was cold in the cup.

But if she was going to be honest, if she faced the truth... she was lonely. She ached from it, a physical pain as real as the spasms in her back when she lifted something too heavy, a pain all the gratitude in the world couldn't erase. Because the hole left with Mark's passing swallowed all the things gone right. Something needed to change.

She got up and went to the window, pulling aside the sun-blocking curtains she needed in Utah summers and on winter nights like this one, where temps dipped into single digits. The sky was black, speckled with bright stars. A storm had passed through a few days before and replaced an awful brown inversion that had lingered like a bad bout of flu with clear air and a fresh coating of snow. No moon, but the snow still reflected light.

Then, shivering because she kept the room cool at night, she dived back under the covers, pulling the plush microfiber blanket close around her, sinking into its warmth.

Tomorrow.

With that, she slipped into the off-and-on-again sleep that now was an established part of her nights.

The next morning she took action. She called the minute she thought Jessie would be awake.

"Hey, Mom. What's up?" her daughter asked in a groggy voice.

"I've made a decision," Beth said. "I—"

"You're going to do it?" Jessie asked, the sleepiness instantly gone. "Brian's really a nice guy. I mean, he'll never be Dad, but Tyler thinks he's great."

Beth scrunched her eyes closed. Tyler was Jessie's fiancé. She'd forgotten about Brian, a widower who was a friend of Tyler's parents. "No," she managed, then in a firmer voice, "No, I don't want to go out with Brian." Year three had also been the Year of Dating. At best it had all the fun of getting her socks wet on a rainy day's walk. At the worst, excruciating. "No. I've been thinking about this for a while. I'm going to get a dog."

There was a moment of silence. Finally, "A *dog*?"

"For company," she said.

"You need *human* company," Jessie said. "You can't hide from life forever."

Hide from life? She'd done everything but wear a goddam spotlight.

"Many women in my demographic prefer life alone," Beth said cooly. "You know as well as I do that being alone is better than being in a relationship that isn't working." Before Tyler, Jessie had had a close call with an engagement to a man who clearly wasn't a good match. Beth's personal name for him had been "the jerk," but she'd kept that to herself.

How could any new relationship be as good as what she'd had with Mark? No one wins the lottery twice.

"Maybe I'll be ready down the road," she continued into Jessie's silence. A long, narrow, winding road. She loved her daughter and couldn't have survived the last three years without her, but Beth had to live her own life.

"What if you get a dog and don't like it? You can't just discard it. A dog is a ten or twelve year commitment." Jessie could have been reading one of those moralizing Facebook memes. "Dogs are a lot of work, you know. And you don't even like Loki much."

Beth had to admit her daughter was right. She *didn't* like Loki much. Loki was Jessie's aptly named miniature Yorkshire terrier, a barky, annoying, needy animal that spent most of its time shaking and begging for affection. But fortunately not all dogs were like Loki. Weren't there as many different types of dogs as there were people? She just needed to do research.

Jessie, never one to give up easily, said, "I still think you ought to give Brian a chance. Tyler's folks have known him for years. Lost his wife to cancer, but—" she added hastily "—that was almost four years ago."

Beth had exploded once when Jessie had suggested a potential date with a man who'd been widowed less than a year.

"A *year*?" she'd shouted. "Just shoot me now! He's going to be a hot mess."

No, she didn't want to meet Brian. She wanted to learn as much as she could about dogs, about different breeds, which ones shed a lot, which ones didn't bark or shake all the time. Surely, there could be a dog out there that would fit into her life, become a friend to take on walks, and snuggle against on lonely winter evenings. A dog that would alert her when someone was at the door but was otherwise quiet. She just needed to do her research. And make a list. A nice list that would lead her to the dog of her dreams.

Jessie was saying something about Brian.

Suddenly impatient—so much research to do—Beth took the path of least resistance. She loved her daughter, who was, after all, only trying to help. She sighed, scrunched her eyes up one more time. "Okay. One date with Brian. But don't get your hopes up."

BETH MET BRIAN AT PIZZA AND MORE IN PROVO, A NEW place that her daughter recommended. Beth had insisted they come in separate cars. She never gave strange men her address, even ones vetted by people she knew. You couldn't be too careful these days.

"The food's wonderful," Jessie had told her. "And now that

you're a dog person, you ought to like the place because they allow dogs." Beth heard the smirk in her voice.

"Only the canine kind, I hope," she'd retorted, and Jessie had laughed, but then in an earnest voice had said, "Just give him a chance, okay?"

"Okay," Beth promised, even though the idea of dogs being there piqued her interest more than meeting Brian.

After a few humiliating experiences when she'd first tried dating again, Beth made it a habit to arrive early. She quickly discovered that she became too nervous to really look at the menu and had consequently made some poor food choices given that she tended to be a sloppy eater. The stain from the time she'd had barbecued ribs had never come out of her favorite blouse.

So she arrived promptly at 5:10 for their 5:30 date. Usually she was a bundle of nerves, but tonight she was just eager to see the dogs. She'd been researching them all week at work, and now she would be at an actual laboratory for studying how dogs acted in public.

She found a parking spot near the restaurant and was grateful she and Brian had agreed that a weeknight would be less crowded and that earlier would be better than later. The single-digit cold bit through her coat as she crunched across the snow to the entrance of Pizza and More. But inside, she was greeted by steamy, fragrant air in a welcoming place, rustic, with dark wood paneling and furniture.

A smiling young woman—maybe about Jessie's age—with a name tag that read "Kelsey" raised her head and smiled.

"For one?" she asked cheerfully. No judgement in her voice.

"Two," Beth said. "I heard dogs were allowed here?"

"Sure! In the atrium." Kelsey gestured off to the right.

"Could we be seated there?"

"Of course," Kelsey answered warmly. "Would you like to go to the table now or wait for the rest of your party?"

"I'll wait. But could I have a menu?" Beth took one of the seats lined up by the doors, which let a blast of cold air in every time someone walked through.

She had decided which pizza to order by the time Brian arrived at 5:28. At first glance, he looked good. Great even, as he shrugged out of his puffy quilted coat. Tall, he had the lean frame of a cyclist. Good hair, too, flecked with gray but wavy and over his ears. Was she being shallow or what?

"This way." Kelsey led them through the main area into a spacious room with a glass-paneled ceiling. The floor here was tile and the tables Formica rather than wood—probably easier to clean if a dog misbehaved. She was disappointed to see that the room was only about half full and there were only four dogs.

But Kelsey ushered them into a table next to one of them, a large, orange, curly-haired poodle. Or perhaps doodle. Nobody could tell for sure these days, but she suspected poodle. Either way, really cute.

"Enjoy," Kelsey said, handing them menus.

Brian stiffened. "I'm sorry. Do we have to be in here?" He cast a disapproving glance at the orange dog.

Kelsey looked chagrined. "Oh. Sorry." She turned to Beth. "I thought you requested that we seat you—"

"I did." Beth turned to Brian with the apologetic but firm look that she used at work when she had to deny a patron something they requested. "I really wanted to be in here, if you don't mind." She didn't quite bat her eyes, but she looked up at him imploringly. "I'm, um, doing research on dog-friendly places and wanted to check this out."

The muscles around Brian's mouth tightened. Clearly, he did mind, but he said, without much grace, "Okay." With another hostile glance at the dog, he sank down into the chair. "Not very sanitary," he said in a voice loud enough to make Beth cringe.

The man with the orange dog sat at the far side of his table with a view of Brian's back. He had reddish hair, white in places, and ruddy skin. A round, pleasant face. Intelligent blue eyes. And friendly, she thought. She was pretty sure he'd overhead Brian's complaint and worried he might be offended, but he seemed more amused than anything else. Almost smiling. And then, to her consternation, he looked directly at her. For an awkward moment their eyes locked. Intelligent, Beth thought again. And somehow familiar. Had they met before?

Then, feeling her face flush, she wrenched her gaze back to Brian, and forced herself not to look at the man behind him.

Poor Brian, she thought, who was staring stiff-jawed at the menu. Was he aware of how quickly he'd fallen from grace? Of course, to be fair, his opinion of her must have taken a dive as well.

A skinny young man came by for their drink order, a beer for Brian and a Diet Coke for her.

"Do you not drink?" Brian asked in a careful voice. She wondered if that was important to him.

"I do. A little. But I'm driving." Beth refrained from stating the obvious, but Brian answered the unspoken question with a smile.

"Two beers with a meal won't put me over the limit."

And, in fact, the beer seemed to help. By the time he'd finished the first and ordered another, he grew quite cheerful, even after she'd declined his suggestion that they share a pizza.

"I like to have leftovers," she said. "To take for lunch at work."

He frowned slightly and she suspected he was used to having people follow his suggestions. But then he asked about her work which led to conversation about her job at the library and then his job with a local insurance company. Maybe being in insurance made him more risk aversive, she thought, realizing his remark about sanitation still stung.

By the time their pizzas arrived, he was positively chatty, telling her about his biking and camping in considerably more detail than perhaps she needed. But eventually he turned to her. "Are you doing a paper or something? On dogs?"

Beth, who had been studying an overweight Golden Retriever

under the table of a plump blonde woman, drew her attention back to Brian. "Not exactly. I'm thinking about getting a dog. For company, you know."

"Dogs are a lot of work," he said, sounding like Jessie in lecture mode. "You'd do better with a cat. Can leave them if you go on trips. Not as needy."

Beth, who had cats growing up and loved them, disagreed. She'd seen plenty of needy cats. But she didn't feel Brian was in the mood for a discussion on the topic. "I'm allergic." It was true enough.

Brian nodded sympathetically. "Too bad."

Somehow, Beth lost control of her gaze and looked beyond Brian straight into the eyes of the man behind him, who grinned back at her. They shouldn't put these tables so close together, she thought, irritated. She jerked her head down and tried to listen to Brian, but all she could think of was the man. Where had she seen him?

She realized Brian was talking again. "—big screen, high definition—" he was saying. "Maybe you'd like to come over and watch the game on Sunday?" He smiled, charming and good-looking with his curly hair.

"Game?" she asked. *Focus*, she told herself.

"It's one of the biggest football games of the year." He almost beamed with enthusiasm.

Football? Just shoot me now, she thought. Except she must have said it out loud. Brian's face drained of color, his eyes stricken.

Flooded with shame, because she would never have been so rude intentionally, she stammered, "Sorry. I didn't mean to say that. I... I just don't like football much. But I didn't mean..." Her mouth closed. Brian had stood up.

"I think... I think this has gone on long enough," he said. "Don't you?"

Honestly, yes. She'd known the minute he'd complained about the dogs. She nodded, mutely, tears filling her eyes.

"I'm sorry." His voice softened. "But best to quit as soon as you know."

He must have thought she was crying at the fact he was leaving rather than from embarrassment. She couldn't find any words.

Still in a gentle tone, he said, "I'll get the check. It was, um, nice meeting you. Good luck finding a dog." He turned and hurried out of the room.

Beth stared at the half-eaten pizza on his plate wondering if she'd kept her word to her daughter, if she'd given him a fair chance. Wondered, ashamed, if he'd be sad or bitter as he walked back to his frozen car.

She pushed her own piece of pizza aside, all appetite gone. She usually took all her leftovers, but knew she could never eat this.

She wiped her eyes with her napkin and reached down for her purse.

"Excuse me." The man from the table behind Brian's chair stood in front her, his dog on a leash beside him.

She stared up at him.

"Excuse me," he said again. His voice was full of concern, but there was a certain twinkle in his eyes. "Ginger here is an AKC therapy dog and she thinks you might feel better if you could pet her. She's been worrying about you being exposed to someone who recommended you get a cat rather than a dog. Brutal. No one should have to face that. What do you think?"

Beth couldn't help but laugh. Was that the best pickup line in the history of romance? "Eavesdropper!" She *knew* he'd been listening.

"Your friend had a loud voice," he said without apology.

"Well." She thought a moment. "You have a very well-behaved dog," she conceded. "And beautiful."

The man gripped the back of Brian's chair. "I tell her beauty is as beauty does. Would you like to pet her?"

Beth nodded and Ginger moved forward and placed her head on

Beth's lap. She stroked the dog's head for a few minutes, amazed at the softness of her fur.

"Standard poodle?" she ventured at one point.

That brought a smile. "Yes! People usually think she's a doodle. They're so popular now."

"I've been studying dog breeds," Beth said. And because everything about this man seemed somehow safe, she added, "I think I need a dog. For company."

"Ginger would approve," the man replied.

After a few minutes, Ginger pulled her head away. Beth took a deep breath. "Thanks! I really do feel better!"

"She's good at her job." He stroked the dog under her chin, then straightened up. "I'm pretty sure we've met before. You worked at the Provo library, right?"

"Yes! Still do in fact." Beth frowned, trying to remember. "I'm sorry. You look so familiar but I can't quite..."

"It was a long time ago. You helped my son Adam with a research project on the Omega Nebulae."

And then she recognized him. The father with brilliant but socially awkward son. She'd been impressed by how gently he'd guided the boy into interacting with her, into learning how to do his own research. "I remember! He worked on it for several weeks. How is he doing?"

"Good! Graduating from UVU in the spring." His face shone with pride.

"And... and your wife?" Beth remembered now that he'd been married.

There was a pause. "She passed away. Five years ago. She was sick during that time."

Another silence. Beth noticed there was no ring on the freckled hand clutching the chair. She remembered something else as well. How much she'd liked this man. How interesting she'd found him.

And then, because she was happily married, how she'd quickly dismissed the thought from her mind.

"I'm Beth Thompson." She offered her hand.

"Jim Swenson," he said, taking it.

And if there weren't any visible sparks when they touched, there might as well have been for the way Beth's heart jumped.

With another smile, so engaging as to easily out-charm Brian, he asked, "Mind if I sit down?"

"Sure," she said her mind still reeling from the handshake. "No! Wait!" She squinted up at him. "How do you feel about football?"

———

THEY TALKED UNTIL THE RESTAURANT CLOSED. SHE learned that Adam had been the youngest of three kids, the only one still living at home but with plans to go to Cal Tech after he graduated. Learned that Jim's wife, Sandra, had struggled with multiple sclerosis for most of their marriage and eventually died from it. Learned that he worked as a software engineer for Adobe and loved his job. And learned that he also loved football. He ducked when he told her that, as if she might hit him, and she laughed harder and longer than she had in years.

In turn, she told him about her life, Mark's cancer, Andy on a career path to be a physical therapist, Jessie in nursing school, about her own love for books, which made her job at the library a joy.

Jim loved books as well and they talked about favorite authors and moved on to music, movies and mountain trails. And, of course, dogs. Ginger was one of a stream of dogs that had graced Jim's family's life, and it seemed there was little he didn't know about them.

More than once, as they talked, Ginger got up to rest her head on Beth's lap. She seemed to love having her ears rubbed. Beautiful dog, Beth thought, her hands stroking the soft fur. And then, remembering the warmth of Jim's hand, beautiful man.

Be careful, she warned herself. Take things slowly.

"I think we should take things slowly," he said, as if he'd read her mind.

She nodded, relieved, although to be honest a bit disappointed as well. But it was the wise thing to do.

"Me too."

He reached for her hand then, took it and held it as they talked, held it until the skinny young waiter evicted them. They hastily exchanged phone numbers before bundling up and venturing out to the frozen parking lot, mostly empty now.

Jim stopped by the closest car, a Forester. "This one's mine," he said, clicking his remote. The car beeped. "Let me just get Ginger in —I don't want her paws to freeze."

He opened the hatch and Ginger hopped in, shook vigorously, and lay down.

And then he walked with her as she led him to her car.

"Text me when you get home?" he asked.

She nodded. "I will." She turned to open the door, when she felt his hand on her shoulder. He leaned in and gently drew her to him. "See you tomorrow?" he asked, his voice soft.

"Definitely," she murmured.

He opened the door for her then, and she climbed inside. The seat was cold, but her heart warm, and as she started the engine and slowly pulled out onto the street, she wondered if it might just be possible to win the lottery twice after all. And wondered if she'd just stumbled upon the ticket.

SUSAN J. KROUPA IS PERHAPS BEST KNOWN FOR HER Doodlebugged Mysteries, a gentle cozy series featuring the irrepressible, obedience-impaired sniffer-dog, Doodle. But before she let her writing go to the dogs, she had stories appear in Realms of Fantasy, *and in a variety of anthologies, including* Bruce Coville's Shapeshifters *and*

Writers of the Future Vol X. *Her newest book is* TreeTalker, *praised by the Booklife Prize as "a gripping contemporary fantasy with relatable characters."*

Susan lives in Utah with her husband and Toby, a trouble-prone poodle. You can find more about her on her webpage, https://www.susankroupa.com.

About "The Four Dog Night," Susan says:

"The story began in my mind as the image of a woman staring out into a snowy, star-lit night wondering what she can do to change her life. While I often have the title to a story before I begin writing, in this case I was halfway through before I realized that, like so much of my recent work, the story was once again going to the dogs. Four of them, in fact. I'm not sure how this happens! But I had fun writing the story and I hope you enjoyed reading it."

A Waste of Cycles

DAVID H. HENDRICKSON

As DAWN BROKE, THE SPRAWLING, SNOW-COVERED campus in rural Western Massachusetts felt like a ghost town. Almost all of the university's forty thousand students had completed final exams and headed home for the holidays. Only a few stragglers remained.

Inside the giant athletic complex, alone on the pool deck, Mia closed her eyes and let the once-familiar smell of chlorine flood her senses. It was a sensation she had both loved and loathed in years past. The *grind* of two-a-day swim practices, up at the crack of dawn before school and then back at it again in the late afternoon or early evening. Six days a week. Over and over and over. No letup. It never stopped. Doing her homework on the way to the pool while Mom drove.

The *thrill* of those two-a-days. The *opportunity*. The sweet, blissful opportunity. Yes, six days a week! Yes, opportunity! The opportunity to slice through the water, streamlined like a dolphin, feeling as if she was actually *atop* the water, skimming across the surface. Lungs bursting. Body aching. Over and over and over without letup.

And on those good days, who would ever want to let up? Coach Crowley blowing that shrill, annoying whistle of his to kick off the latest set, the whole list of them spelled out on the whiteboard hanging on the wall at the deep end of the pool below the lime green team banner.

Dryland three days a week *before* getting in the water. Because too much was never enough. All leading up to the exhilaration of competition.

Those were the days. The beauty of the grind. The bliss of the grind. The eventual reward of the grind.

Feeling bone tired all the time. Muscles achingly sore. Ravenously hungry after practice. Until her last two years of high school, stopping at the Mickie-D's a half mile away from the pool—a half mile that felt like a hundred miles—devouring half the menu—she didn't just want a burger, she wanted the whole damned cow—or at least as much as Mom would allow while protesting that Mia was "eating us out of house and home." Substituting healthier choices those last two years, but still ravenous nonetheless. Don't give me just the grilled chicken breast. Give me the whole damned bird. Hell, the whole damned chicken coop. Got to fuel the engine.

Never a question that it was worth it. First-place ribbons and medals galore. A few New England age group records. Only a notch below qualifying for the Olympic tryouts.

The best of times. Her closest friends were other girls on the team. Traveling together to swim meets all throughout New England. Lots of local ones, plus the overnight trips up to Dartmouth College and even to St. John, New Brunswick. She and her friends listening to the same song over and over again on the way, driving Mom and Dad nuts. Which, of course, had been half the fun. The groans and eyerolls! Sweeter than a chocolate éclair! And at night in the hotel room, Mom warning them that if they didn't get to sleep before Dad did, he'd keep them up all night with his snoring.

And then the dream came true, a full ride scholarship to swim here, a perennial power in New England and routinely ranked nationally in the Top Twenty.

Life wasn't just good. Life was great.

The celebratory team dinner. Basking in the praise from coaches and teammates for her dedication, all the hard work, all the sacrifices. And then the following celebratory family dinner at her favorite restaurant. Her family's pride and praise. Her deflection of the praise —at least some of it—to Mom for getting her to all those practices.

The pinnacle of all the many celebrations the family had rejoiced in at her achievements.

Life was truly great.

Until it wasn't.

Until everything changed.

The car accident on a late summer night, the summer that was supposed to lead into her freshman year. Dad behind the wheel, as usual. But tragically so was a hopelessly drunk, stoned-out-of-his-gourd, twenty-six-year-old A-hole traveling the wrong way on the interstate.

Hit them head on. The car all but exploded.

As did Mia's life. Her family, wiped out. Mom, Dad, and even her older brother Joey seated next to her in the back seat, all pronounced dead at the scene.

In the days and months to follow, Mia would often wish the carnage had claimed her, too. Emergency surgery saved her life— barely—but at the cost of both legs. Double amputation above the knee. The fifteen broken bones and torn ligaments in her upper body, a mere afterthought. The emotional wreckage, to be repaired at a later date.

If ever.

And so it was that she sat here on the pool deck in her wheel-chair, her once-strong legs reduced to thigh-length stumps. Her shoulders now muscle-bound and huge. Freakishly so, she feared. Freakishly so, she knew. Her flowing hair still shoulder length and chestnut brown. Her complexion, clear. Her once-brilliant, beaming smile, now but a memory.

A year and a half removed from the nightmare. But who was she kidding? She would never be able to remove herself from the nightmare. It would remain burned into her charred soul until the day she died.

Mia opened her eyes and looked out onto the eight-lane, Olympic-sized pool stretching fifty meters to the far end. The twenty-five-foot-by-thirty-five-foot state of the art scoreboard hanging on the wall at the far end, blank and lifeless. The retractable stands on both sides that could seat over two thousand cheering fans, cold and empty.

Mia drew in a deep breath, took her old green swim team cap off her lap, and tugged it on. While tucking her long hair inside, the cap snapped against her right ear, setting it to ringing. Something that had happened only a million times before. She pulled her goggles on and wheeled herself astride the starting block for the rightmost outside lane.

The lane for the lowest-seeded swimmer. Never her lane back in the day. She was always in the middle. The top seed. The one all the others were shooting for. The one with the target on her back.

Now, she was the bottom seed in the outside lane. The hopeless underdog. Sucks to be you.

But I'm here, dammit! I'm here.

Mia began the transfer from her wheelchair to the starting block on her left. Not much different than the transfer to her bed or a sofa or a chair, a move she'd done what now felt like a million times. She slid her butt forward in the chair, turned slightly away from the platform, pressed her left hand onto it, pushed up and on. From the backpack affixed to the back of the wheelchair, she removed the fold-up half-bench, unfolded it, set the metal brackets, and rested it on the pool deck. Half the height of her wheelchair's seat, she'd use it as the mechanism to get back into the chair after first hoisting herself from the water to the deck.

She had hoped no one would ever watch her through the process, but knew it was inevitable if things worked out with the team. She couldn't just levitate back into the chair. The bench was a necessary evil, as was the emergency pager she removed from the backpack and with a feathery touch, leaned over and dropped to the deck.

She slid her butt to the edge of the starting block, then slid just a tiny bit further and dropped into the cool water.

It washed over her, cool and familiar and wonderful. It had been so long. Almost a year and a half. She had both dreamed of this moment and dreaded it, too.

She checked her goggles and cap. All set. Her heart pounded. Her mouth was dry as cotton.

I'm here, dammit! I'm here!

She'd set no records, win no medals or ribbons. So much had been lost, never to return. So very much. But she was here, dammit. She was here.

She pushed off, using both hands even though all her instincts told her to use feet that were no longer there.

For a brief moment, it was glorious. Feeling herself slip through the water again after all this time. And then it all went to hell.

DESPERATELY TRYING TO STAY AWAKE AND BARELY managing it despite the cold winter wind whipping into his face, Tyler didn't see the woman until she almost ran him over.

He'd never felt more bone-dead tired in his life. He'd been up all night working on an extra credit project to save his grade in Foundations of Algorithms, and he wasn't close to finished. The professor had thrown him a lifeline, but right now Tyler felt more like a drowning man who'd been thrown a two-ton anchor. And it had hit him squarely between the eyes.

Maybe he just didn't have what it takes to make it in the university's prestigious Honors Program in Computer Science and Electrical Engineering. He'd always been the smartest kid in the class in high school, albeit at the special school in Germany for sons and daughters of military people stationed there at the Boeblingen base. And he'd done reasonably well in all his other courses in this his first semester at the school. But the Algorithms class had him wondering if he could add two plus two and come up with four.

The answer *was* four, wasn't it?

He sipped his now lukewarm, bitter black coffee—he'd decided in typical self-loathing fashion that he didn't deserve sweetener until he conquered this project, *if* he conquered this project—knowing that he was already overcaffeinated. But what was the alternative?

Sleep was not an option. He only had two more days to pull off the miracle, and he was so far from being up to the challenge, he couldn't even *find* the challenge. Not even with his own two hands and a flashlight.

An Honors program fraud. He no more belonged in it than on the basketball team. And although he looked reasonably athletic—six feet even, a hundred eighty pounds with broad shoulders and dirty blond hair cut short that would fit the part—he'd learned long ago that he didn't have an athletic bone in his body. It had made his supremely athletic Marine sergeant father furious, prompting him to finally say in exasperation to his wife, Tyler's mother, "Are you sure this kid's mine?" and even mutter unfulfilled, surely-not-serious threats of a paternity test.

His father hadn't been serious, had he? Or had he been dead serious? He was dead serious about everything. Had as many comic bones in his body as Tyler did athletic ones.

Which was why Tyler couldn't get anything less than a C in Foundations of Algorithms. Even that grade would jeopardize his position in the prestigious Honors program. And for Tyler, it was Honors program or bust. His father would accept nothing less. If Tyler were an athlete, like so many of those who were also staying in the Intersession Break housing with him, the normal academic track would be satisfactory.

But not Tyler the Klutz. Who was well on his way to also becoming Tyler the Moron.

He'd hoped the brisk, cold wind on this short walk to the twenty-four hour campus café for a breakfast sandwich would wake him up. Sharpen his senses. Perhaps even, miracle of miracles, give him a burst of inspiration on how to get past what seemed like an insurmountable problem with his project.

But no.

He was still drop-dead tired. His backpack containing little more than a laptop still felt like it weighed ten tons. And he was still stuck on the Algorithms problem.

Still dumb as a rock.

And freezing his ass off besides. Snow flurries had begun whipping through the air, making him blink furiously as they blasted into his face—the gods spitting at him, he thought with rueful, morose humor.

He continued along the massive expanse of the athletic complex on his right, a series of ten interconnected edifices to the university's obsession with athletics at all cost, now barely visible through the thickening flurries. Which was fine with Tyler. Better that he couldn't see a single building at all. The very word *athletics* made him cringe. Reminded him of his father's words of abject disappointment.

Are you sure this kid's mine?

The woman in the wheelchair came out of nowhere—from the athletic complex main entrance off to the right—and almost blindsided him.

Tyler saw her through the flurries at the last minute, just as her cry of warning belatedly registered in his fatigue-addled mind.

Tyler whirled away from her.

Slipped on an unseen sheet of ice.

Windmilled his arms, coffee spraying through the air. Felt himself tilting horizontal.

Turned sideways, instinctively protecting the laptop in his backpack.

And then landing hard on his side. *Oomph!* The remaining coffee —once-lukewarm, now cold—splashed over his face.

Tyler blinked. Either coffee or snowflakes were in his eyes. He wasn't sure which. He blinked again.

"Oh my god, I am so sorry!" the woman exclaimed, eyes wide, leaning forward, her right arm outstretched. "Are you all right?"

Tyler blinked in disbelief.

He'd almost been hit by a goddess in a wheelchair. A *goddess*! Long chestnut brown hair. A cover model complexion so perfect God must have used Photoshop. And the most beautiful emerald green eyes. So very wide now in shock.

Unless of course, he'd hit his head hard, been concussed, and she was hideous.

"I never saw you!" she said, her voice husky with concern. "I'm so sorry! The flurries, you know? I never saw you. Are you all right?"

Tyler swiped the cool coffee and cold snowflakes off his face, blinked yet again, and propped himself up on one elbow.

"I'm fine," he said, shaking his head. "I never saw you coming either. Yeah, the flurries. And sort of deep in thought."

He slowly got to his feet, wincing.

"Sorry about your coffee," the goddess said, looking up at him now from her wheelchair. Looking like an angel. Snowflakes in her hair. "I was probably going too fast—definitely going too fast—but I was hurrying because of... because of the snow, you know?"

She was most definitely a goddess *and* an angel. Not to be superficial about it. He'd dated plenty of girls that offered other than mere looks. But holy smokes, there could be no doubt, possible concussion or not. She was a goddess and a snow-flecked angel.

Talk about thunderstruck! This woman had thunderstruck *and* poleaxed him!

"Don't worry about the coffee," Tyler said, shaking his head. "It was already cold. I was just on my way to the café. I'll get another one there."

"I was headed there myself," the goddess said. "Mind if I join you?"

Did he mind? Tyler almost laughed but kept his reaction to what he hoped was just a very broad smile. "Sure."

"You're sure you're okay?" she asked again.

"I'm fine. Great, in fact."

"Well," the goddess said with a twinkle in her eyes, "at least you stuck the landing."

HE DIDN'T SEEM TO GET THE JOKE, WHICH WAS disappointing. But what could she expect? Fly out of the athletic complex like a bat out of hell, race down the ramp and onto the walkway, almost run the guy over and then expect him to laugh uproariously at your quip?

Not fair.

If he proved to have no sense of humor at all, that would be truly disappointing because he was good looking as all heck. Not that all that stuff mattered anymore now that she was... well... what she was. Good-looking boys didn't need her kind of baggage. They could do better. No need to settle. Although he had seemed to show an instant attraction to her.

Unless she'd been dreaming it.

Of course, she'd been dreaming it. Boys had found her attractive back in the day. Back when she'd been... whole. Vivacious, athletic, cute. That's what they'd said back then.

Now, something else was always the first thing that their minds would come up with to describe her. They wouldn't say it out loud. No one ever did. It was the elephant in the room. Anyone who looked at her, from boys her age to middle-aged men and women to white-haired grandmothers and grandfathers always saw her wheelchair first of all. And rarely anything else.

So she ought to just forget that sparkle of attraction that had seemed to burst all over his face. Especially in those soft brown eyes and winsome smile. She'd been imagining it.

Imagining it because in the instant before he saw her barreling toward him, those eyes and that handsome face had looked so troubled. So very sad.

In all likelihood, she'd been imagining that, too. The troubled sadness. After all, it had only been an instant.

And probably a projection of what had been in her own troubled mind. How as blissful as those first few strokes through the water had been, all the rest of them had been so brutally wretched.

She had once been exceptional, a near-Olympic level swimmer. It had been who she was. Now? She was *nothing*. This wasn't swimming. This was... crap.

She'd lost it all.

Stroke by tortured stroke, the damning evidence bombarded her senses.

It wasn't just that she was out of shape. She could get back the cardio. In fact, she already had most of that back. Cardio wasn't the problem. Neither was it that her mechanics simply needed fine tuning, get the rust off.

No, the problem was simple and inescapable.

There was nothing there... down there. Even if it inexplicably and improbably itched and ached sometimes. There were no knees. No tibia or fibula. No ankles. Nothing to provide the power of her old propulsive kick. Nothing to keep the rest of her body in alignment. Nothing to provide the stabilizing force for the streamlining.

It was all lost and gone forever. Dreadful sorry, Clementine.

Stroke by tortured stroke. The universe rubbing her nose in it. She could never reclaim what she once had. Could never again be *somebody*. Forget about ever again being elite. She could never even regain mediocrity.

Now, she was *a joke*.

Whatever had she been thinking when she considered Coach Abbot's offer that she could still train with the team even if it could never again lead to competition.

"You'll always have a place on this team," Coach Abbot had said, as she informed Mia that her swimming scholarship had been revoked to be used for another young woman who could actually help the team. Who could actually still competitively swim. The coach hadn't used exactly those words, but the euphemisms amounted to the same thing. Not to worry, the coach had continued. The scholarship would be replaced with a virtually equivalent academic one now that... well... not to be indelicate, but now that Mia no longer had any means of... well... of parental financial support.

A place on the team? Train with the team? How humiliating that would be! She was worse even than the most mediocre club swimmers.

She'd be a laughingstock.

Oh, certainly not to her face. There would be the polite smiles, the patronizing encouragement. Even as her pathetic inability to keep up or even stay out of their way made the other swimmers hate her a little bit more each day. And secretly beg her to quit, a day after which they could breathe a sigh of relief.

As Mia hoisted herself out of the pool onto the deck, she swore she would never allow herself to be humiliated like that. Never, ever swim in front of the team. Hell, in all likelihood, never, ever swim again at all.

If what she'd just done could even be called *swimming*.

She showered and changed, and with her fury mounting to near explosive status, Mia flew out of the athletic complex, never wanting to ever step foot in it again. *Step foot in it? What foot?* Good Lord, even the wording behind her own thoughts tortured her now!

Small wonder she almost ran the good-looking boy over. Thank goodness, she didn't. Their near collision and the ensuing conversation on the way to the café had at least begun to get the awful taste of her swimming session out of her mouth. She had trouble feeling totally miserable while looking at him, listening to him, and responding to him.

"The coffee is on me," Mia said as they neared the café.

"I'm pretty sure," Tyler said with a wicked grin, "it was totally on me."

THE TWENTY-FOUR HOUR CAFÉ WAS NO LONGER OPEN ALL twenty-four hours—not with almost the entire student population gone home for the holidays—but they lucked out anyway. It was only open from 7 a.m. to 2 p.m. during inter-semester break, but it was now 7:17 and the strong smell of coffee and egg sandwiches filled the air. Only two other students were in the café, seated at the far end of a row of six tables. The ten-foot-long clear plastic display case showcased a limited supply of bagels, donuts, and pastries, a mere fraction of the usual mid-semester fare.

At the cash register beneath a sign hanging from the ceiling that read ORDER HERE, they placed their order. Tyler argued with what he thought was delightful incongruity that Mia could indeed pay for his coffee, could pay for both coffees, in fact, as long as he paid for both egg sandwiches. The logic was that he was fining himself for inattention that led to the near collision.

"That doesn't make any sense," Mia said.

"I'm failing logic design, too," Tyler said, the far-too-close-to-the-truth words slipping out of his mouth before he realized it. He wasn't going to fail Logic design, but a B- in an introductory Electrical Engineering course like that felt like a harbinger of F's to follow when the EE courses got exponentially tougher.

More writing on the wall that his Honors program days were numbered.

"You're failing? Really?" Mia asked as they headed to a table at the opposite end of the other students. Tyler placed their coffees on the table, then pulled one chair away and stowed it up against the wall so Mia could wheel herself in. "I can't tell when you're serious and when you're kidding."

"Not failing, but...." Tyler shrugged his shoulders and took his seat. He wasn't sure why he was blabbing this way about his troubles to a total stranger and to a beautiful woman no less. Knowing he had to say something more, he added, "It's been a tough first semester."

"Yeah," Mia said somberly. "I get that."

"It's just that I've got to make it in the Honors program," Tyler said. "My father is kind of this classic Marine sergeant type. Well, not a sergeant *type*. He *is* a Marine sergeant. Stationed in Germany. Our whole family is. At Boeblingen. That's why I'm staying on campus for the holidays and until the spring semester starts. Money's tight and my father wants me to 'grow up.' Become a man. He's a stereotype in many ways. Tough on me. Tough as nails. Won't accept anything but my best. But sometimes he overestimates exactly what my best is. I can't live up to his expectations. So I can't settle for anything short of the Honors program or he'll kill me."

A bolt of alarm suddenly shot through Tyler. Here he was talking about the Honors program as if anything else was second rate and yet chances were, Mia wasn't in it. Just based on statistics. Only about ten percent of the student population was in Honors.

"Not that all the other programs here aren't also excellent," Tyler said, trying to cover his tracks. "It's just how my father sees it. The Marine in him."

Mia smiled. "I get it. I'm not in Honors. I'm not offended."

Tyler let out a silent sigh of relief. Whew. Dodged a bullet. He needed to be more careful about what he said. Needed to get talking more about her. Less about him. *Nothing* about him.

Although actually, what he really needed to do, if he was going to be brutally honest, was get away from here and get back to his stuck project. What the hell did he think he was doing? He didn't have time to be flirting with this woman, even if he'd needed coffee and breakfast to keep him going. The project that just might save his butt wasn't going to get finished this way.

A few more minutes, he told himself. Ten or fifteen minutes with her wouldn't make the difference between success and failure on the project. In fact, he felt suddenly energized. He'd been running on fumes when he met her. Now he felt like he could go the next twenty-four hours straight.

Unless that was the coffee. Or hormones.

He grinned.

"What's funny?" she asked.

"Oh, um... I was... I just... I was amazed at how dead tired I was when you tried to run me over." He grinned, raising his eyebrows hopefully. She reciprocated. "I pulled an all-nighter on a project that has me stuck and I was dragging. But now... thanks to you...." He flashed his brightest smile. "Bright eyed and bushy tailed."

"Thanks to me?" Mia asked smiling. "More likely the coffee."

"I don't think so. Keep in mind I was halfway into a cup and was still dragging when we had our... episode."

"Maybe *wearing* that half a cup is what's made the difference," Mia said with an impish grin. "And I've got to say, you wear it well."

Tyler beamed. God, he could sit here all day and talk with this woman. Witty. Beautiful. She had it all.

"Are your parents hardasses like my father?" he asked, wanting to know everything.

Mia's face clouded. She bit her lower lip.

"I'm sorry," Tyler said quickly, knowing he'd stepped in it again. What had he said wrong this time? When would he ever learn to keep his mouth shut? "I didn't mean to pry."

Mia shook her head.

"It's okay. No way for you to know." She took in a deep breath. "My family, both parents and my brother, were killed in the same car accident that left me like this." She gestured with her right hand to her wheelchair. "Not quite a year and a half ago."

"Oh, I'm so sorry," Tyler said, feeling as though he'd been punched in the gut. And if that's how he felt, he could only imagine how she must feel. Just a year and a half ago. Oh my god. He hadn't just stepped in it. He'd... he couldn't even put a label on it. When would he learn to shut the hell up?

"Thank you," she said softly.

"I'm so sorry," he said again. And wanted to say it over and over. Not just because he felt so very, very sorry—felt it like a stab wound —and not just because he also felt so damned embarrassed, but mostly because he couldn't even imagine the pain.

She nodded and mouthed again her thanks, but her eyes looked down into her coffee and didn't look up.

A dark pall fell over the table.

Their egg sandwiches arrived, They ate for a time in silence.

Tyler couldn't think of what to say. Every time he opened his mouth, he seemed to make things worse. But the painful silence stretched longer and longer, more and more painful. It felt like hours.

"How 'bout them Red Sox?" Mia finally said, looking up with a forced grin.

Tyler blinked. "Yeah, how 'bout them?" he repeated robotically, having no clue what else to say.

"So," Mia said, and slowly nibbled at her sandwich. "Tell me about this project of yours."

"What?"

"Your all-nighter project. That has you stuck. Tell me about it. What has you stuck?"

"I... well... you'd have to know... do you know Computer Science? This is normally a sophomore-level class but between me getting AP credit from before I got here and being in the Honors program..."

"Would you rather talk about the night I lost everything?" Mia asked, her voice suddenly brittle. "Or are you going to tell me about your project?"

Tyler blinked.

"The project," he said, swallowing hard. "Definitely the project. Unless of course, you want to talk—"

"No, I don't. Tell me about your project and what has you stuck."

Tyler nodded, a fast and nervous nod, almost as if he was responding to his father with a "Yes, Sir" or a "No, Sir."

But then Mia reached a hand out across the table and rested it on his. Warm and smooth and comforting.

"I'm sorry that got a little rocky there. I'm still a little rough around the edges." She smiled weakly. "Probably going to be that way for a while." She drew in a deep breath. "I want to hear about your project and where you're stuck. Even though I don't know anything about it."

With that soft, warm hand of hers on his, Tyler figured she could tell him to go outside and find a snowbank to dive into and he would. So he launched into a fifty thousand foot view of the project, describing it for someone who didn't know anything about Algorithms or the project, then slowly, methodically began zooming in on the problem area that had him stuck until—

"That's it!" he cried out. "That's it! That's the problem!"

Mia beamed. "You were too close to the problem. Looking in the wrong microscopically tiny location. You couldn't see the forest for the trees. You had to step back and zoom out to describe the problem to someone who didn't know anything about it."

"That's amazing! Thank you!"

"I used to do the same thing—" Mia winced but continued. "I did that for my older brother all the time. I'm glad I could help."

"Wow," Tyler said feeling elation at solving the problem—at *both* of them solving the problem—that had threatened to make or break his project. At the same time, he also felt a shared pain at Mia's memory of her brother. "And I'm sorry it touched a raw nerve."

Mia nodded and waved away the apology, clearly not wanting to linger there.

"I find that exercise often accomplishes the same thing," she said. "It unlocks the brain. Relieves the stress you're feeling so your mind can function better. It can zoom out on the problem, even subconsciously, so you can see the solution. Just like today."

Tyler nodded, not buying it but also not wanting to disagree.

"What exercise do you like?" she asked. "What sports?"

Suddenly, Tyler could only think of his father's disapproval.

Are you sure this kid's mine?

"I hate 'em all," Tyler blurted out. "As far as I'm concerned, they're all a waste of cycles."

Mia paled into an ashen hue. Eyes widened. Nostrils twitched.

From her horrified, mortally offended look, Tyler knew he didn't need to translate the instinctively geeky computer reference of "waste of cycles" to "waste of time." Mia had gotten the meaning loud and clear.

And without question, he had said the most monstrously wrong thing possible. Of course! What had he been thinking? Where had she been coming from when they almost collided? The Athletic Complex! He was the dumbest fool in the universe!

Mia yanked her hand away from his. Her eyes flared with hot anger. Her lips quivered.

"You might think that sports are a *waste of cycles*," she said, venom dripping from every word, "but sports—swimming—was my *life*! It's who I was. It's what I loved. I wasn't just good. I was great! It got me a full athletic scholarship to this place. Probably an empty achievement in your book but—"

"I'm sorry! I never meant—"

"Shut up and listen!" Mia snapped. "You don't get to crap all over everything I've ever done and then not let me speak my peace. So let me tell you, *Mr. Honors Program Pretty Boy Who Thinks My Life is a Waste of Cycles*, when *ever* is doing what you love a *waste of cycles*?

"I loved it like... like Juliet loved Romeo. More! Loved slicing through the water faster than anyone else. Loved the burning in my lungs at the end of a race. Loved everything about it.

"And now I've lost it. Lost it all. I got back in the pool today for the very first time. A year and a half of surgeries! Bones and tendons and ligaments healing. Endless physical therapy. *Endless!* Nine months of PT on my shoulder alone! All to be able to get back into the pool. Why? Because it was my life! Not a *waste of cycles*. *My life!*"

Tyler couldn't speak. Couldn't breathe. What had he done?

"And today I found out it's all gone!" Mia said. "I've lost it all. Just like my family. Lost and it's never coming back. I couldn't do *anything* today. I don't know what the hell I was thinking. Of course, it's all gone. *I don't have any legs!* Do you know how important legs are to swimming? Not as much as the upper body, but you can't swim for crap without them.

"I could have tried it weeks ago. My therapists finally gave me the go-ahead. But I waited until everyone on the team was gone for the holidays. I needed to be alone when I gave it a try. I needed an empty pool. No one looking at me. No one watching me. No one feeling pity or shock or anything. No one else could be there.

"And it's a damned good thing! It was humiliating how awful I was. Thank god no one saw me. I was *pathetic*. My therapists told me to take it easy and have low expectations. But I never imagined how horrible I would be. I really have lost it all."

Tyler's heart broke for her. But what could he say to comfort her? Nothing. If he so much as opened his mouth, he would only make things worse. If that were even possible.

"It crushes my *soul*," Mia said, her eyes filled with pain. "Swimming is who I was and now it's gone! First my family and now this. Yeah, losing my family was even worse, and I'm supposed to be grateful I survived at all. Why me and not them? Yeah, I get it! Yes, I'm grateful, but grateful for what? I lost them and now I've lost the one other thing I could cling to. The one other thing I loved. I've got nothing left.

"That might have had something to do with me flying out of the complex like a bat out of hell. Not just because of the snow like I said, but also because I just had to get away from that place. And I may never go back." She gave a half-snort. "We met and it was funny in a way, so for a short time, you distracted me.

"I pushed that aching in my gut as far away as I could. I've gotten pretty damned good at pushing things out of my mind over this past year and a half. Ignoring the elephant in the room. And you seemed like an interesting person. Good looking and fascinating in a quirky kind of way. Not that someone like me can afford to be picky anymore, but I liked you."

She had liked him, Tyler thought. How was that even possible? He was beneath contempt, yet she had liked him. Until he'd ruined it all. And not just ruined it for him. He'd taken this fragile angel's heart into his hands—this fragile angel who had endured catastrophic loss—and then with thoughtless, careless words deepened her agony.

Unimaginable. He did not deserve to live.

Mia shook her head.

"I could not have been any more wrong," she said, leaning close. "You know what's a waste of cycles? You!"

Mia wheeled herself back, away from the table.

"I need to leave. We're done."

OH, WERE THEY *EVER* DONE. STICK A FORK IN THEM DONE. Burnt to a crisp done. *Finis. Kaput.* I-don't-ever-want-to-see-you-again done. I will piss on your grave done.

And before they had really even started. She had really liked him, Mia thought bitterly. Had felt a little something. She couldn't deny it.

But... *a waste of cycles.*

She lay in the dark on her dorm room bed. Even now, half an hour later, she still felt the steam spewing out of her ears. Her head still wanted to explode. How could she ever have begun falling for that jerk?

A waste of cycles!

The small, spartan room felt stuffy, the bare, unadorned walls oppressively close. On the opposite wall from her bed was a pine wood desk and chair with a matching dresser and mirror. On the far wall, the plain white shades were still drawn, concealing the picture window and maintaining the darkness.

She'd moved two days ago from her usual dorm, which had been fine, to this one, the only option for those staying between semesters. She'd formed an instant dislike for it. She wasn't sure why. Perhaps it was just the looming holidays alone without any coursework to keep her mind preoccupied.

Now, she wondered what else she could use to fill her mind. Certainly not the soul-crushing debacle at the pool. And certainly not Mr. Waste-of-Cycles.

That was two strikes for her. One more and she'd be out. But of course, that was waste-of-cycles thinking.

ALONE IN THE COMPUTER LAB, SEATED AT ONE OF THE thirty terminals lined up in three rows surrounded by custom hardware on tables up against all four walls, Tyler clicked the keys on the black keyboard on autopilot. All the air had burst from his balloon. The terror of failure on the extra credit project was gone. He'd be finished with it soon, thanks to the Mia-inspired breakthrough.

Which was a good thing because all he could think about was Mia and how he had hurt her. He'd never felt worse in his life. What a total and complete idiot he was! He'd dodged one conversational bullet after another, fearing a misstep with this witty goddess. The Honors program. Her tragic accident. And even her deceased brother. Only to blurt out his hatred for the one thing she most held dear.

He wasn't just too dumb for the Honors program. He was too dumb for life.

But what could he do to win her back? Apologize, of course. Let her know that he could not have been more wrong and that, in fact, any sport with her involved would be the most wonderful way to spend every second of every day. Even though he didn't know anything at all about swimming. It would be great, it would be special because of her.

Because he was totally thunderstruck. And not just her beauty. Not even the wit. There was simply something magnetic between them.

But he'd ruined it all.

He didn't get his brilliant idea until hours later, well after he turned in his completed project and only after the most serious of brainstorming. Nothing sensible had come to mind until he finally zoomed out, as Mia had suggested for his project. Only then did inspiration strike. After that, the research was a piece of cake.

He hoped it would make a difference.

THE HUMAN WASTE OF CYCLES WAS WAITING FOR MIA IN the café the next morning, sitting in the same seat he'd occupied when they shared coffee, egg sandwiches, and a delightful conversation until... *a waste of cycles.*

Other than that, Mrs. Lincoln, how'd you like the play?

Mia almost turned and left, but this was pretty much the only place open on campus in the morning. Which was probably why the jerk was here. If he waited long enough, he could be sure she'd show up eventually. It didn't take any serious Honors program debugging to figure that one out.

She noticed that he'd taken the chair at what had been their table and moved it somewhere, probably off in some corner, so she could wheel herself into place, like yesterday.

"Please let me apologize and make it up to you," Tyler said. "I was an idiot and there's really no excuse, but I do want to explain. And tell you something I really think you should hear."

Mia grimaced and took in a deep breath. The smells of coffee, egg, cheese, bacon, ham, and sausage were intoxicating.

"Okay, let me order," she said.

"If you want the same as yesterday, I told the cook in back to be ready." Tyler grinned wryly. "He's been ready for over an hour. I helped him open the place." Tyler spread his hands in a well-what-do-you-think gesture. "And of course, if you want something else, just let him know. His name is Allen. And it's already paid for, if you don't mind."

Mia gave Mr. Waste of Cycles a sideways glance. "I'm not paid off that easily."

"I would never expect it. But when you've dug yourself a fifteen-foot hole and dropped into it, every inch counts."

Mia felt herself melting ever so slightly. An inch or two out of fifteen feet sounded about right.

"Fair enough," she said, and wheeled herself up to the table's edge.

Allen, middle-aged with salt-and-pepper hair and a pronounced beer belly, brought her a coffee with a smile and then rushed back to the kitchen. Clearly down to a staff of one today, which at least for now was sufficient since the place was otherwise empty.

"I told him black with two Splendas," Tyler said. "Right?"

Mia smiled. He'd remembered. Another inch regained on the fifteen-foot hole.

"I am so very sorry," Tyler said. "I never, ever would have hurt you, insulted what you've spent your whole life on, if I had any idea. But there's a reason why I made such a rude comment. You see, my father..." Tyler launched into a description of his father and their relationship and a story that Mia was only half listening to until the pieces began to fall into place. Then she really listened. "So there's no excuse for me insulting you, but that's the background I was coming from."

Mia shook her head, taking it all in.

"He actually suggested a paternity test?" she asked incredulously. "That's awful."

"I never knew if he was actually serious. It's hard to believe he'd really do it. I mean, we look a lot like each other and my mother never gave him reasons to doubt her fidelity. It's ridiculous, really. But when you hear over and over comments like that— *are you sure this kid's mine?*—and you're not good at sports, at least the sports that he liked which were football, basketball, and baseball, it doesn't exactly turn you into a fan. It turns you sour."

"I can imagine," Mia said, in truth having trouble imagining a parent like that.

Yikes.

"If, on the other hand," Tyler said, "I had an athlete I really cared about, I'd become the biggest fan ever. It would be the best part of every day."

"Like who?" Mia asked, mystified by the cryptic words.

Tyler looked at her like she was from another planet. "You! Who do you think? I'd love to see you swim. I'd love to cheer you on."

Mia felt her face grow very hot.

"Oh, no, no, no, no, no. No one is ever going to see me swim again. I'm horrible. It's humiliating. I've lost it all." She suddenly realized what Tyler had meant when he said *an athlete I really care about.* He'd looked at her as if the reference was as obvious as the nose on one's face. It was a measure of how crushing her attempted swim had been yesterday that the word *athlete* no longer registered on her self-radar. The comment had gone totally over her head because she knew she was no longer an athlete and never again would be one.

Lost and gone forever, Clementine.

"If you ever saw me swim now—if *anyone* ever saw me swim now —I'd be mortified."

"No, I wouldn't."

"You would! Trust me. Neither you nor anyone else is ever going to see me swim again!"

"Never?"

"Never! I may never even get in a pool again, regardless of whether or not anyone is watching. It's excruciating to know how much I've lost. How I've lost *everything*! I can't believe I ever enter-tained thoughts of training with the team at the beginning of the next semester. If Coach Abbot ever realized how pathetic I've become, she never would have made the offer. Or more likely, she made the offer knowing I could never shatter my dignity by accepting it. Knowing I would realize how high a level all the other girls are at—*have to be at* to compete—and how now I'm not much more than an eighty-year-old grandma swimming at the Y.

I'm not exaggerating. I've lost it all. I used to be great. Now, I'm nothing."

Tyler nodded thoughtfully and waited for what felt like a very long time.

"I know we've just met, but I like you," he said. "Like you a lot."

"I like you, too," Mia said. "For a time there, I hated you. Despised you. And that fifteen-foot hole you said you dropped into. It was more like a mile deep. You were down in the molten lava. Assuming that's what's a mile down. I'm not a Geology major." She shrugged. "But somehow you've climbed out of that hole. At least most of the way. And I do like you." She grinned and felt that perhaps there was a twinkle in her eyes. "I'm not sure if it's 'like you a lot' quite yet, but you're getting there."

Tyler smiled and reached his hand across the table. Mia took it.

"Okay then, hear me out," he said. "This may be totally presumptuous. In fact, it's totally, one hundred percent, ridiculously presumptuous. But you've seen that when I talk, there's no filter. Seen it the hard way. So here goes. In 2028, I see the two of us in Los Angeles."

Mia frowned. "What?"

"That's not only where the Summer Olympics are held that year," Tyler said, sending a shot of pain into her gut. "But it's also where the Paralympics are held. I researched this last night, but there are different categories for every level of... of... of impairment. Or whatever the correct word is. Ten different levels from S1 to S10. God help me if I say this wrong and drop down again a mile deep into the pit, but you'd be competing against swimmers just like... um... just like... like you. Not the old you. The new you."

Mia rocked back in her wheelchair, stunned.

"But I'm horrible," she said, even as a spark of hope flared within her.

"Maybe you're horrible compared to your old self. I don't know anything more about this than what I read last night. So forgive me if

I say anything wrong. But if you were great before, you can be great again. Just against other swimmers like you. You can't compare yourself now to the old you. That isn't a fair fight. This will be fair. I'm sure it'll take time and training to adjust to the new you. But I sure wouldn't bet against you."

He squeezed her hand.

"And um..." he continued, "I'd like to be along for the ride. As long as things work out between us, of course. Call me crazy, but I believe they will. We've got a chance. A great one. I believe in us. And I'd like to be there as long as you'll have me."

"I... I... I don't know what to say."

But Mia knew exactly what she wanted to say. That this was exactly what she needed. A goal to strive for. A way to continue what she'd spent her whole life trying to achieve, only now in a new way. Now, with a new measuring stick, one that she at least had a fair chance at measuring up to. She certainly didn't measure up now, and maybe she never would, but this was a second chance to do what she loved.

And to possibly do it all with this strange, sweet boy on the journey. Gobsmacked. That's how she felt. Positively gobsmacked.

"Say that you'll think about it," Tyler said.

"I'll do more than think about it," Mia said, already making a mental calendar of training stages. "This is wonderful. Thank you! This was a *great* idea! You have no idea how perfect this was for me. Perhaps further down the road my therapists might have mentioned it. Maybe they didn't think I was ready for it, or maybe they just didn't know. But it sure never occurred to me."

"It's like it was with my project," Tyler said, smirking. "I couldn't see the forest for the trees. My microscopic focus was on the wrong place. Same thing with this. You couldn't see the forest for the trees either. Your microscopic focus was on how poorly your first attempt went yesterday. I could zoom out and take the fifty-thousand foot view. That, plus a few hours of brainstorming and research and, *voilà!*"

"I'm in shock," Mia said, dazed. "I can't totally commit right now. I'm sure I'm a million miles away from qualifying right now. It may be hopeless, but this is so exciting! I am so pumped! I'll have to check what the qualifying times are for the trials."

Tyler blinked. "Qualifying times? What trials?"

Giggling, Mia reached across the table and put her right index finger on his mouth in a shushing gesture. "You need to learn to quit when you're ahead."

He laughed and shrugged sheepishly.

"This is truly wonderful!" she said, and curled her hand around the back of Tyler's neck and drew him close. "I might fail, but this gives me a chance to get my life back. I've got a shot now. Thank you!"

They both leaned forward until their faces were mere inches apart. Emotions bubbled up within her. Mia blinked back the tears.

"And yes," she said, "I want to try this journey with you."

They drew closer still until their lips touched, and they began to kiss. Tyler's soft lips tasted of coffee. Mia thought she had never loved coffee more.

The kiss lasted for the longest, sweetest time and was ever so lovely. And when that one was finished, another began.

At some point though not soon, their lips parted for more than mere seconds.

Mia whispered, "L.A. in 2028. The two of us. Book it!"

DAVID H. HENDRICKSON'S SHORT FICTION HAS APPEARED in Best American Mystery Stories, Best of Thrill Ride the Magazine, Ellery Queen's Mystery Magazine, *and frequently in* Pulphouse, Thrill Ride, Mystery, Crime, and Mayhem, Heart's Kiss, Fiction River, *and other anthologies. He is a multi-finalist for the Derringer*

Award, and was honored with the 2018 Derringer for Best Long Story. He has released ten short story collections. He co-edits with Annie Reed the quarterly anthology Romance for All Seasons.

His first novel, Cracking the Ice, *was praised by* Booklist *as "a gripping account of a courageous young man rising above evil." He has since published seven additional novels, including* Offside, *which has been adopted for high school student required reading.*

Hendrickson has published three nonfiction books and over fifteen hundred articles and features. He has been honored with the Joe Concannon Hockey East Media Award and the Murray Kramer Scarlet Quill Award.

Visit him online at www.hendricksonwriter.com. Sign up for his newsletter and get a free book!

About this story, David writes:

"I've interviewed and written about quadriplegic athletes, culminating in my book Travis Roy: Quadriplegia and a Life of Purpose. *It became inevitable that the emotional impact of those discussions and friendships would eventually give birth to quadriplegic or paraplegic characters in my fiction.*

"Since my daughter Nicole was one of the top distance swimmers in New England through her teenage years, I naturally gravitated to a paraplegic swimmer in this story. As for Tyler, I was a software engineer for decades until retiring to become a full-time writer and still teach Computer Science part-time at two universities. Long, long ago, I was in Tyler's shoes and was fortunate to receive shockingly effective 'debugging' help from my non-engineer wife Brenda similar to what Mia gives Tyler. And what a happily-ever-after that has been!"

Blue Christmas at the Starlight Lounge

STEPHANNIE TALLENT

EVERY YEAR, ON THE FRIDAY CLOSEST TO THE ADVENT DAY of Blue Christmas, the longest night of the year, I go to the Starlight Lounge in Gardena to sing karaoke, alone, in a private room I book a month in advance.

The Starlight is a typical cheap, strip-mall Los Angeles Korean karaoke bar. I love it. I'm there several times a month with a group of gal pals, the She-Wolf pack. We sing the '80s New Wave and hair metal of our high school years, and always hit a couple songs off the soundtrack of Grease.

The after-party at the Starlight has become part of our Friends-giving celebration, too.

That's when I made the reservations for tonight, 7 p.m. I'd even picked my favorite room, the second on the left. Room Two. Roddy, the manager, hadn't been there, and the new kid Jenisse was totally lost on the computer booking system, but she'd written my name—Catie with a C—on the freebie Sierra Club calendar hung from a nail on the wall behind the desk.

She swore she'd let Roddy know.

Looks like she hadn't.

"I'm sorry, sweet pea. You're not on the schedule," said Roddy. Tall, thin, and of indeterminate age, he was currently dressing up as a Korean version of Robert Smith from The Cure, complete with a shock of spiky black hair, deep red lipstick, and eyeliner so thick you could measure the width in quarter inches. He looked fierce and fabulous, even in the harsh fluorescent lights illuminating the cluttered Formica check-in counter.

I wished I looked that good.

I settle for cute, most days. Wavy brown hair with salon highlights that covered the inevitable gray, a genetically blessed athletic build, and hazel eyes. Like every other girl next door, ageing into her late 40s.

"Check again?" I asked, leaning over the counter and nearly dislodging the bowl of those hard, flat, round red-and-white peppermints—Roddy told me they were Starlight mints—that sat next to a beatific Lucky Cat wearing a tiny Santa hat.

Roddy had gone all out, decorating the Starlight for the holidays. A brightly lit fake tree, flecked with fake snow that dusted the linoleum floor underneath, filled the corner nearest the front door. Glitter cardboard snowflakes hung on threads from the acoustic-tiled ceiling, sparkling as they twisted. Cinnamon-scented candles battled the piney odor of industrial-strength cleaning fluid and the ramen place next door.

The snowflakes extended down the corridor that stretched back to the main bar with the open mic. A series of windowless rooms, the private rooms, lined either side of the corridor.

The mints were always there, not just for Christmas. I don't think anyone ever ate them. The one time I'd tried one, the plastic wrap was glommed onto the mint, the candy was so soft it was chewy, and it tasted like the stale memory of peppermint mixed with disinfectant.

I poked at the Lucky Cat, causing its paw to rock up and down, as Roddy squinted at his computer monitor like staring at it would magically update the schedule.

"Nada," Roddy said finally.

"Look," I said, pointing to the calendar on the wall behind him. A sad-looking polar bear perched on a tiny ice floe for December. "Look. There's me. Jenisse put me on the calendar."

He peered at the wall calendar, at the scribble on today's date, then turned back to me.

"I'm really sorry, sweetie," he said. "You never got in the computer. We're all booked up. I'll give you half off your next reservation. And a free drink tonight, if you want to head back to the bar."

As tempting as the drink was—the Starlight was known for its craft cocktails that could compete with any trendy Arts District bar —that's not what I needed.

"There's no one even here yet. Can't I just have my room for a bit? Or *any* room?"

He shook his head. "It's booked for seven o'clock. If the person doesn't show, it's yours, but all the other rooms are booked for a big holiday party."

It was ten till. Maybe I'd get lucky and whoever had booked it would be a no-show.

"What about tomorrow?" I asked.

"Booked through the holiday. Nothing till after New Year's. I'm sorry, Catie," he said.

"I'm going to wait just in case," I said. I had my whole playlist planned out.

I always sing "Blue Christmas" at least once, in honor of the day. But I often sing all those other nostalgic holiday songs, too, in between the gaps. "White Christmas." "Auld Lang Syne." "Have Yourself a Merry Little Christmas."

And sometimes I'll come up with a theme, veering away from Christmas songs.

This year, I'd decided the theme was "blue."

I'd worked on the playlist all week, scribbling it down in between appointments. I work as a locum tenens vet, filling in as needed at clinics. I had more work than I wanted. Sometimes I was busy, sometimes everyone wanted to see Dr. Regular and my schedule was light. I didn't take it personally.

Tonight's playlist included "Blue Christmas" three times, a record for me: starting off with it in style of Elvis, then midway screeching to an instrument-only track by the Misfits (yeah, they did a cover!), and finally doing a singalong with Harry Connick Jr.

Then I went rando. "Blue Light" by Mazzy Star, "Blue Bayou" by Linda Ronstadt, "Forever in Blue Jeans" by Neil Diamond. I even included "Pale Blue Eyes" by the Velvet Underground—I could listen, and sing, to Lou Reed all night, and I think I do him credit.

And lots more. I think blue must be one of the most common colors in songs. How could it not, when you have an entire genre of music named after it?

I always finished any session with the Cowboy Junkies' callback to "Blue Moon," wrapping it back to memories of when I was a kid, regardless of any theme.

Every Blue Christmas, my dad dug out his boxes of 45s and spun that singular 1954 cover of "Blue Moon" Elvis recorded at Sun Records.

The snaps and pops of the old vinyl added to the otherworldliness of Elvis' vocals on that cover and to the clip-clopping backing rhythm.

I'd sit on our old scratchy couch, inhaling the stale cigarette smoke that infused the plaid fabric (everyone smoked in the '70s, it seemed, including Mom and Dad), mesmerized by the yellow and black label revolving on the record player, while my dad hovered over the player, ready to gently lift the needle when the song ended.

"Pretty special, huh, kiddo?" he'd always say at the end.

"It's the best," I'd reply. "Play it again?"

Dad's 45 was a demo, not an actual release—that came a few years later, after RCA purchased the rights—and that 45 was his most prized possession.

I couldn't sing the actual Elvis version, especially not as the last song of a karaoke session and expect to leave the room with my mascara intact. So it never made it onto any of my playlists.

The doorbell tinkled behind me, and a gust of cold air blew in. Even Southern California gets cold in the winter—well, cold for us Angelenos. I shivered in my jeans and navy-striped cotton sweater and scooted away from the counter to give whoever was coming in room.

Wowza.

Apparently hot Santas are a thing this year. I saw a Target commercial with a decidedly un-jiggly Santa getting into a pickup to go work at Tar-Jay, and another commercial, same guy, with him already at work. Cute.

This guy, bundled up in a navy and white Norwegian sweater, snug-in-all-the-right-places faded jeans, and beat-up black cowboy boots, would give *that* Kris Kringle a run for his money. His face was tanned, even at this time of year, and his silver-streaked light brown hair was tied back in a curly ponytail. He looked my age, late 40s, or even a bit younger.

Pale blue eyes met mine briefly and he smiled, a flash of even white teeth, before he sauntered to the counter.

Cowboy Santa, for sure.

Roddy was glancing at me, furtively waggling his eyebrows, before focusing on cowboy Santa dude.

I always came with the She-Wolf Pack, never a guy. Roddy, who seemed to have a endless stream of cute boyfriends picking him up from work, likely knew *I* didn't have a boyfriend.

He was right. Pickings were slim once you reached my age and you were a workaholic. Crap, pickings were nonexistent at my age regardless.

"I booked a room? Room Two?" hot cowboy Santa said. "Jace Krasowski?"

Ah.

There went my chance of Blue Christmas karaoke.

"There's a small problem," said Roddy. "That room accidentally got double booked." Roddy pointed at me. "Catie booked it, too."

I projected *WTF* at Roddy, hard as I could. He ignored me.

"We could share," hot cowboy Santa—Jace—offered. Oh, his eyes were pretty. Like the crazy husky puppy I'd seen that morning.

"That's really nice of you," I said. "But I was planning a solo sort of thing."

"Me too," he said, unruffled. "But, spirit of the holidays and all that, I bet we could work it out."

He smiled, a smile that warmed me from my toes on up. And up.

And stopped around my middle, but who's counting? Or whatever.

"Um." Oh, yeah. Real smart, Catie.

"We could alternate songs."

"I'm not that good of a singer."

"Neither am I."

Nothing available till after New Year's. What was worse? Compromising, or outright skipping?

Skipping. Skipping was worse. I didn't want to skip.

"I have a song list in mind," I said. "For my songs."

Oh, real smooth.

"Sounds great."

Roddy led us to Room Two. The overhead lights were on, dimmed to halfway; Roddy flicked on a second switch, and projected red and green dots spotted the walls.

All the private rooms were set up with a loveseat and a couple of chairs or a U-shaped sectional sofa, a coffee table, and a big screen TV. Room Two had the loveseat/chair combo.

You can order drinks or snacks to be delivered to your room. It's an awesome setup. If you've booked the room later in the evening, you can smell the fried dumplings and sugary fruit cocktails from previous customers, and the floor is sticky and crunchy at the same time.

If you get there early, like I prefer to do for these solo sessions, the rooms hold a hint of the industrial cleaner from the early morning hour scrubbing.

All I could smell was a woodsy vanilla scent that had to be Jace. Vanilla shortbread and campfire. Nope, that wasn't me drooling.

I dumped my bag on the armchair farthest from the door, then sat at the far end of the loveseat. The large screen TV was mounted on the wall, opposite the loveseat. A red plastic three-ring binder, swollen by pages of song lists stuffed into sheet protectors sat on the coffee table, next to an iPad tablet for sending the songs to the TV. (You could also Bluetooth your phone to the TV set, if you couldn't find your song. I've only had to do that once or twice.)

"Can you bring a couple bottles of water?" I asked. "And an order of egg rolls? Put it on my tab?" I emphasized *tab*.

"Let me—" started Jace.

"You had the more valid reservation," I cut in. "Let me do this, at least."

"Right back with those rolls," said Roddy. "Have fun, kids!"

Jace sat in the armchair nearest the door after Roddy swooped away.

"I'm Jace. Just to be official."

"Catie." I twitched nervously. This was a bad idea. I could barely talk right now, let alone sing.

"Come here often?" he asked, cracking a smile. "It's my first time here. I moved to LA from Austin last summer."

"Isn't that backwards?" I asked. Oh, crap. Open mouth, insert foot. "I mean, don't most people move from LA to Austin? Tech stuff or whatever?" I plowed on. "And, um, I come here at least once a month. Usually twice. With friends. Usually. Except for this time, every year. For Blue Christmas. It's my thing."

"Ah. Okay. Yes, I moved from here, to Austin, then back here. And yes, tech stuff. Gaming stuff, actually. But tell me about Blue Christmas." He leaned forward, eyes intent on mine.

"Blue Christmas is the longest night of the year. It's the time to remember loved ones we've lost. Or other things we've lost. I don't worry about celebrating it on the actual day. I just try to schedule it on the Friday closest. I pick a theme to help reflect on the past year." I was babbling. I had to stop babbling.

"Sounds like what I do," said Jace. "Or maybe the opposite. I pick songs to help me think about the upcoming year. Solstice. Longest night. But after that, the nights are getting shorter, and the days longer. You said you had a playlist? What's your first song?"

This, I could answer succinctly. "'Blue Christmas,' in the style of Elvis."

Jace laughed. "Makes sense. Go ahead. Then I'll do my first song. But you can't laugh at it."

He was making *me* go first? "No, you first."

"I know this is really messing up your thing. But maybe we could sing it together? Take turns on the lyrics? As a warmup?" he said.

He was nice, but he wasn't going to give up.

I queued up the song and passed him one of the mics. "I'll start," I said, just because I knew he would argue I should since it was my song, and the clock was ticking on how long we had the room for.

The music filled the room, and the lyrics, each track highlighted as it came up to sing, scrolled across the TV screen. I started, my voice hesitant at first; then, as Jace smiled, his expression nonjudgmental, I relaxed.

My voice was a warm contralto. I wasn't *great* by any stretch, but I enjoyed singing and had splurged on some remote lessons with a voice teacher in New York, just to try to make the most of what I had.

Jace joined in on the second couplet. I sat back, enthralled; his voice, an expressive baritone, rounded out the lyrics with reserved, but full, emotion. I nearly missed joining in about snowflakes falling.

We finished the song together, our voices harmonizing.

I'd gotten to the point I wasn't usually nervous about singing in public. One on one, especially with a handsome stranger, and for this longest night of reflection, was a different story, but Jace made it easy.

The door cracked open.

"Wow," Roddy said, setting the crispy, golden egg rolls (four on the plate, and a bowl of sweet-and-sour sauce for dipping—my stomach growled) on the coffee table, then handing us the bottles of water and a handful of brown paper napkins. "You kids sounded great."

"Thanks," I said. "Now stop listening at the door."

"You're no fun, sugar plum." Roddy left and shut the door with a definite click.

"What's first on your list?" I asked. I pushed the tablet to Jace.

"You're gonna laugh," he said.

"No, I won't." And I wouldn't. Rule One of karaoke was never, ever laugh at anyone. Not at them, not at their voices, not at their song choices (unless they were very clear they were making a joke with their choice).

"'Here Comes the Sun,'" he said, fingers tapping the tablet's screen. "You said you come up with a theme? This year, mine is sun songs."

"Optimist," I noted. "Mine this year is blue. Though I always do 'Blue Christmas.'"

"Blue? Pessimist?"

I shrugged. "It's been a tough year." I grabbed an egg roll, dipped it into the sweet-and-sour, and took a big bite.

Sauce dripped down my chin and onto my sweater. Of course it did.

"See? Bad things."

"Or good," said Jace, swiping the sauce off my chin with his finger and licking it.

I gulped. Hoo boy. "Stay away from my sweater." I poured some water on one of the napkins and wiped at the dribbles of sauce. I succeeded in getting tiny brown pieces of the napkin stuck in the sweater.

He laughed. "Wouldn't even dream of it. Unless you asked." He smiled, slow and sexy. "Okay, same as the last song, we take turns, but this time I'll start."

Was he flirting with me? He *was* flirting with me!

The simple picked guitar notes expanded into the lusher arrangement as the song proceeded, and he started singing. I joined in on the first chorus. He sang the verses, and we both sang the chorus. It just *worked*.

"It's a good song," I said as the last notes faded away.

"It's a *great* song," he said. "It's the one I always start with. No matter how bad the previous year, I remind myself things will get better."

"Was the last year bad?"

He crunched into an egg roll, avoiding the sauce, then dabbed at the crispies stuck to his lower lip. I watched, wishing I had the guts to wipe them off myself. It'd been forever since I'd flirted with anyone with less than four legs. Smooching up to a Golden Retriever puppy or snuggling a fluffy kitten didn't count.

"There were good parts and there were bad parts," he said. "Our gaming company got bought out by one of the big fish in the pond end of last year. I made a bunch of cash. That was great. But half my team got fired after they swore they'd keep our team intact. And then they said they were closing our Austin HQ, and anyone who wanted to stay on would have to move.

"So I moved out here. I still have my house in Austin. It's handy for South by Southwest gaming expo, I guess. I don't see moving back there anytime soon, though." He finished the egg roll and wiped off his hands. "Your turn."

"My year?" I asked.

"Song. We'll get to your year after."

"Okay. Here's one that's more optimistic. And close to a karaoke standard." I mentally tossed the planned order of my playlist out. I could do more upbeat. A strong beat and a simple picked and strummed melody filled the room. I stood, tapping my foot, and belted out the first line of "Forever in Blue Jeans."

"It's too early for Neil Diamond!" he protested. He stood as well, knocking into the coffee table, and joined in.

We danced around the tiny room as best as we could. I tripped over the table and he held my elbow, keeping me upright and sending butterflies spiraling in my stomach.

On the last chorus he lowered his own mic and leaned in at my mic, his eyes closed in concentration. I stumbled over the words, my lips only the width of the mic head away from his.

The notes trailed off and he opened his eyes. "That was fun. My turn."

A snappy beat and an energetic horn section filled the room.

"Oh, yeah." I grinned, clapping with the beat. Katrina and the Waves. "Walking on Sunshine."

He took the first stanza, we both sang the chorus, then I sang the next stanza—wondering, hoping, he was single and hoping that having us sing a song about how great it was to hook up with someone was one more flirty overture.

"That song just banishes gloom," he said, flopping on the loveseat and pushing up the sleeves of his sweater. He patted the cushion next to him. "Now tell me more about you. Your year."

"Nothing exciting like yours," I hedged, sitting next to him. Our thighs brushed. The loveseat was small.

"Fair is fair."

"You just told me generalities," I said. "I need details."

"Okay. My best friend, the guy I developed the game that made us famous with, well, he got let go. It wasn't my fault, but he blamed me. He got back at me by fucking my fiancée, who didn't want to move to LA anyways."

"Jeesh. That really sucks." I didn't dare ask if he'd found someone else. If he'd gone through any needed rebounds.

"Maybe it was for the best," said Jace, shrugging. "They ended up getting married at Thanksgiving."

"I don't have anything to compare to that. I mean, nothing seems to change in my life. Just the same day, different place, different season. I work as a vet. I love being a vet. I book myself solid with work. I don't have time for anything else. But it seems like I'm just spinning my hamster wheels."

"That's funny. Hamster wheels."

"That's me, funny girl."

"What do you want to do? To get off the hamster wheel?"

"Sing the next song. This was one of my mom's favorites."

A slow thumping bass filled the room. "Blue Bayou." I stood so I could gesture, singing of yearning and past happiness, and a love left behind, and hope of maybe, just maybe, finding that happiness again.

He watched as I sang, swaying to the music.

"That was great," he said, as I settled back next to him. "I gotta ask. Is there someone?"

"Nope, to my mom's chagrin. She's given up on grandbabies," I said lightly. On the rare occasions we spoke, Mom hadn't given up on nagging me about it, though. "You?"

"Work, work, work. And I know it sounds totally L.A., but I've been taking acting classes at night. I've started doing some voiceover work on some of the smaller games. It's fun. And nice thing about a big company, they're shutting down for break, so I do have some free time now. In between projects, so that helps, too."

He grabbed another egg roll, eating it in a couple bites, then pushed the plate towards me. "That was a long-winded way of saying no, there's not anyone. Gotta admit, I was happy when that guy said the room was double-booked with you. You looked so cute. And pissed off."

"I have great resting bitch face, don't I? Blue Christmas karaoke is my thing. I've never shared it, before."

"Sorry you are?"

I snagged the last egg roll and dipped it into the sauce. This time I managed to not drip sweet-and-sour all over myself. "Sorry it's the last egg roll."

"I'm sure that guy will bring us more."

"Roddy? He'd love to find out what's happening in here."

"What is happening in here?" Jace leaned towards me, blue eyes warm.

"Karaoke. Whose turn is it?"

"Mine." He reached out and curled a strand of my hair around his finger. "Pretty."

"You have to pick a song," I said, voice breathy.

The door opened. "Strawberry margaritas on the house!" said Roddy, beaming, carefully setting down two large Mason jars full of clear ice cubes and pink liquid. "Macerated farmer's market fresh strawberries, fresh squeezed lime juice, lime bitters, Cointreau, and of course Daddy Julio and a vanilla sugar and salt rim. Happy holidays, ducklings!"

Jace had let go of my hair as soon as Roddy barged in. Sadly, he didn't reach for it again after Roddy left. "Strawberry margaritas?"

I lifted the closest jar. "Don't knock it till you try it. The Starlight usually ends up in the top three cocktail bars in the South Bay. To Blue Christmas." We clinked jars.

"To serendipity and sunshine." He sipped tentatively. "It's actually really, really good."

I shrugged. "He knew he had to have give me something good for spying on us." I raised my voice. "Go away, Roddy!"

"You're no fun!" Roddy called back.

"Are you going to check to see if he left?" asked Jace after a minute.

"Nah. But seriously. Your turn."

"I've lost my place." He stretched, causing the bottom edge of his sweater to pull up just over the waistband of his jeans.

My breath hitched. Dude! Seriously?

He tugged the sweater back down. I swore to god, if he winked, I was going to toss my margarita at him. And then hold myself from licking it off him, because darn it, they were too good to waste.

"Why do you do this every year?" he asked. "Why sad songs?"

I sighed. "They're not all sad."

"What do you end with?"

"'Blue Moon Revisited, Song for Elvis.' Cowboy Junkies," I admitted.

"That's the version where the lover is *dead*. That is so dark."

"It's an homage to Elvis."

"Who was dead."

"Well, yeah. But it's my closing song because of my dad."

I related the story of Dad's demo 45, how he would play it for me, once a year. How special that was, that he would share something so precious with me.

And then I told him something I'd never told the She-Wolf Pack.

"Dad left us at Christmastime, the year I turned thirteen. Mom was so pissed, she threw all his records into the garbage. The trash men came before I could dig them out of the dumpster." I paused. "He got married to someone else six months later. Didn't have time for me after that. He died my senior year at vet school.

"So there's a lot tied up in all that. I do love that recording. It's sad. Elvis skips the last bridge and final verse, where the singer does find someone to love."

"Kind of how you've treated yourself, all these years, sounds like," Jace noted quietly.

I didn't want to argue. "Serious trust issues, for sure." I swirled the Mason jar, watching the ice cubes spin and catch the light.

Jace tapped at the tablet, then stood. He held out his hand. "Come on."

The strains of "Blue Moon" echoed in the room. Not the clip-clop beat of Elvis' version, but something fuller, rounder, lusher. I placed my hand in his, let him draw me close. He was just tall enough for me to nestle my head against his neck.

Jace whispered the lyrics as he guided me around the room. We both knocked into the coffee table twice before he gave up, and he tugged me closer, only our feet shuffling in time with the music.

The version he picked turned the blue moon gold, with hopes of a future. Not alone.

He kissed the top of my head as the music ended. "I don't usually feel a connection like this with someone. Never so soon."

"Me neither. Ever." I looked up at him. "Our two hours are up. I'm not ready for this night to end."

"Is the ramen place next door any good?" he asked.

"It's fantastic."

Jace stroked my cheek then traced his finger across my lower lip. It was like Christmas morning and Thanksgiving dinner and the crackles of an old 45. "Ramen sounds great, then. And ramen with you sounds amazing. But you have to know, I don't really know what's going on with my job. That's why I'm taking up the voiceover stuff."

"You have a great voice."

"But I don't know what's going to happen. Where I'll end up. L.A., back in Austin, where."

"That's not a bad thing," I said. "Uncertainty. Change. Year in, year out, I do the same thing. Gets old."

"I do always land on my feet," he said.

"I'm thinking I'm ready for a change," I said.

I stood up on tiptoe, brushed his lips with mine.

"Maybe I'm ready for a little sunshine."

STEPHANNIE TALLENT IS A 1989 WEST POINT GRADUATE. Since then she's served in the Army as a Military Intelligence officer, gotten a Zoology degree, went to vet school, worked as a small animal veterinarian, and designed and published knitting patterns and books.

Throughout all that she's always wanted to be a writer, and she's finally put all her type A, soft-spoken, liberal, invisible middle-aged woman focus on that goal, writing everything from fantasy to science fiction to mysteries to romance.

She loves karaoke and sings with enthusiasm, if little skill.

Check out her website at www.stephannietallent.com

About "Blue Christmas at the Starlight Lounge" Stephanie says:

"This story combines so many fun things: private-room karaoke, tasty craft cocktails, a range of great music.

"My dad was an avid music lover, with a large collection of records from the 1950s and 1960s. I grew up listening to those records. He didn't have the described demo of 'Blue Moon'—I made that up for the story—but he did have an early 45 by the Beach Boys on the X record label.

"Unlike Catie's father, my dad and mom remained happily married until he passed in 2014."

Reindeer Heart Collision

DAYLE A. DERMATIS

BRYONY STOPPED AT THE EDGE OF THE PARKING GARAGE to pull the hood of her burgundy rain jacket up against the December drizzle. No self-respecting Portlander used an umbrella, not even in torrential rain. She'd never heard of a reason why.

December in Oregon rarely meant snow unless you were in the upper elevations. Snow was largely for the mountains. It might snow occasionally in the city or suburbs, which would shut things down for a day or two because there was no infrastructure to deal with it. Icy roads were a greater responsibility.

She couldn't dawdle any longer. She had to face the coming chaos. Stepping onto the sidewalk, she headed for her office.

Woodsport Village was largely a misnomer, as the only foliage in the medium-to-high-end shopping area were those carefully maintained in concrete planters decorated with an Art Nouveau rose design. The buildings were laid out mostly on a grid with roads and sidewalks—they were just connected rows of stores rather than houses or condos.

Big-box stores—Barnes & Noble, The Container Store, Crate and Barrel, the Apple Store—anchored the area, bringing people who'd then drop money at the boutique shops for children's clothes, cocktails, and paper products for those who had the time to fill out party invitations with fountain pens.

For food, there was everything from the ubiquitous fancy steak place, an oyster bar, and a boba tea room, to fast-food shacks serving overpriced burgers, Korean-Mexican fusion, and pizza with creative toppings.

Before she left home each morning, Bryony assembled a bento box that she now carried in her oversized tote-slash-purse.

The upper stories of the buildings held offices for a dentist, an esthetician, and the Village administration, among others. Bryony worked for the Village—and therein lay the looming nightmare.

Christmastime added a whole new dimension. The piped-in music turned to cheerful holiday instrumentals, and the black Victorian-esque gazebo was fitted with heavy plastic sides and cover, with heat lamps within. A massive decorated fir dominated the crossroads where the walking and driving roads met, with Santa's house nearby.

And this year, the powers that be had decided a scavenger hunt would bring in even more shoppers.

A project they'd dropped in Bryony's lap, and which commenced today.

The shops wouldn't open until ten, which gave Bryony time to go over the plan one last time. She mentally mapped which shops she had to visit as she rounded a corner...

...and smacked face-first into a goddamn reindeer.

GODDAMN STUPID HEAD GAVE HER NO PERIPHERAL VISION, and not a lot of forward vision, either. It made no sense for her to be wearing it. Right now, all Susannah knew was that she'd smashed into someone. She ripped the reindeer head off.

And, unusually for her, was momentarily speechless.

The woman sprawled on the ground was *gorgeous*.

Her hood had fallen back, revealing a cute bob of ebony hair streaked professionally with electric blue, a color that almost matched her vibrant eyes. She wore a dark red raincoat over wide-legged black pants and mid-heeled black boots.

Her glossy lipstick, Susannah couldn't help but notice, was nearly the color of her raincoat.

Susannah was all for beautiful women falling at her feet—just not because she'd physically knocked them over.

"I'm *so* sorry!" she said. "This thing has no peripheral vision."

She tucked the reindeer head beneath one arm and stretched out a hand—a hoof? Really just an oversized mitten—to help the woman up.

"I've heard of Grandma being run over by a reindeer, but I'm not quite old enough for that," the woman said as she accepted the aid and stood. She bent down and picked up her large black leather tote.

Susannah tried not to gawk.

"I work in the management office," the woman said. "I didn't know we'd hired any costumed actors. How did you get stuck with the gig?"

"Would you believe it's community service because of parking tickets?" Susannah said with a grimace.

The woman snort-laughed, which somehow sounded utterly charming.

"I'm Bryony," she said. "If you need anything, just call the office —or stop in. Same place you were interviewed."

"Thanks," Susannah said. "Have a great day."

Sadly, she knew whether she did her job right or screwed it up, Bryony's day was going to get even worse.

Either way, she'd probably never see Bryony again.

BRYONY STOPPED INSIDE THE GLASS DOORS AND TOOK A deep breath. Ahead of her was an elevator; to her left, tan carpeted stairs. The offices were on the second floor. Shiny red and green garland wound up the banister, and tinny piped-in holiday music reminded her that she was in a time of jolly-ness and holly-ness.

The woman who'd run into her had set Bryony's heart racing. She was stunning.

Liquid brown eyes (rather like a reindeer), full pink lips, small scar bisecting one of her eyebrows. Long blond hair braided and wrapped around her head, no doubt to keep the reindeer head from messing it up.

Bryony was amazed she'd hadn't stuttered, or lost words entirely, while talking to her. The reindeer woman had had that effect on her. She pressed a hand to her chest, willing herself to breathe normally.

A part of her knew she should be angry that her boss—or whoever—had hired more actors than just Santa and his elves without telling her.

The other part of her... well, meeting the reindeer woman made up for any lack of office communication. More than worth it.

Bryony started up the stairs, mentally slapping herself for not getting the woman's name. But it would be in the computer system.

THE REINDEER WOMAN'S NAME WAS NOT, IN FACT, IN THE computer system, unless Bryony was looking in the wrong place.

The office was dark when she arrived, which was unusual, but after she unlocked the door and went in, she saw a light on her phone blinking.

Of course Chester, her boss, had called in sick. Of course he had, on this crazy day. But from the message he'd left, he did sound awful —his throat was so raspy from coughing that she could barely understand him.

When she pulled her phone from her tote, she saw he'd texted her as well.

Her boots made no sound on the gray carpet as she went to the tiny break room to start the coffee maker. A large map of the Village took up one of the eggshell-painted walls in the main room, which included a waiting area with orange, midcentury modern inspired chairs and a kidney-shaped wooden table with chrome legs.

As the aroma of life-giving beans filled the office, she opened her laptop and did a search for the seasonal hires.

Odd. The only temporary hirees she could find were Santa and his elves. Maybe an elf had decided to try something different?

Then again, the woman had said she was doing community service, so maybe she wouldn't be in the system at all. A handshake deal between Chester and... whoever assigned the reindeer woman the position. A judge?

Bryony didn't have much time to think about it—with Chester out, she was already being swamped with phone calls and emails. Problems with store heaters. A leak in a ceiling; flickering lights. Questions about the stupid scavenger hunt.

But beneath it all, the reindeer woman's lush pink lips lurked in Bryony's memory.

Her phone dinged, reminding her that it was time to check in on the stores that were stops in the scavenger hunt and make sure they were prepared. Thank you, past me, she thought.

A final swig of coffee, then she grabbed her jacket and headed for the door.

JAMESON'S FINE JEWELRY WASN'T A HIGH-END JEWELRY store, at least not on par with the likes of Cartier or Tiffany's. It wasn't low-end, either, given the upscale nature of Woodsport Village.

It made sense, Susannah thought. The really high-end places had excellent security systems, their personnel was carefully trained and always on the lookout for suspicious behavior, and the safes were a bitch to get into. Plus they had security guards on top of everything else.

No, Jameson's was just right. All of its offerings were very, very nice, but not unique enough that the jewelry couldn't be resold later without raising suspicion.

This close to Christmas, shoppers would be tense, sometimes even testy, and with the scavenger hunt going on as well, stores would be crowded. Which meant individuals didn't stand out as much, and employees' attention would be stretched thin.

Susannah thought about all of these things as she passed by the store, noting the nondescript doors between Jameson's and the next store (perfumes and bath-and-beauty products, their scents warring and making collateral damage of hapless passers-by when the door was open) that led to upstairs offices. Simple white letters embossed on the glass doors mentioned a dentist, a law firm, and a drafting firm.

That would be one place someone coming from Jameson's could duck into. Especially if they'd already checked it out and knew where the back door was.

The parking garage was nearby—another place relatively easy to disappear into.

Susannah walked around the block, waving at the early shoppers and even stopping for a picture with a couple of tiny children on their way to Santa's, their parents beaming, all the while making a mental list of places someone could disappear.

They should have done this earlier, she and her partner, but there had been obstacles and some confusion. She didn't think things would go down today anyway.

Not that she had any power to make decisions.

She passed another set of double glass doors. According to the neat white letters, upstairs there was a Lasik center, a yoga studio, and Woodsport Village Management.

Bryony's office.

Susannah allowed herself a moment to daydream. To imagine getting coffee with Bryony, making her laugh, laughing in return. To find out what it would feel like to kiss those glossy burgundy lips....

But it was only a daydream—it could never happen.

Happy endings were too complicated for someone like her.

Movement inside caught her eye. Someone was coming down the stairs, which faced away from the door at the top, then turned one-eighty at the landing.

Susannah recognized the raincoat and wide-legged black pants. It was as if she'd manifested Bryony by thinking of her.

She dashed around the corner and power-walked away, hoping Bryony would go in a different direction. The less they interacted, the better for both of them.

And hopefully Bryony would be safely back in her office before anything went down.

THE DRIZZLE HAD STOPPED, HOPEFULLY FOR A WHILE, because less rain meant more happy shoppers. And a happier Bryony, who was able to leave her hood down.

She had a list on her tablet of things to check in each shop that was participating in the scavenger hunt, and extra supplies in her tote just in case. Only the small shops were participating; coordinating with the anchor stores and their many employees would have been too much work on both sides.

Her first stop was Curds and Corks, a shop that didn't, despite its name, sell wine and cheese, but rather accessories for cocktail parties: cheese plates and knives, napkins with cute sayings such as *Of Course Size Matters—Nobody Wants a Small Glass of Wine*, cruets for flavored olive oil and little shallow dishes to pour it in, and more cocktail swizzle sticks than you'd need even if you threw a party every evening for a year.

Armand let her in, showed her where the stuffed candy cane was semi-hidden behind the ice buckets, and confirmed that he had the scavenger hunt cards, which each shop would initial when the candy cane was spotted.

She visited Glowing Gifts Candle Emporium, the children's clothing boutique, the boba tea room, the essential oils and perfumes shop, and the leather goods shop, where she briefly fondled the buttery-soft oxblood leather jacket she'd been coveting before she left.

She'd started around the outside, then up and down each street, until she was back to the office. Everyone was sorted—in fact, things had gone more smoothly than she'd expected.

It was only after the shops had been open for a while that she realized she'd somehow skipped the damn jewelry store.

SUSANNAH HAD TO DUCK TO GET INTO JAMESON'S FINE Jewelry, thanks to the antlers. The suit made her bigger, clumsier, and she hated taking up so much space. The last thing she needed was to accidentally knock over a display.

Honestly, the reindeer suit was a stupid idea—but she didn't want to be recognized.

Inside the store, greenery and sparkly ornaments in purple and silver, and muted instrumental holiday tunes, made things feel festive.

She already knew the placement of all the security cameras. Another plus of the season: people wore scarves and hats that obscured their features, distracting reindeer-antler or mistletoe headbands, and, in her case, full-on costumes. The extra bodies would also make it harder for someone watching the security feed to see exactly what was happening, or who was doing what, if the *who* in question was canny enough to use the obscured lines of sight.

Susannah viewed it all with a practiced eye.

Any time now.

She couldn't linger all day—that would be too obvious—but she'd switch with another member of her team as per the schedule, and be available outside if or when she was needed.

She posed for pictures and made overly dramatic gestures worthy of any character at Disney World. Because nobody knew exactly where her actual head was, they couldn't tell where she was really looking: at the jewelry cases, at the clerks sliding velvet trays out from the cases to let a customer examine a ring or necklace close up, at the door to gauge an escape route.

She saw two things almost simultaneously, and cursed:

Bryony walking into the shop, and the glint of a handgun in a man's pocket.

At which point, she made a decision that could possibly end her career.

Her team could handle this.

She needed to get Bryony out of there.

BRYONY WAS SURPRISED TO SEE SUSANNAH IN JAMESON'S. Shouldn't she be out doing reindeer holiday things in the central plaza near Santa's cottage?

Of course, if this *was* Susannah, because there could be other reindeer she hadn't been warned about.

She was going to have a sit-down with Chester when he recovered and was back in the office.

But she didn't feel annoyed at the moment. She was imagining

Susannah's crown of blond braids and those ripe lips curving into a smile at the sight of her. She felt herself smiling in response.

Next time she ran into the reindeer, she was going to slip Susannah a note with her phone number and a suggestion of coffee or a drink that evening. She wasn't usually so forward, but in their brief contact this woman had somehow gotten her hooks into her—in a delightful way.

First, though, work. She looked around for Juliette, the store manager, to touch base about the scavenger hunt...

...when suddenly a big reindeer arm wrapped around her and half-dragged her out the door of the shop

---

SUSANNAH HELD ON TO A STRUGGLING BRYONY WHILE trying to pull the reindeer head off with one hand, which was about as easy as it sounded. As in, not at all.

"What the hell?" Bryony was saying when the head finally came off.

"Trust me," Susannah said, dropping the head and pulling Bryony across the road and behind the planter on the sidewalk. "Please?"

She mashed at her in-ear communicator, but of course the padded hoof-mittens were too bulky to activate it. Swearing, she grabbed the hoof with her teeth and ripped it off. The faux fur tasted like something she didn't want to think about.

This reindeer suit was the stupidest idea ever, and she was going to rip her boss a new one over it.

"It's about to go down," she told her team, but she was wrong. It had already started going down, but the man standing outside Jameson's Jewelry—the lookout she hadn't spotted because she'd been inside—was yelling into his own earpiece and pulling out a gun.

"Get down!" Susannah said, dragging Bryony down and half-covering her.

Not a moment too soon, because a bullet winged the planter, sending chips of concrete flying. Susannah felt one scratch her face as musty-sweet dust filled her nose.

"Not the planter!" Bryony wailed. "We just had them installed!"

Susannah shushed her as she drew her own gun from the pocket inside the reindeer suit sleeve. "Not now. I need to focus."

Focus, and ignore the screaming and pounding footsteps from all directions. She hoped the shoppers all had the good sense to be running away.

She rose up enough to peer through the evergreen bush decorated with white lights and red and silver ornaments.

The lookout had taken shelter behind a planter in front of the jewelry shop. It looked as though the thief or thieves inside the store were keeping customers from leaving. She cursed. She couldn't do anything while the lookout had a bead on her.

Into her earpiece, she let her team know there was an active shooter outside and an unknown number of perps inside. She had to take the lookout out before it would be safe for them to handle the store.

"Who even *are* you?" Bryony asked, but her voice was thin with fear.

The lookout shifted. Bracing her wrist on the edge of the planter, Susannah aimed and shot.

And missed.

The man had flattened himself to the ground but rolled so he was looking around the far end of the planter. Before she could take another shot, he did.

Susannah fell back as the bullet hit her shoulder, fierce, hot pain slicing through her.

BRYONY'S EARS RANG FROM THE GUNSHOTS. SHE SAW Susannah fall backwards, saw the rip in the reindeer suit, and knew crimson blood would bloom soon.

Grabbing Susannah's gun would be a useless endeavor; she didn't know how to fire one.

Don'tbesickdon'tbesickdon'tbesick.

Breathing deeply—it was that or hyperventilate—she peeked through the decorated greenery.

A gun fired, and she couldn't hold back a shriek.

But it hadn't been aimed at her. There was a man around the corner from Jameson's, where the cutesy children's clothing shop was. After firing, he'd ducked back.

He was wearing a red-and-green elf costume.

At this rate, Santa and Mrs. Claus were going to show up with shotguns.

Dimly, she heard Susannah speaking, probably to her team.

Susannah had a team? What the jingle balls was going on?

There had to be more reinforcements coming, but she didn't know how badly Susannah was hurt. She'd seen thriller movies. She knew how long these shoot-and-fall back things could drag on.

What she didn't know was how long it took someone to bleed out.

Frantically casting about for some idea, anything, she caught a glimmer out of the corner of her eye.

In a dip at the edge of the wall behind them, where rainwater would be funneled and then flow to discreet drains, was her bento box. It must have fallen out of her purse when she'd collided with Susannah that morning.

She stretched across the sidewalk and scrabbled for it, her fingers sliding on the stainless steel. Finally, she got a good enough hold to roll it towards her.

On her knees, she looked through the little evergreen trees again.

The guy behind the other planter was focused on the corner where Susannah's guy was.

She rearranged herself until she was in a crouch.

She felt a touch on her leg. Susannah shook her head, mouthing something Bryony couldn't hear through the ringing in her ears.

Shaking her own head, without giving herself time to rethink, she stood and hurled the bento box across the street.

As she dropped back down, she saw that she'd actually nailed the guy in the head. Not hard enough to knock him out, but enough to distract him so another elf coming from the opposite direction was able to tackle him.

After that, everything blurred into mayhem. Elves seemed to pour in from all directions. One of them bundled her off while another tended to Susannah, and she never got to see how it all went down in Jameson's.

Which, when she was able to think about it, kind of annoyed her.

Most importantly, though, she worried about Susannah, because nobody was telling her *anything*, even after she'd *told* them she was in charge of the shopping complex.

BRYONY WAS TREATED FOR SCRATCHES AND A BANGED-UP knee—from when Susannah had pulled her down onto the sidewalk —and released into the custody of the FBI, who wouldn't answer most of her questions.

Once they were comfortable that she hadn't been in on it, hadn't been hurt too badly, and wasn't going to sue them (which wasn't stated outright, but Bryony could tell), they released her. Even drove her home, the black-suited agent still refusing to respond to her queries.

Chester called her, apologizing profusely with what little voice he had left, and gave her the next week off. He'd been sworn to secrecy about the operation and hadn't expected to fall ill, and honestly, she couldn't blame him on either count.

The news reported that Major Crimes, with assistance from the FBI, had stopped a spree of multiple-state jewelry store robberies. Her part in the melee wasn't mentioned, thank goodness. The only name mentioned in any of the articles was the police spokesperson.

Bryony still didn't know Susannah's last name.

Or how to find her.

Or if she'd ever see her again.

She went back to work after two days off, because she was going stir crazy, and because she felt bad at Chester having to work while he was still so sick. She had her hands full with the scavenger hunt, as well as the uptick of shoppers due to the exciting events that had occurred at Woodsport Village.

"It's as if they *want* to get caught up in a shootout," Bryony remarked to Chester on the phone.

He coughed. "The stores aren't complaining, so neither am I."

On Friday, Bryony was eating lunch out of her new bento box— the previous one having disappeared, and she wondered if it had been collected for evidence—when the office door opened.

They almost never got drop-in visitors, and Bryony knew no one was scheduled on either her or Chester's schedules. In fact, neither of their desks directly faced the door.

A woman came around the corner. Tall, lithe, with lush wheat-blond hair spilling loose over her shoulders. Big brown eyes.

She wore jeans, brown boots, a white button-up, and a brown leather jacket, although the jacket was draped over her shoulders because one arm was in a sling.

It was, improbably, the sling that jolted Bryony's brain, which had slammed to a halt at the gorgeous woman in front of her.

Susannah. Even more stunning with her hair down and in normal clothes. Bryony's belly fluttered.

"Oh," she said stupidly. Then, "I'm so glad you're okay. They wouldn't tell me anything."

"I'm glad *you're* okay," Susannah said, relief palpable in her voice. "Nobody who worked here was supposed to get caught up in the sting. You were so impressive, though. You really kept your cool." Without asking, she dragged a grey padded straight chair in front of Bryony's desk and sank into it.

"Stop. I was not cool at all. I was terrified."

"Terrified or not, you may have saved my life. You distracted the shooter long enough for my team to get there. You've got a hell of a throwing arm."

Bryony tried not to squirm in her seat, unsure if her desire to squirm was from embarrassment or delight. "College softball," she muttered.

Then she realized that while she'd been worried, she'd also been mad. "You lied to me—you said you were doing community service for parking tickets."

Susannah had the good graces to look abashed. "Actually, I didn't lie. I asked if you would believe that's what I was doing."

"And I did." In hindsight, it was a pretty lame story. In her defense, she'd been distracted. "Are you even allowed to talk to me now?"

"Not about operational details," Susannah said, "except to say it was a success."

"Can you tell me if you're with the FBI or the local police?"

Susannah blew out a breath. "FBI field officer, stationed in DC. But..."

"But that might change," Susannah said.

Admitting that made her a little lightheaded. She thought she'd known her career path, but now everything had gone pear-shaped.

In potentially really good ways.

This beautiful woman with electric blue streaked through her hair cocked her head. "Oh?"

"I've been offered a promotion." The words made Susannah breathless. "To head the field office here in Portland." The person who'd insisted she wear the stupid reindeer outfit wasn't in anyone's good graces. Reshuffling would happen—in such a way that a certain position would be open and Susannah was strongly encouraged to accept it.

Pink tipped Bethany's cheeks. "So you might end up being local."

"I think I like it here." Oh, she sounded lame. It wasn't about the milder weather than DC, or the amazing hiking in the Columbia River Gorge, or the laid-back attitude, although all of those things had spoken to her.

It was about the blushing woman sitting in front of her, who made her stomach do somersaults. Beautiful, brave, resourceful.

"I'm hoping so." Susannah pointed at her sling with a grimace. "Meanwhile, I'm obviously on medical leave, so I have some free time. Can I take you out to dinner to say thank you?"

Bethany laughed, a sound that made Susannah's heart flutter. "As long as it's not a restaurant in Woodsport Village, absolutely yes."

Dayle A. Dermatis is the author or coauthor of many novels (including snarky urban fantasy Ghosted *and YA lesbian romance* Beautiful Beast*) and more than a hundred short stories in multiple genres, including fantasy and SF, romance, mystery, thriller, and YA.*

Called the mastermind behind the Uncollected Anthology project, she also edits anthologies, and her own short fiction has been lauded in many year's best anthologies in erotica, mystery, and horror. Her romance has been published in Heart's Kiss *and various* Fiction River *anthologies, among others.*

Dayle eloped properly in Gretna Green, Scotland, rode off on the back of a motorcycle, and hasn't looked back since except to smile and sigh happily. Unsurprisingly, she writes romances that are sometimes sweet, sometimes spicy, sometimes spooky, and sometimes funny, but will always make you smile and sigh happily.

An unabashed romantic, she lives in a historic English-style cottage with a wild and fae back garden, and whenever she can, she travels the world for inspiration and loses herself in music.

She'd love to have you over for a virtual cup of tea or glass of wine at DayleDermatis.com, where you can also sign up for her newsletter and support her on Patreon.

For the story that would eventually be called "Reindeer Heart Collision," Dayle says:

"I knew I wanted to write a romantic suspense. My first mental picture, though, was of a woman rounding a corner and running smack into someone wearing a reindeer costume. If this was going to be a romantic suspense, then the reindeer-clad person had to be dressed that way for a reason other than hanging around Santa's Grotto... And off I went.

"Sometimes, as they say, the magic just happens."

Christmas Baggage

LISA SILVERTHORNE

WITH CELL PHONE TO HER EAR, JORDAN MCKENNA CALLED her boyfriend for the third time as she paced in front of the crowded Sea-Tac baggage carousel. Late December's snow-fragile gray light hadn't quite reached baggage claim's cavernous basement. And it was chaos.

She cleared the call. Tyler still wasn't answering.

Granted, he didn't know she was flying into Seattle a day early to spend a romantic Christmas together at his place. Like they'd planned. But her call going straight to voicemail made her anxious. Heavy snow was beginning to fall. All the way north to Bellingham and south to Portland. The predicted Christmas Eve storm had arrived a day early, too.

The air felt electric, that jittery calm before the storm that made her feel a little manic. Even if she didn't know where she was sleeping tonight. When that snow arrived, the entire city would shut down.

She had to get hold of Tyler. Soon.

She and Tyler had taken their relationship long-distance until Christmas when her contract job ended, Facetiming or talking on the phone every night. She hoped to swap her iPad for an engagement ring this Christmas.

Everything about getting back to Seattle had been perfect— almost magical.

She'd gotten the last seat on an earlier flight and ahead of the approaching fifty-year winter storm. Her ugly old black suitcase, packed full of gifts, had magically weighed in at exactly fifty pounds, too.

Home a day early.

Everything had come together. Except her and Tyler.

The bone-jarring buzz startled her, light on the baggage claim flashing. Bags were incoming. Like an airstrike.

People rushed toward the carousel in a wave of desperation and winter coats. To spot their bags right when they came off the over-head chute. Because the rest of the conveyor was lava. And people refused to waste an extra three minutes lumbering around to an open spot, preferring to Chuck Norris the surrounding crowd with a roundhouse luggage pull right in front of the luggage chute.

With a fifty-year snowstorm coming, hand-to-hand luggage removal was acceptable. No matter the casualties.

Like the sound of a jet engine, the conveyer began to move, shiny metal plates clacking.

The herd of travelers rushed it, crowding around the baggage chute four and five deep like velociraptors hunting prey. Now she remembered why she hated travel days. She didn't want to become the Highlander just to get her luggage before everyone else.

It seemed like forever before the first bag, damp with snow, thunked down the chute and onto the turning carousel like chum.

Sending the waiting travelers into a feeding frenzy.

People pushed and shoved. Rammed their way to the exits, no matter who got in the way.

Jordan glanced out the window. Big, heavy snowflakes began to drift past. Time to join the assault.

She weaseled her way closer to the carousel's luggage entry chute as she searched for a hotel room on her phone.

In case she couldn't reach Tyler.

The air had a faint citrus and aggression smell, scented with pine, fear, and fresh falling snow, marred by whiffs of car exhaust from the nearby exit doors decorated with wreaths and garland. Christmas music drifted above the barely controlled panic in baggage claim and she almost laughed when she realized it was "Let it Snow, Let it Snow, Let it Snow."

The roar of conversations was a heavy drone as she joined the push toward the baggage carousel in an all-out frontal assault that would make Patton proud. Jordan refused to star in her own Lifetime original movie, *Christmas at Sea-Tac*, by getting stuck here when they closed the airport.

She glanced at her phone again. Why hadn't Tyler called her back?

Tense and anxious, she fought to stay in front of the baggage carousel, ready to grab her ugly black suitcase. She patrolled her tiny but critical spot like a chihuahua fresh from someone's purse.

Maybe Tyler was still at the office?

The floor behind her was a minefield of backpacks and briefcases. One wrong move and the crowd's undertow would banish her to the outer edges of the carousel, losing precious minutes to escape the airport. It was already getting dark outside and snow was falling.

But hey, what would Chuck Norris do? He'd make it out. All was fair in love and war and Christmas travel.

It took forever until her bag slid onto the carousel. Along with four other beaten-up black suitcases.

Now, she had to pick her nondescript black bag out of a lineup. All black luggage looked alike. Why hadn't she remembered that?

She grabbed the handle of the first black bag just as a tall, handsome blond guy in a gray business suit, shiny black shoes, and a charcoal wool coat reached for the same bag.

Three other guys in suits pushed toward the conveyor beside him, nearly knocking her and the blond guy over.

But blond guy was faster.

He reached for her bag.

His hand fell on top of hers. And those crystalline blue eyes connected with her green gaze. All she could do, in the middle of this Christmas travel warfare, was stare.

But his hand. Mulberry silk soft. Beach bonfire hot. And for a moment, it felt like... magic.

Until the man on her left, wearing a puffy green coat and jeans, elbowed past her. Breaking the spell.

Suddenly, she felt underdressed in her oversized red sweater, black sneakers, and black flared yoga pants. Her mahogany hair was pulled back in a thick ponytail at her nape with a black scrunchie. Stretched to its maximum capacity with her hair ready to expand like the universe. At least she'd worn makeup today. For Tyler who seemed to like her smoky green eyes and matte red lipstick—but not her curls.

Next to this blond guy, who looked like he just stepped off a Paris runway, she looked scruffy.

"Excuse me," he said, tugging on her bag. "That's my bag."

"Your bag?" Jordan frowned. "No, it's mine."

"How can you tell?" he demanded, an edge in his voice. "Half the bags coming down are black."

"It's got the appropriate number of battle scars on it," Jordan replied with a decisive nod.

"So does mine—and a tag," he said, voice rising as Jordan kept staring into his pale blue eyes, so bright against his thick, tousled blond hair, chiseled nose, and perfect oval face.

God, he was way too attractive for his own good.

Especially in that expensive charcoal gray suit that had Armani written all over it. Wonder what he did for a living? Ran a small country? Inherited a bottomless trust fund? Starred in the newest superhero movie? Probably a massive jerk.

"Don't let it go around!" he shouted as the bag they both clutched started to get away. "Pull it!"

He yanked on the handle, but he was too far away to get enough leverage to drag it off the conveyor. Especially with Jordan in front of him.

"I'm trying!" she shouted and grabbed the bag's side handle, wrestling it like a rodeo steer.

Maybe it did belong to mister male model here? She wasn't sure. But she didn't like his tone now.

Finally, she yanked the bag off the conveyor. Damn! All hundred pounds of it.

The black suitcase swung around, knocking two people out of her way.

And hit mister male model square in the chest.

Dropping him.

"Oh, God!" Jordan cried, kneeling beside him on the floor. "Are you all right?"

"Nice arm," he said in a strained voice as she helped him sit up.

Until she saw her bag getting away on the carousel.

"No, no, no!" she cried.

He fell backward as she let go of him to chase her bag.

Leaping between two people, she grabbed the handle before the bag entered the Mordor of baggage claim. The burning lava side where no one dared go until the bag reappeared on the other side again. Like the dark side of the moon.

Yanking the fifty-pound dead weight off the carousel, it spun her around.

She and the bag both slammed into mister male model who had just gotten to his feet. Knocking him and his bag to the floor.

Again.

"Shit! I'm so sorry!"

"Is it the suit?" he shouted as he struggled to his feet. "Do you have something against men in suits?"

"Just men with black suitcases, apparently," she said with a groan.

He snapped his suitcase up from the floor and backed into Jordan, nearly knocking her and her luggage over. Rolling over her foot.

She shrieked. Like he'd just set a minivan on it.

Turning, she hopped on one foot.

"Is it the yoga pants? Or the color red you hate? No wonder it's such an angry color."

"I'm sorry," he said, frowning. "Are you all right?"

She nodded as she put her foot down. "I'm sure a prosthetic will fix it right up. Eventually."

His frown darkened.

Contrite? Or annoyed? She couldn't tell. Maybe both.

He stared for a moment or two, looking her up and down. Was that a good stare or an I'm memorizing this woman's appearance for the police station lineup of redheads in red sweaters brandishing black suitcases as deadly weapons.

Two men in dark suits and trench coats, looking like CIA agents, shoved their way between her and mister male model, trying to grab their own black luggage. She side-stepped the two aggressive and not nearly as attractive men.

Finally, she opened the black tag holder on her suitcase and confirmed it was her bag.

Time to leave before she accidentally put this hot blond guy in the hospital. Or he broke her other foot.

She pulled her phone out of her pants pocket and redialed Tyler one last time as she rolled her bag away from the carousel. To the right. Where mister male model stood in front of her, checking the tags on his bag.

And nursing his wounds.

The call didn't go to voicemail this time and she waited for Tyler to pick up.

Until a familiar song rose above the din of baggage claim noise. But it wasn't just a song. It was their song.

A ringtone.

A cold chill danced across her heart as the intense strains of "Someone You Loved" by Lewis Capaldi echoed through baggage claim. Hers and Tyler's song. His ringtone for her. But he couldn't be at the airport. He didn't even know she was here yet.

The song continued from somewhere behind her.

She turned. Toward baggage carousel thirteen, phone against her ear. And froze.

A woman in a tight green dress with long, wavy blond hair ran toward a tall, brown-haired man wearing an orange parka, jeans, and the light blue V-neck sweater Jordan had given him for his birthday.

Oh. My. God. That was Tyler. Her Tyler.

He swept the woman into his arms and kissed her hard on the lips. The woman returned his kiss with a long, passionate smooch. He gripped her hand and they rushed off together with a small pink suitcase in tow.

Stunned, Jordan watched the whole surreal scene replay behind her glassy eyes.

Him kissing another woman. Holding hands. Ignoring her calls.

Pain radiated through Jordan's chest, anxiety fluttering into her throat and down into her stomach as she dropped her phone against her side.

Shaking, she moved on autopilot now. Her shock was the only thing keeping that first flood of tears in check as her bottom lip trembled, her stomach sick.

Mister male model whirled around, gripping the handle of his black luggage like he was about to fling a shotput for the world record. And fell over her suitcase which she had inadvertently shifted directly behind the poor guy.

He tumbled over her bag headfirst, his suitcase the only thing keeping him from faceplanting against the bright tan travertine tile.

"Oh, not again!"

Jordan shoved her phone in her yoga pants pocket and helped the guy up, knocking over two more black suitcases into a four-bag pileup while their owners waited for other bags at the conveyer.

"Are you a hired assassin?" mister blond model demanded. "Because you're very good at making this murder look like an accident."

"I'm so sorry," Jordan cried. "Really I am."

As she got him to his feet, the button on his coat caught in her hair and pulled her black scrunchie free. Into an explosion of mahogany curls that tumbled around her shoulders like they'd been shrink-wrapped for hours and then released.

He stumbled over the bags again and grabbed hold of her to keep from falling. She held onto his arms, keeping him steady, mortified that she'd caused him to fall so many times.

"I'm really sorry!" Jordan cried, still gripping his arms. "Are you all right?"

But the words soon fled as she stared into his big, crystal blue eyes for a second time.

And saw stars.

He stared back at her, his gaze locked with hers, looking startled. No, surprised. And all she could do was stare. At the pale blue shimmer as his pupils widened, his mouth open as time stood still for a moment. Or a century. She couldn't tell and didn't care either way. He was so attractive, distracting from the image of Tyler kissing another woman right in front of her—while ignoring her calls.

"I'm... I'm sorry," he said in a bright, buttery voice that resonated like the patter of rain against glass. "Didn't realize you were behind me. I didn't hurt you, did I?"

People rushed past on all sides, but Jordan only saw them in a blur of colors and shapes at the periphery of her vision. She was transfixed by him as the compact space between them halted all time and movement. He smelled delicious—like hazelnuts and woodsmoke.

"I'm fine," she said, barely finding her voice.

He nodded and handed her the black hair tie. And unhooked a wild mahogany curl from his sleeve that had been tightly sequestered into loops until her spring-loaded scrunchie gave way.

"Your hair..."

Embarrassed, Jordan tried to smooth the tangle of curls. "I know. Looks like a brush fire. Or hair salon explosion."

He shook his head. "No... ditch the scrunchie. The curls... they're—exquisite."

The sudden, loud ring of a phone broke the spell between them.

Still staring, he reached into his pocket and put his phone to his ear.

"Yeah?"

He seemed as out of sorts as she felt. Had he hit his head? Or felt time slow like she had? That was silly. Guys didn't feel that sort of thing.

Did they?

"Olivia? Sorry, baby... connection's flaky."

He smiled at Jordan and turned toward his luggage, sliding up the telescoping handle. But hesitated a moment.

"Where am I?" he said into the phone and then pulled it away from his ear. "Merry Christmas," he mouthed to Jordan.

"Merry Christmas to you," she said.

His smile was big and warm as he stared at her one last time.

And put the phone back to his ear.

"I'm... at Sea-Tac," he said. "Just got my bag," he said as he wheeled his luggage away from the carousel. "Yeah. Storm's hitting right now."

His blond model looks, commanding voice, hazelnut and woodsmoke scent, and those starry blue eyes faded into the crowd.

Jordan felt her heart sink. Wanting to run after him. But that call was clearly from a girlfriend.

Lost two guys in one day. That was a record.

She refused to call Tyler again after what she just witnessed. Guess she was spending Christmas alone in Seattle. Broken-hearted. Getting to the ferry at Anacortes in a fifty-year snowstorm wasn't happening. Tomorrow, she'd try to get to Anacortes and catch the ferry. Tonight, she still needed a hotel room.

Teary-eyed, she searched for a hotel room again. After nearly a dozen sold out messages, she booked a room near the airport. It was probably the last hotel room left in the city.

Worst Christmas ever.

Cody Penton had no intention of proposing to Olivia Emerson-Hilliard this Christmas.

He glared at his phone as he sat in the drafty waiting room of Northwest Car Rentals, his blond hair disheveled by snow and wind, and waited for the keys to probably the last available rental car at Sea-Tac.

The long, narrow but well-lit space was crammed full of people. Lines went out the door into the falling snow, dozens of travelers with black bags stoically waiting around half a dozen rental counters, hoping to snag a rental. The counters were right beside each other, signs brightly lit, and adorned with wreaths, garland, red bows, and blinking Christmas lights. The air smelled like rewarmed coffee and falling snow, the roar of too many voices filling the space.

Even without the snowstorm, Olivia would have found another excuse not to pick him up at the airport. Much of the time, he felt like an afterthought to her.

And now, he waited for a rental car. With chains.

She didn't understand how difficult this Christmas was for him.

The first one without his dad. As the first anniversary of his death fast approached, Cody's grief was still raw with firsts. And this first Christmas without the old man was eating him up inside.

With both parents gone, Cody, an only child, met with a buyer in L.A. yesterday who made him a very lucrative offer for Dad's company. Cody told them he'd be in touch after the holidays. Running his own software development company from his Bellevue condo was enough. Besides, he knew nothing about Dad's hotel revitalization business.

Today, he'd boarded a plane back to Seattle. To spend Christmas with Olivia's family in Anacortes. She'd gone up a few days ago. Texting him for days about plans and arrangements. Dropping hints about what she expected out of this trip. Out of Christmas.

Him to propose.

But after three years together, their relationship felt more like a business transaction. And Olivia's callous response to his father's death hurt as much as her insistence that he should be over it by now.

The last thing on his mind right now was merging Emerson-Hilliard with Penton, Incorporated. Or selling Dad's business.

Had fate intervened with this massive storm?

He stared at the car rental app still open on his phone. With its confirmed reservation for a car. If only he'd gotten that lucky with a hotel room.

He doubted the roads would be open tomorrow because the storm was expected to last into tomorrow afternoon. He sighed. He just might have to sleep in his rental car.

Worst Christmas ever.

But still—the memory of that beautiful redhead and those wild, sexy curls made him smile. Clouded his head. Along with those smokin' hot yoga pants showing off her tall, lean body and some very nice curves. Her green eyes had enchanted him. Distracted him.

No, transported him.

His phone rang again. He glanced at the screen. Olivia.

Groaning, he shifted in the hard plastic chair and put the phone to his ear, "Jingle Bell Rock" playing through the building. He leaned on his black suitcase, yawning.

"Yes, Liv," he answered. "No, I'm still in Seattle like the last time you called. Renting a car. Yes, I know it's well after six. I won't get to Anacortes tonight. No... it's impossible."

Didn't they just have this conversation?

She thought she could just magically will the roads to stay clear and open long enough for him to drive an hour and a half up to Anacortes. Even though it would probably take five and a half hours now—if he was lucky.

But she expected him to just rent a car, because there were so many to choose from, drive like the roads were clear, and magically show up on her parents' doorstep. He flinched. With a ring.

Because she wanted it to happen.

For as long as he'd known her, Olivia Emerson-Hilliard always got what she wanted. Even if her parents had to pay triple for it. Money solved everything in her world. And she never had enough of it.

"If Sea-Tac doesn't have one, you need to try around the city. And then try Paine. Or an Uber." Olivia's voice was shrill against his ear, and he held the phone away from it.

He'd tried enough pain over this last year. Including the beating he'd just taken at baggage claim. He knew she meant Paine Field in Everett, but he resented her attitude. Like he was too stupid to manage on his own.

"I'm working on it," he replied. "Everyone's trying to rent cars right now."

"Well, work harder! Someone has to have a car for rent!" she said. "You've got to be in Anacortes for family dinner tomorrow. Try an Uber."

Again, he pulled the phone away from his ear as Olivia's shrill voice filled his head, demanding that he find a way to Anacortes.

Tonight. Right.... No Uber or Lyft drivers were out on these roads tonight and if they were, they were charging a fortune for it.

"If you can't manage it," she said in her most dismissive tone, "Dad will make it happen. I'm sure he can arrange a rental from somewhere—"

"I said I've got it handled," Cody snapped, an edge in his voice.

He'd grown tired of her always thinking he wasn't smart enough to manage his own affairs. Or that her dad could throw around money and solve the problem.

"Then I'll see you tonight, Cody."

His thoughts drifted.

Away from Olivia, the entire damned airport, the fifty-year storm, and the Christmas battle for luggage and rental cars. All of it fell away at the memory of that beautiful redhead's sparkly green eyes, like lights on a Christmas tree. Until she'd shouted at him about the luggage.

But before that, he couldn't look away. Didn't want to look away. She'd smelled so soft and inviting, like lilacs and linen hot from the dryer. Despite her trying to assassinate him with his own luggage, he wanted to get her name. Her phone number. Ask where she saw herself in the next five years? But he wasn't a cheater.

He was still with Olivia. A decision he questioned.

Besides, that redhead probably had a boyfriend. He smiled. And a coupla pairs of nun-chucks with his name on them, hidden in her assassin's luggage.

"Olivia," he said in a firm voice. "A blizzard's dumping nearly two feet of snow from Portland to Bellingham right now. There's ice under that snow. Even if I could rent a snowplow—or a damned Zamboni—those roads will close. I'm not going anywhere tonight except a hotel near Sea-Tac. I'll call you tomorrow."

"But I *want* you here at my parents tonight, Cody."

He knew that tone. That veiled threat beneath it. If she didn't get her way, her father would get it for her. And she would take whatever (or whoever) completely out of the equation to make it happen.

A bitter smile touched his lips. He looked forward to seeing her stop a snowstorm and magically transport him to Anacortes. Still, he was tired of her always demanding (and getting) her way.

"Liv, stop. It isn't happening."

He didn't want to tell her that he might be stranded tomorrow night, too.

"Call me tomorrow," she said in that dismissive tone, when she couldn't get her way. "With good news about your dad's company."

Cody frowned. "What good news?"

"That you sold it for three times its worth."

Like she was ordering him to sell it.

"Still considering the offer," he said in a quiet, distant voice. "That company meant a lot to Dad."

"How much was it?" she asked, pressing for specifics.

Like she always did. Her father was almost a billionaire. Why did she even care about his father's much smaller company?

"I'm not discussing this right now. Goodnight, Liv."

"Your dad's dead," she said. "He won't mind if you sell it."

Cody bristled. This wasn't some stranger. This was his dad. His best friend.

"Goodnight, Liv," he said with a growl.

"Goodnight, Cody," she said.

He cleared the call, angry and exhausted as he checked the hotel app again, but there wasn't a single room available near the airport—or anywhere. Reasonably or unreasonably priced.

He dropped his phone into his coat pocket and loosened his burgundy tie. After unbuttoning the top two buttons of his gray dress shirt, he peeled back the tag flap on his suitcase.

Jordan McKenna
(360) 378-5555

He smiled at the memory of the hot redhead with the curls and curves. But slowly, it dawned on him that this suitcase wasn't his.

Dammit!

That last faceplant over her luggage. They must have gotten their bags mixed up.

He snatched his phone out of his pocket and quickly dialed the number on the bag. Jordan McKenna. At least he had that gorgeous redhead's name. And cell number.

FEELING DISTRAUGHT, TEARS RUNNING DOWN HER cheeks, Jordan wheeled her black suitcase into a shotgun style, industrial, low-end motel room. The narrow room was painted cinderblocks and echoed, brightened by cream-colored paint, patterned carpet that could have hidden blood stains and brain matter in its nauseating rust-colored design. But the king-sized bed looked soft and clean, white sheets crisp and smelling like lemons.

She set her mint green backpack on the fake cherry dresser/desk combination against the wall opposite the bed. A big screen television perched on a dresser beside a desk and rolling black desk chair. A framed print of Elliott Bay hung on one wall and a print of the Cascades at sunset hung over the bed. The heater rumbled beneath rust-colored drapes with blackout curtains underneath. A small round table and two gold chairs sat in front of the window.

It wasn't the Edgewater, but it was warm and dry. The first-floor room had doors into the hallway and the parking lot with a heavy-duty deadbolt on both doors.

Jordan plopped down on the bed, muted olive green and rust colored damask bedspread and forest green blanket turned down, revealing two crisp white pillows.

Her phone rang.

Wiping her eyes, she grabbed her phone, frowning at the unrecognized number.

She didn't want to answer it.

Until a text popped up on the screen.

Pick up. Luggage guy from the airport.

The blond male model in the Armani suit! How did he get her number?

With shaking fingers, she answered the call.

"Hello?"

"Jordan?"

She frowned. How did he know her name?

"Who is this?"

"My name's Cody Penton," he said. "I was the luggage fall guy at baggage carousel fourteen."

She smiled. Dreamy, hot luggage fall guy. Well, he got the carousel number right. But she had to be sure.

"How do I know it's really you? We didn't exchange names. Or numbers."

He sighed. "Look at your luggage tag."

"My luggage tag?"

What would that prove?

"Just... look at it. It'll explain everything, I promise."

He sounded tired and exasperated. And she felt a little bad for him. Was he stuck at the airport? While she was in a room for the night.

But he'd left before her.

She rose from the bed and stepped over to her suitcase. And peeled back the luggage tag.

Cody Penton
(206) 385-5555

"Oh, my God!" she cried, a hand to her mouth. "I've got your bag!"

"And I've got yours," he said.

How did they manage to switch bags?

"Look, I've got a rental car," he said. "Tell me where you are and I can bring your bag to you."

She went quiet for a moment.

"You got a car?" she cried.

"Yeah," he replied. "I'll probably have to sleep in it. Not a room left in the whole damned city."

"I've got a room," said Jordan in a shaky voice.

The line went quiet.

"What... you got a hotel room?"

"Uh huh," she said, her voice softer than she'd intended. "But you got a rental car. That means you won't be stuck in Seattle for Christmas."

"No, but I just might freeze to death before I get to Anacortes."

Anacortes? That's where she needed to go!

"Cody, you can't sleep in that car," she said. "You *will* freeze to death."

She gazed around her room. And felt guilty.

"Listen, I need to catch the ferry at Anacortes," she said. "And you need a place to stay. What if I share my motel room with you tonight? And you share your rental car with me tomorrow? That way, we both get where we're going alive for Christmas."

The line went quiet.

She paused. Too scary? Considering she'd almost given him a concussion. Okay, several.

"Cody? You there?"

"All right, Jordan," he said. "You've got a deal. Tell me where you are and I'll be there shortly."

"Seattle Airport Motel, room 114. Sorry, it was all I could get. It's definitely not the Hilton, but they have a restaurant. With a bar."

"Then things are looking up. See you soon."

She cleared the call and turned around.

Oh my God. This room only had one bed.

She called the front desk.

"Would you have a rollaway bed avail—no? Thanks for checking."

Again, she turned to stare at the king-sized bed.

Sleeping with a stranger in a strange motel with only one bed? This was straight out of a bad TV episode.

How bad could it be?

Then she smiled. A smokin' hot, blond male model stranger. Who liked her curls. Probably due to multiple concussions, but regardless, they'd get through tonight and then she had a ride to Anacortes!

She moved his suitcase over against the wall and not five minutes later, a knock resounded on the door.

Feeling first-date nervous, Jordan rushed to open it.

Cody Penton. With her black suitcase, tie undone, dress shirt unbuttoned at the neck, and a weary expression on his smokin' hot oval face, those crystal blue eyes tired but sparkling.

"Hey, Cody," she said and opened the door wide. "Come on in."

He smiled as he walked past her, pulling the suitcase but stopped in mid-stride. Eyes wide.

Staring at the bed.

Finally, he whirled around, fear burning in those blue eyes.

"There's one bed," he said. "There's only one bed."

Jordan nodded, sliding her phone into her pocket. "I called the front desk and tried to get a cot, but they were out."

Shaking his head, he let go of her suitcase and moved toward his bag against the wall.

"I can't do this," he said and started toward the door.

But Jordan grabbed his arm.

"If you sleep in your car, you'll freeze to death," she said.

"Then I'll head back to the airport."

"And then drive treacherous roads without sleep?"

Finally, he turned around.

"Jordan, my girlfriend will lose her mind if she finds out I shared a hotel room with another woman."

God, he was thoughtful. He was a stand-up guy, and she admired the hell out of this man who was willing to freeze to death rather than upset his girlfriend.

"Cody," she said, catching herself from laying her hand against his arm—bad timing. "It's a fifty-year storm. Trust me, this is the last hotel room in Seattle. Would she rather you froze to death?"

He sighed. "Yeah. She would. And she'd bury me, knowing I'd been faithful while spending every penny of my estate on a grief trip to the Maldives."

Jordan laughed. "Then don't tell her." God, that sounded awful, didn't it? "Or tell her I'm a guy."

A light went on in his eyes. "Jordan!" he cried, grabbing hold of her arms. "That's brilliant. I'll tell her you're a guy."

Then he turned back to the bed. "You have a jealous boyfriend? That's a black belt? World heavyweight champion?"

She shrugged. She didn't know anymore. Tyler found someone else while she was in Ohio on a contract job. But if Cody knew she was newly single, like an hour or so ago, things might get weird between them. Sharing a bed and all.

"I got a last-minute early flight," she said. "He isn't even expecting me until tomorrow." All true. "I just won't mention it."

After hearing that, he relaxed a little. He pulled off his coat and wheeled his suitcase over to the table. He draped his coat on the back of a chair and sat down. Laying his suitcase on the carpet, he unzipped it and pulled out a dark blue sweater, jeans, and some tan loafers.

"Hungry?" he asked.

"As stuffed as I am on those three tiny airplane pretzels I had with my Coke Zero, I could eat. Everything on the menu."

He laughed. "I'll change out of my work clothes and we can go investigate this restaurant."

He took off the black dress shoes and slid his feet into those lived-in tan loafers.

"Although, if it's anything like this carpet, we may be dining from the vending machines."

Jordan chuckled. "I saw that they had the finest in ruffled chips and November was a very good month for cheese puffs."

His expression brightened.

"And the finest plastic-wrapped pastries in Seattle. Circa 1975."

"Nothing but the best—at triple the gas station prices," said Jordan.

His humor was a lot like hers, setting her at ease. He seemed more like a real person than the male model business persona she'd pinned on him at the airport. Tyler rarely made dumb jokes, much less riffing jokes off hers. She liked that.

Chuckling, he rose from the chair. "Thanks for going along with my bad sense of humor. Drives Olivia nuts. She's always telling me to leave the comedy to the professionals."

Jordan frowned. "She's the one that's nuts."

He carried his clothes past her and changed in the bathroom. When he came out, he looked even hotter in jeans. She sighed. She could really fall for a guy like Cody Penton.

She grabbed her small black purse out of her backpack and slid out a room keycard, handing it to Cody.

"Just in case you go on a vending machine pastry run," she replied.

Grinning, he took the card and pulled out his wallet. He put the key inside and slid his wallet back into his pocket.

"Ready?" he asked.

Jordan nodded and he opened the door into the hallway.

THE SMALL, DINER-BRIGHT RESTAURANT WAS PACKED, NO seating available, so Cody and Jordan ordered a couple of cheeseburgers to go. For twenty minutes, they stood by the cold windows, watching the snow pile up. About three inches on the ground, big, heavy flakes falling.

Jordan looked excited by the snow. At the airport, she seemed angry and flustered, but here at the hotel, she seemed so different. She watched the snow like a little kid and her excitement was intoxicating.

Jordan looked up at him, grinning as she pushed open the door into the snowy parking lot. And stepped underneath the twinkling multi-colored lights above the restaurant door. Colored lights illuminated her hair and face, igniting those fiery curls with a red and purple glow.

As she walked out into the heavy snowfall.

She held out her arms, twirling around, big flakes collecting against her curls and clinging to her long, dark eyelashes.

Laughing, she danced in the snow.

Cody was entranced. The snow was magic and she enjoyed every moment of it.

And that was totally intoxicating.

Olivia refused to even get her hair wet. Hated rain. And tolerated snow at Christmas. She hated the Pacific Northwest weather. But he loved it. It took him back to being a kid on Bainbridge Island.

His phone buzzed. He slid it out. Text from Olivia.

Have you found a way up to Anacortes yet?

Damn! He shoved the phone back in his pocket. He'd had enough of her pushing to get her way. Everything about Olivia was pushing for her way.

He shoved open the door and rushed outside into the falling snow.

The world felt so quiet and fragile. And so magical covered in inches of wet, heavy snow, the sounds of traffic—and planes—quiet now.

"Isn't it amazing?" Jordan asked.

She held out her tongue, catching snowflakes, and then laughing.

Cody held out his arms and closed his eyes, letting a tough decade slough away, transporting him back to Christmas on Bainbridge Island. Coming home on the ferry from Seattle with Dad, carrying bags of presents while Mom picked up pizza at a local favorite, King's Pizza.

He remembered one Christmas when snow started falling as they opened presents and ate pizza. Afterward, he and Dad had a snowball fight in the front yard. It was magic.

It was the first the memory of his dad that hadn't quite hurt so much.

Smack! A snowball hit him square in the face. Followed by Jordan's hysterical laughter.

He opened one eye. As another snowball hit him in the chin.

Woman had great aim.

"You really wanna go there?" he shouted with a devilish grin and bent down, grabbing a slushy wet handful of snow.

Another snowball hit him in the chest. Followed by Jordan's musical, hysterical laughter.

"Oh, it's on!"

He chased her across the parking lot and beaned her with a snowball. Retreating to grab another handful of snow.

Laughing, he fired off another one, hitting her in the cheek. She laughed harder and scrabbled for another handful of snow. He lunged for more and ran into her, the pavement beneath the snow slippery.

Jordan lost her footing first, grabbing hold of him to keep from falling. Dragging him down with her, into a snow drift beside the building. They both faceplanted into the drift.

He laughed hysterically and struggled to his feet, his jeans wet and snowy now. Like her yoga pants. He helped her to her feet, her hair covered in snow, turning those fiery red curls into glorious ringlets.

She was so beautiful and for a moment, she took his breath.

He stared into her bright, wonder-filled green eyes.

"Are you all right?" she asked, still laughing.

"Never better," he answered as he helped her out of the snow.

He brushed off his jeans while she shook out her hair and those incredible curls. He reached out and brushed snow out of a tangle of curls over her left eye. Staring into her eyes.

She watched him in silence, green gaze intense.

In that moment, what did she see? He felt lighter somehow. She'd gotten him past his grief for a little while and she didn't even know it.

"Liar," she said. "You were faraway for a few moments there. Everything okay?"

Cody glanced down at his snowy loafers.

"First anniversary of my dad's death is coming up," he answered finally. "And for a while, you made me remember a wonderful Christmas snowball fight with him."

"Like this?" she said and hit him with another snowball.

Grinning, he looked down at the snow covering his sweater and grabbed snow off the bushes. Hitting her in the shoulder with a snowball.

"Grief is tough at Christmas," she said, brushing snow off his sweater. "If it helps to talk about him, I'm a good listener."

"Thanks," he said. "I appreciate that."

Olivia would never listen to him talk about his dad's death. She always changed the subject, avoiding anything unpleasant. To money. The offer for Dad's company. How much his estate was worth.

"Let's go check on our food."

After a couple of Pyramid Hefeweizens on tap at the restaurant's tiny bar, Jordan and Cody brought their food back to the room. They sat down at the small table by the window, watching the wind whip the snow into tall drifts across the parking lot.

Cody got quiet after he pulled out his phone, mood darkening. Worrying her.

"Is someone from work texting you?" Jordan asked finally.

He looked puzzled.

"Because that's the face I make when someone I don't want to hear from texts me," said Jordan. "Like work."

He sighed. "It's Olivia again," he said. "She keeps demanding that I get to Anacortes tonight. Like I'm not even trying."

Jordan sat back in her chair and tossed her trash into the brown paper bag on the table.

"Unbelievable... storm's moving north," said Jordan. "We'll be chasing it all the way there tomorrow—if we can even get on the roads. Why isn't she worried about you getting there alive? Or that you're safe?"

Even now, that would have been her concern if Tyler had been driving from Seattle to Anacortes in a massive snowstorm.

Cody shoved his trash into the bag.

"A very good question."

He slid off his loafers, his mood still dark. He was no longer that fun guy trading snowballs with her in the snow. He was quiet and brooding. But she didn't know him well enough to tell him that his girlfriend was probably a raging narcissist. Or bring up the fact that she'd seen her boyfriend kissing another woman at the airport.

After throwing the bag in a small white trashcan beside the dresser, Cody moved to his luggage and began sorting through it, stacking several little presents wrapped in gold and red paper on the table.

"Taking inventory?" Jordan asked.

He nodded. "Making sure I didn't forget anyone's gift. Olivia would stroke out."

Jordan put her suitcase on the desk and began checking her own gifts, making sure she had gifts for her sister and brother-in-law. Seeing the four small presents for Tyler hurt. Made her eyes tear up.

She noticed that Cody's gaze had drifted to her presents.

"Those for your boyfriend?" he asked.

"Some of them," she replied. "The others are for my sister and brother-in-law on San Juan Island."

"Nice," he replied as he packed the presents back into his luggage. "I hear the island's beautiful."

Jordan turned around. "You've never been?"

He shook his head. "Lived in Seattle, Bellevue, and Bainbridge Island, but never got up to the islands."

"Well, if things go south with your girlfriend, you've got a place to stay on the island. At my sister's B&B."

At last, he smiled, shades of that dark mood retreating. "Good to know."

By the time ten-thirty rolled around, they were both yawning. And nervous.

Jordan pulled out a pair of gray leggings and a purple T-shirt to sleep in and took a shower. Brushed her teeth. She'd wash her hair tomorrow at the B&B.

When she came out of the bathroom, he'd taken the blanket and folded it on one side of the bed. He draped the bedspread on the other side by the window. Two pillows on either side. With a notice-able gap between them.

"I hope you don't mind, but I... arranged things," he said.

Did a good job. Better than she would have done.

"Looks good to me," she said, smiling. "Thank you."

He held up his hands. "And I promise to be a gentleman."

"And I promise to mind the gap and stay on my side," said Jordan.

After sharing an awkward glance, he rushed into the bathroom with a small black leather bag. She heard him brushing his teeth and taking a shower as she put away her toiletry bag.

Nervous, she sat down on the side of the bed with the blanket and set her phone on the nightstand, plugging in the charger.

In a few minutes, he hurried out of the bathroom dressed in a blue and green plaid pair of pajama pants and a gray T-shirt and put away his leather bag. He sat down on the bedspread side and plugged in his phone to charge. It buzzed against the nightstand.

And again.

The third time it buzzed, he jerked it off the table. Thumbs flashed across the screen and then he practically threw it onto the nightstand again.

"Everything okay?" Jordan asked.

"Fine," he said, angry and tight-lipped.

"Turn off your phone," I said. "Or you won't sleep."

The phone buzzed again. With a growl, he shut off the phone.

His girlfriend seemed like a narcissistic piece of work. What did she expect the poor guy to do in the middle of a massive snowstorm?

"Lights on or off?" Jordan asked.

"Off," said Cody.

"More heat or cold?"

"Cold," he said.

Worked for her.

She rose from the bed to check the heater's settings, putting it on low. He checked the parking lot door's deadbolt and she checked the hallway door. After turning off the lights, she sat back down on the bed. The nightstand lamps were the only lights in the room.

Taking a deep breath, Jordan crawled under the blanket, facing away from the hottest guy she'd ever met, and turned out her light.

"Sleep well, Cody."

"You, too, Jordan."

With eyes wide open, she stared at the wall, waiting for him to turn out the other light. Only bathed in total darkness would she let go of enough nerves to fall asleep beside a man she'd only met this afternoon. Who smelled like hazelnuts and woodsmoke.

Click.

All the lights went out, drone of the heater the only sound in the room.

For what felt like an hour, she was afraid to move, afraid to breathe. Afraid to turn over and accidentally set something awkward in motion.

SOMETIME AFTER MIDNIGHT, CODY HEARD JORDAN'S steady even breaths whisper above the heater as he hugged the pillows under his head, afraid to move. Afraid to make an inappropriate move in his sleep. But his eyelids got heavier until he sank into an exhausted sleep.

And dreamed.

About that last night at the hospital. Dad's breaths had been so shallow and labored, a rattle in his throat as he called for Mom. Cody held his hand, telling him it was okay to go to her. Lying that he'd be fine, the pain so sharp in his chest that it stung his eyes. The pale blue hospital room got so dark and cavernous, so many lights flickering and shuddering, so many beeps and trills and buzzes. The lights in the dark room made Dad's shadow twist and rise along the wall in terrifying proportions.

Dad shouted and shuddered, the vital signs monitor jolting with every labored breath. As the numbers and indicators began to drop.

Dying of cancer, he'd gotten pneumonia. Cody refused the treatment that would have prolonged his life. A week or two at most. Letting him go.

It was the hardest thing he'd ever done.

And he'd told no one, especially Olivia. He'd done it out of love. It was what Dad wanted.

But he still had nightmares about it.

"Cody?"

The voice was soft beneath Dad's shouts and the machine beeps, growing louder until it filled his head.

Finally, he lurched up from the pillow with a gasp and dropped his face in his hands.

"Cody? Are you okay?"

Hands rubbed his shoulder in the dark.

"Sorry I woke you," he said in a drowsy voice, not quite sure where he was, the room so dark and unfamiliar.

That wasn't Olivia's voice.

But he was grateful. She would have told him to get over it and go back to sleep. Because she'd never experienced a single moment of trauma. At twenty-two, her obscenely wealthy parents had shielded her from everything.

"Don't worry about that," said the female voice, still rubbing his shoulder. "You were calling for your dad."

He was shaking, the dream—no, the memory—haunting him. He hated how Dad died and he hated that he had to make such a terrible decision as withholding treatment. It made him feel like he'd murdered his dad. It was the thing he couldn't talk to Olivia about. She'd just tell him it was the best choice and to get over it.

"Bad dream about the night he died," he said, his voice breaking.

Dammit. He felt like a fool. Like a little kid afraid of the dark.

"What happened?"

He hesitated as her arm went around his shoulders, her left hand still rubbing his shoulder.

"You don't have to talk about it," she said in a soft, soothing voice. "It's okay. But I'm here if you do."

"I...." He pulled in a painful breath, bowing his head. "I let him die."

"What do you mean?" she asked.

He leaned against her, smashing his eyes closed, the pain of the memory radiating. It was the one thing he couldn't admit to himself until now. Until the nightmare. That he'd let his dad die.

"I let him die," he repeated in a tight voice, his chest aching.

She put both arms around him, holding him close, rubbing his back.

"He was dying of cancer," he said, pulling in a hot breath. "When he got pneumonia, I...." Another heated breath, his eyes stinging at the realization of what he'd done that night. "Oh, God... I let my old man die, Jordan. My best friend. I just let him lay there and die."

Her arms tightened around him.

"You let him go, Cody," she insisted. "You didn't kill him. You let him escape the pain and the cancer. Months of suffering."

He put his arms around her and pulled in a shaky breath, his body cold and trembling. Pressing against her warmth and comfort. Something Olivia had never done. Grief was weakness and comfort was coddling. She'd never experienced grief. He'd gone through his grief alone for almost a year, living with this horrible decision he'd been forced to make.

"It was an act of love, Cody," she said as he laid his head against her shoulder. "One of the last things you could do for him was let him go."

"Olivia says I just need to get over it."

"No, you just need to get through it," she said. "There's no time limit on grief and only you get to decide how long that takes. Not Olivia or anyone."

Her words calmed him and her embrace warmed him, kept him from walking the floor and blaming himself until the sun rose. Like most nights when he had this nightmare. Or when he was with Olivia, forced to keep everything inside. To himself. After nearly a year of it, he was exhausted.

She held him until he yawned, his eyelids drooping. Slowly, she laid back with him against the pillows. Bridging the gap. Still cuddled against her, he closed his eyes. And with Jordan against him, he fell asleep.

A deep, satisfying sleep.

Her warm, comforting presence chased away other nightmares and he slept through the rest of the night.

When he woke up, he was alone in the bed. The smell of warm hazelnut coffee drifted through the room.

He glanced at the clock on the other nightstand. After seven.

Stretching, he sat up and ran his fingers through his hair.

Jordan was in the bathroom, door closed. A fresh pot of coffee steamed in the coffeemaker, a paper cup beside it.

Crawling out of bed, he put on his loafers and poured a hot cup of coffee, adding the powdered creamer to it. Better than no creamer. He swirled it around in the cup and sipped it.

As Jordan came out of the bathroom.

For a moment, they stared at each other. Feeling awkward.

He felt embarrassed about last night. Dealing with something so intense and personal with a stranger.

"Sleep well?" she asked and hurried past him.

"I did," he answered between sips of coffee. "And you?"

"I did, thanks," she said and put a small makeup bag into her luggage.

And zipped it up.

"I checked the highway reports," she said, moving him gracefully away from the awkward subject. "And I-5 North has one lane open, chains required."

"Good news," he said and finished the coffee. "I'll get dressed and we can get on the road."

He tossed the cup and moved to his luggage.

———

JORDAN SAT WITH HER PUFFY BLACK COAT OVER A GREEN sweater and black yoga pants, her luggage and backpack beside her, waiting for Cody.

He seemed okay this morning, but she still felt terrible for the guy after that awful nightmare. And nearly a year of dealing with all that pain and grief and blame alone. His girlfriend seemed unaffected by anything but herself. He seemed almost embarrassed this morning, but he'd needed someone to talk him through that pain last night. And tell him that he hadn't done anything wrong.

She didn't even know this woman and she already detested her.

In a few minutes, he came out wearing a red and black flannel shirt, black T-shirt underneath, jeans, and hiking boots. His hair was damp and combed into place, sexy blond stubble along his jaw. He grabbed the handle of his suitcase.

"Ready?"

Jordan nodded.

She left both keycards and a tip on the table and they went out to the parking lot. To a small black Kia. Half-covered in snow drifts.

Using his sleeve, Cody brushed the snow off the back passenger side window, snow dusting the air, and unlocked the door. He opened the door, reached in, and grabbed a scraper from the seat pocket. One of those long ones with a scraper at one end and a brush at the other. He closed the door and moved around the car, brushing away the dry, powdery snow from the windows, the rear window, and front windshield.

With only traces of snow on the windows now, Cody opened the backseat door and hefted both bags into the car. They piled in front, the black interior still smelling new. He started the engine, turned on the heater, and inched the Kia out of the parking lot, headed toward I-5 North.

Few cars were on the roads. I-5 looked like an arctic wasteland with snow drifts and ruts of ice covering lanes north and south.

He gripped the steering wheel with both hands, a look of intense concentration pinching his features as he drove about twenty miles an hour, the chains biting into the ice underneath the snow. Trees and countryside glistened with a white sheen of snow, a winter wonderland as the sun rose.

Jordan felt his tight grip on the steering wheel as the tires struggled to stay in the ice ruts. What should have taken an hour and a half became three hours. Then four. The rasp of chains against ice and snow was a constant inside the car, drowning out the radio. She turned it off.

His phone sat in the cup holder between them, ringer and vibration turned off. But Jordan watched text after text roll across the screen. Olivia.

She seriously disliked this witch. This entitled woman had no idea how treacherous these roads were and how stressful driving on them was for her boyfriend. Instead of letting him concentrate, she was blowing up his phone with stupid texts, demanding responses, and expecting him to let her know exactly where he was at all times.

At least she was interested. Tyler hadn't even bothered to call her back. She could be lying in a snow-filled ravine, trapped in a rental car, and he wouldn't even know it. Or care.

"Let me know if you get sleepy," she said.

He smiled. "Facing my mortality every mile on this ice and snow is doing a fine job of keeping me awake."

Jordan laughed.

"Your girlfriend has sent you like fifty texts since this morning."

He rolled his eyes. "Before we left the room, I texted her that I'd let her know when I got close to Anacortes."

Jordan turned her head sideways, reading another barrage of texts that hit his phone.

"She's demanding to know how much," said Jordan, shaking her head. "What does that mean?"

"It means," he said with a snarl, his grip on the steering wheel tightening. "She wants to know how much Acclaim Suites offered for my dad's business."

His girlfriend's father was rich. Why did she care how much Cody got offered for his dad's company. Was she making sure he had enough assets to suit her?

"Checking your net worth?" Jordan asked.

"Seeing if I'm worth marrying," he added. "She all but said that she was expecting a ring from me this Christmas."

A cold chill shuddered through Jordan. He couldn't marry this harpy! She'd make him miserable. More miserable.

"That's... really... cold," she said finally.

"That's Olivia," he said, his gaze fixed on the road.

"And that works for you?" she asked, glancing at him.

Might as well put it out there. She couldn't believe someone like Cody wanted a woman like that.

He exhaled, part laughter, part sigh.

"The first year we were together was great," he said, his gaze not leaving the road. "When Dad got sick, she changed. Got annoyed whenever I talked about his treatments. His health."

Because narcissists hated it when the attention went to someone else.

"When he died, her focus shifted to his estate. And his company."

Making sure her boyfriend's net worth was worth bragging about.

"What's your boyfriend do?" he asked.

129

"He's a lawyer for a medical tech company here in Seattle," Jordan answered.

"Why hasn't he bothered to check on you?" Cody demanded.

"I'm not supposed to be flying in until this afternoon," she replied.

"Not even a text?" Cody glanced over at her. "If you were my girlfriend, I'd have been blowing up your phone. Making sure you were safe."

She wanted to keep up her charade, but she couldn't lie to him. Not now.

"Okay..." Jordan said with a groan, feeling her eyes sting. "Truth. I called him from baggage claim yesterday and his ringtone for me went off nearby. I turned around and saw him kissing another woman. He hasn't returned my calls. Merry Christmas to me."

She bowed her head, biting her lip to keep the tears from filling her eyes.

"My God... Jordan." He glanced from her to the road and back again. "I'm so sorry. And you've been dealing with this since yesterday?"

She nodded, staring at her feet. And then melted when she felt his hand against her arm, rubbing it.

"For what it's worth, this guy is a total idiot. Doesn't know what he's lost."

She felt tears well up and she swiped at them, trying to extinguish them so Cody wouldn't see.

"I thought everything was fine," Jordan said, fighting back the tears.

"Maybe it was," he said, his gaze encompassing her. "Maybe he just met someone that set his heart on fire? Something he didn't plan."

She stared at Cody, at the wistful look in his crystal blue eyes. He was so hot. So sweet. Why couldn't she have met him instead of Tyler? Why did he have to have a girlfriend?

"By the way," he said. "Thanks again for last night."

"Of course," she said, turning her head away to wipe the remaining tears away. "You grieve as long as you need to about your dad. It's an expression of love not weakness."

When she looked up, he was smiling.

"Thank you," he said in a quiet voice.

He turned his gaze back to the road, tires and chains thumping against the icy ruts.

In a few minutes, they passed a sign for Marysville. Still about an hour away from Anacortes. The roads seemed to be getting a little better as they traveled north. Trees and landscape were still blanketed in snow, but that crunchy layer of ice seemed thinner. Mostly snow.

Just outside Marysville, the driver's side tire blew.

Cody fought the swerving car onto the side of the road. And turned off the motor. After hitting the parking brake, he popped the trunk.

"Let's see what's in the trunk," he said, getting out.

"I'll help," said Jordan, opening the passenger side door.

When she followed him to the trunk, he was smiling.

"Not used to anyone offering to help," he said as he opened the trunk.

Beneath the liner was a rudimentary jack. And a real tire!

"Look at that!" Jordan cried. "No donut."

He nodded. Relieved. "Chains won't fit a donut."

He pulled out the scissor jack and Jordan picked up the tire.

"Jordan, really," he said, his hand on her shoulder. "You don't have to."

"Why not?" she said. "My dad taught me how to change a tire. If we work together, it'll go faster."

Cody's smile turned into a grin as he watched her carry the tire over in front of the vehicle. He knelt in the snow and positioned the jack, but she laid her hand on his shoulder.

"Might want to loosen the lug nuts first," she said. "Just a little. A quarter turn. Helps keep the jack steady."

"Right," he said, looking nervous as he swiveled the jack handle. "A quarter turn."

He was going to blister his hands without gloves. She reached into her coat pockets and pulled out a pair of black stretch gloves.

"Here," she said. "Put these on."

He accepted the gloves, sliding his hands inside. With the lug wrench, he loosened each lug nut a quarter turn and then jacked up the car. And began removing the lug nuts. She gathered each one in her coat pocket as he lifted off the flat tire, setting it aside.

She glanced over her shoulder at the road, afraid a car might slide onto the shoulder or sideswipe them. Seeing I-5 so desolate, not a single car headed north, it made her anxious, so she kept checking. Listening.

Finally, in the distance, she heard the crunch and whisper of tires. She glanced up. A car headed north. She glanced at Cody, so thoughtfully changing the tire, making sure she wasn't stuck out in this storm. A warm blush touched her cheeks. She'd keep him safe.

After she'd collected all the lug nuts, Jordan knelt beside him and together, they lifted the tire onto the axle, fitting it over the lug nut posts.

"Ready to go," she said as he grabbed the lug nut wrench, but she grabbed hold of his arm as the whisper of tires drew closer.

"Wait for the car," she said, staring into his eyes, wanting to wrap her arms around his neck and kiss him.

"Why?" he asked in a raspy voice, a smile lifting the corners of his mouth.

"Just keeping you safe," she said softly, falling into his crystalline blue eyes.

God, she wanted to kiss him!

His hand gripped hers a moment and she gasped, but realized he was retrieving lug nuts.

Sighing, she handed the rest of the lug nuts to him one-by-one as she glanced at the empty road until the tire was secure.

Finally, he stood up, undoing the chains hanging on the flat tire. He spread the chains out in front of the tire and climbed into the car. Starting it, he lifted the parking brake, and inched forward until the tire was centered on the chains. When he shut off the car, Jordan bent down and began fastening the chains in place.

He rolled down the window.

"You know how to attach chains, too?" he said.

She nodded. "Dad was thorough."

He put the flat in the trunk and closed it as she climbed back into the car. He reached up to start the car, but Jordan laid her hand on his sleeve.

"Hungry?" she asked.

"I could eat," he said and then frowned. "Why?"

She opened her backpack and held it out to him.

"Scored the finest vending machine fare this side of Oregon," she said with a chuckle.

He laughed and pulled out a bag of ruffled chips. "You had me at Ruffles."

Quickly, he finished off the small bag of ruffled chips and then started the car, pulling back onto the almost empty interstate.

They headed north again. Toward Anacortes.

He glanced at his phone, scowling at the text messages and then finally called her back on speaker.

"Olivia," he said, a sharp edge to his voice. "I told you I would contact you when I got close to Anacortes. Why are you blowing up my phone like this? You're on speaker, by the way."

"Why are you ignoring my texts?" Olivia snapped. "I need to know where you are."

"I'm outside Marysville," he said with a grumble.

"Marysville!" The woman sounded furious. "That's an hour from here. And you couldn't be bothered to call or text me that."

He bristled. "I'm calling you now. Blew a tire and just finished changing it."

She was quiet for a moment or two.

"I hope you're bringing me the gift I asked for," she said, changing the subject.

His laugh was incredulous. "And what is that?"

"The sale of your dad's company," she said and pulled in a breath. "And that engagement ring you promised."

Oh, no! He couldn't be getting engaged to this woman? He couldn't!

Jordan turned and stared at him like he'd lost his mind. He shook his head and leaned toward his phone.

"Liv, I've decided not to sell Dad's company."

"You what?"

Jordan couldn't help but smile at this woman's comical outrage.

"Dad and Mom built that company together," he said. "It started with saving the inn where they spent their honeymoon. Now, the company rescues old hotels across the country and revitalizes them. I want that to continue."

"You're keeping it?" she cried.

"I am."

"Cody!" she cried. "We talked about this."

"No, you talked about it," he said. "I want to continue my dad's vision."

The phone was quiet for several long moments.

"Don't bother with a ring," said Olivia. "I wouldn't marry a man who chose his father's business over me. In fact, don't bother coming here for Christmas either."

Cody grinned. "Merry Christmas, Olivia."

Olivia growled and the phone went dead.

Still grinning, Cody turned toward Jordan.

"Well, that was easy," he said with a laugh and settled back in his seat. "I never dreamed she'd dump me for keeping my dad's business, but I'm glad I found out now."

Jordan turned to him, smiling. "So, we've both been dumped for Christmas," she said.

He nodded. "Looks like it."

He drove on in silence and Jordan wondered what was running through his head, but he got quiet as the roads got better. North around Burlington, the roads were just snow. Cody pulled over and together, they removed the chains. Back on the highway, they turned left onto the US-20 spur. Headed toward Anacortes.

"Where will you go for Christmas, Cody?" Jordan asked.

He shrugged. "At this moment, I have no idea. How far to the ferry terminal?"

"About thirty minutes."

Twenty-five minutes later, Jordan's phone rang.

She slid it out of her pocket. Her heart dropped. Tyler.

"Tyler," she said, trying to keep her voice from breaking.

Cody kept glancing over at her.

"Where am I?" she repeated. "I'm about five minutes from the Anacortes ferry terminal. Why?"

Tyler paused. "What? But your flight from Cincinnati is boarding."

She pulled in a deep breath. He needed to know that she knew everything.

"I got a seat on a flight yesterday," she said. "Called you several times when I got into Seattle. But you never picked up. Well, you picked up a blonde, but not my calls."

The line went deadly quiet.

"What blonde?"

Jordan laughed bitterly. "The one you picked up at baggage claim thirteen yesterday. Green dress. Pink suitcase. I was at fourteen, Tyler. I saw everything."

"Jordan, I—" he stammered. "Can we talk about this? Please?"

Her eyes began to sting.

"It's way too late for explanations. And I don't care how you met or when. We both know it ends here. Enjoy the holidays. Blocking you now."

She cleared the call and blocked his number.

"You okay?" Cody asked.

She bit her lip as it began to quiver. "No... but someday, I will be."

He reached over and slid his arm around her shoulder, pulling her against him. He smelled like hazelnuts and woodsmoke and she wanted to lose herself in that intoxicating fragrance.

"That's what he gets for cheating on his smokin' hot girlfriend."

Cody thought she was hot?

He turned into the ferry terminal surrounded by tall cedars and firs, blanketed in white snow, the deep teal bay calm against the small squat terminal building perched on its edge. Two large parking lots with sixteen car lanes, numbered in white, were mostly empty despite the ferry arriving at any moment.

He pulled over before he got to the pay booth.

"I can walk down from here," she said and turned toward Cody, gripping his hands. "Thank you for getting me out of Sea-Tac on Christmas Eve."

"Thanks for the night in your bed," he said and cringed, smashing his eyes closed. "That didn't come out right, I—"

She laughed, keeping a smile on her face, but she didn't want to say goodbye to Cody Penton. She wanted to throw her arms around him and kiss him hard on the lips.

"Anytime," she said, wincing. "I mean, you're welcome."

"You made the worst travel experience of my life a lot of fun, Jordan," he said. "Thank you."

"Thank you for not murdering me in my sleep after I gave you a dozen concussions at baggage claim."

She threw her arms around him and hugged him. His arms tightened around her and they hugged for several moments.

"Where will you go for Christmas?" she asked. "Now that you've escaped from Olivia's clutches?"

He shrugged. "Not sure. Guess I'll head back to my place in Bellevue."

She brushed the hair out of his eyes. "Offer's still open to stay at my sister's B&B on the island. She'll have a room available."

He paused, like he was waiting for something. She'd just invited him to her sister's B&B. Wasn't it obvious that she liked him?

"Thanks, but I should probably head home," he said finally, looking a little dejected. "You're staying with family—I don't want to intrude."

He was letting her down easy. Finding a way out of this situation. And that made her sad.

No use prolonging the pain. He wasn't interested.

Sighing, she got out of the car and opened the back passenger door. She grabbed the suitcase behind her seat. She hefted her backpack on her shoulder and closed the door. With a wave, she wheeled her luggage along the smooth asphalt past the ticket booth, heading toward the terminal to buy a walk-on ticket for San Juan Island. Feeling like she'd just left her heart behind.

If he'd wanted to stay with her, he'd have said so.

Wouldn't he?

The luggage wheels slid in the snow as she walked down the road and across the parking lot where six cars were lined up. Cody Penton would be a hard man to get over. And she already missed him. Why hadn't she told him she wanted to spend Christmas with him?

She got halfway to the terminal when a horn honked behind her. She turned.

Cody! He'd changed his mind. Her heart fluttered as he drove the black Kia into Lane Four and rolled down the window.

She rushed toward him, expecting him to say he was crazy about her.

"Wrong suitcase," he said.

She frowned, her heart dropping. "What?"

"You took the wrong suitcase, Jordan," he said.

What? No way! Not again. She just assumed he'd put her bag behind her seat when he loaded them into the car.

Mortified, her cheeks burning, she rushed over to the car.

"Are you serious?" she cried.

He nodded.

She opened the tag and sure enough, she'd grabbed Cody's bag. Again.

He got out of the car and put his bag back inside. He opened the other door and she moved toward it.

As she reached for the other bag—her suitcase—he laid his hand on her arm.

"Wait," he said. "Jordan... I don't want to say goodbye to you. These past two days have been so much fun and so comfortable and... well, amazing. And I don't want that to end. I don't know if you felt the same way, but—"

She stared at him, trying not to smile. "You switched the bags, didn't you?" she said.

He bowed his head. "Guilty. I put your suitcase behind my seat and mine behind yours." He sighed. "It was my last resort."

She took hold of his hands.

"It worked," she said. "I don't want you to drive off and never see you again."

"What?" His eyes were wide with surprise.

She nodded. "Yes, that's right. I'm crazy about you, Cody. And I don't care if you sell your dad's business or not."

He pulled her into his arms and kissed her. It was fire and heat and Christmas magic all rolled into his hazelnut and woodsmoke kiss, and all she wanted for Christmas was Cody Penton.

With no gap between them.

She smashed her mouth against his with an urgent, aching kiss that staggered him a moment. And then he pulled her into his arms, holding her tightly as it began to snow again.

Arm and arm, Cody walked her around to the passenger side and opened the door for her. Jordan climbed into the car. And back into Cody's arms as the arriving ferry's horn blew one long blast. For the best island Christmas with Cody Penton that she'd never expected. And whatever came next.

AWARD-WINNING STORYTELLER LISA SILVERTHORNE HAS published over 25 novels and 150 short stories in SF/F, romance, and mystery. She writes heartfelt, atmospheric, and magical stories.

Her short fiction has appeared in publications from: DAW Books, Fiction River, Roc Books, WMG Publishing, Prime Books, and Pulphouse Magazine. She is also a Writers of the Future award winner. Discover more about her work at: LisaSilverthorne.com.

About this story, Lisa says:

"This tale began while I was shopping for a new suitcase and decided against buying the cheaper black suitcase. They were so prevalent and easily confused with someone else's bag. But the what-if bore its way through my brain, mixed with a storm I got caught in one Christmas while trying to get to Sea-Tac, and became part of the meet-cute/conceit for this sweet romantic tale.

"On second thought, maybe I should have bought the black suitcase and gotten it mixed up with some handsome guy's bag at the airport?"

The One-Hit Wonder of Mulberry Court

ANNIE REED

ONCE, BACK IN THE '90S, JERRILYN MEADOWS WENT FOR A visit to her old elementary school. The visit had been officially sanctioned, of course. Even in the '90s a strange adult couldn't just walk into an elementary school and go unnoticed or unchallenged.

She'd been invited to talk to the combined sixth-grade classes about the importance of education and staying in school even when the going got tough. Which just happened to be the theme of her latest book.

She'd brought along her dog McGillicuddy, an Irish Setter mix she affectionately called Big Mac. She'd based the doggy hero in her book on Big Mac. She figured the visual aid would keep the kids from squirming in their seats too much during her talk, and she'd been right.

The book itself was a short little novel about how scary it was to leave behind the relatively safe confines of elementary school where recess was still a thing and sixth-graders were the top of the food chain. The dog in her book helped his sixth-grade buddies deal with the structured and fairly grown-up world of middle school. With his undaunting heroism and relentlessly happy doggy grin, Big Mac's doppelgänger even convinced his owner not to run away from home because the kid was afraid he'd disappoint his parents.

The book hadn't been her one and only bestseller. That would come later. The book wouldn't have even garnered any notice except she was a local author, a hometown girl who'd made good—at least by local standards. Jerrilyn had been back in town to visit her parents for the holidays, and it turned out her father was friends with one of the teachers at her old school.

The rest, as they say, was history.

The kids had paid more attention to her dog than they did to her, which was fine. A few parents had shown up for her talk as well, standing in the back of the room so as not to distract their kids. Most of them had applauded when she was finished. The kids just wanted to pet her dog.

Everything about the school had looked so small to her that day. From the kids to the classrooms all decorated for Christmas to the auditorium itself. When she'd been in sixth grade, the auditorium with its vaulted ceiling and hardwood floor and old-fashioned elevated stage complete with red velvet curtains edged in gold trim had looked enormous. Like it belonged to the giant who'd been so perturbed when a boy named Jack invaded his space.

It was all a matter perspective. Time plus distance plus age distorted a person's memories. Or maybe the distorted perspective of childhood was the culprit. Children thought about the world in relation to themselves, especially at Christmastime.

Some people never outgrew the childish notion that the world revolved around them. Others learned their lesson the hard way, when the world rose up and smacked them in the face with a healthy helping of *who are you again?*

Jerrilyn hadn't thought about that day in years. How many was it now? Twenty? Twenty-five? Good lord, where had the time gone?

Here she was again, back in her hometown on another cold December day, shivering on the front stoop of her parents' house, the key to the front door in her hand.

Decembers in Northern Nevada were cold. How could she have forgotten that? She should have worn a thicker jacket. Some puffy thing packed with goose down or maybe something more environmentally friendly. She certainly should have worn a hat. Her mother used to knit the things one after the other, giving most of them away to charity.

Jerrilyn had never learned to knit. Or sew or do any of the crafty things her mother used to do. These days Jerrilyn spent her free time reading books and thinking that she really should try her hand at writing them again. For herself, if for no one else.

It was a nice thought. One that comforted her late at night when a turn of phrase she'd just read made her blink before she read it again just to bask in the images the words brought to mind.

I used to be able to do that, she'd think to herself. Followed quickly by *what's with this* used to, *chickadee?*

Chickadee. That's what her father had called her. His little chickadee.

He'd been her strongest cheerleader. The one who'd celebrated each of her successes, no matter how small.

Her mother? Not so much.

The key to the front door felt like ice in her hand. She should have worn gloves too. Did she even own a pair? Probably not. She lived in southern California these days, the land of sunshine (and smog) and beach bunnies who looked good in strappy two-piece bathing suits.

Jerrilyn wasn't in half-bad shape for someone in her late fifties. But strappy suits with straps that wedged into places where no self-respecting piece of clothing should wedge were definitely not something she planned to wear. Ever.

She knew she was stalling, letting her mind wander around all sorts of nonsense just to avoid using the key and going inside.

Would the house look the same inside as what she remembered? Probably not. She hadn't been here since her father died nearly fifteen years ago.

Now her mom was gone too.

They'd never been close, Jerrilyn and her mom. To put it mildly.

Her dad, though?

He got her.

He'd never cracked open a novel in his life, but once she started reading, he took her to the library twice a month and let her browse the stacks in the children's section to her heart's delight. When she was in third grade he bought a bookcase for her room and told her it was just for her. Then he went about filling it with well-worn books from used bookstores. She reread each of those books so often they started to come apart and she had to shove the loose pages in and rubber band the covers closed.

When she'd started writing her own stories in middle school, her father read each and every one. He always proclaimed her latest was the best thing he'd ever read.

Her mother sometimes read the same stories, but always with the corners of her mouth just waiting to pull down when she pounced on some error.

"That's nice, dear," was her standard comment when she finished reading.

The person who'd coined the phrase "damning with faint praise" must have had her mother in mind.

Would the house have any trace of her father still inside? Her mother'd had a decade and a half to redo the house to fit her own personality.

Maybe that's why Jerrilyn was so hesitant about unlocking the door and going inside. The house was her mother's home now. Jerrilyn felt more than a little like an unwelcome invader.

But her mother had left everything to her. House, contents, and the little bit of money she had left in the bank.

The lawyer had explained it to her in a brief call the week before. When he'd told Jerrilyn that her mother had died.

He'd been solicitous in a professional way, offering to help with whatever she needed. At least he hadn't seemed surprised—or worse, disappointed—when it became clear Jerrilyn hadn't even known that her mother had passed away.

So here she was. Jerrilyn Meadows. The one-hit wonder of Mulberry Court, an icy cold key in her numb fingers, not quite ready to go through her mother's things. Decide what to keep—probably nothing—and what to give away. She couldn't quite stomach the idea of an estate sale, one of the possibilities the lawyer had mentioned.

If she was lucky, she could get in, do what she needed to do, and make a quick getaway. Escape back to the land of sunshine (and smog) and bikini-clad beach bunnies who made her feel every one of her years.

It was a nice thought. A comforting thought.

Life, of course, had other plans.

———

HER FATHER'S OLD SOFA WAS GONE.

Jerrilyn used to sit next to him on that sofa while he watched television. She'd usually have her nose in a book, but he didn't mind. He'd wrap one arm around her shoulders, and she'd snuggle next to him and read while her mother sat in an old rocking chair, working on her knitting.

They never sat next to each other, her parents. Never held hands. Never kissed each other goodbye or goodnight. She'd never wondered why when she'd been a kid. It was just the way they were.

The old rocker was gone now too. In fact, the living room looked more like something out of a minimalist decorating magazine than her parents' home. The furniture, what little there was, was utilitarian, the colors muted tans and beiges, with none of her mother's handmade afghans or throw pillows to break up the monotony.

The old dining room table was still in its usual place. But its polished oak surface was bare, and all four chairs were neatly pushed in.

Jerrilyn left her bag on the table and draped her coat over the back of one of the chairs. She'd expected to feel like a stranger in her mother's house. She hadn't expected to feel like a potential renter checking out a furnished apartment. Even the walls were bereft of artwork.

The kitchen at least looked semi-lived in. An old-style coffeemaker sat on the counter, an empty dish rack next to the sink. The refrigerator was small and at least twenty years out of date. In fact, it very well could have been the same one her mother had been using the last time Jerrilyn had been in this house.

They'd had a horrible argument that day, the last in a long line of arguments.

Her father's funeral had been the day before, and the refrigerator was crammed full of food her parents' friends had brought over to the house. Jerrilyn had been trying to rearrange all the odd-shaped plastic tubs of leftover food when she realized her mother was taking all of her father's clothes out of their closet. Separating what could be donated, what merely had to be thrown away.

It had been too much too soon. Jerrilyn's emotions had still been raw, and she'd said things to her mother she'd never thought she would say.

They'd both said things that couldn't be unsaid or unheard. Or worst of all, unfelt.

She'd left the house that day vowing never to come back. Her mother had told her not to bother.

She hadn't spoken to her mother since. Now it was too late for do-overs.

Or start-overs.

That's what her father used to tell her whenever she felt like she'd failed. "Just do a start-over, chickadee," he'd say. "You'll be surprised how much easier things will be if you just try again."

The eternal optimist, her father. If he'd ever realized some things couldn't be done over, he'd never let on. At least not to the child she'd been.

She couldn't start over now. All she could do was get this job done so she could go back to her life in California. That wasn't going to happen if she stayed in the kitchen staring at that small refrigerator with its spick-and-span surface marred only by a single kitchen magnet holding a business card in place.

The rest of the rooms in the house, save one, looked as Spartan as the living room and dining room. Even her mother's bedroom looked like no one really lived there. The dresser had a single mirror on top, positioned exactly in the middle. All her mother's clothes were either hung up in the closet or neatly folded in dresser drawers. The bed had exactly two pillows, one bedspread, and one afghan folded at the foot.

Where were all the rest of her mother's handicrafts? Had she stopped creating? Stopped sewing? Stopped knitting, maybe because her fingers had stiffened with arthritis?

The thought made Jerrilyn sad. Handicrafts had been her mother's only creative outlet. Even cooking had just been a chore, like cleaning house. A necessary evil that someone had to do so the family could eat.

Jerrilyn got her answer when she made herself go into her old bedroom. She'd put off looking at her old room because she knew her mother would have erased any hint that the room used to belong to a daughter with an actual personality. No doubt her mother had turned that room into more of the same monotonous blandness that had invaded the rest of the house.

She was half right. Her mother had transformed Jerrilyn's old bedroom, but not in the way she'd feared.

The room was a riot of color.

Clear plastic storage tubs stacked along one wall held skeins of yarn in a rainbow of bright colors. Two different sewing machines, each on its own table, took up most of the wall space beneath the room's high window. Her mother's old rocker was shoved in a corner next to the room's tiny closet. A towering stack of folded fabric in a variety of colors and patterns threatened to spill off the rocker's narrow seat.

The drapes over the high window were open wide, and the clear, cold, winter sunshine lit up the room like a meadow of wildflowers on a bright summer day.

After the muted sameness of the rest of the house, Jerrilyn's old bedroom felt like someone had actually lived here. It took her breath away.

She trailed her fingers over the surface of one of the sewing tables. The sewing machine was threaded with bright red thread, and cut pieces of fabric in a red-and-green holiday print were scattered on the table. Jerrilyn had no idea what her mother might have been making, but clearly she'd been in the middle of creating something before she'd died.

The only available space to sit was an old office chair in front of the sewing machines, but Jerrilyn could see her mother spending all of her time here. Happily—or at least what passed for happy for her mother—working on her crafts. There was even a small clock radio on top of a small, pale yellow bookcase.

Had her mother ever listened to the radio when Jerrilyn had been a child? Or had the only sound in the house come from the TV in the living room, which her father left on whenever he was home?

Jerrilyn couldn't remember. There was no TV in the living room now.

She was about to leave what had clearly been her mother's favorite room when she took a second look at the bookcase.

She'd left her old bookcase behind when she'd gone off to college. She'd always intended to come back for it, but life, not to mention a series of half-hearted relationships, had gotten in the way.

This was her old bookcase. Her mother had repainted it a pale yellow, her favorite color. A framed wedding photo of Jerrilyn's parents sat next to the clock radio on the top shelf, and the shelf underneath held a few looseleaf binders and slim, oversized books that looked like pattern books from the titles on the spines.

But the bottom shelf held novels.

Her novels.

All of them.

Children's books. Young adult books. The middle-grade book she'd spoken to a bunch of impatient sixth graders about that long ago day in December when the kids couldn't wait for winter break to start because that meant Christmas Day wouldn't be far behind.

And next to all the other books was her one bestseller.

The sight of that novel sent chills down Jerrilyn's spine.

She'd written it after that last disastrous argument with her mother. Written it in a white-hot heat, pouring all of herself into telling the story of a young woman coming to grips with the death of her father, the only steadying influence in a life dominated by her unfeeling, disapproving mother.

Writing the book had been cathartic, in a way. She'd nearly shoved it in an electronic drawer, intending to lock it up and throw away the key, until her agent had cajoled her into letting him read it.

The book had sold for the highest advance she'd ever received. Not mega-bestseller levels of money, but enough to sock away against potential lean times.

The book's success had caught Jerrilyn totally off guard.

What was that old saying? About how writing was easy—all you had to do was sit down at the keyboard and open a vein?

She'd half expected her mother to call her after the book started getting some attention in literary circles. When she didn't, Jerrilyn figured her mother hadn't read it, like she hadn't read any of Jerrilyn's other books and had only looked at the stories Jerrilyn had written in school because it had been expected of her.

Instead of being relieved when it became clear she wouldn't be getting an angry phone call from her mother, Jerrilyn became increasingly worried that she'd gone too far. Revealed far too much about her own life in the guise of fiction. Whenever she sat down to work on a new project, her imagination served up the disapproving look her mother always gave her whenever she read one of Jerrilyn's stories.

Eventually Jerrilyn stopped trying to write.

Her single bestseller, what reviewers called the best book she'd ever written, turned out to be the last book she would ever write.

She'd become the proverbial one-hit wonder, an overnight success who'd toiled away unnoticed for years only to be destroyed when success finally found her.

Jerrilyn stared at the shelf holding her novels. The bottom shelf, of course. Had her mother been proud of Jerrilyn's accomplishments, or had she simply kept the books out of a sense of maternal obligation?

Far too late to ask. No start-overs possible this time, Dad.

As it turned out, this time neither one of them was quite right.

DARIUS MCKINNON MET JERRILYN AT HER MOTHER'S house the next morning at eight.

The day had dawned even colder than the day before, if possible. Jerrilyn had arrived at her mother's house early enough to brew a pot of coffee in the old-fashioned coffee maker, which was just a larger version of the single-cup coffee maker in her hotel room.

Jerrilyn had found filters in one of the cabinets the day before but decided to bypass her mother's half-empty can of generic grocery store coffee. Instead, she'd picked up a fresh pack of Columbian blend at a chain coffeeshop that morning.

The aroma of fresh-brewed coffee helped make the house feel lived in. So did turning up the thermostat. Her mother had always set the thermostat at an energy-saving sixty-eight degrees in the winter months. After years of living in Southern California, sixty-eight was just too damn cold.

By the time Darius arrived, Jerrilyn had downed half a cup of black coffee and ditched the sweater she'd worn on top of a comfy holiday sweatshirt she'd purchased at a local mall the day before. She'd also gone through the fridge and thrown out most of the food, although there'd been very little. Her mother had either been eating like a bird or fixing single-serving frozen dinners.

Darius was nothing like she'd expected. She'd talked to him briefly on the phone the day before. His name was on the lone business card tacked on the fridge. The card was for a business called Helping Hands and identified Darius as a Donations Coordinator.

She certainly didn't know where or how to donate her mother's remaining things. Contacting someone like this might be a good way to start, especially if his services weren't too expensive, so she'd called him.

His voice had been pleasantly deep and rather youngish sounding. When she explained who she was and why she'd called, he told her he was familiar with her mother.

"I've been helping her downsize," he'd said.

When she asked about his fee, he told her he didn't charge for his services, which amounted to making sure donations went to the non-profits best suited to receive them.

She might have ended the conversation there. Southern California was a ripe stomping ground for scam artists who offered services that were too good to be true, with the true cost only coming up after it was much too late to back out of the deal.

But her mother had clearly known this man, and her mother had never taken anything at face value. If her mother hadn't vetted the guy and his business to her satisfaction, she would have thrown his card away.

"You must be independently wealthy if you don't charge," Jerrilyn had told him.

He'd chuckled. "It does keep me busy," he'd said.

When she opened the door, she expected to find someone in their thirties. Instead, a man who was clearly in his sixties stood on the front stoop.

"Darius McKinnon," he said, nodding toward her and giving her a little half smile. "You must be the famous Jerrilyn Meadows."

He didn't hold out his hand for either a handshake or the more common fist-bump, for which she was grateful. She was too busy being gobsmacked.

Famous?

She wasn't famous. She wasn't anything other than a middle-aged woman dealing with one of the unavoidable tasks that fell on the adult children of recently deceased elderly parents.

She managed to stammer out some sort of response before she invited him inside.

She offered him a cup of coffee, serving it up in one of the two mugs she'd found in the cupboards.

"Hope you don't take it with cream," she said. "I don't have any, although I think there's some sugar around here somewhere."

"Black is fine."

Their fingers touched briefly when she handed him the mug. His were warm even though he hadn't been wearing gloves. Hers were still chilly enough that she'd topped off her own coffee just to heat up the mug.

There was a moment of silence as they stood in her mother's small kitchen sipping at coffee that was too hot to chug down. Jerrilyn spent the time trying not to feel awkward, wondering what exactly he'd heard about her and where he'd heard it from.

She didn't think she'd ever met him before. He was handsome enough that she felt she'd remember meeting him. He had deep blue eyes beneath brows that were only slightly bushy and as salt-and-pepper as his full head of hair. He didn't have a beard, at least not in the way she thought of a beard, but he wasn't exactly cleanshaven either. The scruff on his chin and cheeks might have been the result of getting up earlier than normal, or he might be one of those men who only shaved before special occasions. When he'd smiled at her on the front stoop, small dimples had appeared in his cheeks. She had a feeling those dimples might appear more pronounced when he chuckled like he had on the phone.

Which made her wonder if the dimples and chuckle would be accompanied by a mischievous glint in his blue eyes.

She gave herself a mental shake. Just because she was standing in her mother's kitchen with a handsome stranger close to her own age didn't mean she should start acting like a lovesick teenager.

"Explain to me how this works," she said, then realized that might have come out too harshly. "I mean, why you don't charge and how did you come to help my mother—what did you call it? Downsize?"

He took a sip of his coffee. "Fair questions," he said. "I don't charge because I retired with a decent pension." He shrugged. "I don't need the money."

That would be a foreign concept to half the people she knew in California. No matter how much money some people had, it never seemed to be enough. Jerrilyn wasn't exactly retired. Officially she had a real estate license, but in reality she simply helped friends navigate all the convoluted steps involved in finding a place to live. The perks of investing the money she'd made on her one bestseller in markets that hadn't actually tanked.

"Your mother," Darius started, then his expression sobered. "I'm sorry. I should have conveyed my condolences on your loss. She was a nice woman with a kind heart."

Jerrilyn blinked. She almost blurted out, "You are talking about *my* mother, right?" before she caught herself.

Instead she thanked him. "We weren't close," she said. "You probably knew her better than I did."

She expected him to be shocked. He had said her mother was nice woman, after all.

But he simply nodded. "The older we get, the harder it is to stay in touch," he said, and left it at that.

The silence this time was less awkward.

She broke it by asking him if her mother's downsizing had been a recent development.

"I don't know how recent it was," he said. "But she'd apparently read one of those articles about how hanging onto things that don't bring joy is toxic. The 'less is more' argument. Tiny houses. Spartan lives."

The way he'd said "tiny houses" made her think he wasn't on board with that trend. She tended to think the whole tiny-house trend was just another way to try to convince people they'd be happy with the fact that tiny houses and closet-sized apartments were all most people could afford.

"One of her friends at the senior center put her in touch with me," he said. "We went through the house, decided what to donate, and I suggested where it would do the best good."

He told her a lot of the furniture had gone to the local SPCA thrift store. Including, it turned out, her father's old sofa. Darius had arranged for the SPCA to pick up the furniture and had been at the house to make sure everything had gone smoothly.

Clothing had gone to a Catholic charities shop along with excess dishes and kitchenware. Some items went to the Habitat for Humanities store.

Then there'd been all the afghans her mother had made, along with scarves and hats.

Those went to homeless shelters. Darius had delivered them himself. Baby blankets had gone to a women's shelter.

Jerrilyn hadn't known her mother made baby blankets, and she told him that.

"She taught a class for that at the senior center," he said. "She said it kept her busy."

By this point they were walking through the house. He told her he thought he could arrange to donate pretty much everything that was left. Including all the fabric and yarn in her mother's craft room.

"The senior center will take a lot of it," he said. "They have craft classes. Your mother took a ceramics class there at one time, I believe."

There wasn't a single ceramics item in the entire house.

"What did she do with what she made?" Jerrilyn asked.

Darius shrugged. "Gave it away, I imagine. In fact, there was only one thing she wouldn't let me touch."

He gestured toward the bottom shelf of the bookcase in the craft room.

"Your books," he said. "She told me they were the only things in this whole house that she couldn't bear to part with."

———

OVER THE NEXT FEW DAYS JERRILYN AND DARIUS SORTED through her mother's few possessions. He arranged for the furniture to be picked up—by the SPCA again, an amazing accomplishment considering it was only a couple of weeks before Christmas—and took boxes of clothing and kitchenware to Goodwill.

"You'll want to keep the jewelry, of course," he'd said.

Not that her mother had much. A few necklaces and brooches. She didn't want him to think badly of her, so she said yes, she wanted to keep them. She could always decide what to do with them later.

When he invited her to go with him to drop off her mother's yarn, fabric, and both of the sewing machines at the senior center, she said she'd be happy to do that. Darius had become a comforting presence in her life. She hadn't expected to make a friend while she was in town, and she looked forward to seeing him every day. She made sure she had a fresh pot of coffee ready for him every morning, and after he mentioned the house seemed so quiet, she kept the clock radio on, tuned to a local soft rock station.

She'd even started to daydream about him when he wasn't around. She realized those daydreams could be dangerous. It wasn't like they lived in the same town, after all, and he was just being nice to her. But the possibilities were still pleasant to contemplate.

After they unloaded the last of the donations at the senior center, the woman in charge of the craft classes was so effusive in her thanks that she made Jerrilyn uncomfortable.

"Are you sure you don't want to keep any of this?" the woman asked. She looked like the quintessential, pleasingly plump version of a grandmother, what with her short curly white hair and gold-rimmed half-glasses low on her nose.

"I never learned to do any of this," Jerrilyn said.

The woman looked incredulous. "Really? Your mother was such a wonderful, patient teacher."

Again. Here was another person telling her about a version of her mother she'd never known. The mother of Jerrilyn's memories was a hypercritical woman who'd never approved of anything Jerrilyn had ever done.

"I guess I didn't have an aptitude," she said.

"That's right," the woman said. "You're the famous writer." She squeezed Jerrilyn's arm gently and gave her a smile. "Your mother was so proud of you, you know."

Jerrilyn muttered her thanks, but she couldn't look the woman in the eye.

Her mother had been proud of her? When? Certainly not when Jerrilyn still lived at home, or even after her first few books had come out. Her mother had never said a thing about them.

Jerrilyn hurried out of the senior center, leaving Darius to finish up inside. The parking lot was half empty. She leaned against his truck, arms crossed in front of herself, hands tucked beneath her bent elbows to keep her fingers warm.

The senior center occupied a standalone building in the middle of an older subdivision. Half of the houses in the neighborhood were decorated for the holidays, deflated blowups lying flat on winter brown front lawns, holiday lights turned off to conserve energy. There must have been an elementary school nearby. She heard a buzzer signaling recess, followed by the happy sounds of children released from their classrooms to burn off excess energy running around outside.

Why couldn't her mother have told Jerrilyn she'd been proud of her when it would have mattered? Why were Jerrilyn's memories of her mother always dominated by her mother's disapproving, turned-down mouth?

Then there was the other thing that was bothering her. Had, in fact, been keeping Jerrilyn awake at night.

Why the hell hadn't she swallowed her own pride and contacted her mother these last fifteen years? Been the bigger person? Been the one to attempt to mend their broken relationship?

Because she'd always thought she'd have enough time to do that?

Like she always thought she'd have time for a proper relationship?

The only long-term relationship she'd witnessed firsthand, the one between her parents, had always seemed so cold. So loveless, but had it always been that way? What if her mother had mellowed in the years after Jerrilyn left home, and she just hadn't seen it?

What if her mother's need to rid the house of her father's things so soon after he died was the only way her mother could cope with the sudden loss of the man she loved? Instead of understanding, of being there to help her mother cope, Jerrilyn had blown up at her. Blasted her mother with all the pent-up frustrations of a childhood spent never knowing if her mother was proud of her.

If her mother had really loved her.

Apparently she had.

"Kinda late to find that out now, mom," Jerrilyn muttered under her breath.

It only took Darius a few minutes to finish up inside. When he got to the truck, he had an expression of concern on his face.

"You left in a hurry," he said. "Are you all right?"

She gave him a half-smile. "I suppose I just don't feel famous," she said, more to get herself back on an even keel than anything else. "I've been meaning to ask why you said that when you met me."

Now he looked uncomfortable. "I have a confession to make," he said.

She raised one eyebrow and tilted her head. He wasn't giving off any vibes that made her uncomfortable. In fact, she'd grown more comfortable around him than she had with anyone in a long time.

"I introduced myself to your mom when I found out she was your mother," he said. "I sort of followed your career for a while."

Her career? "My writing?" she asked.

He nodded. "Yeah."

"Why in the world would you do that?" she asked, too startled to keep from blurting out something fairly rude instead of keeping it to herself.

"You gave that talk to my kid's class," he said. "Sixth graders. You had your dog with you. I was one of the parents at the back of the auditorium. I liked what you had to say, so I bought all your books. I gave them to my daughter, but I read them too."

All her books? Even the last one?

All of a sudden she was too nervous to ask.

"Why did you stop writing?" he asked. "You were good. Especially that last book, the adult one. That was—"

"A long time ago," she said.

Her heart was sinking. She'd started to think it might be nice to find out if they could take this burgeoning friendship of theirs and transform it into something more. But if he'd read that book, the novel she'd poured so much of herself into—so much of her self-absorbed, self-indulgent self—would he even want some kind of a relationship with her?

Then something new occurred to her.

"Is that why you keep telling me what a great woman my mother was?" she asked. "Because the person in that book was such a..." Go ahead and say it, she told herself. "Such a horrible mother?"

He tilted his head back and gazed at her with blue eyes that had gone dark with some emotion. "That's... I always thought that was fiction, but I'm guessing it was more than that, wasn't it?"

She looked away from him. Another buzzer somewhere in the neighborhood signaled the end of recess. She felt colder than she had in a long time, and it wasn't just from the chilly December day.

"Even made-up stories have some basis in truth," she said. "With that book, there's more truth to it than fiction." She rubbed her arms against the cold. "At least from my perspective."

The perspective of a child who'd felt ignored by her mother. But over the last few days, her perspective had certainly changed. The world she'd known as a child was smaller now. Smaller and colder and very, very far away.

"You know," Darius said. "I'm a lucky guy. I managed to stay friends with my ex, and my daughter calls me twice a week to shoot the breeze. She hasn't made me a grandfather yet. To tell the truth, I'm not sure I'm ready for that. Most of the time I don't think I'm old enough to be a grandfather. I know not everyone's so lucky."

"No?" she said, still not looking at him. She didn't want to see the disappointment in his eyes when he looked at her.

"The thing I'm feeling especially lucky for right now is meeting you and getting to know you as a person," he said. "I'd like to keep getting to know you, if that's something you might be interested in."

"Really?"

Now she did look at him. There was no judgment in his expression, no disdain pulling down the corners of his mouth.

"Yes," he said. "Really."

He took her cold hands in his warm ones. His fingers felt wonderful wrapped around hers.

"One thing I need to know up front though," he said. "Are you still a dog person?"

The question came so out of left field that she couldn't help it, she laughed. "I suppose so. I haven't had a dog in years."

"But the dog you brought with you that day, that was your dog, right?"

"McGillicuddy was certainly mine," she said. She hadn't had the heart to get another dog after Big Mac had passed away at the ripe old age of eighteen.

"Good," he said. "Because I'm a dog person. And that," he added, his blue eyes twinkling, "would definitely be a deal breaker."

"So I take it you have a dog?" she asked.

"Two, in fact," he said. "A setter and a Heinz-57 mutt."

He was still holding her hands. She didn't exactly feel the zing of instant attraction, but holding hands with him was warming more than just her fingers.

It was too late to reconcile with her mother, but she had learned that her mother had somehow managed to resolve her own feelings toward her estranged daughter. Maybe knowing that was enough for Jerrilyn to mark paid to that particular part of her life and finally let all the old resentments go.

Let herself live a little.

Even let herself explore the possibilities of a new relationship that might actually go somewhere.

She tilted her head just a little as she grinned up at Darius. She'd never noticed before that he was just a couple of inches taller than she was, which was just about perfect.

"When do I get to meet your dogs?" she asked.

His smile widened, and those dimples in his cheeks made him look a good ten years younger. He took a key fob out of his pocket and unlocked his truck. Then he helped her climb up onto the passenger seat.

"How about now?" he said. "I'll even spring for coffee."

She settled onto the soft leather of the seat. The inside of the truck smelled like him, she realized now. It was a good smell and something she could definitely get used to.

"Sounds perfect," she said.

ANNIE REED'S BEEN CALLED ONE OF THE BEST WRITERS OF her generation and for good reason. An award-winner in multiple genres, her stories have appeared in six year's best mystery, crime, and thriller volumes, including an amazing three years in a row in the prestigious Best Mystery Stories of the Year *from series editor Otto Penzler. She's a multiple Derringer finalist and frequent contributor to* Pulphouse Fiction Magazine, Mystery, Crime & Mayhem, *and* Thrill Ride Magazine. *Her recent novels include the sweet holiday romance* A Christmas Reunion *and* Wedding Belle Blues, *written under the pen name Liz McKnight.*

Find out more about Annie at anniereed.wordpress.com.

About "The One-Hit Wonder of Mulberry Court," Annie says:

"This story started as a memory I had of being in elementary school sitting on the polished hardwood floor of what seemed to me at the time to be a huge auditorium. It was the last assembly before Christmas vacation. Each class was grouped together, all of us impatient kids who

couldn't wait for the last bell of the day, so the teachers distracted us by having us sing all the old Christmas carols. What would that be like for an adult going back to their old grade school to talk to those impatient kids? How would she keep their attention?

"I mashed that idea with a recent trend in downsizing. You know, the idea of getting rid of everything that doesn't bring you joy. I'm not sure if there are actually people like Darius who specialize in helping people find the best places to donate all that downsized stuff, but I really liked the idea.

"The story that resulted is a slow-burn romance, which is one of my favorite types of romance to write."

Deerly Undeparted

ROBERT JESCHONEK

JULIANNE THISTLE WAS LOADED FOR BEAR.

Whoever was pounding on her front door at six o'clock in the morning was going to catch *hell*. *So what* if she lived in the woods now, way out on Buck Ridge Road, where maybe *other* folks tended to wake up early? It was still *her* God-given right to sleep as late as she chose without some *mook* banging the *bejezus* out of her door.

Wrapped in a heavy flannel robe against the early winter chill, she pushed her shoulder-length chestnut brown hair out of her face as she stomped barefoot over the cold hardwood from her bedroom to the living room. All the while, the pounding never stopped.

It was a good thing she didn't own a *rifle*, she thought as she reached for the doorknob. Not that she'd ever *use* one, gentle soul that she was... much like her late Aunt Peggy, whose house in the Western Pennsylvania woods she now inhabited after thirty-five years of urban existence.

"All right, buddy!" She cranked the knob left and whipped the door open with an attitude. "*What* is your *problem?*"

It was then that she got a look at the guy who'd been doing the knocking, and her breath caught in her throat.

Actually, he looked a little surprised, too. His dark brown eyes flashed, set deep amid chiseled features framed by wavy black hair and a close-cropped beard.

His handsome face and muscular form, clad in a dark brown corduroy jacket over a tan hoodie and faded jeans, were not exactly what Julianne had expected to see on the other side of her pummeled door.

"So, uh... right." He cleared his throat and frowned as if trying to regain his own level of pissed-offedness. "My *problem* is...."

"Yeah?" Julianne planted her hands on her hips and cocked her head to one side, presenting her best Tough Woodsy Chick pose... though she'd only been living out there on her own for a total of three whole weeks. Before moving out there after inheriting the place from Aunt Peggy, she'd been pretty much the *opposite* of a Woodsy Chick, in fact... more like a hard-bitten City Girl who'd only made occasional visits to her country-based kin over the years.

The guy shook his head, cheeks flushing with... what? Frustration at losing his manly momentum? A rising tide of returning rage? Then he forced out one more word, as if that explained everything: "*Them.*"

And he turned, stepped aside, and gestured at what currently occupied Julianne's front yard.

At which point, Julianne's eyes flew wide with surprise and delight. Excitedly, she tossed her head, not caring how her sleep-mussed hair might look at that especially joyful moment.

"Omigod!" She pushed past him, heedless of the dusting of snow on the planks of the front porch. "My beauties! You brought *friends!*"

Perched above the top step, she beamed as she gazed out at the vision of wildlife spread before her. Her entire front yard, from porch to tree line, was crowded with whitetail deer—mostly doe, a smattering of fawns, and a few snooty bucks lording it over the herd like royalty, keeping watch while the others fed.

"Just *look* at them!" she said softly, forgetting her annoyance with the door-pounder. "There were only a *handful* a few days ago! Now, there must be at least *two dozen*."

"No kidding," snapped the guy. "That's exactly the *problem*."

"Only if you hate *nature*," said Julianne. "And by the way, keep your *voice* down. You'll scare them *away*."

"Good! That'd be perfect!"

With that, he started shouting and clapping his hands at the deer. "Go away! Get outta here!"

All two dozen animals flicked up their heads at once, ears twitching, onyx eyes glued to his noisy presence.

"Cut it out!" Julianne grabbed his closest forearm and pulled, breaking the rhythm of his clapping. "They're innocent animals, and they have every right to *be* here."

"Not if they keep using my *property* as their personal *salad bar* and *toilet*." Angrily, he jerked his arm from her grasp.

The sudden move bumped her off balance, and she tipped forward. Before she could stumble or fall, however, he caught and held her firmly.

"Sorry." He held on to her a moment longer, looking flustered. "Are you okay?"

Meeting his gaze, she felt a pulse of warmth deep in her chest in spite of the cold. As much as she thought she should dislike him, she got the feeling there was more than negativity going on under his surface.

"I'm good," she said, regaining her footing... then slipping just a little on a patch of ice.

"Let's get you inside." Supporting her with an arm around her back, he turned her toward the open front door. "Make sure you didn't twist anything."

She hesitated, narrowing her eyes at him. "What did you say your name was?"

"I didn't, but it's Walden. Walden Collier. I'm your next-door neighbor."

"Like, five acres over *that* way?" She bobbed her head left, to the west. "Does that even *count* as next-door?"

"Ask *them*." He glanced at the herd milling in the yard. "They cross *my* property to get to *yours*, so yeah... pretty sure they'd agree we're neighbors."

Julianne frowned, then smirked. "'Walden,' huh? What kind of name is that for a nature hater?"

"I don't *hate* nature." He sighed with exasperation. "I'm not hateful. Not a hater."

"Well, *good* then." Maybe there was hope for him yet. "So stop *acting* like one, or my *deer friends* might get the wrong idea about you." *And I might, too.*

Then, she turned and let him guide her to the front door.

Keenly aware of the two dozen pairs of obsidian eyes that watched them every step of the way into the house.

———

"NICE PLACE." WALDEN LOOKED AROUND THE LIVING room after he'd helped Julianne to the sofa. "Not *too* rustic."

She nodded. "Thanks." He was right, the house was comfortable and contemporary inside, though the exterior had the look of a rough-hewn cabin. "I probably wouldn't be living here otherwise."

"You don't mind the rustic *wildlife*, though." He arched an eyebrow in her direction.

"It's all part of the package, Wally." She found a hair tie on her left wrist and used it to wrap a tidy ponytail so she wouldn't look quite so scruffy. "I *can* call you Wally, can't I?"

"Walden's good. And you're...?"

"Julianne." She reached for a handshake. "Juli, for short."

He returned the shake with a smile. "So, uh... maybe we should start over, huh?"

"You *think* so?" She smirked.

He nodded, looking a bit sheepish. "The 6 a.m. banging on the door was over the top. I apologize."

"It *wasn't* the best approach," she told him. "My coffee maker doesn't even start brewing till 7:30."

"I'm up at 5 every day," said Walden. "Sometimes I forget not everyone's an early riser."

"Don't have to worry about *that* if you use *this*." She pulled the phone from a pocket of her robe and shook it. "Ever hear of *texting* or *voice mail?*"

"I didn't have your number."

Well, maybe you should. "I'm just saying, there's rude..." She pointed at the front door. "And there's *less* rude." She waggled the phone.

Walden looked confused. "Okay."

"Good." She snapped her fingers as if the matter were settled. "Starting over."

"Starting over."

They traded phones then, each entering their number in the other's list of contacts. When that was done, they traded them back and put them away.

"Now you can call instead of hammering on my door before sun-up," she told him. *Not that I'll answer, because my phone will be off that early....*

"Likewise."

"Just, if you can't get me at first, leave a message," said Julianne. "I have meetings for my day job sometimes, so I can't always answer."

"What's your day job?" he asked.

"Marketing specialist." She gestured at a doorway leading off the living room. "I work from my home office, but I still have to be on deck when I'm needed."

"I get it." With that, Walden turned, and a framed photo on the end table by the sofa caught his eye. It was a shot of Julianne's Aunt Peggy and Uncle Lucky from years ago, somewhere in the great outdoors. "Sorry for your loss, by the way."

"Thanks." Julianne nodded. "My aunt's the reason I have so many deer friends, you know. She specifically *requested* it."

"You mean...." Walden hiked a thumb in the direction of the front yard.

"It's in her will as a condition of taking ownership of the house and property. She wanted the local deer fed and looked after in the winter, when food gets scarcer in the wild."

"Hold on." Walden frowned. "Do you mean to tell me you've been *feeding* them?"

"Just scattering some field corn around," said Julianne. "And some oats and hay and deer pellets."

"*This* is why my property's a wreck." Walden suddenly looked angry. "Because *you're* setting up a *buffet* in your yard."

"I only started last week," she explained. "How much damage could they *do* in that short amount of time?"

Walden's cheeks reddened. "How much *damage....*""He closed his eyes for a moment, and the muscles in his square jaw twitched. Then, he shook off whatever was straining his self-control and blinked. "You don't get it, do you?"

She felt hurt. Whatever disagreement was in play here, she didn't want him to think less of her. Something in those flashing dark eyes of his still caught her like the bait on a fisherman's hook.

"I'll tell you what." He zipped up his jacket. "Why don't you come by my place later? I'll show you around."

She thought for a moment, then nodded. "Okay." She couldn't deny she was curious. In all her visits to Aunt Peggy and Uncle Lucky, she couldn't recall spending time at the Colliers' place. She barely even remembered Walden's folks.

Just one memory jumped out at her, from when she'd been a

little girl. Walden's dad and Lucky racing around in a pickup with her on the front seat between them, chasing people off their land.

Because it was posted private property, no hunting allowed. Signs nailed to the trees left no room for misunderstanding.

"Sounds good," she told him, more curious than ever. Did a love of deer and the need to protect them not run in his family? "I've got some time this afternoon."

"I'll see you when I see you." He opened the front door. "But your deer friends aren't invited, if you've got any pull with that bunch."

"No pull, sorry," said Julianne. "I'm pretty much just their lunch lady."

JULIANNE FELT A LITTLE NERVOUS WHEN SHE GOT OUT OF her black Jeep Cherokee in front of Walden's house. She wasn't sure what to expect, and she couldn't say for sure if her attraction to him might be leading her astray somehow.

Tugging up the collar of her black sheepskin-lined jacket, she took in the view, impressed at how new the outside of the place looked. The battered old clapboard farmhouse she remembered was now covered in updated white siding and a new red metal roof. The front steps, wraparound porch, and picture windows all seemed to have been recently upgraded, as well... and a sign she'd never seen before hung from a crossbar surrounded by spiky green holly bushes along the sidewalk from the driveway.

Mountain Laurel Getaway, it read. Behind it stood the figure of a young deer, head dipped as if to nibble the deep green leaves of the holly.

Julianne took a step toward it, then jumped and yelped when the deer raised its head to meet her gaze. Until that instant, she hadn't realized it was anything other than ornamental statuary.

Dropping bits of holly from its muzzle, the deer hopped out of the bush. On the way over, its rear hooves knocked the sign from one of its hooks on the crossbar, leaving it to dangle from the other, off-kilter.

"Hello, little friend." Julianne smiled. "Do I know you?"

As if in reply, the deer drew up one foreleg and stamped the ground with its hoof.

"What does that mean?" Julianne stamped her own foot on the ground. "Are you trying to say hello?"

This time, the deer pulled up its other foreleg and repeated the motion.

Julianne did the same. "Well, hello to you, too, then." Impulsively, she took a step forward.

Without hesitation, the little deer whipped around and bolted off into the woods, its fluffy white tail bouncing at full attention behind it.

Suddenly, she heard Walden clearing his throat nearby and spun to look in his direction.

"Exhibit A." He marched over and gave the sign a kick, so it rattled around on the one attached hook. "See what I was talking about?"

Julianne glanced after the deer, which was well out of sight. "What does it mean when they stomp the ground like that, anyway?"

"Probably 'See ya, wouldn't wanna be ya.'" Walden waved for her to follow as he started across the yard. "Now come on. Let the grand tour begin."

"Exhibit B." Walden crossed the gravel driveway and stopped, sweeping an arm from left to right to indicate the yard before him. "This is what happens when enough deer spend their staycations on your property."

Julianne frowned. The snow-dusted ground was torn up in all directions, the brown turf cratered with hoofprints.

"Exhibit C." Walden's brown work boots crunched the churned earth as he walked through the mess, pointing at piles of coal-black pellets along the way. "More deer droppings than you can shake a stick at."

"Wow." Julianne followed, trying hard not to plant a foot in one of the piles. "I haven't even seen *that* much in *my* yard, yet."

"Because they leave it all *here* on the way *there*," said Walden. "Or drop it off on the way *back.*"

"Right." Julianne had to admit, she hadn't thought about it this way before. She'd been too caught up in granting Aunt Peggy's wish —and enjoying her personal interactions with wildlife—to think about downstream or upstream impacts of her actions. If anything, she'd only ever thought of herself as *helping* Mother Nature by feeding her denizens in need.

"This way to Exhibit D." Walden led her around the corner of the house, gesturing at the scraggly remnants of barren twigs clawing out of the flower beds spanning the cinderblock footer. "And no, these particular plants *aren't* supposed to be leafless during the winter. All their foliage has been *stripped* by your friendly neighborhood deer friends."

"But I put out *more* than enough *food* for them at *my* place."

"And that draws more *animals*." He sounded like he genuinely wanted to help as he explained it. "Word gets around, right? All the friends, relations, and hangers-on show up from miles around... and that's what leads to all *this*. Maybe they get to your place, and it's too crowded, or they just fill up here because they're too lazy to go the distance. Next thing you know, this place is a total *deer sty...*"

"Deer sty? Is that a thing?"

"...and all my hard work to get ready for the grand opening goes out the window." Walden let his arms fall at his sides with a smack of frustration.

Julianne remembered the sign. "Mountain Laurel Getaway, you mean?"

Pride flickered in his eyes. "Exactly."

"You're turning the place into an inn?" she asked. "A bed-and-breakfast?"

"That was the plan when Dad left it to me. I was living out of town, working construction, and I came back after he passed to turn it into a business." He kicked one of the scraggly plants with the toe of his boot. "Little did I know the *deer* would take it over. I mean, we always had them around out here, but never *this* many."

Looking around, Julianne saw more patches of ruptured ground, piles of droppings, and snags of stripped-bare plant life. She felt a stab of guilt at the thought that something she'd done had led to this mess.

So maybe the six o'clock wakeup call had been right on time after all... if not overdue.

The question now was what, if anything, was she going to do about it?

"Okay, look." She nodded at the barn across the side yard from where they stood. "You got a wheelbarrow and some shovels in there?"

"I do, but...."

"Then let's get going." She headed for the barn, waving for him to follow. "I wonder how much of the deer staycation mess we can clean up together?"

A LOT, AS IT TURNED OUT.

Between the two of them, they shoveled loads of droppings into the wheelbarrow, hauled them out into the woods, and dumped them in an out-of-the-way spot. They raked up swaths of the torn-up ground, smoothing out many of the bumpiest spots. They dug out and toted off the dead snaggles of barren brush, adding them to a burn pile at the edge of the property.

Then they fixed the *Mountain Laurel Getaway* sign that the little stamping deer had knocked loose on its way out of the holly. They secured it to both hooks on the crossbar, then stepped back to admire their work.

Julianne nodded as she pulled off the leather work gloves he'd loaned her. "Looks pretty good, wouldn't you say?"

"Thanks for the help," said Walden. "So when can I expect you tomorrow?"

"Huh?" She shot him a look of disbelief. "But we're done, right?"

"For now, but they'll be back. With lots of friends, no doubt. And they'll tear up my place all over again."

Julianne blew out her breath in frustration. "What if I stop feeding them on my property? At least for a few days?"

"That's not how it works."

"But won't they spread the word? Won't they stop coming after a few days?"

Walden shook his head. "Once they lock onto a food source, it takes longer than that to break the habit. It can take weeks. Months, even. They're *smart*. They don't *forget* that easily."

Julianne frowned. "Isn't there anything you can use to keep them away? Like deer repellent and such?"

"Yeah, but nothing's foolproof," he told her. "And even if it was, the amounts I'd need to treat this property—and keep doing it on a regular basis—would be astronomical."

"So you're telling me all this was for *nothing*? All the work we just did?"

"It's a start," said Walden. "But the grand opening's a week from today. My first guests arrive Saturday. I can't imagine the place being ready by then if the deer keep coming... which they will."

Disappointment and annoyance rippled through Julianne. "You're telling me there's no way to fix this?"

"Canceling the grand opening, probably. Refunding the guests."

"But that isn't fair. You've put so much *into* this place."

He shrugged. "No one ever said Mother Nature was fair."

Then, with a sigh, he turned and marched off to put away the wheelbarrow and implements, leaving Julianne to consider just how unfair things could be.

Especially when she'd just started to get the hang of this seemingly decent guy, only to discover they could never truly be together because of the mistakes she had made.

BY THE TIME JULIANNE GOT HOME, THE HERD FROM THAT morning had moved on. The front yard was trampled and piled with droppings, but the two dozen deer were gone.

So was most of the feed she'd put out along the tree line the night before. She saw shreds of hay and yellow kernels of field corn scattered in the buckled muck, but the bales were gone, the baskets empty. The deer had cleaned her out, as they always did.

Now, she was faced with a decision. Should she put out the next spread or stop feeding the creatures?

She needed to honor Aunt Peggy's wishes, and she *loved* spending time around the deer. On the other hand, she didn't want to make things any worse for Walden... but why bother trying, if it was already too late for that? Fixing the situation didn't seem to be an option.

Aunt Peggy had left clear instructions and money to cover the costs of feeding and upkeep, so maybe she should just stick to the original plan. Or maybe she could keep going but change things up a little to limit the impact on Walden's venture.

The deer had come to depend on her, but maybe she could still change their habits without letting them down.

THAT AFTERNOON, WHEN JULIANNE PUT OUT THE FEED, she moved it away from the house. She set up stations in the woods as far as she could from Walden's property, hoping to redirect the traffic flow away from Mountain Laurel Getaway.

Would it be as much fun as waking up to a herd of beautiful deer milling around her front yard? No way... but she could still hike out to the feed stations to spy on them when she pleased.

And maybe their patterns would shift, at least a little, over time. Maybe the bulk of the destruction would play out along a new passage in the woods, leaving just a few stragglers to wander near the houses as they'd always done.

If that meant Walden thought better of her, so be it. There might not be a love connection after what she'd done to scuttle his grand opening, but she didn't want there to be blame or hostility between them.

In a place like Buck Ridge Road, especially during the cold and snowy winters, staying on good terms with your neighbors was important. Even a transplanted city girl knew that much.

IT WAS STILL DARK THE NEXT MORNING WHEN JULIANNE'S phone rang. "Damn!" Rolling over in bed, she saw from the digital clock on the bedside table that it was 5:45 a.m.

Bleary from sleep, she fumbled for the phone, angry that she'd accidentally left it on overnight. She barely spotted the name on the screen before the device slipped from her fingers and crashed to the floor.

Walden Collier.

Why the hell did I give him my number?

Cursing, she slid her legs off the bed, leaned down, and fished the phone from the cold hardwood between her bare feet. She let it ring three more times, during which she thought hard about hanging up... then decided against it.

"Hello?" She knew her voice was raspy, but it couldn't be helped.

He, on the other hand, sounded wide awake... and in a hurry. "Juli, this is Walden."

"What do you want, Walden?"

He paused, and something clattered on the other end of the call. "I need you to come over here."

Julianne scowled and rubbed the side of her face. "Can it wait? It's not even six in the morning!"

"Not really." He grunted, and something clattered again. "I think you should get over here right now."

"Is it the deer again?" Her mood was *not* improving as the call continued. "Because I'm *not* coming over to clean up every morning, Walden."

"Just come over, okay? Trust me. It's important."

With that, he hung up the call, leaving her sitting there on the edge of the bed, wondering.

Just how important was it that she rush over to his place at six in the morning instead of flipping over and going back to sleep?

As Julianne rolled into Walden's driveway, the first thing that caught her attention were the two lawn chairs set up in the middle of the yard. A few feet in front of them stood a chrome tower as tall as she was, with a cylindrical copper base and a conical cap like a silver gardening hat. When she flicked off the headlights, she could see the clear cuff under the cap was glowing bright blue, which made her think it was a propane heater.

She was baffled as she got out of the Jeep. She'd been expecting to see a throng of deer ripping up the yard, or at least the evidence of a fresh round of devastation... but things looked generally as tidy as she'd left them.

So why had Walden insisted she race over?

"HEY!" HE CALLED OUT FROM NEARBY. "OVER HERE!"

Turning, she saw him waving from near the tree line, no more than thirty yards away. His face glowed in the beam of a flashlight, his smile incandescent.

Curiosity piqued, she worked her way over to him. "What's up with the wakeup call, Wally?"

If the nickname annoyed him, he didn't show it. "Shhh." He held an index finger to his lips like a librarian. "This way."

They proceeded toward the tree line, stopping a few feet from what at first looked like a brown patch of grass. When he trained his flashlight on it, though, she quickly realized what she was actually looking at.

"Omigod!" she whispered. "It's just a *baby!*"

A tiny fawn blinked up at them, gentling nuzzling the air in their direction. Her big eyes were glossy black, her fur light brown and mottled with white patches.

"I've never seen one so *tiny*," said Julianne. "It's *adorable.*"

"I found her there this morning when I came out to start my chores," said Walden. "Curled up under the trees like that, all alone."

"Abandoned?" asked Julianne. "The poor thing!"

"No, no. She'll be fine." Walden crouched down with his hands on his knees, barely three feet away. The fawn made no move to get up and approach or get away from him. "You'll see."

"But doesn't she need someone to take care of her? Isn't that why you called me to come over?"

"Nope." He got up from his haunches, lightly took hold of her arm, and guided her back from the fawn. "I just thought you'd want to see her up close... and help me keep watch for a bit."

"Keep watch?"

"Sure." He led her across the yard to the lawn chairs. "She could use a babysitter, so why not us?"

SIDE BY SIDE, THEY SAT ON THE LAWN CHAIRS, WARMED BY the blue glow of the propane heater cooking away in front of them. For extra warmth against the pre-dawn cold, he gave her foil blankets and a thermos of piping hot coffee.

None of it fully warded off the chill, but she found she didn't mind so much as dawn drew near. Her mind was mostly on the vigil... and him.

He'd surprised her with this. Just when she'd thought there was no hope for the two of them, he'd given her reason to think they might yet find common ground.

"I'm calling her 'Bambina,'" he said between sips from his own steaming thermos. "What do you think?"

"I love the movie *Bambi*, so sure," she said. "Bambina it is."

"I'm glad you agree. It just seemed to fit her, you know?"

She nodded, watching as Bambina briefly raised her head, her pointy little ears fluttering. "Isn't it late in the season for deer to have babies?" she asked.

"As a rule, but it still happens sometimes."

"And, what? Their mothers just leave them behind like this?"

"They do," said Walden. "They drop off their fawns where they know they'll be safe, and then they go off searching for food."

"Because food's scarcer in the winter?"

He shook his head. "It's the same any other time of year. The mother drops off the baby with a sitter while she goes to work."

Again, the fawn's little head popped up as if she knew they were talking about her.

"And the mother isn't worried something might happen to her little one?" asked Julianne.

"Not with us sitting here."

Julianne leaned closer, feeling his muscular arm pressing against hers. This moment was like nothing she'd known in the city or foreseen when she'd moved out to Aunt Peggy's place. Even more than witnessing the herd clomping through her front yard, it made her feel in tune with the natural world, connected to something more special than watching TV in an urban apartment or going downtown to bars or shows.

Somehow, it felt more *real* than all that. And *he* felt more real than any of her past boyfriends had felt, more authentic and down-to-earth.

Through the simple act of sitting on a lawn chair, watching over a baby deer, she felt a sense of wonder and warmth that completed her in ways she hadn't known she'd been incomplete.

A LIGHT SNOW STARTED TO FALL AS THE SKY BRIGHTENED slightly.

"It won't be long until dawn," he told her, checking his watch.

"I wonder when the mother deer will show up?" asked Julianne.

"Hard to say," said Walden. "Could be today, could be tomorrow." He sounded like he knew this from experience.

"You've done this before, I guess? Babysat left-behind fawns?"

"Couple of times, with my dad. He was a true believer in looking out for the wild creatures of the world—deer, especially."

"Aunt Peggy was the same way," said Julianne. "She used to say deer were her spirit animals. That's mostly why she wanted them taken care of after she died, I think."

"Good for her. They're beautiful creatures, for sure."

"Even when they're destroying your landscaping and ruining the grand opening of your inn?"

"Even then."

Suddenly, a gust of frigid wind whipped past, and Julianne shivered at the cold. Walden leaned closer and wrapped an arm around her, shielding her from the worst of the chill.

"I never hated the deer, you know," he said softly. "I said before, I'm not hateful, especially when it comes to beautiful creatures."

Eyes locked with his, she felt herself being swept away by the magic spell weaving itself between them. The arm he'd wrapped around her was welcome, the nearness of his smile and softness of his words even more so.

When he leaned in to kiss her, she did not push him away.

Just as their lips pressed together, though, the sound of a snapping twig interrupted their union. Breaking the kiss, they both looked in the same direction at once, toward the sound of the snap—which was right where the fawn had been lying.

It was then that they saw Bambina up on her feet, standing side by side with a doe that could only have been her mother.

Silently, the two animals stared at them, and they stared back. The snow continued to fall between them, getting heavier.

Bambina drew up her right front leg, then stamped the ground with it.

Tears rolled down Julianne's face as the deer turned and bounded off into the woods, their white tails disappearing amid the curtain of falling snow.

ONE WEEK LATER...

The snow on the ground was a foot deep, but the driveway was clear when Julianne rolled up to Walden's inn.

It was a perfect day for a grand opening, what with the cloudless sapphire sky and the bright winter sun making the snow glitter and twinkle like diamonds. Even the deer seemed to be on their best behavior; she could see they'd left trails of tracks through the snow without ripping up the ground or scattering droppings in the most conspicuous places.

Not that any of that would be a problem, not anymore. Not since the place had been rebranded.

"Hey, Juli!" Walden hurried out the front door in his corduroy jacket and hoodie, waving a champagne bottle. Things were coming together for him, and it showed. "You're just in time!"

Grinning, she got out of the Jeep and crossed the snowy yard in her fur-lined boots. She was so glad to see him, it was hard to imagine she'd only known him for a week.

Sometimes, a week was all it took, though.

"Come on, let's do this! The guests are due any minute now!"

Laughing, she followed him to the sign by the sidewalk—the *new* sign, the one they'd installed as part of the rebranding. It didn't say *Mountain Laurel Getaway* anymore.

And *that* was all thanks to *her*. The idea had come to her that night, a week ago, when the two of them had babysat little Bambina... and Walden had fallen for it all the way.

Just like *she* had fallen for *him*.

"Ready?" he asked.

"Yes!" she said. "Ready!"

"All right then!" Walden raised the bottle high and held it aloft a moment, sunlight flashing from its smooth, emerald surface. "I christen thee...."

He swung the bottle down, smashing it over the sign, sending champagne splashing over the newly engraved lettering... the new name of the inn, dreamed up by Julianne and approved by them both.

If you can't beat 'em, get rich off 'em. That's what she'd said... and so, they'd turned the property's biggest challenge into its biggest asset.

"I christen thee…" He corrected himself. "*We* christen thee… the *Deerview Retreat*. A deep-woods inn for anyone with a passion for wildlife. *Deer*, especially."

Beaming, Julianne applauded. She loved the concept, loved the name.

And, as anyone watching could tell from the way she kissed him, she loved Walden Collier like a deer loves the woods.

ROBERT JESCHONEK IS AN ENVELOPE-PUSHING, USA Today *bestselling author whose fiction and comics have been published around the world. His stories have appeared in* Heart's Kiss, Pulphouse Fiction Magazine, WMG Books' *Holiday Spectacular, and many other publications. His young adult fantasy novel,* My Favorite Band Does Not Exist, *was named one of Booklist's Top Ten First Novels for Youth. He won an International Book Award, a Scribe Award for Best Original Novel, and the grand prize in Simon and Schuster's Strange New Worlds contest. Visit him online at www.bobscribe.com. You can also find him on Facebook and follow him as @TheFictioneer on X and as @bobscribe.bsky.social on BlueSky.*

About this story, he says:

"Years ago, during an especially cold and lengthy winter, my wife and I decided to put out some field corn to feed the deer passing through our neighborhood. The hungry deer quickly found and made the most of the corn, and we loved it! Every morning, we saw those beautiful creatures in our front and side yards, gobbling up the kernels we had cast on the ground.

"Unfortunately, as in my story 'Deerly Undeparted,' our good intentions soon led to overpopulation. Before we knew it, whole herds of deer were showing up each day to enjoy the field corn buffet, forcing us to buy more and more feed to keep up. The deer also left ample drop-

pings and tore up the turf... and did similar damage to the yards of our neighbors. We quickly realized our suburban neighborhood was not conducive to this arrangement, especially as the deer ate every other bit of vegetation they could find on our property and adjacent lots.

"We ended the feeding experiment, but it still took a few seasons for the deer to stop flocking to our yard in great numbers in search of goodies. They don't seem to hold it against us, though: fawns still love to congregate under our trees, frolic on our grass... and, yes, eat everything in sight. But we don't mind, and the neighbors don't seem to mind, either."

The Nice Capades

MELISSA YI

MAC GRIPPED HIS SON GREYSON'S SWEATY LITTLE PALM with one hand and the skate bags with the other, pressing the lock button and hip checking the car door closed while his older daughter, Poppy, splashed ahead in the brownish slush blanketing the rink's rectangular parking lot.

"Stay with me, Poppy," Mac warned her as she crested the front bumper of his beat-up Kia. Greyson had lost a glove, but Mac didn't want to search for it now.

A car stopped to let the trio pass to the second row of parked cars, and Mac nodded his thanks, recognizing the driver as one of the hockey players he'd coached two years ago. The driver saluted back, accelerating slowly so as not to splash them with salted snow.

Everyone in Glengarry, Ontario knew to keep an eye open for kids around the Ice Palace, but Mac had parked next to an unfamiliar red Toyota Sequoia. Glengarry got more out-of-towners closer to the holidays, and some of them popped up at the free public skate. You couldn't trust strangers to stop, especially when the sun set around 4 p.m. in December, decreasing visibility of even the brightest pink jackets that both his kids loved.

"Look both ways," Mac instructed his kids before doing the same at the final lane before the arena's entrance. A single dad could never be too careful with his kids, and as a hockey coach, Mac felt like the whole town was made up of his kids.

Poppy stomped back to their side. "I'm ten years old, Dad. I'm not a baby like Greyson." Her last stomp sent slush spraying toward her little brother."

"I'm not a baby!" Greyson yelled, jumping back to avoid the sludge.

Mac almost lost a grip on his slippery little hand. Then Greyson yelped because his dad had squeezed too hard.

"Enough." Mac eased his clutch on Greyson's wrist and pinned Poppy with a glare and his coach voice.

Her little shoulders sagged. She twisted her brown ponytail around a gloved finger. "Sorry, Greyson. You're not a baby. I'm old enough to walk across the parking lot by myself, though."

Was she? A snowflake touched Mac's left cheek, startling him. Not for the first time, he wished his ex-wife hadn't left him without a road map, or left him, period. He gazed at the swirl of snowflakes now highlighted by the rink's lights. "Let's talk after skating, okay?"

"Okay. But since I'm old enough for my own phone, I'm old enough to look for cars!" Poppy skipped toward the black pressure mats in front of the rink's automatic doors, and Greyson called, "Me! I want to do it!"

Mac laughed and released his son to pound his little boots over the carefully shoveled concrete curb. Poppy paused so that they could jump on the mats together, splitting open the doors.

Mac hustled after his kids into the Ice Palace, ignoring the trophy display case on his right so he could nod at the volunteers setting up at the table by the front doors. The 50/50 draw was a big fundraiser for their minor hockey league team, the Williamstown Whips.

Behind the volunteers, the rink took up pretty much the whole bottom floor of the building. Most onlookers grabbed a rinkside seat, which meant taking a quick right to push open a door on the wall of Plexiglas and concrete surrounding the rink. That wall helped keep the cool air in and reduced their electricity bills.

But Poppy headed straight toward the end zone and draped herself over a row of red metal chairs set in the concrete floor. The red chairs were ideal for families to stay warm while watching the Zamboni, the ice resurfacing machine that hypnotized every child five and under. Mac let Greyson skip ahead and join his sister on the chairs.

There weren't a lot of places to hide on the left, what with six change rooms, locked admin offices, and a canteen. Even if the kids took off upstairs, that only led to one big room with a rink viewing area, nowhere they could get into trouble.

At the opposite end zone, the scoreboard displayed the time in bright red numbers: 5:40. Twenty minutes till the free skate. Plenty of time for his kids to shed their boots and lace up their skates.

"Can we have popcorn?" Greyson asked, bouncing up on his toes.

"I brought carrots." Mac dug an economy-sized bag of washed baby carrots out of his back pack.

"Awww!" Greyson rolled his eyes.

"Get changed. Room number 1, okay?" Mac loaded his kids up with the skating bags and waved them into the first white painted brick room. Meanwhile, Mac stopped at the canteen next door to drop the carrots on the counter. He made sure not to cover up the sign under the Plexiglas that announced the Glengarry Ice Palace's zero tolerance policy toward abuse of any kind.

"Thanks, Mac," said the teenaged canteen volunteer from behind the bags of chips and the popcorn. She headed for the Slushie machine for her next order. This was why Mac shored up everyone's diet by giving away fruit, vegetables, or protein whenever he dropped by.

"Hey!" called a little voice behind him.

Mac twisted around to face the red chairs where Poppy and Greyson had sprawled earlier. Every onlooker, from grandparents to toddlers, now gawked at the ice.

Mac followed their gaze to the single woman on the rink right now, standing at centre ice, and his heart tried to punch out of his chest.

Mac pressed his hand to his sternum and reminded himself to breathe. Something about this curvy brunette lit him up, and not only because she wore green leggings and a red parka like one of Santa's elves. But she wasn't from around here. He would have remembered the bright light in her brown eyes and her round cheeks. Everything about her made him want to smile.

Then the woman visibly took a breath, placed her skates at 90 degrees, and tried to push off into a one foot glide on her left.

Mac took a step. He could tell immediately that she hadn't balanced her weight over the skating hip. She set down her other skate, caught her toe pick, and crashed on her knees and hands.

Mac sprang to the end of the hall, toward the other inner door to the arena. He caught himself already pushing the door open.

This was a grown woman. He had to get his kids.

But now that he'd broken the seal around the arena, cool, moist air billowed in his face, and he could hear another woman cursing in a low voice that raised the hairs on the back of his neck as well as his arms, underneath his jacket.

"Daddy? Daddy, what are you doing?" called Poppy. She and Greyson padded toward him on their ice skates, their blades cushioned by the black rubber floor laid down on the hallway. "It's not time for the free skate yet, see?" Poppy pointed at the scoreboard clock's red numbers glowing at them from the top of the oval.

"Right. Not time yet," Mac agreed, but he still waved his kids ahead of him, into the small waiting area to the left of the end zone, outside the rink boards. Here skaters and players waited to go on and get acclimatized to the colder rink temperature. Or in this case, eaves-dropped.

A sixtyish blonde in a fitted track suit and custom figure skates banged her clip board on the boards, yelling through the Plexiglas at the brunette now brushing ice dust off her knees. "You do everything wrong. You say you skate, but you do not know how to tie your skates or use your toe pick. You. Waste. My. Time."

The brunette's eyes widened. She opened her lips to reply.

The blonde coach spat out, "And you are too fat."

Mac's arms shot forward, and the next thing he knew, he'd leaped over the boards like he'd been tapped for a penalty kill while Greyson called after him uncertainly, "Daddy?"

Mac stepped onto the ice, using his 5'11", 180-pound ex-hockey body to physically block the brunette skater from this demon coach like the defence man he used to be. "That's enough," Mac growled.

The coach glanced at Mac, her words halting for one second before she visibly dismissed him.

Mac pointed to another anti-abuse sign hung on the Plexiglas door through which more children now piled into the waiting area. Mac said two words, very clearly. "Zero tolerance."

The coach snorted. "What are you talking about?"

"Abuse," Mac told her.

Along with the parents and children now flooding into the rink's waiting area, twice as many peered at them through the Plexiglas. They all knew and trusted Mac from growing up with him, hockey, or from school with Poppy and Griffin. Even the tots blinked at him, registering the severity of his tone. They couldn't wait for him to fight.

Meanwhile, Poppy filmed them all with her phone. Mac shook his head at her, but the phone stayed up. His daughter had a mind of her own.

The beautiful brunette blinked at Mac and said, "It *is* abuse, isn't it?"

"Sure is," Mac said over his shoulder, partly because he could listen to that honey of a voice all day. He felt his face flush. In high school, they called him "Fiver" because he used to be known for speaking five words or less. He didn't enjoy the spotlight. His ex-wife had been the talker.

The brunette faced the demon coach and planted one hand on her shapely hip. "If you have comments on my form—how to execute a spin faster, for example—please tell me that."

The coach sneered. "Why should I do that? No one will look at your spins. They will only see your enormous body moving across the ice, like a whale!"

The woman froze at the criticism before she cocked her head to the left and replied, "Whales are beautiful."

Mac nodded in agreement before he told the coach, "Get your things."

"What are you talking about? She has paid for an hour of coaching." The coach eyed Mac up and down and clucked her tongue. "You are stealing her time. She has nine minutes left."

Mac's left eyelid twitched, a sure sign he was going to blow. They could plug the scoreboard into him right now, he was that wired. He opened his mouth one more time.

The brunette beamed at him before she told the coach, "He's right. I wanted to get 'the best' coach and maximize my time, but all you've done is berate me for the body I was born with, without offering one thing I can work on. I'll post a review online. Goodbye."

The coach sheathed her skate blades with a pair of plastic skate guards, snatched the teal water bottle and the luxurious jacket and boots she'd hung on the boards, and stormed out of the rink on her skates, already shouting on her phone.

"What a meanie," Greyson said, watching the coach go.

The other kids stomped their blades on the rubber padding, laughed, and clapped their hands.

Normally Mac didn't let his children badmouth an adult, but this time, he wished he could bang his hockey stick on the boards himself. He had to bite the soft inside of his cheek and say, "Manners are important," before he turned back to the brunette. "Sorry about that."

She tossed her hair, which was so shiny that it reflected the ceiling's fluorescent lights. "Thank you. You saved me from nine minutes of abuse. My name's Natasha."

"NATASHA," SAID THE MAN WITH THE KINDEST BROWN eyes Natasha Goodluck ever seen in an adult. Yes, he was easy on the eyes, with a strong jaw, a nose that had been broken at least once, and the kind of build that looked like he could chop firewood, but as a hockey player, she'd met and played bigger and better-looking guys.

She'd never seen this kind of gentle, thoughtful expression, though, with laugh lines bracketing his eyes. Plus the sound of her name on his lips made her shiver.

She hid that by saying, "Yes, my name is Natasha Goodluck." Then she waited for him to laugh at her. The cluster of kids watching them giggled, the sound echoing throughout the arena.

"Mac," he said, holding out his hand to her. "Allen McMaster, but everyone calls me Mac."

Since she'd been trying out figure skating instead of playing hockey, she wore no pads or gloves. The cool, bare skin of her hand touched his before she almost jumped back. Although he held back his strength, barely touching her, his roughened palms and callused fingertips created a spark that felt like it should be visible to their little audience.

She and Mac stared into each other's eyes until a boy yelled, "Are you okay, Natasha?"

She tore her gaze toward a little guy barely visible over the boards, his face hidden by a hockey helmet complete with a wire shield. He wore a bright pink jacket and matching mittens that made her smile.

She gave Mr. Pink the thumbs up. "I'm all right. Thank you for asking."

"Greyson," Mac supplied the name, in a low voice.

"Greyson," she repeated. It matched little boy's blue-grey eyes.

Pop music blasted through the speakers, and kids and their families cheered. Natasha realized it was time for the free skate, when the rink opened to the public at no charge. She hadn't come to one of these in well over a decade. She used the ice to train and to play. She generally avoided this free-for-all where everyone from great-grandparents to tiny tots would clamber onto the ice for an hour, and you had to cut around little ones pushing triangular skating aids to keep their balance. Natasha remembered older kids shoving the skating aids down the rink at each other, back and forth, possibly taking out the odd skater or two like bowling pins. But public skating was a good way for kids to get their energy out and for families to reconnect, and from the way Mac smiled at everyone, it seemed like a town reunion.

A woman who looked to be in her seventies opened the rink door and gracefully sailed onto the ice, her burgundy skirt fluttering like a flag. Families poured onto the rink like colourful, helmeted ants taking over a wedding cake.

"That woman was very mean to you," said a girl with the same bright pink jacket and the same serious eyes as Greyson, although hers were brown instead of blue-grey. Hopefully Mac and his partner hadn't named her Brownie. This girl tossed her brown ponytail over her shoulder before tugging Greyson onto the ice, unblocking a stream of skaters behind them. "No one should talk like that!"

"You're right, Poppy," said Mac.

Natasha smiled. The girl was a firecracker. That was a much better name than Brownie.

"I'll never hire her again," Natasha told the little family.

Two boys booked it down the ice, hollering the whole way, their shouts bouncing off the ceiling.

"Sometimes it's hard to stand up to bullies," said Poppy, before she skated backwards away from them, her hips torquing and her blades carving C-shapes.

Greyson scampered after her, nearly as fast, even though he was about half his sister's size.

"Bullies," Natasha repeated, and winced so hard that her face hurt. Every day, she stood up to people in her finance job, or when she suited up as #17, but as soon as she tried on figure skates, she paid a bully to coach her.

'I should get my skates,' said Mac, but made no move to leave. In fact, he put out a hand to steady a little girl in a yellow jacket who wobbled by them on her skates. "You okay? People like that give coaches a bad name."

"You're a coach?" Natasha asked. Mac standing on the ice in his boots meant that she, boosted up a few inches in her blades, stared directly into those deep eyes.

Mac watched her right back, and she became conscious of everything: his breath, the sound of blades cutting the ice around them, the faint smell of hot dogs and popcorn in the air, and a little boy moaning behind them, "Could you get out of the way?"

Natasha swiveled to apologize to that boy. He clomped past them on his skates, clinging to his dad with one hand and the boards with the other.

Mac gestured them closer to the middle of the arena, out of the way of the beginners. "I coach U8 and U12 hockey. I play for the Glengarry Guards too. You probably never heard of any of us. What brought you to Eastern Ontario to rent out the rink?"

Natasha blushed. She didn't want to sound like she was bragging, plus she heard the swoosh of his kids skating back toward them, but she believed in telling the truth. "I'm visiting my grandparents, who wanted to retire to a small town. Then my agent got a call for a potential new show called *Blade Boss*."

"*Blade Boss*," Mac repeated, nodding at Greyson and Poppy, who both accelerated forwards before they tried to spray ice at them in a sudden stop. "That sounds familiar, but sorry, as a single dad, I can't keep up—"

Single dad?

As in single?

As in dateable?

Natasha's head wrenched toward his, and their lips hovered an inch apart, hers parted in surprise.

"*Blade Boss*? So cool!" squeaked Greyson's voice.

Natasha released her breath and smiled down at the little boy, who wiggled with puppy-like joy.

"Your agent?" Poppy asked.

Mac's eyebrows drew together. Natasha wanted to smooth the furrow out with her index finger.

Poppy practiced her crossovers while she explained, "We saw it on the news. *Blade Boss* will be a reality TV show where a figure skater and a hockey player get paired up and compete against the other teams to raise money for charity."

"A reality TV show?" Mac sounded like he'd heard of the concept, but had never watched one. Somehow, Natasha believed it, in this little town. "Is that why you hired that d—uh, woman?"

Natasha nodded. "That figure skating coach advertised that she was driving from Montreal to Ottawa and was willing to take on a student on the way. I thought the timing was impeccable and booked her."

"Then she said you were fat!" Greyson put in, wiggling his hips, maybe to practice skating backwards, maybe to imitate Natasha's weight. She bit her lower lip hard enough to hurt.

Mac placed his hand on his son's shoulders. "That was very wrong of her. Natasha is an athlete who needs muscle to compete. And if she wasn't, it would still be wrong, because you can be healthy at any size."

"Exactly." Natasha squatted so she was more Greyson's height. "I can't drop weight for the show, even if it makes it easier for my partner to carry me. This is my hockey season too. I play for the Roanoke Rebels."

When she stood up, a smile broke across Mac's face. "I thought you looked familiar."

His enthusiasm made Natasha's heart flutter as much as his kind eyes had earlier. The skating song switched over to a hard-driving rock ballad that made her want to pump her fist too. "You know my team?"

"I love hockey. I follow everything. Minor league, major league, men's, women's, it's all one sport."

A single man who respected women's hockey! Natasha couldn't resist a quick celly, or celebration, which she usually saved for scoring a goal. She cut a quick circle around them, the confident scrape of her blades overriding the music, before she bent down on one knee and pretended to play air guitar in time with the song.

"You should do that on the show!" Greyson called after Natasha, and when she skated backwards toward them, only catching her toe pick a little, Mac nodded at her.

She smiled and looked away, knowing that Mac was silently pointing out her grace on the ice, despite the figure skates' toe picks, now that she'd gotten rid of the demon coach.

"Natasha's a left wing," Mac told Poppy, who had pulled out her phone to video her celly.

"You know my position?" Natasha asked. They said the way to a man's heart was through his stomach. The way to Natasha's heart, and more, was to praise her hockey.

"All about your position," Mac said, straight-faced.

Natasha nearly choked while one of Mac's eyelids dropped in what might have been a wink. Yup, the man was flirting with her.

Poppy piped up, reading from her phone. "Even though 90 percent of the population is right-handed, over 60 percent of the NHL shoots left-handed like Natasha."

"I can't wait to see Natasha with a stick," Mac told them. "Want to go practice skating now?"

"No, we want to skate with you!" Greyson bladed around his father and Natasha, while Poppy showed off the beginning of a spin.

Natasha stayed in place. She hadn't been to a public skate in a long time. It was chaos. Behind them, a boy dropped to the ice and wiggled like a worm, forcing other kids to skate around him.

Mac touched Natasha's elbow and brought his lips toward her ear. "I'm sorry that my kids won't let you go. Do you, ah, have anyone who'd mind if we spent time together?"

His voice cracked on the last word, which made Natasha smile, press her hand on his, and whisper back in his ear. "I'm free. Would you like to go out for dinner after skating?"

"Watch out!" Mac coiled one arm around her and thrust the other palm forward to block a kid in a camouflage coat barreling toward them. Mac spun and managed to release the kid further along the rink while keeping the other arm around Natasha.

Her hero. She wanted to kiss him.

"Yes to dinner," said Mac, not even breathing faster, "if you don't mind my plus two. My parents or brother should be able to babysit another night too. That is, if you want."

What a gentleman. Mac's body felt blissfully warm, a haven on this cold rink. He smelled like coffee and shampoo and man. Natasha stared into those beautiful eyes, close enough to count each eyelash, and brushed her nose against his, imagining that she could feel the bristle around his mouth. "I want."

They didn't kiss. Not with dozens of little eyes fixed on them and multiple more skaters threatening to mow them down. But he took her hand in his, and she caught her breath at the feeling of his skin on hers.

He grinned, and she could see him handing her a hot dog, and her settling into a red chair beside the two littles so she could bite into it. She pictured the four of them tossing snowballs at each other. Aloe, her black lab mix, would jump in the air to catch every ball. She imagined teaching Poppy and Greyson how to shoot left or right-handed on the homemade rink in her back yard while Aloe galloped in the snow around the rink, woofing with joy.

And from the way Mac smiled back at her, he couldn't wait to turn those dreams into sweet reality.

MELISSA YI IS AN EMERGENCY PHYSICIAN WHO BELIEVES in happily-ever-afters. She is best known for her crime-fighting doctor heroine, Hope Sze, but as a Canadian living in the cutest small town, Melissa could not resist penning the Glengarry Guards hockey romance series, which has been collected in the omnibus Home Ice. *Melissa has also climbed aboard the Jane Austen train with her novel* Pride & Provocateur, *where Mr. D'Arcy is a tech bro in Dildo, Newfoundland. http://www.melissayuaninnes.com*

About this story, Melissa says:

"I've always admired the artistry and strength of figure skating, but only recently appreciated the grit and teamwork of hockey. Why not join both sports in a romance?

"Mac is the seventh Glengarry Guard, the oldest player, the only coach, and the only one with kids. I knew Natasha would match his loyalty and humour. Her character is an homage to strong female hockey players who competed on the reality TV show The Battle of the Blades, *like Natalie Spooner.*

"I started taking skating lessons myself last year. Fun, frustration, and friendship, and only one nasty fall so far. Sort of like what author

Kristine Kathryn Rusch says about writing: 'Have fun. Go play.' And I do love coming home afterward to my husband, kids, and dogs, and drinking hot cocoa with real chocolate. I'd love to keep in touch on social media (https://linktr.ee/melissayi) or through my newsletter (https://melissayi.substack.com/). Thanks for reading, and stay warm!"

Under Cover of Night

CATE MARTIN

THERE WERE NO BUSY NIGHTS AT THE CLEAR LAKE FAMILY Restaurant. This was a fact that Ginnie Schrader knew well by now.

Back in 1926, when Gran had bought the property for a steal, she had promised Ginnie they'd be making money hand over fist. With the new Highway 10 that was going to be linking St. Cloud with the Twin Cities right out their doorstep, and with so many people buying cars these days and just driving them around the countryside, they were ideally located. Close enough to town to catch everyone coming back from up north, but far enough away from the Twin Cities that no one would want to wait that long for good food. And with the lake view through the many windows out the back of the restaurant, they were sure to be a draw.

But that had been two years ago. Lately, Gran had shifted to putting all the same expectations on the next year, because the government promised the highway would be paved by the end of 1929. People were particular about their cars, Gran said. Unpaved roads were a deterrent. So many axle-ruining potholes. But once that divided highway was fully paved....

Well, then the talk went back to those hand-over-fist promises.

Ginnie sighed as she looked around the empty dining room, every table cleaned to a sparkling shine and waiting to be of service. Her hands still smelled lemony from the polish she'd used on all that wood just to have something to do. But now she'd run out of busy-work tasks.

She turned to look out at the equally empty parking lot in front of the building, then at the snow-covered lanes of the divided highway beyond, and sighed again.

There were no busy nights, but there was usually a reliable trickle of regulars. Enough people passed by on their way to and from the Twin Cities and St. Cloud to at least keep their little business afloat.

But not on a night like this. Not when the snow that had started out as a pretty silvery dancing of flakes in the light of the nearly full moon had deepened into a dark smear of icy clumps carried on howls of wind.

That wind whistled down the chimney of the river-stone fireplace and rattled the glass windows between her and the ice-covered lake outside.

It was just the two of them, running the business together. Even so, she could ask Gran for the night off and go home early, except there was no way she was going to try traveling through that storm. You'd have to be crazy to even contemplate trying it.

But a gleam of light coming from the highway caught her attention, and she realized that someone was just that crazy. Pulling the folds of her hand-knit cardigan a little more closely around her, she stepped nearer to the window by the front door. The cold from the storm outside was radiating in through that glass, intense enough that her breath fogged even though she was still inside.

But she was curious. Who was driving down the highway that was all but invisible under the deepening drifts of blowing snow?

At first, all she could make out were the headlights, swerving and angling up and down as whatever vehicle was approaching slipped on icy patches or rolled in and out of potholes.

Then it drew close enough for her to make out details. It was a car.

More specifically, it was a taxi.

But that made even less sense. It might be a taxi out of St. Cloud, but she didn't think so. No, it looked posher than the taxis in that town. It looked more like it came from the Twin Cities. But who would take a taxi so far, and on a night like this?

She was shivering now despite the thick cardigan, but she moved even closer to the window, hoping for a glimpse inside the car as it made its way past her Gran's restaurant. Who could be out in this weather?

Only it didn't go past the restaurant.

It sort of turned, but mostly slid, into the parking lot that was little more than a gravel patch off the highway.

And then it just sat there.

Ginnie frowned as she leaned so close to the window her forehead was touching it now. She thought she saw two people inside that taxi. Two men. But they were both sitting together in the front of the car. Which was a little strange for a taxi.

Then the passenger door opened, and someone stumbled out. Definitely a man, although he was so bundled up in a hat with flaps, a dark wool coat with a turned-up collar, and layers and layers of bright red muffler, that being male was all she could guess about him. Male and tall.

The man turned to close the door and immediately slipped in the snow. He caught himself with the hand still holding the door handle, but in a way that made Ginnie wince in sympathy.

The man had stayed on his feet, but his shoulder was surely paying the price for it now. He had wrenched it pretty good.

She watched as the man pushed away from the door again. He stood for a moment with his gloved hands out in front of him. He looked for all the world like a toddler braving a second try at his first steps.

He nearly fell again when he turned to close the car door behind him. But then he made his way oh so carefully over the snow-covered gravel to the front door. He stamped the snow from his boots before reaching for the handle to the front door.

Then visibly jumped when he saw Ginnie there watching him. She was dressed in her waitress uniform, but given that her hand-knit cardigan went down to her knees, she wasn't surprised he didn't notice it right away.

"Oh, pardon, miss," he said. His voice was doing a good job of demonstrating why that garment around his face was called a muffler. She could just barely make out his words. But his eyes were wide and friendly.

And the most intense shade of green she'd ever seen. Like he was a living promise that this cold, blue weather would be gone in time, and the warmth and greenery of spring would follow.

"Are you lost?" Ginnie asked. Because if it was food he was after, he wouldn't have left the other man out in the car. Not even if he was just a driver. It was too cold for that.

He took a moment to unwind all those layers of scarf, then grinned at her. Like his eyes, his smile was wide and friendly, if a bit chagrined.

"'Fraid so," he said. "We were expecting some snow, but not all this. And we should've reached where we're going by now, but we don't seem to be getting any closer."

"Wow," Ginnie said. And not just because, with his muffler and his hat both off, she could see his face clearly now. And what a face it was. But no. Mainly, it was his voice. How strange that a voice, just a voice, could make her feel all warm inside.

But his questioning look wanted an answer. So she settled with, "You're not from around here."

"Well, no," he admitted. "Is it that obvious?"

He looked down at his clothes. The black wool coat over what looked to be the charcoal gray trousers of a two-pieced suit were nondescript enough. They didn't exactly go with the heavy-duty boots and fur-lined hat with flaps he was wearing. Those were more like what her uncles would get decked out in before going deer hunting for the afternoon.

And the red scarf? She couldn't imagine any outfit where that would look like it fit. It was so oversized, almost more a shawl than a scarf. And so brightly, eye-catchingly red.

But she just gave him her brightest smile even as she led him closer to the warmth of the fire crackling in that that river-stone fireplace. "It's your accent," she told him. "Where are you from?"

His green eyes narrowed at her, as if uncertain if she was teasing him or being sincere. But he seemed to fall down in favor of the latter. "Eastern Tennessee," he said at last. And she was certain the accent he had been trying to suppress before was stronger now. Like he was letting it show in his voice, just for her. "From the hollers, although not so deep in the hollers as some of my cousins. I reckon you'd've had trouble understanding more'n a few words out of them. I've been working in Minneapolis for a spell, but I guess not long enough to polish off all my twang."

"Not quite. But I like it," Ginnie assured him.

And she did. Something about the rise and fall of his words, so different from the steady, sober tone of her own German-descended family, made her feel completely at ease. Warm and comfortable.

"I do get comments," he said with another flash of that disarming smile.

She just smiled back at him, basking in the glow of being near him. She tried to remember the last time she'd spent more than two minutes with a man who wasn't either twenty years older than her, or a cousin. But she came up empty.

But he was bouncing on his toes. Only ever so slightly, but enough for her to remember that he wasn't actually there to eat.

"So where are you trying to get to?" Ginnie asked. "You're most of the way to St. Cloud on Highway 10, you know. If you just keep on going the way you have been, you'll get there. Although I wouldn't want to guess how long that would take in this weather."

"It's a doozy, isn't it?" he said. "We get snow back home now and again, but nothing like this."

"I'm surprised your driver agreed to take you out this far on a night like this," Ginnie said.

That seemed to fluster him. He looked out the window towards the car with the dark shape of the man still waiting behind the wheel inside. Then he looked down at the lengths of red muffler in his hands.

Then he looked up at her and hit her with the full wattage of that chagrined smile again.

"Well, I can't drive in this. Never learned how. Back home, when it snows, we mostly just hunker down and wait it out. But...." And there he leaned in to speak close to her ear as if about to tell her a secret. "I'm paying him double."

Ginnie felt a shiver run up and down her spine at the touch of that warm breath.

A man in a wet wool coat had no business smelling so good, either. Not at all.

She ducked her head a little and twisted a lock of her bobbed brown hair behind her ear, needing a moment to regain her composure. Then she said, "Where are you trying to go?"

"Ah, sorry. You asked before," he said. "It's a farm near here, belongs to a man going by the name of Paul Schrader?"

"Paul Schrader?" Ginnie repeated. Of course, she knew at once who this man meant. Paul was her uncle.

But Paul, like most farmers in Stearns County, didn't care for unexpected visitors.

"How do you know Paul?" she asked.

"Would you believe we're long-lost cousins?" the man asked. His smile wavered ever so slightly.

"No, not really," she said.

"Yeah, I don't have any family at all in this neck of the woods," he said. He was gesturing with his chin towards the windows at the back of the restaurant, as if to point out the neck of the woods he was referring to. But the sight of the view out of those windows distracted him at once. "Wow," he said. "Now that I'm not out trying to drive through it, it's actually kind of pretty. Isn't it? Like a kaleidoscope of white."

Ginnie turned to look out the windows at the snow dancing over the surface of the lake. There was not even a hint of moonlight through the clouds above, and everything was a muted swirl of wind-tossed snow in hypnotic spirals. There were no individual flakes in weather like this. It was like an angry, white blur of motion.

But now that she was seeing it through his eyes, it definitely had its own beauty.

Although he was also right that it was definitely prettier when you weren't out in it.

"You should see it after the storm passes," she told him. "When the moon is shining on that lake, and it catches every flake of snow. It's like spun sugar. Or like a crystal menagerie."

"I would love to," he said at once, his eyes smiling into hers.

He sounded like he was accepting an invitation.

Wait, had it sounded like she had just extended an invitation?

Yeah, she decided. It had. It had sounded just like that.

And she wasn't sorry. It might be outrageously forward. Especially as she had yet to even ask him his name.

But she knew. The racing of her heart was telling her. She wanted to see this man again.

"No, I'm not related to Paul Schrader," he said, startling her into paying attention to the actual conversation again. "I just have a legal matter to discuss with him. Nothing life-threatening. Just something to clear up before the end of the year. Can you give me directions to his place? I'm sure we're close."

Ginnie was about to speak when Gran suddenly banged a large

cast-iron pan down on the cooktop back in the kitchen. Ginnie and the man both jumped in surprise. At least she had known Gran was back there, futzing around her kitchen. The man might have thought they were all alone inside that restaurant.

Then she realized that somehow they had been touching each other. She didn't know when exactly it had happened. When they'd both been looking out the windows at the lake and the snow? But somehow, her hand had ended up clutched in both of his.

She couldn't even recall when he'd taken those gloves off.

But she missed the warmth of his skin the minute he snatched his hands away from hers.

Then Gran was slamming her way out of the kitchen, drying her own hands on the food-stained apron she always wore over her faded, decidedly old-fashioned gray dress. Ginnie was pretty sure that dress dated back to the Civil War, but Gran never threw anything away if she could eke one more use out of it, so the dress stayed.

As she crossed the room with her most determined stride, Ginnie saw that Gran's steel gray hair was escaping from its tight bun at the nape of her neck. Like even her hair wanted away from whatever angry outburst was about to come.

"Gran," Ginnie said, swallowing hard. Was she about to get a talking to for being overly familiar with the customers?

But Gran just ignored her, pushing past her to stand with her fists planted on her wide hips and glare up at the young man who was a good foot taller than her, at least.

"Young man," Gran said.

"Robert Tate, ma'am," he said, and thrust out a hand.

Gran stared at the extended hand until he finally—awkwardly— retracted it.

"This dining area is for customers only," she said. "Now, I'll walk you to the door and tell you how to get to Paul Schrader's farm. But I expect you'll leave then and not return. Understood?"

"Yes, ma'am," the man—Robert Tate, apparently—said.

But over the top of Gran's head, his eyes met Ginnie's with what she was sure was real regret that their conversation was coming to such an abrupt end.

She regretted it too. But what could she do? He would get his directions and get back into his car, and that would be that. She'd never see him again.

Ginnie was so shocked by her grandmother's sudden unfriendly behavior that she almost missed what her grandmother was really doing.

And once she did figure it out, she almost gave the whole charade away by bursting out with the truth.

She might have made a meep of sound. Certainly, she felt Robert's green, green eyes on her again, this time with an unspoken question in them.

And she was certain her cheeks were flushing a deep shade of pink. But still, she got her head straight in the end. She twisted that cardigan tightly around her again in her nervousness, but she said the words she had to say. No matter the regret that still clenched at her heart.

She had to follow Gran's lead.

"That's right. That's how you get to Paul Schrader's farm. You can't miss it." And she summoned up a smile that she hoped looked convincing.

But the arching eyebrow over one of those green eyes told her really, she probably hadn't.

"Thank you both so much," Robert said as he tugged those gloves back on and started winding the lengths of muffler around his neck. Then he nodded at Gran in a gesture of thanks. "Missus...." He broke off, like he'd caught himself about to call Ginnie's Gran "Missus Gran" before realizing that couldn't possibly be her real name. "Um, ma'am," he amended.

Gran said nothing. She just waited with her arms folded for him to go.

But she scowled as Ginnie ran past her and after Robert, meeting him just before he could disappear out the front door.

"I'm Ginnie," she said, ridiculously breathlessly.

"Ginnie," he said. His voice was muffled once more, but the eyes were as communicative as ever. Warm and inviting.

"Short for Virginia," she added. Stupidly. But it wasn't like she could tell him her last name.

"I hope to see you again soon, Ginnie. But not in the middle of a blizzard next time. By moonlight."

For a moment, they both just stood there, like neither one wanted to be the first to look away from the other.

But then he was gone.

And Gran made a loud huffing sound behind her.

"I get it, Gran," Ginnie said. Even though she stayed at her post by the window, watching Robert once more make his toddling way back out to that taxi with its waiting driver.

"You were going to send him straight out to your uncle's farm without so much as a warning first," Gran grumbled as she headed back towards the kitchen, stopping in the doorway to pick up the phone that hung on the wall there.

"Do you *have* to call the sheriff?" Ginnie asked. "Isn't it enough that you already sent Robert to the Widow Muller's farm instead of Uncle Paul's? If they even get there without putting that car in a ditch, they'll surely leave after the Widow Muller has given them her full tour. They always do."

"Foolish girl," Gran said as she waited for someone to pick up the other end of the line. "Of course we have to call. That boy was a fed. And the feds never come alone. How these two got so lost from the others is a mystery, but it's a guaranteed fact that there *are* others. And who knows where they are now?"

Ginnie chewed at her lip.

He hadn't *looked* like a fed. Maybe under that wool coat he'd been wearing the same sort of suits the Bureau of Investigation agents always wore. But he was so young, and his face had been so open and kind.

And honestly, what federal agent had such a strong accent? Some of them definitely came from New England, sure. But from the south? With those warm, homey tones?

"He was a fed," Gran said, as if reading Ginnie's thoughts. Or correctly interpreting the reason Ginnie's hands were still twisting and twisting at the knit fabric of her cardigan. "Although what they're doing, riding into town in taxis at night in the middle of a snowstorm, is beyond me. They must really be getting desperate to catch someone doing anything illegal."

"Yeah," Ginnie said, but only under her breath. Gran had finally gotten the sheriff's wife on the line, and from there, everyone in the area would soon know to hide their moonshine, burn their mash, and take apart their stills before their farms were searched. "Who around here would be caught doing something illegal?"

It was the family business, after all. Without the bottles of whiskey Gran was selling out the back of the kitchen, the trickle of customers coming in through the front door was never going to be enough to keep them open until the highway got paved. And she got her whiskey from all four of her sons, always careful not to pick a favorite.

Still, Ginnie didn't particularly like it.

And she *had* liked Robert Tate. There had just been something about him. She wasn't sure exactly what it was, but she was sure she would know. After a second meeting, she would know.

Only now it didn't seem likely that second meeting would ever come.

Ginnie looked up as another hard blast of wind shook the walls of the restaurant around her.

The lake really was so much prettier in the moonlight.

ROBERT TATE SLUMPED LOWER IN THE SEAT OF THE borrowed—or rather, commandeered—taxi, trying to warm his gloved hands by burying them deeper in his armpits. The car's heater was running as hard as it was able. It just wasn't doing much. Not against this cold.

Another blast of wind rocked the car, blowing it sideways hard enough for the tires to brush up against the snowbank that more or less defined the edge of the highway. Robert had to take his hands out of his armpits to brace against the dash.

But Pete Foster, his senior partner behind the wheel, just laughed. He did that a lot. At Robert's expense. And not in a good-natured way.

Only this time, Robert was sure he wasn't overreacting. He was sure Pete was the one not taking this storm seriously.

"Hey, the woman in that restaurant didn't seem to think this was a normal sort of weather," Robert said defensively.

But also slowly and carefully. Because after several minutes of lovely conversation with Ginnie, now he was back with Pete. And when he was talking to Pete, he really couldn't let his native accent slip out.

Pete would take any opportunity to tease him mercilessly, and the red scarf Robert's mother had knit for him was target enough.

Sure, the length, width, and color of the garment were all different kinds of too much. But she didn't know what winters here were like. Robert hadn't even known. Not until this storm blew in and they'd all hopped into waiting taxis to sneak into the county under the cover of night and storm when no one would expect a raid from the Bureau of Investigation.

This was his first winter here in the Midwest. And, if anyone had asked him, he was pretty sure he would've said he'd rather not experience his first proper blizzard from the passenger seat of a car Pete was driving. Pete didn't so much navigate a car as point its front end in a direction, hit the gas, and hope for the best.

No, if anyone had asked Robert how he'd want to experience his first real Midwestern blizzard, it would've been more like what he'd almost had back at that restaurant. A warm fire at his back, a gorgeous view before him, and an even more gorgeous woman at his side.

But switch out the dining room with all its tables and chairs for a comfy little couch and a blanket big enough to cover both of them. Then we'd be getting a lot closer to ideal for Robert.

Pete laughed again as they hit another patch of ice and the entire car started to rotate underneath them before the tires caught and pulled them out straight again.

Robert felt sick to his stomach. This was definitely not how cars were supposed to move.

But he sat up a little straighter when a snow-caked willow tree suddenly emerged from the storm. It was off to his right, so there was little danger that Pete would hit it. Although Robert wouldn't bet money on that.

But it was one of the landmarks the older woman had given him. The angry one with the thick arms and the stocky posture.

Who had shared the same blue eyes as her granddaughter. He had never thought of blue as a warm color, but the two of them were making him question that assumption.

Well, the old woman's eyes had been warm with angry heat. But the warmth in Ginnie's eyes had made a very different impression on him.

"That's the tree," he forced himself to say, pointing it out to Pete.

"I saw it," Pete said, leaning forward over the steering wheel to rub the frost from the windshield with his sleeve. Not for the first time.

"Nearly there, then," Robert said.

Pete just grunted.

Robert wasn't sure how to tell his senior partner that he suspected the directions were all a lie. It's not like it would be surprising news to the man. The farmers in this county lied to federal agents as if it were some sort of sport they were all engaged in and someone was definitely keeping score.

"Turn at the broken-down fence," Pete grumbled, remembering the directions Robert had given him after getting into the car. "Yeah, this all looks familiar."

"You've done a lot of raids out here?" Robert asked.

But Pete was back to just grunting in response. He rubbed at the window again, flakes of frost covering the dashboard like another, smaller blizzard of snow.

"It's just, it's all families out here," Robert said.

Pete shot him a sideways glare. "It's all families where you are, too."

"I know," Robert said. Although he very much regretted sharing his family history with Pete. He had thought his partner would respect him more if he knew that Robert had joined the BOI despite his extended family's many rum-running members. That he might see Robert as exceptional, choosing a life in law enforcement when the opposite path had been so much easier.

But that wasn't how Pete saw it. No, when Pete looked at Robert, it was always with suspicious eyes. Like maybe Robert was some kind of plant, secretly working for the other side.

For his part, Robert had been hoping his career would look more like being one of the Untouchables, taking on the really, truly bad guys. Taking them down and making the world a safer place.

But he had never been up against an actual gangster. No, so far his whole job was riding along on these raids. Helping tear a farm apart in search of evidence of whiskey-making.

Trying not to feel the eyes of the farmer and his family as they watched him tear up the floorboards or bust up the walls of their homes.

Their *homes*.

And for what? For a law that this particular county had over-whelmingly voted against enacting.

These people were breaking the law, sure. But they were breaking it because it was a bad law they disagreed with.

In a way, they were living their lives with more integrity than he was. And he kind of respected them for it.

"Yep, definitely familiar," Pete said, then swore as the car hit another patch of ice.

Robert held on for dear life as the car spun around in two complete circles and then another half turn before finally smashing into the snowbank with a soft thump. A wave of snow leapt up into the air outside Pete's door but was quickly caught up in the dance of the blowing winds and carried off with the rest that was still falling from the sky.

Pete swore again and struck the wheel in front of him.

"If it makes you feel better, I think that old woman was lying to us," Robert said.

"Of course she was lying to us," Pete growled. "I know where this road goes. It's that old woman's farm. The one who's always so helpful to let you search everything. Really takes her time with it. Meanwhile, all her neighbors have all the time they need to toss their stills in the mill ponds."

"So, why are we going this way?" Robert asked.

"We can meet up with the others," Pete said. "They couldn't have all gotten lost. Six more cars, someone must've gotten at least a few arrests before the locals were onto us. They're crafty, all of them, but no way in this blizzard they saw all of us coming. Not at night."

"You knew this whole time we were going the wrong way?" Robert asked, honestly surprised.

"Just since the willow tree," Pete said. "Bad news, Tate. We're jammed up in this snowbank. You're going to have to get out and push. But hey, your mama's scarf should keep you plenty warm out there."

Robert said nothing.

But there was nothing to be said. He knew he'd already come to a life-changing decision. And Pete didn't need to know. Because if he did, Pete would probably wait until the car was free, then hit the gas and leave Robert to walk back to civilization on his own.

Not that Robert would mind the walk so much. It would beat being in the car with Pete. Or whatever worked waited for him back at the station, helping to process the arrests the other agents were making.

But it was too soon to walk back to Ginnie. No, that had to wait.

The moon wasn't out yet.

FOUR DAYS AFTER THE STORM, GINNIE FOUND HERSELF once more looking out those windows at the back of the restaurant, out over the moonlit sparkle of snow on the lake. There was no wind, and every star was shining brightly up in that sky.

But it all just made her wistful.

Eleven men had been arrested the night of the blizzard. Six taxis filled with federal agents had slipped in besides the one she had seen. And even though Gran had gotten the word out through the party lines, it had been too late to save everybody.

Eleven men, and none of them her uncles. But they were all surely on their way to Leavenworth by now.

And Gran was still in a mood.

Ginnie turned away from the windows. There were three families enjoying evening meals closer to the fire where it was warmer, but none of them needed anything from her at the moment. Huddling deeper into her cardigan, she wandered closer to the front door.

Just in time to see another taxi easing its way into the gravel parking lot.

She was out the door before she even saw the flash of red muffler as Robert Tate got out of the car. This time from the back seat.

"What are you doing here?" she demanded in a fierce whisper, even though she'd already heard the door slam shut behind her.

"What do you mean?" he asked, looking genuinely confused. "I said I'd be back."

"Well, yes, but obviously that was before I knew who you were," she said. "You have to get out of here before Gran sees you."

"How can your Gran possibly be sore at me? She sent my partner and me to the end of beyond. We ended up stuck in a ditch for hours and missed the whole raid. Which I'm sure was her intention," he said.

"You were going to my uncle's house," Ginnie said.

"Oh," he said, and blinked.

Then he reached a gloved hand up to pull the layers of muffler down from around his face. "I can see how that would change things."

"He wasn't arrested," Ginnie said. Then rushed to add, "And there's no point going out there now, because you won't find anything."

"Hey!" he said, raising both gloved hands in surrender. "I have no intention of going after your uncle. Or any of your family! I just came out here to see you."

"Yeah, right," Ginnie said. Although her heart was doing somersaults despite her harsh words.

"Honestly," he insisted. "I resigned."

"You what?" she stammered.

"I quit," he said. Then laughed, as if he hadn't said that out loud yet, but the words delighted him. "I quit!"

"But why?" Ginnie asked.

"It didn't sit with me right," he said. "I grew up listening to the stories about the Untouchables, and Al Capone, and all that. And I wanted to be a part of it. But this? Busting up stills out in the country where no one is getting shot up in gang wars? It's not what I thought it was."

"So you just quit?" Ginnie said. She wasn't sure if she believed it. No, she wasn't sure if she could let herself believe it.

But that wide, sincere smile was back on his face. And the bright red of his wind-burned cheeks was only making him look more forthright than before. "I just quit. I told you I was from the hollers, and I think I mentioned my cousins?"

"The cousins with the impenetrable accents?" she said.

He laughed. "I did mention them, then! Yep, that's them. They're my mother's people, mostly. And she doesn't like to talk about them much. Because most of them are rum-runners. I reckon it's not too different than what you folks are doing out here. My cousins don't mean no harm. They just want folks to have good corn whiskey. Not the stuff that makes you go blind."

Ginnie smiled up at him. She doubted he even knew how strong his accent had kicked back in. Like talking about his cousins just reminded him too much of home.

But she said, "Actually, what my uncles wanted to brew was beer. And my uncle Felix still does. But the whiskey is far more lucrative."

"And your Gran?" he asked.

"Her Gran sells it," Gran said from where she was suddenly standing in the doorway. Arms akimbo, enjoying the height being at the top of the few short steps gave her. "Because it's lucrative."

"Ma'am," Robert said, touching the brim of his fur-lined hat.

"Don't ma'am me, boy," Gran said with her fiercest glower.

"He quit, Gran," Ginnie said before her grandmother could get fully worked up.

"What's that?" Gran said, caught off guard.

"I quit, ma'am," Robert said. "I'm no longer an agent of the federal government."

"So you're unemployed?" Gran said, narrowing her eyes down at Robert.

But Robert just gave her his warmest grin. "Currently, yes. It seems that way."

"Unemployed, but paying for taxis?" she pressed.

"Well, ma'am, the fact of the matter is, I never yet learned how to drive in the snow," he told her.

Gran said nothing.

Ginnie snugged her cardigan more tightly around her, feeling the cold after so many minutes outside without a coat, even on a night without wind.

Robert just waited to hear what Gran would say. Ginnie admired his patience. She could never stand any of Gran's icy silences.

But then Gran finally broke down and pushed the front door back open. "Come inside, then," she said.

"Gran?" Ginnie asked even as Robert turned to speak to the driver of the taxi. Who appeared to be an actual taxi driver this time and not a federal agent trying to go incognito.

"It's too cold to talk out here. But I know a way to fix both your problems," Gran said.

"Both my problems?" Robert asked, not quite slipping in the snow at the bottom of the stairs before getting close enough to relieve Gran from door-holding duty.

"Yes," Gran said. "You need to learn how to drive in the snow, and you need a job. Correct?"

"That about sums it up, yes," Robert agreed.

"Then I'm going to call the sheriff," Gran said.

"Gran?" Ginnie objected.

"Oh, hush, child," Gran said impatiently. "The boy can't join the sheriff's department if he can't drive a car in winter, can he? Not in Stearns County."

Then she turned and huffed back into the depths of the restaurant.

Leaving Ginnie standing in the snow, looking up at Robert, who was still holding the door.

"I guess I'm staying?" he said as he extended a suddenly glove-free hand down to help her up the steps.

"Well, I find it best to do what Gran says," Ginnie said.

She slipped her hand in his, and it felt so right. Like it had always belonged there, and she had simply never known.

"Come on," Robert said, tucking an arm around her shoulders. "Let's go look at that lake by moonlight."

As much as Ginnie didn't need to go back inside to feel warm, because she was feeling plenty warm there pressed close to his side, she nodded.

The lake was magical in the light of the moon, under the cover of the night.

CATE MARTIN LOVES TO MIX MYSTERIES AND MAGIC. AND she does it a lot. Like in all three of her witch mystery novels series: The Witches Three Cozy Mysteries, The Viking Witch Cozy Myster-ies *and* The Weal and Woe Bookshop Witch Mysteries. *She also loves to mix mysteries and history. Whether that's 1930s St. Paul, Minnesota, like in her Dorothy Lundegaard P.I. short fiction series, or ninth century Norway like in her Ljota and Kiallakr short fiction series. She even loves her mystery straight up, no chaser, like much of her fiction which has appeared in the quarterly magazine* Mystery, Crime and Mayhem. *And her alter ego Kate MacLeod has even been known to mix mystery with her science fiction.*

You can learn more about her work at CateMartin.com and at RatatoskrPressBooks.com.

About this story, Cate says:

"I've always had a fascination with Prohibition, but not just the stories of mobsters and lawmen like the Untouchables. I love the smaller stories, about how those laws impacted normal people. Like my German ancestors in Minnesota, who found ways to be civilly disobedient. The

feds taking taxis through a blizzard at night? Totally a thing that happened. Crazy times, and not a tommygun in sight."

A New Saturnalia

ALEXANDRA BRANDT

JENNA HAD TO PARK THREE BLOCKS AWAY FROM THE COPY Shop on First Street. Cursing holiday shopping all the while, cursing the fact that she had to spend her Saturday afternoon wading through it.

It did nothing to endear her toward Fairwood, a Washington State college town which, being in Washington State, was cold and clammy and cheerless in December—and, being a college town, was doing its best to be The Most Cheerful City You've Ever Seen.

Oh, Fairwood had its charms in other seasons, and Jenna had lived through three winters here so far with few *real* complaints, but this year in particular those extremes irked Jenna immensely—especially since she currently had to slog her way through both to get to her destination.

She was stuck at the very end of the street, where it turned residential and fewer people vied for the spaces. The breeze was especially stiff as she climbed out of her car, blowing the fake-fur-lined hood of her teal wool coat back from her head and throwing her mess of brown curls into even more of a mess, no doubt reddening her pale cheeks and nose.

The cloud cover overhead was thick and gray, and the air wasn't —quite—freezing, but with the windchill and dampness it felt worse than freezing, somehow. At least Jenna was armed for it, with warm craft fair gloves and chunky tan boots which, despite being oxymoronically "recycled vegan leather," were practical enough to be flannel-lined. So her fingers and toes weren't cold. Yet.

So many buildings to walk past, still.

So much Holiday Spirit, trying to fight the winter blues. And failing, because fake warmth couldn't drive off the ever-growing chill between real humans.

Christmas was a veneer, plastering over all the wounds in the world for just one month—and in the end, ripping it off again in January would make the wounds even bigger.

That was what Jenna hated about this holiday season.

Last week she'd sworn to Jesse she wasn't really a Grinch. She just couldn't stand the fakery. Not now. Not when everything hurt too much.

A waft of spices and ginger hit Jenna's nose, causing her to slow down for a moment. The Tea Bar was the last of the (many) beverage shops on downtown First Street, which meant that Jenna had never been inside, only driven past it on her way somewhere else. It sparkled with twinkle lights and looked warm and inviting. It was even decked out in garlands of fragrant, *real* cedar greenery...but no, the candles glowing in the windows were still fake. The sandwich board declared The Tea Bar Holiday Specials, all complicated tea lattes with too many ingredients, heavy on the ginger factor.

So, no...she wasn't in the mood to appreciate overpriced bougie wellness drinks right now. Not even when her mouth watered, just a little.

Maybe someday she'd actually go in. But not today.

Still, The Tea Bar decor was at least classy, compared to the coffee shop on the very next corner—every block needed to have its own cafe, it seemed—with its window decals of twee coffee-drinking penguins and polar bears in Santa Suits. Seriously. Penguins and polar bears were on the opposite ends of the earth! Never mind the Santa suits, they would never be *seen* together in real life!

But then, what was real anyway, right?

That seemed like something Jesse would say, only he'd serve it with a cheerful grin instead of cynicism.

Jenna shoved her hands into her pockets and hustled onward, keeping her head down and ignoring the rest of the shop-fronts. She had her errands to complete, and at least she would get to see Jesse's smiling face as part of it all. If not in person, then at least in print.

The Copy Shop was playing mid-century Christmas classics—or at least songs that were meant to *sound* like mid-century Christmas classics—when Jenna walked in, and someone had strung up red and green tinsel garlands, but it was still mostly utilitarian and joyless, so she wasn't sure why the employees had bothered. The guy at the desk was about Jenna's age—a few years out of college. Maybe he, too, had graduated with a degree that wasn't really... *for jobs...* one might say.

He was surprisingly friendly and cheerful, though, when she gave him her name to pick up the print job.

Although maybe he was smiling because of the *contents* of said print job.

As she pulled one of the posters out to do the quality check, Jenna couldn't keep from smiling herself. She'd have to text a picture to Hannah, Jesse, and the rest of the team immediately. Everyone had outdone themselves.

SATURNALIA REDUX was plastered boldly at the top, the first thing a casual viewer saw—as was right and proper, per their designer, Hannah's friend Chesca. But the second thing you saw was Jesse, in all his glory.

Jenna's best former coworker—and friend—was an utter goofball and the perfect poster boy for the revival of Saturnalia, that ancient Roman winter festival.

Tall and lanky and half-white, half-Korean, Jesse didn't remotely look Roman, and that was kind of the point. But he struck his best "classical" pose, wrapped in a very shiny gold "toga" made from a Mylar emergency blanket. A wild-looking laurel wreath crowned his head—made from boxwood greenery plucked from Hannah's garden, Jenna thought she remembered. In one hand he held an over-sized golden goblet, either a prop from the college's drama depart-ment... or just a super-nerdy possession amongst the bunch of super-nerds that formed their friend-group.

His other hand sported an oversized foam finger, like the sporting event prop, which pointed down toward the main text box, which Jenna thought was very clever.

It had a QR code to the website with more information, a brief explanation of the old Roman holiday (with its three- to seven-day tradition of reversing power roles and giving gag gifts around December 17th), and the following text:

BYOB (bring your own blanket) for a toga, or be supplied with a shiny gold Mylar one! (All blankets and emergency blankets will be donated to Helping Hands shelter afterward.)

Donations of non-perishable food and clothes also welcome!

SUBVERT THE STATUS QUO! Phone bank and letter writing for criminal justice in the afternoon, followed by partying in the evening. Make friends with passionate people doing good work, and then play stupid games with them.

All-day snacking and drinks in the evening supplied by generous donors!

(Then of course there were a bunch of logos from the various places Jenna's team had wangled into donating for the event.)

The Core Four had brainstormed the wording and concepts together a few weeks ago, then sent the contents off to Chesca. It looked good, to Jenna's untrained eye. But mostly her gaze kept being drawn back to Jesse, looking every inch the drama student he'd been before switching to Human Services. He made it look *fun*.

He made everything look fun. Something Jenna had no idea how to do.

But she hoped there would be students in the college that would find an event like this attractive—a chance to do good, to do *something*, when they might be feeling as helpless as Jenna—*and* they could do it even if they were broke.

Because the problem with her peers, passionate though they might be, was they couldn't dump money into all the causes when they already lived paycheck-to-paycheck. So when Jenna had first floated the idea of reclaiming Saturnalia last year, while she and Jesse were still interns under Hannah's benevolent social-justice guidance, they had put their heads together to think of ways to do it that involved as little money as possible.

She wasn't sure it was enough.

Maybe any good that came of it would be as fleeting as the "good" that came from the original Saturnalia in Rome, which went right back to its enslaving ways the moment the festival was over.

Or as fleeting as the holiday season in general.

But she took out her phone anyway and snapped a photo of the poster, sending it to their group text with Rain and Chesca, followed by a bunch of heart-eye and grin emojis. They deserved all the praise for their work, regardless of what came of it.

Later that evening, the Core Four would do a Zoom call to talk about where everything was in the process and what still needed to happen. Jenna knew that Hannah and Rain were juggling family holiday responsibilities, so the bulk of what remained to be done over the next two weeks would be on her own shoulders, with Jesse's help of course. But he also had family, even if he wasn't planning on going home for the holidays until the actual day before Christmas.

And of course Jenna had no one. Not anymore.

But she had this.

And it would probably be enough.

———

THE REST OF HER ERRANDS WERE INCREASINGLY exhausting. Grocery shopping, ATM, distributing a few of the posters in key places (although the bulk of them would go on campus). But everything was so crowded and *loud*—in all the ways—and she was glad to get home as soon as she could, even if there wasn't much that waited for her there, either.

Jenna's studio apartment was cramped, so she kept decorations to a minimum. There were the three potted herbs in the window she hadn't managed to kill yet, and her prized bedspread in lovely jewel tones, which matched the throw rug she'd found at a thrift store. The room was tidy—it had to be, or she would go crazy in this tiny space. It smelled faintly of the white vinegar she used for cleaning, and the fragrant herbal scent of thyme when she ran her hand through the plant before settling onto her bed with her laptop.

The protein bar she munched on was less lovely, only barely resembling the cookie dough it was supposed to taste like, but she didn't have the wherewithal to cook real food right now. Or so she'd been telling herself.

At precisely five minutes before their 7 p.m. Zoom meeting time, she brought her laptop over to the single table in the room, a reclaimed wood affair with vintage vibes that could seat two people at most (not that she had much company here anyway).

She hadn't seen her team in a week, and she missed them. They were the best thing that passed for a social life these days. Her coworkers at her day job—college admin department—were fine, but not really her people. They didn't make her face light up the way it did when Jesse's floppy-haired visage popped onto the screen, for example. (Or Hannah with her fabulous oversized glasses in all the zany colors, or Rain with their bleached hair and matching white cat draped over their shoulder, head-butting them as usual.)

"Hey, all!"

"Oh man, those posters. Jesse, I had no idea you could rock a toga like that. Hilarious!" Rain said, trying to fend off their cat's insistent face.

"What can I say? The thespian needs an outlet." Jesse's big, toothy grin was disarmingly crooked. "Also, thanks so much for taking care of the distribution, Jen! That's got to be a lot right now." The grin dropped into a sympathetic half-smile. How he knew she'd been struggling, she couldn't tell. But he always seemed to be intuitive like that.

"It's the least I could do." And it probably wasn't enough, really. Which brought her to the research she'd been doing for the last few hours.

"So I've been thinking," she started, slowly. "I know a donation drive wasn't part of the original plan. But there are some good organizations also working on clemency for jailed marijuana offenders, just like the letters we're going to be writing, and I thought we could highlight them during that part and ask for donations? I know it's not in the posters, but we could add it to the website, and I'd personally oversee the logistics..." She trailed off as Hannah shook her head gently.

Hannah's smile was sympathetically regretful. "First of all, yes, it's not in the posters—but also we already talked about how we weren't going to ask for monetary donations. That wasn't the point, remember? We're offering an alternative to money when everyone *else* is going to be asking for it. That was *your* idea from the get-go, and I think it's the right one."

Jenna's shoulders sagged. She knew that.

"Also there are likely going to be other people who feel as moved as you do, while they're writing letters or signing petitions with us. We *should* definitely educate them about the organizations doing the work. They can donate money on their own steam—"

"And they probably *will*—" Jesse interjected.

"—and we should leave it at that. Don't you think? You've

already been making so many phone calls for the resources to get this thing going. It's okay to take a break from that and focus on what we've already set up."

It sounded reasonable when Hannah said it.

But Jenna still felt it like an itch under her skin. The need to do *more*. To be more.

But she nodded and instead volunteered to put together educational flyers with all of the resources and organizations to give out to interested attendees.

They proceeded to go over the remaining items for the rest of the two hours. Hannah had put out the word through her social services networks, asking for interested professionals to offer guidance to the guests during the letter writing and also help make connections for people eager to do more. Jenna hoped that would be the long-lasting part of the whole thing.

Hannah, too, was cautiously optimistic. She already had a decent handful of people committing to coming and was hoping for more.

They talked about logistics—food, drinks, venue, the laptops they had finally convinced the computer science department to loan for the day, and of course old-fashioned paper, pens, and envelopes for whoever wanted them.

Then there were the games. Jesse already had grand plans, he said, no need to worry about that part. But they did finalize the rules for what the Monarch of Saturnalia could or couldn't demand, and how the names would be drawn for which guests would get the privilege for the hour. (Like the Lord of Misrule of ye olde days, except with enough restrictions to make sure everyone had a good and safe time. Perhaps a bit sedate by Roman standards... but it needed to be.)

And the gag gifts—Jesse had insisted they were truest to the spirit of Saturnalia (once Jenna had gotten him on a research tangent about it a while back). Some were already in hand and most would be donated the day of, but they still needed to purchase more to fill out the supply. Jenna was familiar with all the thrift stores in town, so she volunteered to be the one to shop for them. Even though the idea filled her with vague queasiness.

As they wrapped up, Jesse said, "I need to stay behind and talk with Jen for a sec after you other two eject. Just some stuff not involving your parts of the job."

This was the first Jenna had heard of it. She tried to search his expression over the screen, but he didn't look like it was going to be about something she did *wrong*, which was of course her first instinct. He looked like the same affable guy as always. But she wasn't sure what he thought they needed to talk about.

On the other hand, she *liked* talking to him, so any excuse, right?

"What's up?" she asked, as soon as the others had signed off.

"How are things going for you right now? Truly?" He leaned forward into the screen. His eyes were soft, concerned.

Had she really been projecting her stress that obviously? That... wasn't great. That felt like being a burden.

"How are they going for anyone, really? Anyone who reads the news or realizes what's happening politically, socially, in the world at large..." The reminder felt like a heavy weight, pressing down on top of her.

Jesse was shaking his head. "You can't let that be everything you think about every day, Jen. That's not healthy. Have you done something you *enjoyed* recently?"

Had she? "I enjoyed looking at those posters," she said, wondering if she could change the subject. But she had a sinking feeling this was the whole reason Jesse had asked for an extra little meeting. "I took care of my plants. I finished my holiday shopping." All online, and all donations to various charities in the name of loved ones. She felt guilty about consumerist shopping. Of course, she also felt guilty about not getting real presents for people.

There was no winning, this time of year.

Jesse squinted at her. "I didn't hear anything actually *fun* in there, Jen. Tell you what," he continued, steamrolling her attempts at protest, "Let's get together tomorrow, *in person*, and brainstorm ways to 'keep Jen from burning herself out before the end of the season.' Coffee, lunch, whatever. My treat. Where is somewhere you would like to try out, but haven't let yourself visit yet?"

Jenna's mind went immediately to the ginger and spices wafting from The Tea Bar. But she really couldn't waste Jesse's money on expensive frou-frou drinks. Or her time. She had more research to do for that document, and thrift stores to visit, and other parts of the project to wrap up. It's not like she would have much time for any of that during the week when she had her regular day job, which always went late, and...

"I can't, not right now." But... she really wanted his company. Was that selfish? "Um, what if—maybe you could come with me when I do some of my thrift store runs? There are a few open on Sunday. And you could help me pick out gifts, since you know what's fun."

"What if we do both? Of course I'd love to come with you. Shopping for weird gifts actually *does* sound like fun. To me, if not to you." He was teasing her.

Jenna couldn't help smiling back. "Team Tennessee, at it again." They'd gotten lightly ribbed during their internship under Hannah for their similar names, and had been often treated as a single unit.

"Yeah, that sounds great to me. But I'm serious about the other thing, too. You come up with somewhere you want to go, and we're going there."

And Jenna found it was impossible to say no. "Fine, but after we hit at least one thrift store first, to assuage my conscience."

THE TEA BAR WAS, ADMITTEDLY, RATHER LOVELY.

It delivered what the glow of lights had promised: warm and peaceful surroundings with live-edge pale wood tables, greenery, and airy white walls decorated with local artists' work. An array of deli-cious smells—and a positive rainbow of specialty hot drinks to choose from. Deep pink beet lattes, golden turmeric, rich green matcha, even royal blue from butterfly pea blossoms.

And the holiday specials, despite having healthful unpronounce-able ingredients, were truly delicious. Warm spices mingled with unexpected yet intuitive flavors like smoke and citrus.

Jesse had insisted they try every single special, if not the entire menu. Jenna balked at so many drinks, so they ended up splitting the drinks between them, after mutually agreeing they didn't care about each other's germs.

It felt casual, cozy, friendly. But also... intimate.

Jenna could slowly feel her shoulders start to relax in the warmth —of the room, of the tea... the spices... Jesse's presence.

She probably should have done this a while ago. Hell, she could have invited Jesse to go with her at any time. He probably would have said yes.

So why hadn't she?

Ever?

She didn't know.

"How do you remember to be soft?" she asked Jesse, after finding herself staring at him for a while.

"I—what?"

She knew it wasn't the word that confused him. Rain had called him "our resident Soft Boy" once and Jesse had liked it so much he started using it to describe himself. But since he'd been talking just now about something cute his nephew had done, she couldn't blame him for looking startled.

She tried again. "Kind to yourself and to others. I think you're good at it. And I'm... not."

"Oh... ah." His eyes crinkled with humor and understanding. His irises were a beautiful warm brown. She hadn't noticed that before.

"Finally figured out what I've been trying to tell you all day, have you?"

Jenna could tell the words weren't intended to sting, but she felt the bite all the same.

He put his cup down. "First of all, you *are* kind—to your friends and the people who need you. And you wouldn't be so passionate about trying to fix the problems of the world if you didn't have an enormous heart. So don't sell yourself short. But no, you're not kind to yourself. And I *have* been worried about you."

She looked down at her cup. The golden tea was starting to go cold. "I... know. But I don't know how to do it in a way that isn't just —superficial self-indulgence."

"Well, asking for help is an excellent first step. You *are* asking for help, right?"

"I guess I am." That surprised her. It hadn't been her intention. But there it was.

He leaned across the table and put his hand on hers. It was so warm.

It felt nice.

And also... were those tingles?

What the hell was that?

But he was talking. She tried to focus on his words.

"You don't need me to mansplain self-care to you, obviously. Or burnout. You were in the same classes as me and read the same books. You know Hannah drilled all those things into us too. So I guess... what's holding you back from letting yourself rest? Are you telling yourself it's only temporary, and you'll rest after the holidays, or...?"

If only.

"I don't feel... *right*... resting," she said, curling her hands tighter around her cup. "I have all the privileges, except being male, I guess. But, like..." She gestured to her white-person self, her nice wool coat, the fancy tea. "I'm not being *harmed* in the same way as others, so how could I possibly feel 'tired' enough to justify resting when other people are fighting for their lives?"

She'd chosen criminal justice as the focus for the new Saturnalia because it felt like a betterment of the Roman "slaves being masters for a day" concept. (In the original version, it was actually horrifically brutal that—after being feasted and showered with gifts—those poor souls went *right back to being enslaved*.)

She'd wanted to take that conceit and make it better, and the closest thing to modern-day enslavement was the industrial prison complex.

But there could have been dozens, hundreds, thousands of other causes to choose from. Mistreatment of immigrants. LGBT+ rights. Voter disenfranchisement. The environment. All of them clamoring for help, immediate and desperate.

She felt like she was helplessly spinning in a void. All the time.

Jesse raised an eyebrow at her, taking his hand away. Jenna wanted to chase his hand with hers, fold it inside her own. A strange urge.

"I'm a straight-passing cis man whose race is considered the 'model minority'—which *is* racist—but my experience is very different from that of a Black person. I've got the privileges too, and I know I will always be doing the work. I believe in the work. But I still let myself rest—and have fun. Am *I* a bad person?"

"Of course not! You're one of the best people I know. But I don't know how you keep all of *this*" —she gestured in a wide circle, narrowly avoiding knocking things off the table— "out of your head and off your shoulders. How are you so... like, actually *joyful?*"

It was Jesse's turn to hold his cup tightly, his expression turning inward. A series of emotions she couldn't quite place moved across his face, before settling into something unexpectedly solemn.

"You think I don't feel despair in the face of all this needless suffering, all the shit that people do to each other in order to keep the shitty status quo? All the things we're slowly losing? The uphill battles for basic rights we should have sorted out decades ago, centuries ago? Of course I worry I'm buckling under it all, like I'm this frivolous, brittle—I don't know—one of those Christmas baubles, and I think I'm useless in the face of it all. And sometimes I do feel like hating myself and everyone else in the world. But I know that's not how I want to live, or who I want to be."

"But then—how do you keep being the person you *are*? Which is none of the things you just said, by the way." Jenna's chest felt tight. She somehow hadn't realized how deeply he'd felt those things too.

"I guess... the more fragile and broken I feel, the more I remind myself to be *kind*. I try to think—the harder the world pushes down on me, the more I reach out to other people. The more I try to spread kindness."

"Like Waymond from *Everything Everywhere All at Once*."

"Exactly like Waymond. Except, you know, a half-Korean queer theater nerd instead of a Chinese immigrant dad."

Jenna laughed, but felt her eyes welling up at the same time.

She'd cried during *that* scene in the movie. Where everything had been awful, nihilistic chaos, and Waymond had just held out that one single thing that gave meaning to a meaningless universe. A choice.

Be kind.

She thought she had taken it to heart. But there was more to it than just doing a series of kind acts, wasn't there? There was something internal. A whole philosophy, a way of being. And Jesse *was* that. A complete goofball who lived kindness to himself and others, who wasn't afraid to be soft. No wonder she loved spending time with him, whenever she could. His warmth spread to her without him even trying.

Jesse ducked his head so that one piece of hair flopped across his face. "Well, that was one thing. And the other thing is you."

She hadn't expected that.

"Me... how? I'm a total downer! We just established this."

"You're not. You're passionate and inspiring. You have a heart that won't quit, even when you're hurling yourself straight for burnout. You care so much! And a lot of people care a lot about *you*. You know that, don't you?"

"Including you?" Jenna *knew* Jesse cared about her. He had done all this for her. She didn't know why she was pushing the question, exactly.

A long pause. "Especially me."

They stared at each other, and Jenna realized she was holding her breath. She couldn't say anything. She didn't know what to say. But this moment felt... like something.

"Oh, hell." He sat back and scratched his head, making his dark hair wilder. "You know I've had a crush on you for like, forever, right?"

She felt like someone had knocked the wind out of her... even as she realized *she'd been hoping he would say that.*

Which was also crazy.

But, like... Jesse had a crush on her? This whole time?

What? How? And also... what?

She knew he was bi, but the only exes he'd ever talked about were men, so she'd kind of assumed his preferences were more masc-leaning. He'd certainly never flirted with any women around her.

She'd once considered asking where he was on the Kinsey scale—like, did he sometimes like women but it was more rare, or...?—but she didn't want him to think she was fishing for herself, or trying to hit on him. Coworkers and all that.

Oh.

Right.

She *was* an idiot, wasn't she?

And also—how long had *she* been into Jesse without even realizing it?

Yeah... a colossal idiot.

A smile spread across her face. She felt giddy. And stupid. And stupidly giddy. "You *like* me!" She put her hands on her cheeks and barely resisted the urge to squeal like a schoolgirl. "You *like-like* me!"

Nope, she was bad at resisting. That definitely sounded like a schoolgirl squeal.

She hadn't felt this happy in a long, long time.

"Okay, are you just straight-up teasing me, or...?" He squinted at her, his crooked smile a bit uncertain.

"No, you dummy. No wait, that's me, I'm the dummy. I'm into you and just somehow... missed it? Probably because I was busy being sad. But you always make me happy. You know that, right? You've kind of been the only thing..." And now she was babbling.

"Well, that doesn't sound great. Wait, I mean—no, it's not great that I'm the *only* thing, but I'm glad I make you happy! And that you like me! But also I didn't mean to derail the conversation—"

Jenna grabbed Jesse's hand and squeezed it. She still felt all weirdly light and bubbly. "You didn't derail it. You just showed me that I missed something big and important because I hadn't let myself be anything other than... I don't know, this Saturnalia machine. And after Saturnalia it would have just been another thing, and another thing."

He was nodding along. "Right. And being happy doesn't mean you stop doing the work. *You* came up with the idea for the Saturnalia *party*. There needed to be fun in order to make the work easier to bear. Right?"

"Right. Yes. Right." And he was right about all that, and she was having a hard time concentrating on it, because Jesse *liked* her and she wanted to throw her arms around him and kiss that crooked smile.

He seemed to catch on, watching her face and grinning. "So we're... a thing? I mean, can you even be my date to the party if we're both co-hosts already? Or since it was your idea first, am I *your* date? Or..."

"Oh, shut up and get over here. I need a hug, like, yesterday. And... kisses? Yes? Are we doing—"

Jesse leapt out of his chair so quickly, Jenna realized he'd already been poised to spring. His arms enveloped her with warmth, sending tingles throughout her entire body. He felt so good, so right, so perfect.

She would never say that a woman was "incomplete" without a man, or whatever reductive silliness still showed up in cheesy romances. But this still felt like... something she had been missing. Or had forgotten.

That bolstering warmth, and care, and support. And love, in whatever form it might take. That human connection, and something more.

That *joy*.

Of course. Because the new Saturnalia—or maybe a *new* New Saturnalia—meant you could be angry and passionate and fierce *and* joyful.

And soft.

And you could hold on to the people who made you all those things, and who celebrated all those things that were already in you.

And maybe that was the only way to survive.

ALEXANDRA BRANDT WRITES SHORT FICTION "WITH *truth and a gentleness that is hard to ignore" (Dean Wesley Smith). A dreamer since childhood, Alex is never happier than when infusing magic (metaphorical or otherwise) into intimate human moments. Her short stories have been published in* Fiction River, Pulphouse Magazine, Selene Quarterly, *and* The Future Fire, *among others, and have also been featured on magazine "recommended reading" lists. Alex lives in the Pacific Northwest, and on the internet at www.alexandra-jbrandt.com.*

About this story, Alexandra says:

"*People point to the Roman festival of Saturnalia as one of the primary influences on Christmas as we know it, but underneath the feasting and gag gifts lies a fascinating upheaval of the class system... that would be inspiring if it lasted longer than a week! So I wondered: 'how could that be reinvented for the struggles of right now?' And what resulted was a story that—well, honestly, it was me giving myself therapy when the world felt especially bleak.*

"*Perhaps more importantly, I took a great deal of inspiration from (and perhaps some liberties with?) my spouse, friends, and family members who are currently doing The Work in social services—and still know how to find joy along the way.*"

Chicken Dance

JOHANNA ROTHMAN

JUST BEFORE SIX IN THE EVENING ON DECEMBER fourteenth, the last rays of the sun fell below the horizon at the Key West Bight, the semicircular protected harbor. The Bight had a twelve-foot-wide smooth, gray, wooden boardwalk that separated the shops from the harbor.

All the lamp posts turned on, their permanent off-white lights illuminating the boardwalk. The town had wound small multicolored Christmas lights around each of the lamp posts and many of the palm trees around the Bight.

Carolyn Stein smiled, delighting in the colors, the background Christmas calypso music, and the enticing odors of greasy and salty French fries, beer, and coconut sunscreen.

She took her "ever vigilant" cop pose—arms across her chest covering the "Ho-ho-ho" on her red t-shirt, feet shoulder-width apart, and eyes scanning the crowd. She stood in front of The Best KW T-Shirts Shop, a one-story, twenty-foot-wide, pastel green building with two-foot-wide horizontal blue stripes. For the holidays, she'd added two six-foot-tall neon pink flamingos outlined with bright white lights to the side of the building.

Because what said Christmas in Key West aside from pink flamingos with white lights?

She was ready for the tourists.

Instead of people, three glossy black chickens swooped in as they stopped and squawked, just a few feet in front of her.

She unfolded her arms. "No, you don't," she said, and wagged her finger at the chickens. "This is a t-shirt shop, not a hen house. It's for tourists, not for chickens. You can't fool me again."

They advanced and swooped to her right.

"No way," she muttered. It was time for her chicken dance. She feinted to her right.

They twisted and swooped to her left.

She stomped and feinted to her left. She hissed at them. "This is a shop for tourists. Stop that right now!" She stomped again. Then took a step forward and jumped, all to make noise.

The chickens fell back.

She stomped forward, her arms extended forward. That made her Ho-Ho-Ho red t-shirt flap in the light breeze. "Oh no," she said. "I'm onto your tricks. You stay out here. I get to guard the shirts in here." She waved her arms back and forth, up and down, as she stomped forward. As long as she could keep the shop's cold air conditioning at her back and the warm, humid breeze at her front, she could succeed.

The chickens fell back again and then swooped off.

Carolyn sighed. The chicken dance had worked again. Key West was nothing like her old home and work in Boston. Thank goodness.

She still could not believe she was no longer a cop. The newly elected sheriff had decided she—she with the most closed cases!—was a DEI hire. Now, her job was to ring up t-shirt and tchotchke sales. Also, to protect and defend the shop from the chickens, drunks, and the oblivious.

It wasn't even hers. Orna, her cousin, had moved down here years ago and bought this shop. Now, Orna had offered her this job and a place to stay while Carolyn figured out her next step. As Orna had said, "You're only thirty. You need a job and a man, not necessarily in that order. Come down and see what you find."

Carolyn thought a job was the first step, not a man. But she and Orna often disagreed on the priorities in life.

Now that the nightly sunset view was over, the tourists had come out to the boardwalk in full force. Both families and friends packed the boardwalk, wandering in and out of the shops, and generally getting in each other's way. With any luck, she wouldn't have to do the chicken dance again tonight. Now, it was just about protecting and defending the shop from the drunks and the thieves. She grinned. Piece of cake.

ALREADY IN DISGUISE WITH GRAY HAIR, A GRAY mustache, and an old, holey charcoal gray t-shirt and beige cargo shorts, Jack Falk weaved across the boardwalk. He'd seen Carolyn do her chicken dance. He'd swallowed his laughter this time because he did not want anyone to pay attention to him. Her chicken dance was just the kind of thing Key West was known for.

He'd met her a couple of days ago in plain clothes—another holey t-shirt and blue cargo shorts. She and Orna were sitting at the local coffee shop on William Street, just one block up from the Bight. He'd waved to Orna who had called him over to meet Carolyn. But because he was in plain clothes, he kept it brief and answered none of Carolyn's questions.

To his cop eyes, Carolyn was clearly unimpressed.

But that was the point back then. He didn't want to be impressive, because he was in full investigation mode. That day, he'd been his normal clean-shaven self.

Now, with the gray mustache, the wig, and the excitement of the chase, the warm breeze from the Bight made him sweat just a little. He was revved up, ready to take down this ring of thieves.

He had zip-ties in his cargo shorts, a small knife in his right shorts pocket, and his small Glock tucked into the right side of the back of his shorts—in a holster. Because he wasn't an idiot.

He really hoped he did not need to use the gun.

He held his clear plastic cup of beer in his right hand, its foam threatening to dribble over the side of the cup. He'd already drenched his shirt in beer, thrown some on his face, and swished around a little in his mouth before spitting it out. He was sure he smelled like a brewery.

He'd learned from previous undercover experiences that cheap beer worked just as well as expensive beer, as long as he generously sprinkled it everywhere.

Weaving in time to the calypso Christmas music, he was glad he wore sneakers instead of flip-flops.

He knew when and where the drop was supposed to be—in ten minutes at the Key West Bight Grill and Bar at the very end of the boardwalk. The thieves had timed it to coincide with the Christmas Lights Boat Parade. All the boats in the harbor lit up all their Christmas lights and created a parade.

Most of the shops closed their doors for the next twenty minutes to see the lights and parade.

Key West was exceedingly good at any celebration, and that included Christmas.

One of the tourists bumped into him as he weaved across the boardwalk, aiming to bypass Carolyn altogether. But the tourist pushed him closer to her, and made some of the beer bounce over the side.

He tried again to weave left, so he could avoid her.

The same tourist bumped into him again. "Sorry, man," the guy said.

Jack thought the tourist was at least as drunk as he hoped he appeared. "No problem, man," he said, partly slurring his words.

The tourist herded him even closer to Carolyn.

What the heck, Jack thought. Just go for it. Maybe she would do her chicken dance for him.

CAROLYN SAW AN APPARENTLY OLDER MAN WITH GRAY hair, wearing a faded charcoal-gray t-shirt and baggy khaki shorts, weaving across the boardwalk. He held a clear plastic cup still mostly full of beer, the foam lurching from side to side with each step. The crowd herded him toward her.

He almost looked like an older, hairier version of the guy Orna had insisted she meet a couple of days ago, Jack Falk. At the time, they briefly talked while she and Orna had coffee, before opening the t-shirt shop.

But she and Jack didn't seem to have much in common. Especially since Jack was cagey about what he did or where he worked. He'd seemed nice enough, but Carolyn was much more interested in direct and honest people these days.

The drunk drawled, "Whatcha got here, little lady?" as he saluted her with his beer.

Some of the beer escaped, dribbling over the side of the cup.

Almost without thinking, Carolyn stepped back. She did not want to smell like beer tonight, not while she was working.

"T-shirts," she said, "but you've had too much to drink to shop now. Come back later when you're drier and more sober."

Now that he was closer, she noticed the gray hair on his head was much grayer than his eyebrows. And his mustache wasn't particularly gray at all. In fact, she thought he looked like someone wearing a wig —and maybe a fake mustache. Both of which were quite good. But to her ex-cop's eyes, still fake.

Even his bright blue eyes looked more like Jack's eyes, rather than the eyes of a drunk. Worse, she thought he looked quite alert to the other people and his surroundings. More like a cop's eyes.

"Okay," he said and offered her a very sloppy grin. Then he drank a sip of beer and belched.

Yeah, drunks. She made sure her smile was pasted on, and said, "See ya!"

She watched him weave away. From the back, she thought he looked a lot younger. And more fit. And he wore real sneakers, not flip-flops or falling-apart sneakers.

If he were young and fit, why would he pretend to be old and drunk?

But, no skin off her back if he wanted to pretend. Part of her wondered what was going on. The other part of her reminded herself that she was no longer a cop. All she had to do was protect and defend the t-shirt shop. And enjoy the Christmas lights.

JACK WONDERED WHAT CAROLYN HAD SEEN AS SHE defended the t-shirt shop. She was just so cute, pretending she was no longer a cop. He didn't buy it for a minute. She was a cop, through and through.

After meeting her, he'd done the bare minimum of investigation because he was interested. Her new boss had laid her off—probably because he was too sensitive about having such a terrific female officer.

Jack would never do anything like that. He couldn't complain about the fact she was here now. Maybe when he wrapped this case up, he could ask her out on a date.

No. Carolyn was a cop from the top of her short, dark curly hair to her serious running shoes. No sandals for her—sneakers, so she could run. And do her chicken dance. She might not have noticed, but she'd danced in time to the calypso music when she'd done the chicken dance.

He was just lucky she hadn't figured out who he was tonight. Maybe his disguise was that good. Or maybe he was just lucky.

He glanced at the cheap analog watch on his left hand and looked down closer to the end of the boardwalk to where he could dump his beer. He only had ten more minutes to get to the end of the boardwalk and meet up with his partner, Dave.

The calypso Christmas music blended in with the excitement of the crowd. Two couples started to rumba—or was that a cha-cha—in front of him, slowing him down.

He had to get to the thieves before they handed off their haul to the people in boats who would meet them at the end of the Bight. Then the people on land would melt away in the crowd. He'd have to find them all over again.

Tonight was the night. He had to be there on time. He had ten more minutes.

He glanced at his watch again. Now, nine minutes.

His stomach churning with excitement—and maybe a few nerves, he found a trash can and threw his beer away.

That's when he touched his left ear. "In place, Dave?"

"Not yet," Dave said. "A little trouble here. I'll catch up."

Jack knew that no plan ever survived reality, but trouble? He'd need backup.

"Should we postpone?"

"No! Tonight's the night."

Jack thought Dave sounded out of breath, but if Dave said to go, Jack would go.

All he had to do was walk down to the end of the smooth wooden boardwalk and meet up with Dave. And put Carolyn out of his mind.

As Carolyn looked down the boardwalk, she saw the drunk dump his beer and straighten up. Aha! That drunk was in disguise.

He was tall, but with all the people in the way—and some dancing to the calypso music—she couldn't quite see what he was doing.

Sighing, she returned to her ever-vigilant cop pose and watched the tourists as they flowed around the boardwalk and in and out of the shop. She sneaked a peek every now and then down the board-walk. She was just curious, she told herself.

Orna bounced out, her frizzy brown, curly hair bopping in time to the music. She looked down the boardwalk and then looked back at Carolyn. She grinned and pointed with her chin.

"You want to go down there and see the dancing?"

Carolyn said, "I think I saw Jack, but he was in disguise. So I could not have seen him, right?"

Orna cocked her head and offered a secretive smile. "Want to find out?"

Carolyn grinned and said, "You bet I do."

"I'll take over from here. Return when you can."

Carolyn used the boardwalk crowd to weave in and out quickly. This was just too good a mystery to resist.

The Key West Bight Grill and Bar was in fine form tonight. The outdoor patio was filled—all twenty tables were busy. The disc jockey had organized a very loud karaoke set. There was a cute couple singing, wearing matching red "Ho-ho-ho" t-shirts, just like Carolyn's. They sang "Baby It's Cold Outside," which Jack thought was nuts. It wasn't cold in Key West, and why sing a song about a man trying to prevent a woman from leaving? He knew there were better Christmas songs.

As he passed the patio, he could smell the fried food, the beer, and even a little of the key lime pie sweetness.

Once he passed the patio, the sounds diminished. He was finally alone. It was much darker back here. The lights from the Bight gave him a long, dark shadow. He glanced at his watch. Four minutes to spare. He whispered, "Dave?"

Dave whispered in his ear, "I'm not going to make it. Abort the mission."

That's when Jack saw two dark-haired men with black bandanas covering their chins walk out from around the outside of the building—from the water side. They must have anchored or moored their boat there because the boardwalk ended where they now stood.

They each wore a black short-sleeved t-shirt, dark jeans, and dark shoes. He couldn't tell if they were boots or sneakers, but their footwear was virtually noiseless on the boardwalk.

They stood there, hands on their hips.

They were only twenty yards away, but that was at least fifteen yards too far.

The one on the right reached behind his back.

That meant a weapon. Jack felt, more than heard, something on his left side.

CAROLYN SIZED UP THE SITUATION IMMEDIATELY. JACK either needed backup or a way out. Well, she could offer both of those options. She hoped he was a righty. His watch was on his left wrist, and he'd held his beer in his right hand, so he probably was.

She gently put her right hand on his left shoulder and lightly squeezed. "Darlin'," she said with a drawl that implied a southern background, not her Boston roots. "You promised to show a girl a good time. I think now's a great time to make good on that promise. I'm up for whatever you want."

She hoped he got the message. Especially since she stood on his left side. She was a lefty, so they could fight—or whatever—side by side.

She suspected he did not want to fight, not on the boardwalk and not during the Christmas lights festival. If she was in charge, she'd want to get these two guys cuffed before they could do anything else.

That's when all the lights went out.

That's when Jack whispered, "I'll go right."

She said, "I'll go left."

Jack said, "Police! Hands up!"

The two of them pounded down the boardwalk to the two men.

At first, the two guys seemed stuck, blinking to reset their eyes. But they started to move forward.

Around them, the entire Bight seemed to hush as people waited for the lights to turn on.

Then all the lights turned on—the various Christmas trees, all the boats in the harbor, all the lights on the buildings.

She heard all the far-off tourist exclamations of, "wow!" and "ooh," and "How pretty."

The two men stopped and blinked again, now that the lights were in their eyes.

Jack reached the guy on the right before Carolyn reached the guy on the left. Jack turned his suspect around and yanked his arm up, across his back.

Carolyn was only a couple of steps behind Jack. But clearly, her key lime pie habit had not allowed her to maintain her speed. She decided it was time to get back on the straight and narrow.

The guy on the left reached his arms out to capture Carolyn. Instead, she feinted right, then stuck her foot out. A slight variation on her chicken dance.

The man tripped over her foot and fell to the ground. She kneeled on the smooth boardwalk and yanked his arms up his back. It felt good to do something useful.

"Cuffs?" she asked.

"Right here," Jack said, and handed a pair of zip-ties to her.

"Thank you, partner," he said and smiled at her.

"You're welcome!" she said and smiled back.

JUST THIRTY MINUTES LATER, JACK CAUGHT UP WITH Carolyn at her t-shirt shop. He'd managed to brush his teeth, take a quick shower, and change into clean clothing at the police station. This time, a light blue t-shirt and dark blue shorts. He felt better just seeing her there.

The odors of French fries, beer, and coconut sunscreen wafted over him like a warm hug. There was nothing like Key West at any time of the year.

She stood there, smiling at all the lights on the boats in the harbor, enjoying the parade of Christmas lights on the ships.

She saw him and smiled even more broadly. "Hey, nice to see you —and not smell you!"

He smiled back at her, appreciating her cop eyes.

"Thank you for your help back there," he said and pointed down the boardwalk. "Dave and a moped encountered each other. Luckily, he's just banged up, but I'm not sure what would have happened if you hadn't been there to back me up. I definitely would have lost the benefit of my disguise and surprise."

"I enjoyed it. Glad you knew what to expect."

"Dave also managed to get backup for the other part of their business. These two stole—tonight, they had a pretty substantial haul of watches, jewelry, and cash. But the other two in their gang were drug dealers. The rest of the department got them. Before the Christmas lights came up."

"Then I'm really glad I was able to play a small part in taking them down. Thanks for understanding."

That's when two dark glossy chickens appeared, swooping in, to land six feet away from them. They squawked and crowed, as they tried to get into the t-shirt store.

Carolyn said, "I've got this. Please stay out of the way."

Jack stepped back, closer to the building. He grinned, knowing what was coming.

She feinted left—the chickens swerved to the right.

She feinted right—the chickens swerved to the left.

She stomped forward.

The chickens backed up.

She stomped forward again—and this time, the chickens took off.

Carolyn smiled at him.

"I really like your chicken dance," he said. "Do you know any other dances?"

She smiled at him, and said, "I do. All kinds."

"When do you get off work?"

Orna came out and answered for Carolyn. "Now, she gets off now. Now, shoo, both of you."

The two of them laughed.

Jack took Carolyn's warm hand and squeezed, just a little. Maybe he'd take her to that place with the sax and the guitar and see what other dances she knew. Maybe a rumba to see how they fit together. Just the anticipation made him want to hurry. He suspected it would be one of the best things he'd ever felt in his life.

She squeezed his warm hand back as they walked down the boardwalk.

MULTI-GENRE WRITER JOHANNA ROTHMAN EMBRACES HER project management roots because they are full of strange characters and unbelievable stories. Since no one would believe any of that reality, she draws from those experiences to write fiction. Her short fiction has appeared in Pulphouse Magazine, Fiction River, *and* Heart's Kiss.

An award-winning author of twenty nonfiction books about managing product development, Johanna incorporates humor—not just practicality—into her nonfiction. All because life is too short to take too seriously.

See her newsletters and all her writing at www.jrothman.com and www.createadaptablelife.com.

About this story, Johanna says:

"Key West is one of my favorite places in the entire world, partially because everyone is a (somewhat) strange character. I fit right in with the street performers, the tourists, and even the chickens.

"Because the roosters and chickens have no natural predators, all the chickens are free range. And every so often, those chickens want to prove that fact to the people."

It Takes Two

KAREN L. ABRAHAMSON

THE FEBRUARY SNOW KEPT FALLING, FILLING IN THE SIX-inch-deep tire tracks as Grant Estevan pulled his battered Ford pickup into the Williams Lake municipal hall parking lot. The snow squeaked under his tires as if pained at his passage. The damned truck heater wasn't working—again—and at fifteen-below his breath had coated the interior windows with a layer of hoar frost he kept having to chip off the windshield. Damn. He should have just rolled over and stayed in bed except...

He needed to deliver the bad news in person.

He pulled into a parking stall close to the front door that was probably reserved, but the snow had effectively coated everything with an equalizer of white. The red and green Christmas lights were long gone off the building's white frontier façade, but in its place were strings of tiny blue lights lighting up the edges of the two-story heritage building and illuminating the snow-smothered bushes and trees so they looked like they glowed from within. All pretty enough for the Winter Festival that started in a week.

Sighing, he turned the engine off, hiked up the collar of his faux shearling jacket and climbed down from the cab. His cowboy boots went right out from under him and he swore as he caught the edge of the door. The new snow hid a sheet of ice. Treading carefully, he headed up the steps and into toasty warmth and the scent of coffee. Trish Worth looked up from the receptionist's desk. Then she arched a brow at him and smiled.

"Grant. I wasn't sure you'd make it with this coming down." She lifted her chin at the glass doors and the drifting flakes beyond.

He chose not to recognize her flirtation just as he'd chosen not to notice every other woman since the car accident that took Carolyn. "The Spring Lake Road was dicey. No plow's been through yet. But the old beater came through." He ran his hand through his mop of hair. Droplets scattered, some landing on papers on Trish's desk. "Oops. Sorry. Her Worship in?"

"Is she ever not? I swear the woman doesn't sleep. She's expecting you."

Resigned to his task, Grant squared his shoulders and headed for the stairs that led up to the executive offices.

Anyone who'd lived in this small town any length knew most everyone of note and Grant had lived here all his life. So had Betsy Beyer who was only a few years older than his thirty-five.

He knocked once on her office door and entered. "You got a moment?"

Blue-eyed, blond-haired Betsy looked up from studying documents spread on her desk. "Grant. I can only give you ten minutes, max. We've got an issue with the new sewage plant and some idiot has sent a letter complaining that this year's Christmas celebration was too Christian." She sighed. "Sometimes I wish I could just be like you and climb on a horse and ride away."

As good a segue as any. He cleared his throat. "About those horses. I came in this morning to let you know there's a problem. I don't think I can provide the grey team of horses to pull the Snow Queen's sleigh. Cassius, my gelding, hurt himself in his stall. He's injured his rear leg. He needs rest and hopefully he'll recover, but it's going to take more than a week."

Betsy blinked up at him as if allowing his words to settle over her. Finally, she frowned. "Are you telling me you can't provide the sleigh? That sleigh is the centerpiece of our winter festival parade. What the heck are we supposed to do with the Queen and princesses? Ask them to trudge through the snow? Put them in a car where no one can see them? How does that fit with our theme of winter heritage?" Her voice had risen. The winter festival was her baby—her attempt to bring in tourism during the worst of Williams Lake's winter economic doldrums that had only worsened since Covid. The city had spent a mint advertising the event and so far it looked like the effort was working because hotel bookings were higher than ever —according to the local news.

"I'm sorry, Betsy. I am. I know you wanted the grey team. But if you'll take a mismatched pair I have a chestnut that can fill the harness and knows how to pull..."

"No. No way. They have to be grey or white to match the blue and white theme of the event. The queen and princesses will be dressed in those colors."

And there was the rub. He could no longer provide what the city needed and that meant he was out the bucks he'd spent to refurbish the bobsleigh and he also wouldn't get paid. Dammit, he needed the money, too. There was hay to buy and rent on the dude ranch to pay. "I'm sorry. Cassius won't have recovered."

Betsy covered her face with her hands. "God, there are times I hate this job. What else could go wrong. I don't have time to look around for another team." Uncovering her face, she looked up at him and he took a step back. White rimmed her lips and the fine web of lines around her now storm-grey eyes had widened into fissures. This definitely wasn't the Betsy she showed to her voters. "Grant, I hate to do this to you, but you signed a contract with the municipality to provide a team of white or grey horses to pull that sleigh of yours.

You either do that or—or maybe your business license won't get renewed."

"Hold on now! I need that license."

She waved him away. "Your choice, of course. But make it elsewhere."

"Betsy. We've known each other forever. Besides, your threat's not even legal."

She flattened her hands on her desk. "Grant. Don't tempt me. I don't have time for this. *You* know the horse community. *You* find another grey horse and get me my team. That shouldn't be that hard, should it?" She hooked her head at the door. "Don't let it hit you on the way out."

He left feeling like he'd been clubbed over the head and trudged down the stairs running through the other horses he knew in the area. Lots of bays and browns and chestnuts. Even a palomino or two and a few appaloosas, but no greys.

"Everything all right?" Trish called as he went past.

"Only if you happen to keep a white horse in that apartment of yours." He shook his head and shoved open the door.

"I don't." She looked at him from the tops of her eyes. "But I was talking to the new probation officer in town. She said she has a couple of Lipizzaner horses. They're white, aren't they?"

"Lipizzaners? Sure she does."

Lipizzaners in Williams Lake were about as likely as the entire Vienna Riding School choosing to relocate here. Originally bred as elite riding horses by the Austrian Habsburg Empire, the breed of famous horses almost hadn't survived the Second World War when the primary breeding herd was about to be left behind the iron curtain. In 1945, it had taken a joint effort of General Patton's American GIs and captured German Soldiers in Operation Cowboy to drive the herd out of the reach of the advancing Red Army. Today the white horses performed classical dressage shows for the public as well as the leaps known as "airs above the ground" in the Spanish

Riding School in Vienna. They were certainly not found on Williams Lake trails. Or pulling a bobsleigh, for that matter.

Trish shrugged. "I'm pretty sure that's what she said. You could ask her... The probation office is just down the hall." A tip of her head toward the rear of the building that housed court staff and a court room.

He let the door bang shut with a sigh, thanked Trish and headed down the hall. At the least he'd meet someone new and find out if there really were white Lipizzaners in central British Columbia.

FOR THE UMPTEENTH TIME THE OLD FORD FISHTAILED ON one of the curves of the Likely Road. He spun the wheel, letting off on the gas until the vehicle straightened and then kept going. Out here, east of town, the snow was falling in huge, wet, white flakes so heavy that he'd had to get out of the truck and clear the wipers twice on his way out of town.

Why the hell was he was doing this? The woman—someone named Jocelyn Payne—hadn't been at work today, but was expected in tomorrow. He could have waited. Except there were only seven days until the parade and in the past it took longer than seven days to break a horse to driving. And the administrative support staff in the probation office had shown him a photo the probation officer had on her wall. A pretty young woman with dark brown eyes and long red hair standing in a green field with two white horses with their heads hanging over her shoulders. So there just might really be two white horses out here that could be an answer to a prayer. So he was here, driving through a blizzard.

The road dipped down, the tall cedar and lodgepole pines rising up like steep walls to either side of the road. At a widening of the road, a small, modular home sat nestled beyond the snowbanks, a snug-looking red barn sitting back among the trees. A coil of white smoke threaded its way up from the home's metal chimney through the flakes.

This had to be the place. He pulled over.

JOCELYN PAYNE HEARD THE DISTANT RUMBLE OF THE truck coming through the ridiculously thin walls of her rental house. She had the wood heater roaring in the kitchen and the baseboard heaters on high, and it still didn't fully cut the chill as she lounged under a blanket on the couch in front of the house's front window. The heating oil costs were going to kill her if the treacherous roads didn't do it first. Less than three months at her posting in Williams Lake and she already hated the place. How the heck was she going to make it the two years before the government would allow her to transfer back to Vancouver? Or at least someplace that didn't have heaps of snow. Someplace where she could go out for a beer and not clear the liquor establishment of patrons just because of what she did for a living.

Damn the Williams Lake View Newspaper for flashing her face on the front page as the new Probation Officer in town. It sure put a cramp in her social life. Not that she'd want to date one of the men she supervised, but where would she meet anyone if not at a lounge or bar? And on-line dating would be too much of a crap-shoot in a town this small. Besides, did she really want a relationship with anyone from this dismal little town when David might be waiting for her in Vancouver?

Might be? He had to be. So why did she care about relationships here?

She sipped her tea and fingered the coiled knot of hair on the top of her head. Her book was about the rise and fall of empires— much more exciting than anything that could happen in a town like Williams Lake. The truck's rumble turned to a roar as it entered the dell her house occupied. The darn trees held in the sound.

But instead of the usual roar past as the vehicle went on into Big Lake Valley, the rumble slowed. Snow crunched out front, and then silence. The thunk of a vehicle door. The crunch of footfalls in snow.

Holy heck! Someone was here. Dropping the book she twisted on the couch to look out. What daylight there'd been through the snow had faded to grey so the world outside was barely illuminated. Now snow swirled in wind gusts and the trees breathed out darkness. When she'd first moved in, she'd been unprepared for, and unnerved by, the total absence of light that was night in the wilds of central British Columbia. She still didn't like to be outside after dark.

And now a dark figure shoved its way through the snow from the pull-out area just beyond the front fence and the gate to her drive-way. Male. Tall. By the way he moved, athletic, too. She thought of the stories she'd been told about offenders hunting down their P.O. And swallowed. Pulled her sweater closer around her neck as feet thumped up her front steps. A heavy fist knocked.

This was one of those moments when she wished David was here. But her boyfriend of the past three years had opted to stay with his legal firm in Vancouver. She'd move back to the city when her two years here were up and then they could be together. She hoped. If David lived up to their commitment and waited...

Leaving her warm cocoon on the couch, she went to the door. "Who is it?"

"The name's Grant Estevan. I live out Spring House Ranch way. I'm doing a bit of work for the mayor and I have a problem I'm hoping you can help me with." The voice came through the door, strong and deep but with a little restless impatience coming through.

She flicked on the outside light and peeked out the window beside the door. High cheek bones placed shadows on his face and a forelock of hair hid his eyes. Shearling jacket that looked a bit light for how the weather had turned. Snow piling up on his shoulders and head. He stood hunched on her doorstep, hands sunk deep in his pockets.

He looked cold. More than cold. Freezing. But he definitely wasn't one of the offenders under her supervision. Of course, he could still be an axe murderer.

Against her better judgement she unlocked the deadbolt and pulled open the door four inches. A bright blue gaze over those cheekbones caught the outdoor light while a five o'clock shadow kept his mouth indistinct. He stuck out a hand forcing her to open the door farther. "Grant Estevan. Hi. Jocelyn Payne, am I right?"

She accepted his handshake—his grip firm, his palm rough with callus—but still wasn't sure if he was safe. Those eyes of his were enough to make a woman sit up and take notice, though. So were the rugged good looks. "Um. Yeah. That's me."

"May I come in?" He cocked a rakish brow at her and she shook herself.

"Um. Yeah. Guess I've heated the outside enough." She stepped aside and he pushed past her onto the mat. She closed the door after quickly sweeping the yard with her gaze. No one else out there. She was alone with this stranger. Turning back to him, she crossed her arms over her chest. "What can I do for you?"

And she felt like an idiot. The guy was clearly cold. The snow on his brown hair dripped down onto his face. She should offer to take his coat. Something warm to drink or eat. A towel. Instead she hugged herself harder and stayed where she was in case he tried something.

The guy seemed to realize that he was standing as far inside her home as she was going to allow. His shoulders stiffened a little and he brushed away the droplets that were getting into his eyes. "Trisha at city hall mentioned you had two Lipizzaner horses. I—I was hoping I could convince you to loan them to me."

It was the stupidest thing she'd ever heard and completely unexpected. She burst out laughing. "And why would I do that?"

He shifted on his feet and his hand sent a spray of water from his hair over the wall and carpet. "It's a long story. It's for the Winter Festival parade. You see the festival is Mayor Beyer's baby and she has her heart set on taking the Festival Queen and Princesses through that parade on a sleigh pulled by two grey or white horses. I happen to own such a pair so the city contracted with me to provide them."

Was this guy ever going to get to the point? He might be good looking, but the way his intense blue gaze bore into her, it was as if he expected her to simply give him anything he wanted. She hated guys like that.

"So if you've got the horses, why do you need mine?"

He sighed and told her about his gelding injuring his leg. "He needs to stay off it for a few weeks and the festival is seven days away." Another sigh. "Mayor Beyer isn't prepared to accept another color of horse so I'm hooped unless I can find another white horse. Or a pair." He gave her a weak smile.

She thought of Huey and Duey snug in their stalls. She'd checked on them only an hour ago. They were the reason she lived in this drafty house this far out of town—it was the only place with a barn and property that she could afford. The two horses had come to her as rescues when a man near Vancouver had decided, after seeing the Vienna Riding School perform, that he just *had* to have a Lipizzaner horse. The man had been abusive to the horses, but soon the bloom had faded off the rose. He'd left the two animals abandoned in a field until someone reported it. The pair of eleven-year-old geldings had been skin and bones when the SPCA had confiscated them. It had taken Jocelyn two years of hard work to rehabilitate them from the neglect and they still weren't particularly trusting.

She wasn't letting some stranger anywhere near them. She shook her head.

"Sorry. I can't help you."

"But it's for a good cause!"

"Doesn't matter. It's not going to happen. I'm sorry you drove out here for nothing, but you could have called. The response would have been the same though. I'm pretty protective of my boys. Besides, they're riding horses. Neither of them is broke to harness."

The guy's gaze narrowed slightly and she tensed. Then his shoulders slumped. "I can't change your mind? I—I've broken a lot of horses to harness. It would help me a lot."

"Nope." She pulled her sweater tighter around her neck and glanced out the window. "The snow's coming down harder. If you want to make it back into town, I suggest you leave now."

He blew out a breath and headed for the door. Pulled it open to allow in a flurry of now-icy flakes and a blast of cold air. "Thank you for your time." But the furrow of his brow and his downturned lips suggested what he wanted to say.

The door shut behind him and his snow-muffled footfalls went down the front stairs. Jocelyn exhaled, all the tension melting out of her as she locked the deadbolt behind him. Some people just figured they could take advantage of a lone woman. Or some men did.

Returning to her book, she shook her head. Her friends back in Vancouver said that she'd become far too suspicious of other people since she'd become a Probation Officer, but she figured the job had simply made her more aware of the risks of living in today's society. So she'd become more careful—or more discerning, as she claimed to her mother.

The truck engine roared to life out by the road and she pulled the front room curtains so she didn't have to see how dark it was—or the way the light from the window caught in the swirl of flakes. She'd be shoveling tomorrow, that was for sure. She sighed and thumped down on the couch with her book.

The sound of the engine outside changed as Grant or whatever his name was dropped the vehicle into gear. The engine revved. Revved again. And again. Against her better judgement she pulled the curtain apart to peek out, just as the truck's brake lights went on and Grant or whatever stepped out of the cab. The thunk of the door closing came clearly through the storm. In the red blush of the lights he went to the rear of the truck and bent down, righted himself and shook his head. Then he reached in the back of his truck and pulled out a shovel. He started digging.

She ducked when he glanced at the house, but was pretty sure he'd seen her anyway. Why the heck was she sneaking around in her house, when he was the stranger? And if she wanted to get rid of the guy, why not give him a hand to dig out his truck?

Besides. It was darned cold out and no one should be stuck in this storm.

Abandoning her comfortable cocoon, she pulled on her parka, mittens and knitted wool tuque with the bright red pompom at the top, then went out the back door where her snow-drifted car was parked, grabbed her shovel and headed for the road.

He'd pulled his truck into the slightly wider part of the road in front of her house just before her driveway gate, which was probably a good idea given the piles of snow in her driveway. The road had apparently been widened here for safety because her house was in a bit of a blind spot.

She came up beside him. "Thought you might need some help." She held up the shovel and read silent surprise on his face.

"Sure. Maybe dig out the other side and I'll see if I can pull out."

She waded through the shin-high and growing drift the wind had formed in front of her fence and started digging. The icy pellets of snow stung her face. The wind was cold enough it ate right through the parka. She should have bought down like her friends had suggested, but hadn't wanted to spend that much money—not when she didn't plan on staying that long in this godforsaken part of the country.

She was sweating and shivering after ten minutes and it didn't really look like her effort had made any difference, but she nodded when Grant said he was going to rock the truck free. He climbed in the cab, revved the engine a bit and then slowly applied the gas and the truck inched forward before losing traction. It rolled back into place and he tried it again, this time dropping into reverse to drive the vehicle a little farther back.

And forward again.

And back again.

The snow was almost blinding in the darkness and the cold had eaten its way into her bones.

Grant revved the engine a little more this time and the truck inched forward then picked up speed before suddenly sliding sideways.

Right toward Jocelyn.

She leapt aside and the truck slid over the spot where she'd stood before coming to rest against one of her fenceposts, the rear resting in the small snow-hidden ditch and decidedly lower than the front tires. Her heart pounded. Blood rang in her ears at how close that had been.

"Dammitalltohell!" Grant slammed out of the truck and stood there considering his vehicle.

The darn truck didn't look like it was going anywhere. It even looked as if the front wheels were off the ground.

He turned to Jocelyn. "You all right? I'm sorry if I scared you. Truth be told, it scared me, too. Damn truck had a mind of its own." He looked ruefully at the Ford. "I'm gonna need someone to pull me outta that depression. You've got a vehicle?"

She managed to stop the shaking in her knees. "Yes. But it's a Mini Cooper. I don't think it's going to be much good."

He looked skyward and sighed. "Guess I better call a tow truck."

"Um. There are usually a lot of people with trucks along the road. They seem like a pretty helpful lot. One helped me when I got a flat."

He looked up at the flakes. "Night like tonight, I doubt it. Not too many are going to be out driving in this. They'll be tucked up in their beds—if they even still have power."

As if on cue, the house lights flickered and then went out. To be snowbound in the dark with this guy who barely acknowledged that he'd almost killed her—it was the last thing she needed.

God, she missed David and the city.

By the truck's running lights Grant read her realization and dismay. He didn't feel much better about the fact that he was here for the night and frankly, given her lack of welcome before, and because no tow truck was going to come this far out of town when they'd have work aplenty inside city limits, he was pretty much resigned to spending the night in his vehicle. If he didn't freeze to death. He did have emergency blankets and such, but still—with a warm house standing right there... She—and the situation—pissed him off.

"I—I guess you'd better come in, then." Her stiff shoulders seemed to have softened. "It wouldn't look good if I let you freeze to death on my doorstep."

At least she was concerned about appearances, if not him. Well—maybe this would give him a chance to convince her to loan him the horses. He'd definitely need to tread carefully, but he could still look for openings.

After turning off and locking up the truck, he followed her inside through a rear door he hadn't seen. It gave onto a small porch area where she toed off boots and pulled off her jaunty tuque before stepping inside a small kitchen where a woodstove burned merrily in a corner. She hung her jacket and scarf on a coat tree by the fire and turned to face him in the darkness.

Her brown eyes were huge in the pale expanse of her face—as if she was frightened. Her red hair was piled high on her head, but the tuque had loosened lovely tendrils that coiled toward her cheekbones.

"Hey—err—I'm sorry the truck nearly hit you out there. I thought you knew better than to stand so close by."

Her gaze narrowed. He hadn't exactly said what he meant to say. "Well, I'm sorry. I didn't mean to scare you."

"You didn't. I've got candles and flashlights, but it's probably best if we call it a night." Her voice was stiff as she dug in a kitchen drawer and pulled out a flashlight that she flashed on. Candles were next, pulled out of the same drawer, with small candle stick holders that could be out of Dickens taken down from a shelf on the wall. In the dim light the kitchen took shape. Simple cupboards and counters —right out of a modular home catalogue. Vinyl floor marked and scarred by years of wear. A plain pine table in what must be the house's only eating area. A photograph above it of an old man in prayer above a loaf of bread. Beyond that, a hallway that led into darkness.

She might be the new Probation Officer in town, but the place didn't speak of the woman who'd moved in. If anything, it was basic, utilitarian, with no indication of her personality. As if she was marking time until she could move on. She wasn't investing anything to make this place her own. He'd seen enough government workers like that. Here and gone in two years max. No investment in the community during those years. No wonder she saw no need to loan him her horses. She didn't give a damn.

He accepted a candle from her and was surprised there were no comments about not burning the place down as she led him to a tiny bedroom with a single bed and pointed out the bathroom across the hall. "I'll see you in the morning, then."

She left him for the room at the end of the hallway and firmly shut the door behind her. If she wasn't so stuck on herself, he'd almost smile. The woman was an enigma, sort of a challenge.

Sort of a turn on with her long red hair, if she wasn't so determined to remain a stranger.

He doffed his jacket and shirt, then climbed in the bed in his jeans. If the power was out he was pretty sure the house was going to be cold by morning. That little kitchen wood burner didn't stand a chance of keeping the place warm—unless someone kept it burning. He didn't figure that a city girl like Jocelyn Payne would know enough to do it.

He dozed off and found himself drifting in and out of dreams about long red hair around smooth shoulders. What the hell was that all about?

He got up twice during the night and depleted the small amount of wood she had stacked on the porch. Beyond the windows, the storm still raged and when he peeked through the living room curtains his truck was lost in darkness and a half-seen drift of white. How the heck was he supposed to train a new team in this? Heck, how did they plan to hold the winter festival at all if the weather continued like this?

It didn't bode well for Mayor Beyer, or himself.

At six am he was fully awake and pulled on his shirt, jacket and boots. The little woodstove was down to glowing coals, but at least the house was moderately warm. He'd turned on the taps in the bathroom to drip to hopefully stop the pipes from freezing.

Outside, the light was flat grey and the air was frigid. It ate right through his shearling jacket and gloves, but he spotted a cord of neatly-stacked wood and an axe. He chopped kindling and split some larger logs that he carried back into the house. The fire fed and coaxed to life, he returned outside.

There was his truck to dig out, but he turned away from the road. The barn sat uphill and sheltered amongst the trees, the main door snuggly closed, but along the right side a pair of horses looked out over stall doors. The darn fool woman had left them exposed to the cold.

From this distance the horses were, indeed, white.

When one of them whinnied, he gave up on shoveling off the truck and headed for the barn. A pair of Lipizzaner horses—how often would he ever get this close to such a thing. Hell, Lipizzaner horses were legends. To a man raised as a cowboy, they were fairy tales. He trudged through the knee-high snow up the slight incline to the barn. At least the wind had died and it might be cold, but the cloud cover meant it was better than it could be.

He had to wrestle with the barn's door because snow blocked the entrance, but eventually he was able to slip inside. Neat little place. Cold, but even unheated it was certainly warmer than outside. Two saddles, one English, one western, sat on saddle trees built onto the wall. Two gleaming snaffle bridles hung there, too, along with brushes and supplies of hoof oil and saddle soap. He glanced back toward the house. Jocelyn Payne might be a pain, but she took care of her stuff.

The horses, too. He peered over the first interior stall door. Lipizzaner horses were born black but turned white as they matured. This gelding gleamed, its white coat immaculate even though he wore thick winter fur. The gelding stood in deep shavings that were mostly clean because he was one of those lovely horses who pooped all his manure into one corner of the stall. A half-empty bucket of water hung on the wall and an empty hay net, too.

The horse pulled his finely chiselled head in from outside, its black gaze wary. It snorted at Grant's presence. He held out a hand, but the animal didn't approach. Odd. Well, that would change, or the horse would starve. He slipped inside the stall and removed net and bucket while the horse remained on the far side of the stall. Then he repeated the process on the second stall. This horse actually came up to him when he held out his hand. Warm breath sniffed his fingers and guard hairs tickled his palm.

"Well, aren't you a lovely beast," he murmured and chanced stroking the horse's face. The animal pulled back, to consider him with almost black liquid eyes. For all the horse was immaculately white, the skin around its muzzle and eyes was totally black, enhancing the impression of intelligent regard. Its arched, white neck was counterpoint to a mane that was a mixture of silver and black threads. "You are, you know. Quite handsome, in fact." He held out his hand and the animal rested its muzzle in his palm. And sighed in a clear sign of relaxation. The horse had accepted him. Grant grinned. A horse's acceptance set a pretty high standard.

"Too bad your mistress doesn't feel the same."

He turned both horses loose into their outdoor pens and then cleaned out droppings and soiled bedding. When he was done, he hung up full hay nets but found the barn water wasn't running. Frozen, probably. "Your owner didn't know enough to keep the water dripping," he said to the pair as he hefted the buckets and headed down to the house.

He'd filled the buckets in the kitchen and was headed back up the hill when the house door slammed behind him.

"Just what do you think you're doing?" The ice in the voice made him consider dumping the buckets right there.

"What does it look like?" He'd tried to keep the question light but was pretty sure she'd hear it came through clenched teeth.

"You're messing with my horses is what it looks like."

He swung around to face her, water slopping over the bucket rims. "I got up early to bring in wood, saw the horses and thought I'd help you out by feeding and mucking stalls. But the barn water isn't working so I'm hauling it from the house."

He watched her throat work as she looked down at the buckets. "Water froze a week back. I've been hauling water, too."

"So shall I continue?" He hefted the buckets.

"Sure."

Could have knocked Grant over with a feather, but he led the way up to the barn and inside where he settled a bucket inside each stall. The first horse eyed him from the pen, but the second came inside and nudged him aside to get at the bucket. The barn filled with the sound of horses sucking water and the warm scent of new hay.

"They're fine-looking animals," he said coming up beside Jocelyn as she hung over the door to the first horse's stall. The second animal tore another bite of hay from the net and munched contentedly.

"They are now. They were skin and bones when I got them and suspicious of everything and everyone. I could barely get a halter on them back then. It's been a long road forward."

"What happened to them?"

She looked sideways up at him. "What does it matter to you?"

He shrugged. "I like horses. Always have. Always will."

She told him a story of abuse and neglect that made his fists clench and his jaw tense. "I hate people like that. Treat a horse as a machine you can throw away when you get tired of it. Doesn't anyone get that these are living, breathing beings?"

He felt her gaze on him. Noticed the furrow of her brow.

"Well, they are. They might not think like we think, but they feel. And the best of them try so hard to please us—actually all of them do if we just give them a chance."

"I know."

It was only two words, but when he looked down at her he read a struggle on her face as she studied him.

"What is it?"

She shook her head and looked back in the stall. "Nothing, really. You like horses, so I guess I shouldn't be surprised. It's just that most cowboys seem so rough and ready with their animals—like they don't get it at all."

She looked sad, standing there, as if she thought every cowboy abused his animals. "I guess you don't know very many cowboys. Sure, there are idiots who treat horses like machines, but there are a lot of good ones, too. They know that working cattle is a partnership. Without a good horse, a rider who listens to his animal, and trust between rider and mount, the work wouldn't happen."

She shifted and he found her looking up at him, an attractive softening around her eyes. "I just heard from work. The highway's closed and the entire town is mostly shut down today due to the snow. Tow trucks are apparently at a premium."

He looked past her toward the road. "So in other words my chances of getting pulled out of that ditch are slim and none."

"Unless one of the locals comes by, I'd say that was the case. I'm sorry. I'm sorry you came all this way for nothing."

It was true, but... He shrugged. "Not nothing. I got to meet a Lipizzaner in person. Two, in fact."

They turned back to the stall. "This is Duey," Jocelyn said softly, motioning at the horse who had been stand-offish to him.

At the mention of his name, the horse left his hay and came to the stall door. He nudged Jocelyn with his muzzle and then turned and surprised Grant by shoving his handsome face into Grant's chest.

"Hey, big guy! How're ya doing?" He smoothed his hands up the sides of the horse's head and scratched around the base of the ears. The horse shoved a little harder into his chest.

"I'll be damned," Jocelyn said. "He never does that. Not even for me." She eyed Grant up and down. "Duey's been the most difficult of the pair. He's been totally head shy. Heck, he'd barely let me near him for the first month I owned him. And he hasn't liked men." Duey gave Grant a little shove with his nose. "Until now."

Jocelyn looked up at Grant as if she'd decided something. "How about we get some breakfast and then take these two out for a ride. I usually ride Huey, so Duey hasn't had a good ride in ages. Then you can say you actually rode a Lipizzaner."

A grin lit her face and it turned the woman he'd thought of as dour into darn-right beautiful.

"Deal." He patted Duey one last time and followed Jocelyn out of the barn, marvelling at the way life could change things. 'Course, going for a ride still didn't mean he had a team of white horses, but maybe he could turn this whole fiasco around.

GRANT WAS NOT TURNING OUT TO BE WHAT JOCELYN HAD expected. She glanced over as she rode beside him, she in her English saddle and him using her western one. He rode easily—as easily as he seemed to do just about everything except get his darn truck unstuck from her driveway. He seemed totally relaxed in the saddle and Duey —amazingly—seemed totally relaxed, too. He certainly wasn't the nervous horse he'd been every time she rode him. His head was down and he simply plodded through the snow as if he was an old hand at it. He kept up with Huey and the two of them were virtually stride for stride as they rode down the pristine snow-covered road.

"These two look like they've worked together a lot. Did they ever do Lipizzaner shows like the quadrilles and so on of the Spanish Riding School?"

"What do you mean?" she asked.

"Look at the way these two are so comfortable shoulder to shoulder and how they seem to actually synchronize their movements. That doesn't just happen, you know."

"Really? I'd never noticed, because it isn't often the two of them are out together. I see what you mean, but I don't know anything about their background. Only where they were before I got them."

Grant's blue gaze studied the geldings and he scratched his chin. "There is another way they could have gotten so clever together."

The soft way he said it put her guard up again. "Do tell?"

He met her gaze, as a snow plow came down the hill, clearing the road. "Lipizzaners aren't just riding horses." The plow's roar almost obscured his words so he was almost yelling. "They've been used to pull wagons for centuries. They're still used in Sport Driving competitions."

He urged Duey off the road into a drift and Jocelyn followed with Huey. The plow roared past sending a silver cloud of snow over them, but the horses only flicked their ears and snorted at all that noise.

"Driving...?"

"Like singles, pairs and four-in-hand driving competitions. Coaches. Buggies. That sort of thing."

She went still in the saddle. "No." Felt a flush of anger at this stranger and herself. She'd almost started to like the guy! "I told you. You are not driving one of my horses in some parade. They might be fine out here, but we don't know how they'd react to a situation like that. And I resent you bringing it up again in such an underhanded way."

She drove Huey out of the drift to the road, turning back toward the house. Damn Grant Estevan. He'd ruined a perfectly nice day and undone any good feelings she might have for him. Give your head a shake here, girl! He wasn't some nice guy who liked horses. He was just some guy working the angles.

He followed her for most of the ride home but urged Duey even with her as they came to her driveway. The plow had sent more snow over his truck and the driveway entrance, but he could almost see the truck's front bumper. With the road cleared it gave him an idea. "Jocelyn, hold on!" She was urging Huey up and over the now massive snow drift. He drove Duey up beside her and put his hand over hers on the reins. "Hold on a moment. I know you want to be rid of me. Well, I want to try something that might make it possible now instead of waiting for someone to pull me out."

He nodded down at Duey, then at the truck. "This saddle's solid and so's he." He patted Duey's neck. "The truck isn't really stuck that badly. Just a little tension on a rope could help me get it out of there and then I'll be outta your hair."

"Duey's not a cow horse. Neither of them is."

"I understand. But let me try and if it doesn't work, you're stuck with me a while longer and I'll dig out your driveway. If it does work, well, you're rid of me. Right? And I'll still dig out your driveway."

She looked up the length of her driveway and the daunting depth of snow. It wasn't an offer to be taken lightly, but this was Duey! She turned back to Grant.

"If there is any sign that Duey is in distress, this is over, no arguments. Got it?"

She read the waver in his gaze, but he nodded. "Deal. You'll be in control of Duey anyway. You'll know. I'll be inside my truck. Now give me a minute."

He backed Duey out onto the road, then dismounted and handed her the reins. Then he grabbed his shovel from the truck, cleared the front end with some quick bladework and worked his way around the sides to clear the tires. Lastly, he pulled a coiled rope out of the cab. He held it up like a trophy. "Gotta be prepared, right?"

He went down on his belly and tied one end of the rope under the truck, then stood up and brushed off his clothes. "Okay. Here's what we're going to do. Luckily ol' Duey here has a breast strap on his saddle, so that should make things easier. We're going to wrap this rope around the saddle horn a few times with you holding the end, along with his reins. You're going to lead him forward until we've got tension on the rope after I start the truck engine. Then I'll try rocking it a few times, but when I wave, I want you to lead Duey forward again so he's helping the truck move until the wheels get traction. If something goes wrong, just release the rope."

The whole thing sounded hopeless. Better to wait for someone with a truck to come by. But if it would rid her of Grant Estevan, she was willing to give it a try. And if it didn't work—well at least she'd have her driveway cleared, because it was an all-day job for her alone.

He wrapped the rope and gave her the end. She rode Huey forward alongside Duey until the rope was taut between the saddle and the truck. The two horses stood patiently waiting while Grant climbed in the truck and started the engine. He was really going to do this. She was letting him try this with one of her horses... with Duey, no less. And yet Duey didn't look like the skittish mess she'd sheltered for so long. If anything, he seemed calmer than her, his ears flicking behind him as if he was fully aware he was attached to something.

The engine roared as Grant rocked the truck. The old Ford shifted in the snow. Then he waved her forward through the open side window.

She clicked her tongue. "Come on, boys. Let's do this!" She urged Huey forward with her heels. Duey dropped his head and seemed to lean into his breast strap. And walked forward like he'd done this a hundred times before. The rope tightened and groaned. But Duey kept walking alongside Huey and the truck moved. Up out of the ditch, up out of the snow, and fully onto the road until Grant waved at her again.

She stopped the horses and backed them up to release the tension on the rope, then leapt down to throw her arms around Duey's neck. "You did it big guy! You did it.!"

Huey bumped her with his muzzle and she stroked his white face. "You did it, too, Huey. You are quite the pair."

"A team. Yes."

Grant had come up behind her, but he said nothing more. He simply unwound the rope and returned it to his truck. He parked the pickup, grabbed his shovel and started clearing her driveway.

It had been a long while since a man had lived up to his word. But maybe that was simply because she worked with offenders. But then David had promised to visit her here, too, and *he* still hadn't come through...

HE COULD READ IT IN HER EYES—THE WAY HER MIND churned over. As she worked alongside him shovelling he could tell she expected him to bring up the borrow-her-horse thing again, but he'd be damned if he would. She'd seen. She knew. Now, just like when he was training a young horse that wouldn't come when he called, he'd let her train herself. Like with a horse, she'd seen enough of him to know she could trust him.

He dug his shovel in one more time and tossed the snow onto the growing ridge along the side of her driveway. Damned thing was long enough most people around here would have a snowblower, but this was a city slicker he was dealing with. He just kept shovelling while she cleaned out around her sorry excuse for a vehicle and started shoveling from the house toward the road. She was surprisingly good at it. Snow flew from her shovel and they were making faster work of the clearing than he'd expected, which was good. He'd had a neighbor go in to check on his livestock and feed this morning, but he needed to get home.

They finally took a quick break for hot chocolate heated on the woodstove until the power suddenly returned and Jocelyn could move the pot to the stove. But neither brought up the topic of the team or the Winter Festival. Instead, he told her about the Williams Lake rodeo and about riding out into the wilderness that surrounded the town. Stories of muskeg, willow, beaver dams, and pothole lakes teaming with trout landlocked after the Spring runoff. Of wild geese flying and swans and pelicans that spent summers in the shallow lakes. Of the terror of wild fires and the smell of the mint that grew in shallow depressions in the woodlands. Of red fox kits playing on Spring green fields.

"You love this place," she said with a charming white moustache of milk above her lip.

"I do. I can't imagine living anywhere else." He sipped his chocolate and watched her. Her dark gaze flickered as she seemed to search her memory.

"I can't remember ever loving a place like that. I mean the city, right? Tall buildings. Bright lights. The culture. The shops. The restaurants." Her throat worked. "The people."

Her voice rasped a little.

"You left someone behind to come here." That explained her a bit.

"Yeah. Maybe. I thought so. We'd agreed this was best for my career."

"So he's waiting for you back there."

"That's what I keep telling myself." She smiled sadly, then took a deep breath. "Listen. I've been thinking about what you asked. About the boys. Given how Duey reacted with the truck, I think I should give you a chance. I'm going to suggest that you head home and come back with harness and a sleigh, while I finish digging out the driveway. If the boys show they can do it without any problems, then yes, I'll loan them to you."

He'd won! He'd bloody well won and he wanted to crow it to the moon, but he didn't want to scare her away. This woman was trusting him. Hell, she'd even allowed him to glimpse her vulnerability and he wasn't going to risk that trust any more than he'd risk damaging trust with a skittish horse. Actually, he'd risk it less, because it was her.

THE SUN WAS EDGING TOWARD THE END OF THE DAY WHEN the Ford truck backed into her driveway. It had a trailer behind it that carried a long, low platform built on sled skids, with a long pole attached to the front end. A double bench seat was bolted to the front of the top. Jocelyn pulled on a coat and boots and went out to meet Grant as he climbed out of the truck.

"Hey! You got the driveway finished!" he said looking around.

"And I've got the sore muscles to show for it." She smiled. "I'm thinking a snow blower might be in the offing."

He grinned. "It did cross my mind, but far be it from me to suggest anything."

"Right. You never suggest anything." She rolled her eyes. "The horses are in their stalls all brushed and ready."

"Then give me a hand, would you?" He motioned her to the truck where he handed her a confusing array of thick black leather straps and a horse collar that he draped around her neck. She staggered under the weight but quickly straightened. No showing she was a weakling. She'd already made a fool of herself this afternoon when she talked about David. Or didn't talk about him as the case may be. In her line of work she couldn't afford to be vulnerable.

After Grant climbed out of the truck bed with his own armload of harness, she stumble-staggered after him up to the barn. Soon the barn rang with the soft sounds of harness hardware jangling and hooves stamping.

Jocelyn shook her head. "I don't believe how calm they are with all that stuff on. They hardly batted an eye."

"Now do you believe that they've done this before?"

"Maybe." But she gave him what she hoped was a wicked smile.

Thirty minutes later they'd shifted the sled from the trailer and the horses were harnessed to the shaft and the chains on their harness attached to the sled. The two Lipizzaners huffed and blew steam in the cold air as Jocelyn pulled on a hat and heavy gloves.

"Grab a seat and we'll get this show on the road," Grant said as he checked the harness.

She took a seat on the bench that was just behind the horses and Grant handed her the lines. When he joined her he had a lantern and a driving whip. "It's getting dark. Don't want to use the road, but we have to for a little way."

He flicked the lantern on, handed it to her and took the lines.

"Giddup, there." He snapped the lines and the two horses set off down the driveway, the sled behind them.

At the road, Grant turned toward Big Lake Valley. "There's a big open area just before the flat where we can put them through their paces."

Another snap of the lines and the horses broke into a trot. "Damn. These are one hell of a team. Look how they accept the bit."

Both horses had their heads down, their necks nicely arched and seemed to stretch into the harness as they went. The drive down the road was uneventful, the sled blades singing on the snow-packed pavement. When they turned off the road onto an abandoned logging road, the volume of snow slowed them, but another snap of the lines and a click of Grant's tongue and the two horses leaned into their collars and took them forward up hill and down. Snow from last night lay heavy on the tree branches, and the lantern light made their passage magical in its golden light. When the trees parted, the dim light revealed a huge open area. Grant guided the horses into a huge figure eight, then urged them into a canter and the snow flew in clouds from their hooves, while steam roared from their nostrils and overhead a full moon rose over the mountains and she thought she might be sick for the beauty of it all.

In the lanternlight Grant was focussed on the horses, his expression rapt and oh so full of wonder. As if he felt her glance, he looked her way and smiled and the night seemed to shimmer.

Until the sled suddenly canted and then turned up on its side.

The horses jerked to a stop as Jocelyn tumbled out of her seat, Grant landing on top of her. She came up sputtering with a mouthful of snow. "What the heck!"

"Sorry! Sorry!" Grant pushed himself up off her. "I got distracted. I..."

He was right there, so close to her, face to face, and then his lips found hers and he kissed her. Warm. She could still taste the chocolate on him and her body weakened.

Then she jerked away. "What the...!"

"Sorry. Lost my head in the moment." He seemed to shake himself. "I accidently sent us up over a gravel pile and the sled tipped." He got up to inspect the horses who were blowing steam in the cold night air. The moonlight placed a silver glare on their black tracks in the snow. "I guess we should head back. We've got our answer, though. This is a driving pair and I would love to drive them in the Winter Festival."

"Yes," she mumbled, mortified. It was bad enough that she'd kissed him back. But she'd enjoyed it and, if anything, she'd kind of like to kiss him again and see what happened. But there was David to think about, and her possible future back home in Vancouver. What the heck was she doing?

ONE WEEK LATER, GRANT DROVE THE HORSES DOWN THE parade route. He could almost swear the two Lipizzaners arched their necks to show off. Mayor Beyer had been ecstatic when she'd seen them, and had told him as much. The sidewalks were packed with people, but he'd told Jocelyn where to stand. He just hoped his plan worked out. It had been an amazing week working the team, enjoying evenings with a woman he realized he'd really come to like. It was a long time coming since he lost Carolyn, but he was beginning to feel alive again.

And there she was. Standing right where he'd hoped.

JOCELYN BOUNCED FROM FOOT TO FOOT TRYING TO STAY warm in the frigid February wind as yet another car float eased down the street with dignitaries waving from inside. Beside her Trish Worth, from city hall, looked like a tootsie roll in an ankle-length down parka that Jocelyn was seriously envying. She wouldn't normally come to a community event like this, but Huey and Duey had a starring role and she couldn't miss that.

Or Grant. Every day for the past week, he'd come out to practice with the team, and every day she'd gone out on the sleigh with him she'd found herself more attracted to him. There was something about his hands. The way they soothed a horse. The way they worked the lines. The way they touched her hand however briefly as he taught her how to drive the sled. David had never had hands like that and she had a hard time remembering what he'd had that attracted her. Each evening she and Grant had warmed themselves with cocoa or something stronger after the horses were stabled and the harness cleaned.

And now the week was over and Grant would have no excuse to intrude any longer. She'd have her life back again, which was a good thing.

Wasn't it?

"That's one heck of a sigh," Trish said.

"It's nothing."

Trish gave her a knowing look. "You know you've had a silly grin on your face all week, right? From what I've heard Grant has, too."

A cheer down the street said the main event must be close. A flash of white and blue and she was sure it was them.

Hoofbeats came on the snow-packed street and classical music played through loudspeakers as Huey and Duey proudly trotted down the snowy pavement. Blue plumes decorated their backs and heads. The bobsleigh had been transformed with navy and white flocking and hay bales covered with white sheets so they looked like the snow. Seated upon them were a bevy of young lovelies clad in pale blue while, at the top, the festival's snow queen wore white with a heavy blue cape cascading over her shoulders.

Seated at the front on a bench covered in blue, was Grant in a white tuxedo jacket and top hat worn over a thick winter jacket. Jocelyn snapped pictures with her phone and couldn't stop grinning. Her horses. Her beautiful white horses out there for everyone to enjoy!

"They're gorgeous," Trish gushed. "The picture in your office doesn't begin to do them justice. You must be so proud!"

And she was. She was as Trish pulled her into a hug. As people around her congratulated her on her fabulous horses. As the team came to halt in front of her and one of the princesses stepped down and grabbed her hand. Tugged.

Mystified, she followed the girl off the sidewalk and out into the road.

"What? What is this?" She looked back at Trish.

"Just go on!" Trish waved her forward and Jocelyn looked up and met Grant's blue gaze. He smiled and held out his hand and she stepped up onto the bobsled to the crowd's applause. Sat down beside him and he settled a blue blanket around her shoulders and looked her in the eyes.

"Thank you," he said and leaned in to kiss her. Lightly as a feather on her lips. He pulled back slightly and she couldn't breathe.

"Thank you, right back," she said and leaned in to kiss him back and he gently caught her chin and kissed her—harder this time. The crowd cheered.

When he pulled away they were both breathless and the crowd was clapping and chanting for more. He flipped the lines at the team and they trotted down the street as Grant caught her hand and squeezed.

Jocelyn wasn't exactly sure where they were going.

But it wasn't going to be to Vancouver.

AUTHOR OF THE WELL-REGARDED PHOEBE CLAY MYSTERY Series, K. L. Abrahamson also writes fantasy and romance under Karen L. Abrahamson. Her latest short fiction can be found in antholo-gies and magazines such as Ellery Queen's Mystery Magazine *and* Black Cat Mystery Magazine. *You can find out about her writing at www.karenlabrahamson.com.*

About this story, Karen says:

"A very long time ago I had the good fortune to live in a small town

where winter lasted ten months and festivals were expected to liven up the cold weather. One year my husband was asked to provide a sleigh for the festival queen and her court in the town parade. This would have been a great honor except, at the time, none of our horses were trained to harness, so we were out in parkas and ski pants training a team of gray horses to drive. I froze, but the horses did eventually stop bolting into snow drifts and became a lovely team. I harvested that memory for this story and made it a little more exotic by having the horses be Lipizzaner's—the famed white horses of Vienna."

Queen of Light and the Perfect Elf

TINA BACK

THE MOMENT THE GRAY SOCCER-MOM CAR PULLED TO A stop in the empty parking lot of the boxy suburban Presbyterian church in the drab crack of dawn, Kara channeled *Die Hard*. She got out of the car, taking the lead with the suave confidence of Hans Gruber, followed by her band of silver-haired mayhem, ready to take the Nakatomi building down. Or the church. Not with explosives, but with well-worn holiday decorations, wrinkly white nightgowns, silver glitter garlands, red silk ribbons and an alarming number of malfunctioning electric candles. And that was just for starters, because it wasn't the Day of Lucia till the ladies in her trail sang off-key like canaries.

Kara had one day to deck the halls for tomorrow's performance. Like Hans Gruber, she had a plan. And a secret: Kara Andersson Kroger loathed Lucia like the Grinch hated Christmas.

She'd never had a choice. She'd been born into it. Once a year, her mom transformed into an Old Country Taliban. The call went out to the far northern immigrant tribe. Come November, the rehearsals were on, and no child of a Lucia devotee was safe. Plied with candy and sweet-smelling mandarins, the children learned the songs by heart before the age of eight. Since there weren't that many of them, Mom had deviously used the local church to procure more innocent children to the cause. To six-year-old Kara's dismay, it had been an astounding success. In horror, she watched the Day of Lucia grow into a community tradition in the years that followed. Of course it was an easy sell when the date of celebration sits snugly between December 1st and Christmas, involves home-baked goods, adorably singing children, and can be blamed on a saint. Kara's mom knew what she was doing.

And because of the way her mom glowed with happy purpose come Lucia season, Kara never came clean about the way she felt about the whole awful thing.

She took the easy way out. She moved away and had a life. Twice. When the latest one crashed in a divorce and mom's cancer turned terminal, Kara moved back. She was fifty, and after mom passed away —kind of idling. Like the engine was running but she had no idea what to do, or where to go next, only that the future better be 100% Lucia-free.

But the Lucia torch had passed to Mom's bestie Asta, another devious woman. It had turned into a Godfather, or a Godmother situation. Kara had no other explanation. She'd left all things Lucia behind, yet Asta and her ruthless silver-haired mob pulled Kara back in, not taking no for an answer. Kara caved. For the last couple of years, she'd become Asta's reluctant Lucia deputy. Kara could feel her mom's circle of friends pinning their hope on her as Asta's natural successor to the title of Lucia General, securing the annual Lucia celebration for generations to come. She didn't have the heart to tell them the truth. This year she'd finally declined. There was too much to do at work, she lied. But then Asta pulled a fast one and broke a femur in October. Here Kara was again, trapped in her mom's California version of Lucia-land.

The plan was beautiful and well tested. The rest of the aging gang of Scandinavian broads knew what to do. The same thing they did gloriously every year: Setting the stage for the perfect Lucia performance.

As always, the plan was doomed from the start. That's why channeling Hans Gruber was the only way Kara could get through the next two days. It helped knowing that while the plan was perfect, there was nothing she could do to pull it off. The John McClanes of near and far had heard the news, they'd seen the fliers and they were ready to Lucia. December 1st their anticipation switched on like clockwork, turning them into a horde of Lucia-craving locusts, demanding sweet saffron buns, mulled wine and crispy gingerbread cookies to be conjured from the frozen voids of Valhalla. The John McClanes and their families would pack the pews, expecting the church to magically glow from an extreme fire hazard of lit candles. They yearned for the magic of the procession. They waited with bated breath for the first faint sounds of the Lucia song from the evening darkness outside, announcing that the one with the crown of lights was coming with her train of angelic children, ensuring that the darkest night of the year had passed, and in her wake, light would return to the world.

Kara sighed. Somewhere between now and then, Hans Gruber would inevitably go out the window.

MAX IGNORED THE HAWK-EYED STARE FROM THE BONY old white woman in the electric wheelchair. He eyed the church warily. So much at stake. First rule of getting anywhere is showing up, that's what he'd told himself. He was trying to get it right this time. "It" being everything that mattered.

The old woman pulled a deep drag on a cigarette, not letting him out of sight. Under the bulky knit cardigan, he glimpsed a bright blue leg brace. "I've been kicked out," she said. "I backed into the ironing board. The foot rest may have bruised Emmy in the shin."

Max glanced at her, not sure if he was supposed to respond or not.

She stubbed out the cigarette on the white plastered wall behind her, checked the stub closely and put it in the pocket of her cardigan. "Kids might eat them. Nobody smokes anymore. Filthy habit." She peered at him again, longer this time. "Nah," she said, "you're not Max Parker, are you?"

"I am." He didn't correct her for adding "-er" to his last name. Better nip this conversation in the bud.

"I'm supposed to keep an eye out for you! You're really Camilla's dad?"

It hurt. She was a stranger and there was no reason he should care, but he did. Cam looked more like her white mother than her Asian father. It was a fact. It didn't mean Cam wasn't his daughter, too. His daughter, now a grown woman with a daughter of her own, who had told him the importance of showing up today, or don't bother ever again. Cam hadn't said the last part out loud. She didn't need to.

The woman beamed at him. "You look younger. But here you are, punctual and in a very nice—" she gestured in his general direction "—suit. I'm Asta. I'll shut up and take you to our fearless leader." She stared at the wheelchair's arm with its many buttons. "It's a rental," she muttered. "It's still hit and miss."

Asta pushed at something. The wheelchair bolted forward. Max took a step back.

Too late. She rolled over his foot with a delighted shriek.

ASTA PUMMELED THROUGH A SMALL ENTRANCE, narrowly missing a bedraggled Christmas tree and the two older women decorating it. They called after her in a sing-song language. Max didn't understand a word, but he picked up the note of exasperation. There was no doubt, his guide was a handful. Max trailed her at a safe distance.

Asta continued. Engine whining, she cleared the rubber threshold ramp to the next room, speeding along the wide aisle dividing the nave into two sets of orderly pews. Max walked faster trying to keep up. He drew the line at running after a woman in a wheelchair down the aisle.

A handful of chatting women pushed new white and red candles into a flea market assortment of ugly candle holders and candelabras. Two more ladies trotted back and forth putting candles on every side table and windowsill. Three enlisted graying husbands or boyfriends tried to bolt and duct tape the remains of a broken Christmas tree back together, while a woman wearing a glitter garland as a necklace cheered them on.

In front of the altar, a twenty-something sound technician with a man-bun argued a point with a woman of tall, lean Nordic build whose crossed arms and arched brow should have told the guy the discussion was over. The red scarf tied around her head and blue overalls made her ooze a "We can do it!" vibe. The "can't" the guy seemed to offer was clearly unacceptable. The young technician opened his mouth to continue. Her eyebrow inched a fraction higher. The temperature of her gaze shot below zero. The technician did the smart thing, closed his mouth and backed away.

Asta pulled to a stop, taking the technician's place, talking sing-song rapid-fire. Fearless Leader's glacial blue-steel glare softened. She listened, then nodded at the poinsettia on the floor that Asta's wheelchair had tilted precariously. While Asta sorted out how to reverse, Fearless Leader summoned Max with a glance.

Natural authority like that was a thing to behold. Max better rein in his inner over-achiever and keep him on a very short leash. She was stylish and pretty. And about his age, fifty or so. He shortened the leash some more. He was a man on a mission. There could be no distractions.

Mid-sentence, Asta switched to English to include Max. "—and you've met Kara, right? When she was Camilla's babysitter?"

After Max had been kicked to the curb and Amanda had returned to teaching.

Kara didn't protest that they'd never met. Max took her Fearless Leader cue and didn't either.

"Camilla said you might be convinced to come," said Kara with a smile.

"I came voluntarily."

She studied him for a beat too long, like a living lie-detector. Speaking the truth, he seemed to have passed the test.

"How long do I have you for?" she said.

Asta sighed happily and put her hand over her heart. Kara point-edly ignored her and continued, "There's the set-up, the perfor-mance, and clean-up shifts. Take your pick. Any hours you can spare will help."

Max shrugged. "Not a problem. I'm here for as long as you need me."

Asta sighed again. Kara cut an icy glare Asta's way.

"No elf costume in the holiday season was a plus," Max said.

"There should be an elf costume," said Asta. "A shirtless one."

"Asta." Kara spoke softly.

"I said it in English?"

"We'll act like adults and pretend you didn't. Just don't do it again, or I'll put you back in charge." Kara's tone was light, but there was no question she'd do it. Firm but fair.

"Come with me," she said to Max.

He shortened his inner leash another inch and followed.

"YOU SEE MY CREW?" KARA SAID TO MAX.

"Active seniors."

Kara smiled. Well-dressed *and* diplomatic, all Hans Gruber could want in an elf.

"They must stay that way," she said, "which means no heavy lifting, no climbing the ladders, no working heavy tools—"

"Drill scare of 2019," Asta piped behind them. "Between the bones, but through the foot."

"—no driving—"

"Last year, Britt and Marianne took the wrong ramp on the freeway and headed for Mexico."

Kara stopped. Asta didn't. "They were chatting and didn't pay attention for an hour or three. Britt is a great driver, really."

Kara waited in frosty silence.

Asta finally paid attention. She sighed loudly. "Yes, general. I'll go supervise the ironing." She added quickly in Swedish, "I bet Max knows how to iron. Look at his collar. Can I—"

She could not. Definitely not.

Asta drove off, parroting Kara's possessive tone. "*My* elf!"

For a terrifying moment Kara didn't know what language either of them had used. Her cheeks burned hot. Great. Hans Gruber never blushed. Probably because he was stuck with an armed Russian drama queen and a sweaty, relentless John McClane. Not saddled with chiseled Max Park in a tailored suit he swaggered the hell out of. Worse, he came with grooming, manners, and something haunted and melancholy inside. Like Lucia wasn't punishment enough? Who put in the order for a hot brooding elf? Kara hadn't known such even existed. More importantly, why was Max here? In the greater Karma scheme of things, she knew exactly why. He was this year's window dressing for whatever curve ball calamity would inevitably make Hans go face first out the window. The only way to prepare for the inevitable was to find out what Max was up to, pretending to volunteer. She had years of experience with elves blackmailed into Lucia service. No eager elves showed up during holiday season looking for unpaid work. They simply did not. There was something else going on. She didn't buy his selfless elf act for a second.

MAX'S FIRST ELF ASSIGNMENT WAS TO CHECK THE flashlights. He corrected himself. *The candles.* As in tiny battery-operated flashlights with a small screw-in light bulb at the top, a white plastic tube to look like a candle, and a red plastic handle. There were two boxes of candles on a side table.

"Everyone in the Lucia procession holds a candle. Except the Lucia, of course."

"Of course," said Max. He pointed a candle at no particular threat, like a baby light sword.

Kara's eyes narrowed. Max froze. Wielding the candle was probably culturally offensive. She asked if he'd been to a Lucia celebration before. Max offered to have a look at YouTube, but she told him not to. "It's different live and it's different here. It's better to just experience it." She pointed to the candle in his hand. "First you check if you can turn it on. That's the ancient model, you turn it on by tightening the light bulb."

There were vintage models in flashlight candles, good to know. The bulb was already tightly screwed on. No light.

Kara sighed. She took the candle from Max and disassembled it in seconds, placing the parts on a stained kitchen towel on the table, much like a jaded action hero prepping for the showdown. The precision stirred things in him.

"Now, you troubleshoot," she said. "It's usually the battery. Sometimes it's the light bulb. There is a newer model with a stupid button. It pinches the smaller kids' thumbs. We call them the thumb eaters. If you hand out the candles, give the thumb eaters to the tweens and older. Unless we run short. Then you hand out whatever still works. If you need spare parts, there are candles that don't work in the boxes."

"Are they marked?"

She flashed a grin. "What would be the fun in that? Just look for loose parts and you'll be fine."

"Written instructions would be helpful."

"There might still be some in the boxes. In Swedish." She shot him a scary smile, all teeth. A very effective stop talking signal.

He asked anyway. "Just one more thing. You said 'whatever still works.' If I put in fresh batteries and check the bulb, shouldn't they work?"

"Yes, they should. They absolutely should." She looked at the box crammed with candles and sighed again. "But they won't." She shot him a pained look. "Just do your best."

KARA FOUND A MOMENT TO PULL OUT HER PHONE AFTER she reset the fire alarm and cleared out the smoke in the weathered kitchen for the third time. She'd left Asta to calm down the baking crew while she went outside to empty the tray of cremated gingerbread cookies. She'd offered to bake them at home, but team "you have enough on your plate, besides we always bake them here" had won. So what if Kara had to reset the fire alarm a couple of times. By now it was tradition.

"About your dad—" she said to Camilla.

"He said he'd be there."

"He's resurrecting candles." Kara snuck a peek through the window. Max had lost the jacket and folded up the pristine white shirt sleeves neatly. The candles were cursed, so she liked his focused frown and determined pout. Suddenly, the candle lit up the planes of his face and there was a glint of satisfaction in his eyes. "He is some sort of candle whisperer," Kara said. She made a face. Hans Gruber never sounded breathlessly impressed. Ever. She pulled herself together. "Why is he here? I'm super grateful, don't get me wrong. But what did he do to deserve a full day with the Lucia crazies?"

"He asked if he could come see Sofia in the performance. He said he was sorry he never got to see me in my Lucia days."

"You used the guilt card."

"Don't feel bad for him. Max collects them. He has lots of regrets over leaving. But I was too young to remember him at all. My grandparents moved in, and grandpa did a great job as a stand-in Dad. I don't feel abandoned. Getting to know a parent as an adult is kind of different. They're people, you know? Dad and I are figuring it out, but it's way harder for him than it is for me. It's like Max feels he can't be forgiven for leaving. And feelings are tricky. Working for it helps him feel he's earning his grandpa privileges. Boss him around. It'll cheer him up. Seriously, I'm doing you both a favor."

"Now I feel guilty in advance for what I'm going to put him through. Thanks."

Camilla laughed. "You two are a lot alike. Asta tried to set you up with him yet?"

"She tried to steal him."

"No way."

"He's wearing a three-piece suit to an elf gig."

"I told him to look nice. You better tell Asta to back off. He's your elf."

Kara closed her eyes and groaned. The fire alarm went off, giving her an excuse to hang up.

She'd been single and fine many Lucias. Now, she was single and fine and fifty. But the Lucia gang didn't see it that way. Every year they tried to set her up with someone, usually the new elf.

It was worse than *Die Hard*. Hans Gruber may end up going out the window, but he never had to deal with well-meaning, ham-handed matchmakers.

THE FIRE ALARM BLARED AGAIN. MAX HELD UP A HAND TO stop Asta who seemed to be going for the indoor speed record in laps while he pasted wintry paper decorations on the walls. "What are they trying to cook in there?"

"Cookies and mulled wine. The wine makes you forget the cookies. It's a tricky combo. That's the fifth time the alarm's gone off, right?" said Asta.

"I think so."

Kara calmly crossed the room and disappeared. A moment later the wailing ceased. Another minute, and she returned carrying a bowl covered with a striped kitchen towel. She headed for the kitchen.

"Uh-uh. Five times," Asta said. "They crossed the line."

No screaming ensued. Max knew someone like Kara didn't need to raise her voice. Pink-faced ladies filed out of the kitchen anyway. They spotted Asta and hurried over, suddenly all grins and conspiratorial whispers. Something made them all giddy. Max didn't understand what they said, but the sneaky glances his way didn't bode well.

"Come on, Max," said Asta. "Looks like you've been transferred to the baking department. A well-rounded elf always comes in handy."

KARA AND MAX BAKED HER BATCH OF DOUGH FOR 200 gingerbread cookies and the fire alarm didn't go off a single time.

He was the perfect elf. She didn't need to translate how thin the dough should be rolled. He'd lived in South Korea, his parents' homeland, and understood three millimeters like a native. Kara baked in metrics but only knew her weight in pounds. Max ran in kilometers but drove in miles. Neither of them could make sense of floating ounces.

The kitchen filled with the sweet spicy scent of perfectly baked, crispy gingerbread cookies. Max made the strong coffee according to Kara's directions and didn't accuse her of trying to ruin people's sleep for a week. They filled the army of thermoses and thawed a mountain of saffron buns. For the first Lucia Kara could remember, she didn't stress about getting everything ready because it turned out Asta was right, a well-rounded elf was always handy. Max was easy company, too.

There were minor disturbances in the force. Asta was hovering but Kara banned her and anyone else from entering the kitchen.

"That's unfair. I didn't break the record in fire alarms," Asta protested.

"You crossed the other line," Kara said sternly in Swedish. "Go away."

Amused, Asta saw straight through her. "Oh, that's how it is?" she said in English. "You want to be alone with him." Asta cackled as she drove off.

Kara hid her face in her hands. Steeling herself, she peered at Max between her fingers.

"I know that's not what you said," he smiled.

"They're trying to set us up."

"I kind of figured that out." Max added, "I don't mind."

Kara's cold, controlled Hans Gruber heart grew a warm silly crack.

"Camilla might be in on it," she said.

"I still don't mind."

She smiled. "This time, I don't mind either."

It didn't derail anything. They continued working like a couple of pros. There was steady glow between them in the kitchen, but they were grown-ups and didn't let it set off the fire alarm.

IT WAS HANS GRUBER SHOW TIME. THE DARK CHURCH was packed. The candles made the hall glow. No matter how hard Kara tried to fight it, the moment everyone stilled in the pews, the Lucia magic did its work. When the first words of the Lucia song made its way in from the outside, Kara started crying. By the time the teens and children in their long white gowns slowly proceeded up the aisle and the glow inside increased from their candles, she was bawling her eyes out. This was her Hans Gruber window moment: Ugly uncontrollable snot-filled crying. The Lucia with the crown made of candles looked like an angel and the bungled Swedish lyrics touched Kara's heart. She saw the misty-eyed way Cam and Max watched four-year old Sofia in her lovely gown, the way people's eyes grew warm and wet. For a moment, Kara believed with all her heart that the darkest time of year had passed, they were in the presence of the harbingers of light, and her mother had been right all along.

It was worth the work. And she just knew the same would be true of Max.

TINA BACK IS A SWEDISH-AMERICAN WRITER-illustrator. Born with a traveling bug, she has lived in Japan, Singapore and California. The places she's called home show up in her art and writing. Tina's illustrations and writings have been published in books for children and adults. You can find her on the web at www.proudlypulp.com.

About this story, Tina says:

"The idea for the story came from grudgingly participating in yearly Lucia celebrations. From the teen fear that a distant Lucia-crazy relative would enter my name in the yearly local Lucia pageant, to the time I had to work the Lucia bouncer shift at the Swedish Christmas

Market in San Francisco, physically denying rabid Lucia fans entry to the packed hall.

"The tears, the lies, the name-calling. Ugh. My best Lucia experience? Singapore, absolutely. Every year, a former Miss Sweden and Lucia fan organized a stress-free event in a church in the pitch dark tropical jungle. Anyone could show up, wear a white gown and a crown, and sing their heart out. Non-traditional and just as beautiful. Well, maybe not the singing."

Although Lucia remains Tina's second least favorite holiday, she's coming around. Slowly. Provided there are enough gingerbread cookies for all and someone else wears the crown.

The Baron and the Hanukkah Miracle

C. S. STEIN

DECEMBER 13, 1817, EREV HANUKKAH

WHEN THE BARON OF NORSHIRE DEMANDED HER FATHER loan him Naomi to create sketches of guests at his party, neither she nor her father could refuse. She begged off initially. Her father pointed out to the Baron that December 13 was the first night of Hanukkah. But their objections fell on deaf ears. The Baron insisted and since the Baron owned the land underneath their home and shop, they could do little other than comply with his wishes.

Naomi bent her head to the inevitable. No point in fighting a losing battle and anything involving a baron, particularly *that* baron, was likely to result in a complete rout. Hanukkah celebrated victory in a war, but it wasn't a hopeless war, nor was it fought for minor reasons.

Which was how Naomi found herself that afternoon sitting in front of her travel easel, dressed in her best Shabbat outfit: a pale blue linen petticoat topped with a blue flowered short gown and dark blue spotted kerchief tied over her bust. She'd topped it with the freshly cleaned, barely stained, linen white apron she normally wore when baking. She wore a lacy bonnet over her carefully braided hair which she'd secured with two simple wooden combs whose tines wove through the braid and kept her hair in place under her bonnet. She hoped this would be enough to discourage any men of the Ton from thinking she was available to them. Though one never could tell with aristocratic men. There were rakes who toppled chambermaids and others with little regard to either morality or consent. Best to avoid them altogether.

She wished she'd come with one of her sisters to act as a chaperone, but they needed to set up the house for Hanukkah, to make sufganiyot, the fried fruit stuffed dough balls that were such an important part of the holiday, as well as to help prepare the dinner. And truthfully her reputation wasn't in much danger at a party. It wasn't as if she were going to the Baron's house alone.

Naomi had taken a chilly corner away from the fire, which she now regretted. But it was a wonderful position for people watching with her back to the corner, her easel in front of her. She could watch the gentlemen and ladies as they circled, flirted, drank, and chatted, illuminated by the grand chandelier with its dazzling crystals in romantic swirls. The chandelier also cast interesting shadows on the elaborate crown molding, shadowy figures dancing across it.

She did a quick sketch of a group of women talking near the fireplace. She wasn't sure what exactly the Baron wanted her to draw, but these women made a nice grouping and were colored like bright birds in their dresses.

Naomi felt like one of those dusty moths that cling to trees compared to the brightly colored, jewel-bedecked butterflies moving through Lady Mellonbury's townhouse. As she looked up from her easel, one of the butterflies approached. Her nearly translucent gown clung tightly to her torso, emphasizing her elegant bust. Its hem and train, though, fluttered as she moved, shifting the light in iridescent glimmers so that the Lady seemed ethereal, like a member of the fairy folk come to make a claim.

The color and movement caught Naomi's attention. She wished she were bold enough to wear something so fashionable, but she'd be embarrassed to be perceived as immodest as these society women.

"Oh, you are the painter," said the young Lady in the glimmering gown. She walked up to Naomi and peered at her over her easel. Her voice was playful as if Naomi were part of some sort of game she was playing and she was expecting Naomi to utter the code word. Her neck, fingers, and wrists were weighted down with shining gold and gems. Or perhaps those were paste? Naomi didn't know. Either way the Lady looked beautiful and slightly intimidating.

Naomi bobbed a curtsy, hoping it didn't look as clumsy as it felt. "Yes, Lady."

"I am told you wish to paint my image."

Naomi had said no such thing, but it was bad business to contradict powerful people. "It would be my honor, Lady."

"Very well. I will sit for you." She looked pointedly at Naomi who glanced around looking for an appropriate place to pose the lady. There was a large blue and white chinoiserie vase she pulled over next to the chairs. The reflection from it and the chandelier would create a soft reflection on the Lady's hair. She tried to set it closer to the warm areas of the room.

One of the ladies seated on a velvet chair near the easel gave up her seat with a nod and quick, "Lady Elizabeth."

This must be Duke Emmingate's youngest daughter. Naomi heard rumors that Baron Norshire was pursuing her for marriage. At the young woman's glance, Naomi rushed forward, repositioned the chair near her easel, and held it as the lady sat.

Resuming her place at her easel, Naomi scanned the room. Some of the older ladies sat on the oxblood velvet divans and sofas, but most people circulated. It seemed to Naomi that they moved in time with the harpist's music, but it was perhaps a trick of the mind. Every now and then a starchly dressed servant passed among the crowd holding a tray of non-pareils, sweet wafers, and pralongs, which were almonds and orange peel covered in caramel. The hypnotic sweet smell made Naomi's mouth water each time. But none of the sweets were for her. They were for the Ton.

The women not being much better than the men, Naomi normally avoided the Ton assiduously. She'd discovered from long hard experience that although many of them admired her art and wanted her to memorialize them, they were bad clients, often insisting that the benefit to her of drawing them was that they allowed her to spend time in their presence. They always added that the beneficial publicity she would gain would be good for her. But of course one cannot eat publicity. Also, Naomi found she didn't like being condescended to. Even their presence wasn't as much of a treat as they thought it was. At least the Baron was paying for her time here, so she didn't need to broach the topic of money as she painted.

Naomi worked quickly, sketching out the outline of the portrait as the fluttery beau monde pranced and posed for each other, the men in their long coats, tight trousers, and pointed shoes, the women in simple dresses that flowed from the bust in a long column elaborately embroidered at the base. She tried to focus on her subject without being distracted by every unfamiliar sight or smell.

Thankfully, Lady Elizabeth ignored them and sat still. She'd positioned herself well. Naomi had only to suggest she turn and tilt her head just a bit more to better catch the light. As she worked, the Lady's companions, one-by-one, made their excuses and drifted back to the festivities. After a time, Lady Elizabeth herself began looking impatient, her eyes darting to either side, trying to see what she was missing. Naomi needed to hurry.

A deep resonant voice broke through Naomi's concentration. Baron Norshire placed his hand on Lady Elizabeth's shoulder as he spoke. "My dearest, I am so glad you consented to have your portrait done."

A sly look passed over the Lady's face in an instant and was gone. Naomi would have missed it if she hadn't been focusing so closely on her. Then Lady Elizabeth's face changed so that she looked like a cat whose tail had been stepped on.

She stood up and stepped away from the Baron. "You!" she hissed. "You arranged this. It will not work. I will not marry you." She turned to Naomi, her eyes blazed. For a moment Naomi thought she would attack her or take the portrait from the easel.

Naomi stepped back. "I'm sorry, Lady." Her voice stuttered as she spoke. "I seek only to please those assembled here."

The lady snorted in what Naomi thought was a very unladylike way and stalked off heading toward the largest group of revelers. But Naomi thought she heard a light chuckle, as if this were all part of some strange game. The Baron followed Lady Elizabeth, his soft entreaties fading as they left her view.

Naomi sagged in relief, though her hands still shook a bit as she put away the paints and stowed the canvas, replacing it with a blank one. She started sketching some of the older ladies sitting on the green divan. She loved the way their conspiratorial smiles and whispered gossip removed years from their faces. Whatever the Baron sought to achieve, it was none of her concern. She just needed to last a short time more.

Her father would be here soon, and they would return home to latkes, the Hanukkah lights, and the love of her family. She could taste the fried potato pancakes in her imagination. Then they would go to the synagogue for the first night's mingling with the rest of the Jewish community. Erev Hanukkah started this year on Shabbat, which meant plenty of time spent with her friends in the synagogue. She couldn't wait.

BENJAMIN'S STOMACH TURNED OVER. THE SYNAGOGUE was a mess. One of the stained-glass windows had been broken. The pieces were scattered across the floor, sparkling in the dim light. The stink of the street and an abundance of light poured through the hole. Clearly that was how the thieves had entered. They broke the window and opened the door once they were inside.

Rabbi Levitan's wife and daughter picked up the pieces and placed the large ones carefully in a box as they spoke quietly to each other, discussing which pieces could be reused when they repaired the window.

Benjamin stooped and began helping, picking up other items the thieves had tossed about, looking for valuables. Prayer books, several yarmulkes, and tallit littered the floor. He picked up a one of the tallit, a blue and white prayer shawl, and folded it carefully ensuring that the fringes were tucked neatly inside to keep them safe. Fringes (or tsitsit) reminded him of his obligations to the Holy One and folding his prayer shawl was something he did each time services were concluded, so bringing this one back in order felt like a bit of a relief in the face of such a large mess.

The large Hanukkah menorah was missing as well as other items, including the silver yad, the ornate silver rod used to point at the text while reading the Torah. Rabbi Levitan himself was speaking to a constable, a slender wiry man with a nervous mien. He was listing everything that had been stolen, which thankfully didn't include the Torah scrolls themselves. Did it make sense for the synagogue to use its meagre funds to hire a thief catcher? Or should they just cut their losses, repairing and replacing what they could? Perhaps hire a guard? That was for the synagogue elders to decide, one of whom was his father. They'd undoubtedly discuss it later.

Finished with the constable, Rabbi Levitan to Benjamin. "Where is your father, Benjamin? I sent a runner to summon the elders. I'd hoped to speak to your father before the others arrived."

"My father is in Paris on business. I'm taking care of the shop in his absence. I will do anything I can to help."

Rabbi Levitan pursed his lips, pushing them in and out, clearly thinking and finally he threw up his hands. "Adonai brings what he brings. He gave us the miracle of the oil, perhaps he will provide another, a miracle of silver, yes?"

That made no sense at all to Benjamin but he slowly nodded, encouraging Rabbi Levitan to continue speaking. Not that the rabbi generally needed encouragement to talk. His loquaciousness was known to all and the frequent subject of well-meaning gibes and jokes by his congregants. The rabbi was like a flowing river of words, mostly good words, but word after word after word. It was quite a change from Benjamin's father whose taciturnity was also routinely commented on. A silversmith, his shop was a place of quiet focus.

"See our synagogue?" Rabbi Levitan gestured around taking in the broken window, the toppled chairs on the bimah, the raised stage where services were conducted and where the ark holding the sacred scrolls was kept. Wrapped in its embroidered blue velvet mantle with the crest of Judah, all that could be seen of the Torah were the large wood rods used to roll the parchment scroll. Placed carefully on the wooden table on the bimah, the Torah was the only item not in disarray.

Benjamin guessed the Torah had been found on the floor. Probably the first thing the rabbi did on discovering the break-in was to right the table, ensure the Torah was undamaged, cover it with its mantle, and place it on the table. The heavy bound book with the Haftorah portion, which would be read for Hanukkah, had been pushed aside to make room for the Torah.

The ark behind them, where the Torah scrolls were normally stored with other items, was open and empty. This synagogue owned just two Torah scrolls and one of them was out for repair. A tear or crack in the parchment made the Torah scroll unkosher and unusable, so it was critical to have at least two Torah scrolls. Benjamin's father had started a collection to buy a third Torah scroll so that there would never be a time when they wouldn't have a kosher Torah for services. It looked like that money would have to go to fixing the synagogue instead. Benjamin sighed at the thought of it.

"All this," the rabbi continued, indicating the debris the robbers left in their wake, "is temporary. What matters is bringing our community together. Hanukkah is far from the most important holiday, but it provides us an opportunity. We haven't the wherewithal to replace all that was stolen, but we can repair the damage and rededicate our synagogue, much as the Maccabees did the temple in Jerusalem."

"There's hardly any time," Benjamin said. "The first night of Hanukkah is tonight."

"True," Rabbi Levitan said, "but Avram, one of the elders, is a glazier. Perhaps he can repair the window. That just leaves the menorah. For the rest, we'll just have to see. We may have to wait until next year to replace everything, but a menorah is essential." Changing the subject, the rabbi added "I trust you'll be here for services tonight?"

"Unless I'm in the shop working on the menorah." Benjamin made his voice light, but his heart was heavy. This was a very bad situation. He stroked his chin, not realizing for a moment that he'd adopted his father's movements while thinking.

Rabbi Levitan was right. They had to have a menorah for tonight's service. Everyone would expect it to be lit before the Shabbat candles. Since the Shabbat candles had to be lit at sunset and it was forbidden to light so much as a single candle after the pair of Shabbat candles were lit and sending their warming light over the assembled, they had very little time to get the menorah ready.

He thought through the problem. The menorah stolen from the synagogue had been a large brass one with a place for the shamash candle, the source of fire to light the wicks pushed into the eight little wells of oil. It stood tall on the bimah, ensuring that everyone could see it. There was no way his family could afford to donate that much silver, and even if they could, he couldn't finish such a large, fine piece in a day or two.

The synagogue door opened as he was looking around for inspiration. It was Mr. Goldin accompanied by his daughter. She looked radiant, dressed in blue covered with little white flowers. Her hair braided and mostly concealed under a lace bonnet couldn't disguise the rich brown, sparkling like coffee from one of the cafes dotting the streets of London. For a moment he couldn't pull his eyes away from her form, barely disguised by the modest dress or her plump lips. Then he realized he was staring at her, and in a synagogue of all places. He dropped his eyes while he tried to reassemble his scattered senses. As he did, he noted that her fingers were covered in red and green paint. How odd.

Menorah. Right. Focus, Benjamin, he heard his father's voice in his mind. He swallowed and deliberately turned back to the Rabbi, who looked delighted. "Mr. Goldin! Naomi! Thank you both for coming."

Mr. Goldin said in his deep clear voice that Benjamin heard often since the man served as the head of the synagogue's building committee and was often making announcements after Shabbat prayers. "We are here to help, Rabbi. What can we do?"

NAOMI AND HER FATHER WALKED INTO THE SYNAGOGUE to find it a mess. The synagogue should be a place of calm and learning. Its scrupulously clean stone floor and walls were kept in perfect shape by the women of one of the congregation's families in rotation but now the floors were covered with glass and debris. Naomi's family had last taken a rotation a few months ago. It wasn't their turn today, but the Rabbi had sent a runner to ask for her father's help and he naturally brought Naomi with him after retrieving her from the Baron's home.

Normally Naomi sat with the other women on the balcony, and she usually accompanied her mother and sisters up the stairs to get good seats. Her familiarity with the main floor was limited. She looked around, seeing the synagogue from a different perspective. The broken window sent a shaft of sunlight illuminating the Torah scroll on the old wooden table that usually held prayerbooks. She would love to paint it just like that, as if it were touched by the Almighty, elevating the simple to the divine.

What truly captivated her attention, though, was the man standing next to Rabbi Levitan. He was perhaps twenty-five, a few years older than her, with soft serious eyes and curly black hair. He had muscular forearms and rough, capable hands. His creamy olive-complected skin was smooth and unmarked by the residue of any pox. She'd seen him before but only from a distance. This close he was quite impressive.

Why was he staring at her? Then, in her horror she realized she was staring back.

She dropped her eyes, her cheeks hot. His gaze felt invasive and yet good at the same time. She glanced up at him through her eyelashes, wishing that her pulse wasn't racing in such an uncommon way or that her skin didn't suddenly feel as if the slightest touch would ripple through her.

The Rabbi spoke into her confused emotions. "Naomi, thank you for coming. Talk to Chavah. She will set you to work. Now, Benjamin, how can we arrange for a replacement menorah tonight?"

Naomi nodded, glanced quickly at Benjamin before joining Rebbetzin Levitan near the windows. She was hard at work picking up pieces of stained glass and sorting them into boxes. Chavah, the rebbetzin, had always been kind to Naomi, but she was an intimidating woman. It was rumored that she was nearly as learned as her husband, Rabbi Levitan. Certainly, she was the one all the women turned to when they needed a religious opinion on a sensitive matter, trusting that if she didn't know she would discreetly ask the rabbi.

"Tsk, tsk," Chavah clucked. "You have come dressed in your fancy clothing. I have no use for cleaners who can't kneel down in the dust."

Naomi laughed at that. The floor was clean enough to prepare dinner on. "I am here to help. Dresses can be cleaned."

Chava pursed her lips and shook her head. "No. I would not have you look frowsy for your Hanukkah celebration. We are still trying to make a complete list of the items stolen to give to the thief catchers. Look around and if you think something is missing, make a note of it. You can write, can't you?"

"Of course. I read and write in English, Spanish, and French and I can read my prayers in Hebrew, though I am not as learned as you are."

Chavah smiled. "English will do. You have been in this synagogue your entire life and you have a gift for art. Use your gifts to observe and make a list of everything you don't see."

"The practice of art is to notice those things one sees, not things one does not."

"A poor practice it is then. For it is the things that are invisible like hatred or the Almighty or love that truly change the world. Now look around while we finish picking up the glass."

Naomi nodded, took the proffered paper and pencil and began her list. If the thief stole the menorah, perhaps he was after the fine metal items. Sure enough, the silver filigree yad, used by the Torah reader to point out the passage, was missing. The thief must have thought the elegant swirling filigree design made from intricately curved silver threads running along its length was a piece of jewelry. Certainly, it resembled some of the fancier hair ornaments she'd seen. Though she herself didn't have anything quite so fancy.

She looked for the Shabbat candlesticks and found them in the cabinet where they belonged. Perhaps the thief hadn't realized it was a cabinet since it blended into the decorative woodwork carved with depictions of the Shabbat essentials: candlesticks, the braided challah bread, a spice box, and a wine goblet.

As she worked, she found herself unconsciously moving nearer and nearer to Benjamin. Was he the son of Mr. Argentiere the silversmith? He must be, mustn't he? She was sure she'd seen him with his father. Where was his father?

She told herself that she was just curious about the arrangements her father was making. Her father offered to create a large wooden stand tonight. Benjamin offered to modify silver cups to make the oil cups that would need to be lit for Hanukkah. Naomi didn't know how her father would get it done on time. Or whether Benjamin could meet his obligation. But her task was to list stolen items, so she focused on that. Or at least she focused the best she could with Benjamin in close proximity. It seemed to her that her entire body buzzed when she stepped close to him. When she thought no one would notice, she watched him as he spoke and gesticulated.

Eventually, Benjamin and her father left to craft the menorah cups and the wooden holder.

Naomi continued her task while she talked casually with the other women as they set the room to right. She handed her list to Naomi, though she didn't know that she'd remembered everything missing.

Chavah looked around with a smile of satisfaction. "Nicely done, everyone. Tonight, when the Sabbath Bride enters her home, she will find it ready for her and ready for Hanukkah. There is nothing holier than making space for Shabbat. Now go home and do the same for your houses."

But when Naomi arrived home, she found an urgent summons waiting for her from the Baron of Norshire: a demand that she appear before him immediately with the picture of Lady Elizabeth. She sighed but packed up to go, looking for her sister, Dinah, who would make an adequate chaperone. It was bad enough that she'd been alone in Lady Mellonbury's townhouse, but at least that had been a house party. She couldn't protect her reputation if she were alone with the Baron in his private residence. What would people think?

THE BARON'S TOWNHOUSE WAS ONE OF THE GRANDER ones on Arlington Street. Benjamin stared at the imposing door, gathering courage to knock when he was joined by Naomi Goldin carrying a large sketchbook and a pencil case and a younger woman that had to be Naomi's sister based on the same chestnut brown hair, large brown eyes, and similar bone structure. The sister had a book that she was clutching. It looked like one of those dreadful women's drawing room stories that were so popular.

"It is good to see you again, Miss Goldin. This must be your sister. What brings you here?"

Naomi smiled and it was dazzling. His heart began pounding in a thoroughly inappropriate manner. "I was summoned by the Baron. I am not certain as to why. Dinah insisted on accompanying me as a chaperone."

With some relief he turned toward the younger Miss Goldin, catching her as she was rolling her eyes. "Very wise, Miss Goldin. One cannot be too careful with one's reputation."

"I guess," said Dinah Goldin. She fingered the novel, looking at it longingly.

Benjamin knocked on the imposing door. A fat, imperious butler welcomed them into the house, closing the door against the cold. The warmth of the residence greeted them. Benjamin was glad to hand his coat over. The butler then hurried the three of them across a marble floor in the elegant foyer. Benjamin caught sight of a variety of intricate silver candelabras that he thought his father might have crafted for the Baron. The largest stood almost three feet high, its five branches shaped like vines curling around tree limbs. The delicacy and precision of the work was a marker of his father's work. It had been placed on a carved stone tripod table with Egyptian figures holding up the tabletop. The candelabra drew the eye up to a ceiling, pale blue and painted with clouds.

They were led into the Baron's library where they found the Baron sitting behind a large wooden desk festooned with carved wooden birds of various types. Benjamin thought one was a crane, but he wasn't positive.

"Mr. Benjamin Argentiere and Naomi and Dinah Goldin, Sir," the butler said as he motioned them in. The smell of old books, leather, and brandy greeted him as he entered.

The Baron raised his head and narrowed his eyes glaring at Benjamin. "You are late. And where is your father?" he said, irritation lacing his voice.

Dinah took a seat in an overstuffed chair by the fire, opened her book and started reading, ignoring the rest of them. The Baron didn't even seem to notice her. Naomi proffered her sketchbook to the Baron who bent over it and nodded.

Benjamin bowed. "My deepest apologies. I didn't get your invitation until I arrived home. I came as soon as I could. My father is in Paris. I am his representative while he is away."

In fact, Benjamin had arrived home only to learn that he had a summons from the Baron of Norshire. Dave, one of the apprentices, looked quite panicked by the visit, which probably meant that the Baron's runner had threatened him with dire consequences if Benjamin or his father didn't appear promptly at his townhouse. He realized that he had no choice but to go. The Baron was powerful enough to destroy their business with just a word. If he were truly angry, they could lose their lease. He couldn't put his father in a position with the Baron that would result in harm to his business or his father's reputation.

Nonetheless the Hanukkah menorah dilemma was also a flaming problem. So, he took the time needed to instruct Dave and the other two apprentices on what he needed them to do with the cups to make them oil pans for the menorah, gave them strict orders to start immediately, putting aside the rest of their commissions, and then set off to the Baron's townhouse.

The Baron nodded, not at all mollified by the apology. "Since you are both here, we can discuss the important commission I need the two of you to undertake. It must be completed by tomorrow."

"Tomorrow?" Benjamin and Naomi's startled voices rang in unison.

The Baron nodded, clearly pleased that they understood. "Tomorrow. And if I do not have it before tomorrow's soiree, I shall be most displeased." His voice dropped and a chill entered it that caused the small hairs on Benjamin's neck to stiffen. "There will be consequences."

"What can we do for you, Sir?" Naomi's voice sounded clear and unafraid. She had courage, Benjamin thought. Or perhaps she didn't understand the gravity of the situation.

"I am proposing to Lady Elizabeth of Emmingate at tomorrow's ball. It is imperative that she accept."

A cloud passed over Naomi's features. "Lady Elizabeth, Sir?" She tapped her drawing. "This Lady Elizabeth?"

"Indeed so! She needs proof of my serious intent. Her father needs to know of my wealth. And her mother needs to know of my good taste. That is where you come in." He ran his finger gently across the drawing in what was almost a caress. "I need a silver box with her painted image on the front. It must be fancy and worthy of a Duke's daughter. Perhaps with our names entwined."

"By tomorrow?" Benjamin choked out. "That is impossible."

Naomi's eyes dilated in shock. "Tomorrow?" she whispered. "Surely not?"

"Nothing is impossible to a man of industry and intelligence."

"But...."

The Baron pushed his hand through the air. It was an aggressive move that showed a man fully cognizant of his power over them. "I will not hear objections. Your father would do this for me. You will as well, or you will endure my displeasure."

Benjamin gulped. He noticed that Naomi had retrieved her pad and started sketching. She was a quiet girl. So, it was up to him.

"Sir, tonight is the first night of Hanukkah," Benjamin said. "It takes time to make these things. We have other obligations."

The Baron shook his head, his lip quirking. "Your father once told me that Jews work on Hanukkah. This is work. I expect it to be done."

"It would take a miracle."

Naomi spoke at last. "Sir, if it were just the Lady's fine head, would that work? Perhaps on wood set into the silver box?"

The Baron nodded slowly.

Naomi turned her attention to Benjamin. Her eyes sent promises, but of what he didn't know. He only knew that he wished those promises were of a more intimate sort. "Could you set a panel of wood in the box? Would that be difficult?"

"I could. The difficulty is in the fine silverwork."

She nodded her head, already back with her sketchpad. She was the most unusual woman Benjamin had ever met. Not that his experience with women had much breadth. He mostly knew his sister and her friends, a giggling, unserious group. He watched her work, her head bent, a slight smile curving her extremely kissable mouth. He needed to focus.

He pulled his gaze back to Baron Norshire and made a counterproposal. "Baron, could we have a week? Will you delay your proposal?"

Naomi cleared her throat. When she spoke her voice was as silky a voice as Benjamin had ever heard. "Mr. Argentiere is right. A delay will work in your favor. The Lady fled you earlier. Perhaps you should let her cool down before you propose."

The Baron shook his head sadly. "There is a deadline. If I cannot persuade her, and more importantly, her father the Duke, she is due to leave on a ship to the Continent where she will meet other men. I have only this opportunity. I cannot wait. That is why the box you make must be so beautiful it takes her breath away."

Naomi nodded and resumed sketching furiously.

Benjamin felt a heaviness descend upon his limbs. There was no right answer here. Either way they would fail. He should tell the Baron that this was impossible and advise him to find a new plan to win Lady Elizabeth. He tapped his fingers on the desk and looked around the library, noticing the quantity of silver items for the first time. The Baron had excellent taste and a real passion for small silver boxes. It made sense that he wanted a box for the woman he wished to marry.

"Sir, perhaps we could modify one of your fine silver boxes," Benjamin said, pointing at one that seemed like a good size. "It would look better, would be faster, and you would not be out of pocket quite as much."

The Baron, whose face had been descending into a dark red angry tone lightened. "A box for a bride?" he murmured to himself. "A good trade." He steepled his hands and gave a little nod. "Very well. But it must be beautiful."

Naomi turned her sketchpad over. She'd drawn an elaborate fili-gree design consisting of delicately curved leaves and stems with tiny roses bent from silver, the elaborate swirls and bends lent an airiness to the design. "Would this design do, Sir?"

Benjamin shook his head vehemently, trying to catch her before she got them further into hot water.

The Baron smiled. "It would indeed. Young man, look around my library and pick the box best suited. I shall return momentarily."

As he left, Benjamin whispered to Naomi, "What are you about? That will take a week or more to do that design."

"You don't trust in Hanukkah miracles, Mr. Argentiere?"

He could easily be persuaded by those dark, melting eyes, he thought, but he shook his head. "In my experience what we call miracles are the result of hard work."

Now she was laughing at him. He could see it in the set of her cheeks and her eyes which danced in the light. She motioned to her sister. "Dinah, please come over here and let down your hair."

Dinah hesitated but a moment, then removed her shawl where it covered her head and pulled two filigree silver combs from her hair, a perfect match for the design Naomi sketched.

Naomi made a little flourish as she presented the silver combs to Benjamin. "We Jews are children of miracles, are we not? Could we have survived so long without Hanukkah miracles?"

He stared into her eyes, which were filled with mischief and triumph. It could work.

"How long would it take to make the item if you had these? And your clever suggestion of a finished box?"

"How long will it take you to paint the inset?"

"Not long. I already have the sketches I made at the party and the Baron has approved them. I can have it done by this afternoon. Can you do it all and still be ready with a menorah for the synagogue?"

"God willing." He placed the combs in his pocket, much to the irritation of Dinah.

Naomi saw her sister's frown and patted the younger girl's hands. "You shall have my fanciest combs, Dinah, whichever ones you want. Just help us with this."

"Momma will notice."

"Leave it to me to explain."

THE BALCONY THAT CONSTITUTED THE WOMEN'S SECTION of the synagogue wrapped around the room. A railing kept the women safely in place. Wooden chairs that matched the ones the men sat in on the ground floor formed two rows on the balcony. There weren't enough seats if all the women in the community attended, but except for the High Holidays, most women took time away from synagogue to make food or take care of children or just because the synagogue was focused on the men.

Those women who attended brought babies, knitting, and prayer books. They chatted quietly, stopping to recite the necessary prayers or wipe the nose of a toddler before resuming their quiet gossip. They dressed in their finest, wearing their expensive perfume, and for those who could afford it, fur wraps. It was a medley of fragrances from baby poop to French perfumes and leather.

That evening, Naomi sat nervously wrapping and rewrapping her shawl. Nearby Dinah showed off her new combs to her friends who were suitably impressed and talking quietly, their heads angling together. Naomi's own hair was braided up and under a shawl held in place by a few ordinary pins. Perhaps she would get new combs with her share of the money. Or perhaps not if the Baron didn't pay.

Her father claimed that as unpleasant as he could be, the Baron was a man of his word. Money. Mmmm. Having money of her own would be a delightful and new experience.

If this worked.

If the baron was happy.

So many ifs.

She had finished her portion of the work, using one of her father's scraps of wood from another project. Painting the portrait a second time was easy and fast, and she'd sent it to Benjamin in just a few hours. She hoped the work had gone well for Benjamin.

She looked over the balcony at the assembled men, her eyes searching for him. There was Papa, looking fine in his best coat. He stood up when the service was almost over to announce that there would be a collection to replace the items stolen and to pay for thief catchers.

"Gentlemen," he said, his voice serious and earnest, "it must never be understood that the Jews of London can be robbed with impunity. I urge you to donate generously so that we may catch these reprobates."

After the service she went slowly down the stairs, hoping she would see Benjamin. Her heart sank when she realized he wasn't there. It wasn't just that it meant that they might have failed, she actually missed him. She remembered his fine features, his curly black hair, his slight scent of lavender and cloves. What did it mean that he was missing Friday night services? She determined she would look for him when she returned to synagogue the next morning for Saturday morning's Shabbat services.

SHABBAT MORNING BENJAMIN WOKE UP AND CHECKED ON the silver box. He'd worked through the first night of Hanukkah and into the night, when Shabbat began, until he'd finished the box, allowing everything to set overnight. He hoped no one would find out that he'd worked on Shabbat evening. His parents were in Paris, so as long as no one told on him, he'd have no problems other than those imposed by his own conscience.

He picked up the box. It was a thing of beauty with Naomi's painting and the filigree combs transforming it to something truly special. He was amazed that Naomi had finished the painting so quickly and had it delivered to him that afternoon. He wished the box was a present from him to Naomi. Since she'd given up her combs for the joint effort, perhaps he would make her a better set of combs.

He wrapped it and called for a runner to bring it to the Baron. Then he dressed for morning services.

Naomi ran up to him after morning services. His gaze lingered on her as she ran down the stairs seeing the energy and lightness in her step. He felt his heartbeat moving in time with her steps. He breathed in the light floral musk of her and wished they were somewhere private.

"Is it done?" she asked.

He nodded. "I sent it to the Baron along with our bill."

Saturday night, the Havdalah ceremony at the home of Naomi's family marked the end of Shabbat with the light of the braided Havdalah candle, the strong smell of dried oranges, cinnamon, cloves, and rose petals from the spice box, and a sip of sweet red wine. That evening Naomi's parents invited Benjamin's family over for dinner to celebrate Havdalah and the second night of Hanukkah with them.

The living room of their small townhouse was filled with chairs pulled from other areas of the house. Benjamin was seated at the adult table, while Naomi was seated with her sisters at the children's table. He wished she'd been seated near him. The air filled with the smell of fried latkes and sweet sufganiyot. The noise level with the adult conversations of politics and the raucous dreidel game at the children's table was loud and joy filled. But Benjamin felt as if he were in a silent tunnel, focused only on Naomi. She occasionally glanced at him under her lashes and his heart trilled.

With Havdalah came another Hanukkah miracle. A knock at the door announced a runner with prompt payment from the Baron and a scrawled thank you note. The timing was fortunate. With Shabbat over, they could again handle money and attend to financial matters.

"It looks like the silver box and the Baron's ardent declaration of love so enchanted Lady Elizabeth and her father the Duke of Emmingate that she allowed him to press his suit," Benjamin said, reading the note. "Further, she has delayed her trip to the Continent until the new year to allow him time to woo her properly."

Naomi laughed. "I knew something was going on there. Lady Elizabeth is a clever woman. She has plans and they clearly include the Baron."

"I think the Baron may truly love her."

A smile transformed Naomi from merely beautiful to angelic. "I told you that Hanukkah miracles are real. Look at all we did in just one day."

He nodded. "We make a good team."

She went shy suddenly, blushing and smiling a secret little smile and twisting a bit. "We do," she said.

"Perhaps we should explore that further. After all, some Hanukkah miracles are better than others. We might find that the best miracles are yet to come."

She patted a tendril of hair that had slipped from her shawl and gazed up at him. "I'd like that."

He'd start on a set of combs for her tomorrow.

C. S. Stein is the pen name of Carolyn and Steve Stein. Steve is an award-winning military historian, specializing in military history and strategy. He's written seven books, spanning topics in military, maritime, and sexual history, including his popular volume Military Strategy for Writers.

In addition, Steve and Carolyn have written several gaming books and short stories together. They bend toward historical fiction. Carolyn writes short stories ranging from historical fantasy to romance to science fiction, and has been published in a variety of venues.

C. S. Stein can be found at https://cs-stein.com.

This story, they say, resulted from a challenge.

"Could we come up with a story set within the Regency period, centering on Jewish characters and a Hanukkah theme? Since Jewish

characters could not be dukes or earls or marry dukes or earls, and since most Regency stories were about the Ton, this was a stumper. We came up with the idea of a silversmith, a synagogue with a missing menorah before Hanukkah, and a Baron with a problem. The story took off from there.

"It's a Regency story with a Regency romance, but it is told from the point of view of the middle-class Jews observing the hijinks, whilst falling in love on their own."

A Major Christmas Eve

ROBERT J. MCCARTER

I FIRST MET CLAIR THOMPSON ON A FROSTY NEW YEAR'S Eve day in 1971 when we were sledding down the steepest, scariest hill around. I was eight, she was nine, and she was about three inches taller than me and appeared to be much older. That day I, literally, looked up to her.

She had red hair in tight curls that snuck out from under her white knit hat with a big yarn pompom on top. Her blue eyes were as intense as the crystalline blue sky and her face was freckly even though all that remained of summer were a few brown leaves stubbornly clinging to the scrub oak trees that were scattered amongst the tall, snow-flocked pines. Her coat was redder than her hair and she had on some of those fancy ski pants so that her jeans weren't soaked through like mine.

The first words Clair ever said to me was, "Race ya?" She had this lopsided grin on her face that told me two things. She liked to compete and she was used to winning.

We were on top of "Sledder's Hill," a hill so steep that any respectable adult would absolutely not let their kids sled down it without supervision. Well, any respectable adult these days. This was

1971 and the rules were different. That said, this was a steep and scary tree-covered hill perched above a city park with a wide bald spot that attracted daring sledders of all stripes like bees to the spring flowers.

That winter the snows had come heavy and hard. It had been unseasonably warm the previous day, softening the snow some but then it had snapped cold, hardening the snowpack. Last night a brief storm had flocked everything with fresh white. The sun was out and it was cold, the sledding just couldn't get any better.

We both had Flexible Flyer sleds, the ones with wooden bases and metal rails, not the silly plastic things you see these days. I eyed her up, noticing that she was heavier than I was so gravity was on her side, but my runners were waxed and I was ready to go and I sure didn't want a girl to beat me.

"Sure," I said and turned to my buddy Clint Evans who was next in line. "Will you start us?"

Clint was my age and about my height but was clearly destined to be a football player, where at that age I looked like I was destined to be a basketball player. Clint was missing one of his front teeth and eagerly nodded his assent with a gape-toothed grin.

Clair and I stood there, our shoulders nearly touching as we held our sleds, ready to leap onto them and start the thrilling, eye-watering plunge down Sledder's Hill.

"On your marks!" Clint said.

"You ain't gotta chance," Clair said to me.

"Get set!" Clint yelled.

"Wanna bet?" I countered.

"Sure," she said, her words quick to get them in. "Five bucks."

"Go!" Clint shouted.

After that day on Sleder's Hill, I didn't see Clair Thompson for almost fifty years.

I remember that day as this sparkling, shiny representation of the best part of my childhood. Exciting. Brisk. Flocked in snow. Full of laughter, thrills, and fun.

Clair won the first run down the hill, so I challenged her to race back up to the top of the hill, which was no picnic given how icy the snow was under the fresh powder.

I won the climb up and then the second run down.

After a while Clair wasn't a girl to me anymore, not at that age where I was so suspicious of girls and catching "cooties." She was just a friend. We went at it for hours, betting and racing under the sparkling blue skies with laughter our near constant companion.

When the sun started sinking to the horizon and our competition was even with each of us winning eleven times, we stood at the bottom of Sledder's Hill looking at each other. For the first time in hours, staring at her ruddy cheeks, the red of it seeming to merge her constellation of freckles into an ocean of them, I realized that she was a girl and I was a boy and that someday that just might mean something.

At that moment, I didn't know her name and she didn't know mine. We had just been kids together doing something we both loved so much.

"That was great," she said. "Thanks."

She turned to go and I said, "Wait!"

I felt my cheeks redden because the stupid word had just snuck out without my brain fully evaluating the implications. I knew she was from out of town and visiting her uncle. I knew she lived in Southern California and there were no good sledding hills or snow to speak of.

I realized I didn't know her name and suddenly it was very important that I at least know her name.

"I... Ummm..." I stammered. "What's, you know, your name?"

Her head cocked to the side and her blue eyes got all intense and she took a step forward. "Why do you wanna know?"

"It's... you know... been fun. And I just wanna know who I had the best sledding day of my life with."

I'm quite sure my cheeks were redder than Rudolph's nose by several shades.

Her face was relaxed and still while my heart hammered hard in my chest so it could pump most of my blood supply to my traitorous cheeks. But then her face broke into a smile and I swear it was like the sun coming out after a terrible storm. It was so bright it seemed to warm my very soul.

She stepped up to me and extended her mittened hand. "Clair Thompson. My name is Clair Thompson. And yours?"

I took her hand in mine and said, "Billy Major. Really glad to meetcha."

FAST FORWARD TO 2020. I'M FIFTY-SEVEN-YEARS OLD, widowed and running "Major Books." It's located in the historic red-bricked downtown of the same mountain town that contains Sledder's Hill, the town I've spent my entire life in.

These days the city does their best to keep people off Sledder's Hill. There's been a few sad accidents and the world seems much more serious than it did back then. I know I am much more serious.

When you're a kid it all seems like possibilities, but as you age the reality of limitations set in. Beyond making a living there are harder things to deal with like cancer and a seriously empty nest when your daughter leaves for college after your wife has shuffled off her mortal coil.

And being a business owner is no picnic. Don't get me wrong, I love it. I get to spend my days around books and people who love books, but it's harder keeping a bookstore afloat these days than it used to be.

Perhaps it was all of this, perhaps it was the slow work of time, but the next time I, literally, ran into Clair Thompson, I did not recognize her, which was, probably, for the best.

"HEY, JANNIE," I CALLED FROM THE VERY SMALL AND VERY crowded storage room of Major Books. "Where's the copies of *Little Women* we got in? The movie is a Christmas release, we need to get those out."

We called it a storage room, but it was about twice as big as a modest coat closet with just enough room to squeeze in between the shelves on three sides.

I love the smell of the room, all fresh paper and ink, whispering of unimagined adventures yet to be experienced. I don't know about you, but reading has, quite literally, saved my life more than once. When the dark times come, you can always find a friendly place to escape to in the pages of a good book.

"Top shelf," Jannie called. "Right side. In the box marked 'Little W.'"

Having aging eyes and still fighting wearing the readers—if I can find them—plus having employees younger than my daughter leaves me in this situation fairly often. They write small and sloppy, which works for younger eyes but not for my decidedly middle-aged eyes.

I snagged the two cases of books from the top shelf while at the same time assuring myself that this qualified as exercise and my growing midsection still wasn't that bad. Besides, now that Paula was gone, who the hell cares anyway?

The books are movie tie-in with a shot of Saoirse Ronan as the defiant Jo March on the cover.

To tell you the truth, these tie-in books are not my favorite for a couple of reasons. While I'm sure Ms. Ronan does a fine job as Jo March, it puts an image into the reader's head instead of letting them create their own images. And while these tie-in books often move pretty quickly, they age just as quickly.

My eight-year-old promise of height did not come to pass, so as I maneuvered around customers and between shelves of books and tourists tchotchkes, with the two cases of heavy books and some *Cosmopolitan* and *Wired Magazine* stacked on top, it was a bit of a trick.

I know better. I should be carrying less. I should be taking care of my back. I should not be risking running into a customer like this, but I was in a hurry.

"Got the new Patterson, Will?" Henry Martin asked as I scooted by with my too-heavy load.

I discarded Billy not long after I met Clair Thompson and go by Will now.

"Up front," I said. "New Pattersons are always up front."

The store is long and narrow with high ceilings with the original stamped-tin ceiling tiles of this historic building. There are tall bookshelves along the walls, a central corridor, and smaller bookshelves arranged at a slight angle off of it. The floors are hardwood and what walls are exposed are a lovely light blue.

On the thin section of wall above the bookshelves are lots of mountain-town-type decorations. An old sign declaring how many miles to the Grand Canyon, antique skis and toboggans, an old miner's pick axe, and along the back wall was my trusty Flexible Flyer sled.

It 'tis the season, so the place was decked out for it with tinsel garlands hanging from that high ceiling with shiny blue, red, and green oversized ornaments hanging from them. There are multiple elves on shelves holding small placards pointing out great gift giving ideas—and a place to buy your own elf to sit on a shelf. There were live poinsettia plants on empty places on the shelves, and gold and silver bows here, there, and everywhere.

In the small open-ish area in back of the store was a live, in-a-pot Christmas tree decorated with the same colors as the ceiling with brightly wrapped faux presents underneath.

I truly love this place. Many days I think running it will be the death of me, but I do love it.

It's not only the books, there's so much of my Paula in it. This was her dream, not mine. I was content with my small accounting business, but she thought what our little town needed was a great bookstore.

So we built one. With sweat and credit and sleepless nights and lots of gray hairs. It was touch and go for the first five years, but it ended up taking and Paula was right, it was exactly what this little town needed.

After we lost Paula's hellish fifteen-month battle with pancreatic cancer, I almost closed the store because it was just too much. There was too much of Paula here and it hurt to be close to it.

But time mellowed that and I'm glad I kept the store because down each aisle is a memory or many memories. The controversial title we debated stocking, the argument we had over what font to use on the wooden signs that mark the sections—she wanted sans-serif while I was stuck on serif. And this time of year all the little Christmas touches she insisted on that bring the season to life.

When you look at a store like this with the thousands of products each in its own place but making a cohesive whole, it's easy to overlook the tens of thousands of decisions that went into creating it, the seemingly endless long nights, the love it took to get past all the hard parts.

Honestly, I wouldn't recommend starting a business like this with your spouse unless you are very comfortable working on your relationship, because if there are cracks in it, they are going to come out.

I managed to make it to the front of the store without hurting myself or colliding with a customer. I even dropped off the magazines at the rack along the wall with no trouble.

I was very focused and this is why I didn't notice the woman browsing the bargain table.

At the front of the store we have two display tables, the "spotlight" table, where I was setting up *Little Women*, and the "bargain" table. This was Paula's idea since some folks only want bargains and some folks want the latest and the greatest.

I used the utility knife that is always in my back pocket, opened the cases up, and started setting up the movie tie-in copies of *Little Women*.

It was a Tuesday morning, which isn't a busy time. So while Jannie was busy with the books—having been an accountant full time, I am happy to let her be our bookkeeper—I was doing setups and fussing over the store like with the *Little Women* spotlight.

It was when I stepped back to admire my work, which consisted of low shelves showing off the book with backups arranged into a large "W," that I felt myself collide with another human being.

"I'm so sorry," I said as I turned around and took a real look at the customer.

She was a tall woman, somewhere in her fifties, with sky-blue eyes and curly red hair that she was gracefully letting slide towards gray. She was wearing a long brown coat and remarkably sensible shoes, hiking boots to be specific.

Paula always encouraged me to notice shoes, particularly women's shoes. She told me that there's a lot that can be gleaned from that choice and the condition of the shoe.

The customer had a cup of coffee in her hand, and I could see that the bump I had delivered had sloshed it onto some of the books on the bargain table.

"I'm so clumsy," she said.

"It was me," I insisted. "Don't know what it is about getting older, but I seem less aware of my surroundings than I used to be."

She stopped and looked me up and down. At this moment I most certainly did not recognize the girl I had spent a day sledding with all those years ago. That girl was hidden behind nearly fifty years of life, but it seemed like maybe she recognized something about me.

At work I have what Paula termed a "professorial" appearance. That day I was wearing jeans, a button-down tan shirt, and a gray tweed jacket complete with elbow patches. I too was letting the gray invade my brown hair, not because I liked it but because there was no way in hell I was going to start dying my hair and worrying about roots showing. I definitely didn't have time for that.

"Have we met?" she asked, a small smile playing on her lips somehow drawing attention to her abundant freckles.

"Maybe," I said. "If we have, it was probably here. I practically live here."

She shook her head. "No. I've never been in here. I live in L.A."

"I'm sorry," I interjected, hoping my smile would communicate the spirit in which the comment was intended. There was something about her and for some reason I wanted to make her smile.

She did smile slightly and shrugged. "It has its advantages. My uncle just died. I'm here taking care of things."

"Oh," I said. "I really am sorry. Who was your uncle? Town this size, there's a good chance I knew him."

Something passed over her face. It was just a moment, but she looked much older and much sadder. "Evan," she said. "Evan Michaels."

I nodded. "I heard he was sick, sorry to hear of his passing. I did know him, he loved old-school mysteries. Christie. Hammett. Spillane. Chandler. That kind of stuff."

She nodded and sighed. "Yes. That's what brought me in. He has quite the collection. Do you buy used books?"

"Sometimes," I said. "First editions and collectables for sure. Just depends. Feel free to bring them in."

I turned to grab the empty boxes and head to the back when she said, "Are you sure we haven't met?"

I wanted to say something silly, like "I'm sure I would remember meeting someone as lovely as you," but that's not the kind of cheesy line I would have said even when I was young. The feeling surprised me. A lot. I still missed Paula in too many ways to count.

"We have now," I said, turning back and extending my hand. "My name is Will Major."

She took my hand, her grip quite strong. "Clair Smith."

I blame it on the change of names, my first and her last. This was the second time we had met, and while she had an inkling, I was clueless.

The former home of Evan Michaels had a smell to it. It was dark, sour, biological, and strong. It was a very human smell but not the good kind, not even the bad kind. It was the horrible kind. It was the smell of failing biology. It was the smell of death.

It hit me hard the moment I walked in. Clair Smith had called the next day asking if I would come view the collection since it was so large.

When you run a business, you have a lot of rules, a lot of premade decisions that are in place to save you from the cognitive load of making those rote decisions and saving capacity for the novel problems that hit you all the time. And my answer to this question was always no. But I had said yes. And because of our bump yesterday, I brought coffee and had a cup in each hand. After Clair opened the door and I stepped in, I smelled that horrible smell.

The reason the smell hit me so hard was because I knew it well. Paula had wanted to die at home, and I had gotten to know that smell, and it had taken me months to clear it out of the house and even longer to clear it out of my nose. The smell was one of the things that haunted me most about her death.

I didn't get far into the house, just to the tiled entryway. I didn't see much, a mirror on the wall, a dark bookshelf with a ceramic bowl that had some keys in it, pegs on the wall a little further in with a red down jacket hanging from it.

I couldn't breathe. My chest clamped up. I felt like I was dying.

Clair Smith was there saying things to me, but I don't remember any of her words. They were urgent, short words filled with concern. I remember shaking my head. I remember trying to speak and it coming out as something strangled and ugly. My hands clenched up and hot coffee went everywhere, scalding my hands. I stumbled backwards out of the house and fell into the snow.

A thought hit me as I struggled to breathe, as my chest felt like a rhino was squatting on it. It was a simple little thought. *Here I come, Paula.*

It was a stupid thought. For me, at least.

I am decidedly unsure about the afterlife. From my point of view it's way too hopeful of a thing that doesn't really jive with the reality of life. Maybe there is one, maybe there isn't, but I seriously doubt us lowly, fallible humans with our many, many versions of what it might be have it right.

And then I heard a voice. A female voice tight with empathy, wet with pending tears.

"Will! Will! Stay with me, Will!"

Maybe this is just a story I am telling myself, but it felt like that voice was calling me back. That without that voice I would have died and found out if there was an afterlife... or not.

And then I saw eyes, blue eyes that were like the crystalline sky behind them that was framing the face that contained those eyes. That face was vigorously freckled and liberally wrinkled and those eyes were so familiar and compelling.

"The ambulance is coming," those eyes said. I know eyes can't speak, I knew it in that moment, but it felt like those blue-blue eyes were speaking to me. "Stay with me, Will!"

Because of those eyes I wanted to stay.

It wasn't like they were like Paula's hazel eyes. It wasn't the past calling but the future.

I tried to speak. I tried to tell those eyes I would love to stay with them if I could, but it came out as something that sounded like, "Occack-ack."

HOSPITALS ARE EMBARRASSING FOR THE PATIENT.

Your dignity doesn't matter. At all. Your modesty is irrelevant. Your comfort is just in the way. Survival at all costs is the order of the day.

Being a patient in a hospital is like being swallowed by a machine that seems to be barely interested in you as a person, just in your numbers, just in what is "vital" about you.

I'm not saying it shouldn't be that way. When your mission is to save lives, you have to discard a lot of niceties. And I'm not saying everyone in a hospital is like that, there are a lot of beautiful caring souls there, but the system itself tends to strip you of your basic dignity and anonymize you in the name of survival.

That smell I was hit with in the former home of Evan Michaels is the worst smell in the world for me. The second worst smell is the smell of a hospital. It's those same biological scents masked with strong cleaner and a heavy dose of antiseptic on top.

After Paula came home for hospice, it was my fervent hope that I would never set foot in a hospital again, much less enter one feet first on a gurney with a metaphorical rhino still squatting on my chest.

I soon found myself in a small curtained area hooked to

machines, with an IV in my arm, and Clair Smith standing nervously next to my bed.

My clothes had been taken and I was wearing one of those ass-exposing hospital gowns, but since I was in bed covered in a worn sheet and a thin blanket, at least exposure of my old ass wasn't eminent.

"Sorry," I said, my voice a froggy croak. I was still in a lot of pain and was having trouble breathing, but it wasn't as bad as it had been.

"Don't be," Clair said, a small smile on her face.

It might seem like a weird thing, but I noticed that she had nice lips. They weren't thin, barely-there lips, and they weren't overly plump augmented lips. They were just nice, real lips a proper shade of red. Whether she had lipstick on or not, I couldn't tell.

When I was sure I was dying, I had been obsessed with her eyes and now I was obsessed with her lips while so very vulnerable and lying in a hospital bed. What the hell was going on?

"I called the store," she said. "It was the only number I knew to call. Someone named Jannie said she's on the way and will call your daughter."

"Thank you," I said.

I must have been staring at her because she looked behind her like she was making sure it was her I was looking at.

"I'm sorry," I said again, my voice a little clearer.

"Do I have something on my face?" she asked, patting at those lips I had been staring at.

"No," I said. "There is something familiar about you."

"Right?" she said with a furrow of her brow, taking a step closer to the bed. "I can't figure it out, but it feels like we met before. Like we did something important together."

I nodded, trying to push back the vulnerability and embarrassment of my situation and focus on this intriguing mystery.

My hands hurt from the spilt coffee. I wanted to pull them out and examine them, but I couldn't bear any more vulnerability. At least not physical vulnerability because I said, "I think I owe you an explanation for what happened back there."

She bit her very nice lower lip and nodded.

"My wife, Paula," I said. "She died just over two years ago. At home. She had pancreatic cancer. The smell of the house took me back to... well...."

"I'm so sorry," she said. "I've been trying to air the place out. That terrible smell just won't leave."

"It takes a while," I said.

"So you don't think it was a heart attack?" she asked.

"Honestly," I said, doing my best to put some energy into my voice, "I'm rooting for a panic attack. Way easier to deal with."

She cocked her head to the side and stared at me.

"What?" I asked, looking around like she just had. "Do I have something on my face?"

She laughed. It was brief but her cheeks got rounder and her eyes narrower, and I wanted to hear her laugh more.

"Nothing on your face," she said. "It's just that my late husband, Al, he would have hoped for the heart attack, not wanting to be the kind of person who has a panic attack."

I did my best to smile. "I used to be that way," I said. "But life has tenderized me quite a bit in the last few years."

"I hear you," she said with a knowing nod.

We chatted until Jannie arrived and then she graciously excused herself.

I missed her presence when she was gone, and I felt so very guilty about that.

JANNIE CLARK WAS A TWENTY-YEAR-OLD NEO-GOTH GIRL with dark brown eyes, jet black hair, black lipstick, and enough piercings and tattoos to make an old guy like me rather uncomfortable.

She was petite, slim, and favored black jeans and black tops with some kind of lace involved.

Her favorite holiday was Halloween, her favorite movies were *Beetlejuice* and *Labyrinth*, and she loved Edgar Allan Poe.

Paula had hired her as a part-time employee at Major Books when she was fifteen. After Paula got sick, Jannie stepped up and kept the place afloat while cancer ravaged Paula's body and our lives. At this point she was the official manager of Major Books, and I both loved her like a daughter and didn't quite understand her just like my own daughter.

"Mr. Major," she said after Clair left. "You still got game!"

Jannie liked to call me "Mr. Major." I think at first it was part of her Mormon upbringing that she was starting to shake off. After that I think it was because she liked the way it sounded.

"What?" I asked, my voice back to normal, the rhino having vacated the vicinity of my chest and gone to squat on some other chump.

"Red likes you," Jannie said, her thick dark eyebrows wagging. "I mean, here you are having epically embarrassed yourself, laid out in a hospital bed, and you're making her laugh."

My cheeks felt hot and I shook my head. "She's just being nice."

"Calling 9-1-1 and calling me was 'just being nice,'" she said. "Hanging out with you in a freaking E.R. after knowing you for five minutes is more than being nice."

"Freaking" wasn't the word Jannie wanted to use but that Mormon upbringing was still exerting its influence.

I kept denying what Jannie had to say, and she kept insisting it was true until the doctor came in and gave me the good news that it had only been a panic attack and that my hands were not badly burned from the coffee and just needed a special salve.

Satisfied that I wasn't dying, Jannie went back to the bookstore and I got to lie in the hospital bed wondering if I had made Clair

Smith laugh, and, in equal parts, hoping that I had and feeling terribly guilty about it.

I LOVE MY WIFE.

To this day I love her. Shortcomings, flaws, and all, I love her and I think I will love her until the day I die. And depending on the afore-mentioned afterlife thing, maybe even after I die.

For the first year after her death, I wasn't sure that I would always love her, not in a bright or wistful way. The last fifteen months of her life were hellish—there is really no other word to describe it—and after her passing that is what stuck with me the most, and that damn smell.

But then the trauma began to fade and I remembered how we had met in high school putting on a production of *Our Town*. I played George Gibbs and she played Emily Webb. It was the six weeks of practice and all the scenes together that got me through my awkward teenage shyness. It is bitterly ironic that George loses Emily in that play, and decades before I lost Paula we had played it over and over and over again.

I remembered the long-distance years when we went to colleges in different states. I remembered our small wedding held in an aspen grove, the gray clouds only threatening to douse us in rain. I remembered the hard years of getting my accounting practice going while Paula taught at the local grade school. I remembered Paula's pregnancy and when April, our only child, was born. I remembered her burning passion to create a bookstore in our small mountain town and her insistence that "Major Books" was the perfect name. And most of all I remembered all the hard days that were made bearable by having a steady partner to walk the exceedingly bumpy and winding road of life with.

It wasn't a perfect marriage, not in the normal way you might think of the word "perfect," but Paula insisted it was. When asked about it she would say something like, "It's a perfect marriage because we still love each other and we're still married. And more importantly, we still really like each other. No one gets out of life without a lot of bruises and bashes. A perfect marriage is one that lasts with love and companionship intact. Period."

And ours did last until death did she part.

This was why I felt guilty about my obsession with Clair's eyes and her lips. I had loved. I had lived with a wonderful partner. And it had ended, as it must. Starting something new just felt wrong. Even thinking about starting something new felt wrong.

So when I got out of the hospital later that day, I went about my life trying to forget about Clair and her crystalline blue eyes and her lovely expressive lips.

———

"OKAY, HERE'S THE FIRST EDITIONS."

We don't have an office at Major Books, and I was behind the counter going over the bookkeeping Jannie had been doing. I was deep in the numbers—which I still really loved doing—and little else besides the words and a loud thump on the counter had registered.

When I looked up, Clair Smith was standing in front of me with her lovely blue eyes and fascinating lips, her gray-streaked curly red hair escaping out of a white knit hat with a big yarn pompom on top.

My mind was in a strange state and I just sat there staring at her hat blinking too much, my brain trying to draw at the many decades old memory of our glorious day on Sledder's Hill.

"Will," she said. "Are you okay? Please don't make me call 9-1-1 again."

I smiled and met her crystalline blue eyes. "I'm just fine. And please excuse my most ungraceful display of PTSD. I hope the coffee I spilled didn't damage anything."

"No harm at all," she said with a small smile. "But take some of these books off my hands and we'll call it even."

"Done," I said, pulling a first edition copy of *Murder Is Easy* by Agatha Christie out of the sizeable box. It was a bit worn, as you would expect, but in good shape. I carefully opened it and found that it was signed and the signature looked authentic. "Okey-dokey. This is worth real money," I said.

"How much?" Clair asked.

"Conservatively," I said. "Ten grand."

Clair stood there staring at me, blinking too much.

"Are you okay?" I asked. "I'd hate to have to call 9-1-1."

She shook her head. "Seriously?"

I nodded. "Yeah."

The next thing I pulled out was a 1931 first edition of Dashiell Hammett's *The Maltese Falcon*. "This one isn't signed but it's probably worth close to a thousand."

She was blinking too much again and staring at the book. The cover really didn't look like much compared to new books, but I love those old, simple covers.

"Really," I said, so deep in the moment that there was no room for guilt. "And I'd be happy to call 9-1-1 and return the favor."

She shook her head again and placed her hand on mine. "You have no idea, Will. This is just the best news. My uncle had considerable debt and this will make all the difference. Can you help me?"

"Of course," I said, the treacherous words sneaking out before my guilt could snap in and stop them. The fact of the matter was I really liked the feel of her hand on mine. "It's going to take some time to get accurate values and figure out how to approach this."

"I've got five more boxes in the car," she said. "Why don't I get us some coffee."

I have rules as to how I run my business. I do buy rare and collectable books, but I never go through them with the customer. I do that when the store is empty and no one is here. But it seemed my rules and my guilt were out the door.

I felt like a teenager again. All I wanted was for those amazing blue eyes to connect with mine while she touched my hand again.

After Clair left, Jannie sidled up and whispered, "Mr. Major still got game."

"Jannie!" I said, using my dad voice.

"You need to invite her to the Feast," she said. "She would come. I can totally feel it."

I shooed her off, pushing the thought away, and dug into the box of beautiful old books.

———

THERE IS A TRADITION PAULA INSTIGATED AFTER WE opened the store. It's called the Major Christmas Eve Feast. We move some racks and set up long tables in the center aisle of the bookstore for friends and family and we have a meal together.

There are four rules to the Major Christmas Eve Feast. No talking politics. No talking religion. You must wear an ugly Christmas sweater. And absolutely no presents. As Paula used to say, "Your presence is our present."

It's a potluck, everyone bringing food and wine, all of us crowded around the table amongst the books and decorations with lots of love and laughter.

That tradition had been on hiatus for the last two years, but Jannie and my daughter April begged me to bring it back and I relented because I really missed it.

Christmas Day is for your family of origin, but the Major Christmas Eve Feast is for the family we have created here at the bookstore.

And honestly, that was what Paula wanted to create with Major

Books. A family. We have local author readings, book clubs, story time for kids, jigsaw puzzle nights, and many more events.

The store is mostly books but really it's all about community.

All of this is to say that the Major Christmas Eve Feast was a big deal for the store and an expression of what we were trying to do, so it had to come back even without Paula, but the thought of inviting another woman to it was approaching sacrilegious. If I could invite another woman into that part of my life, what part of my life couldn't I invite another woman into and what did that say about my "perfect" marriage with Paula?

CLAIR SMITH AND I SPENT MUCH OF THE NEXT TWO AND A half days going through her uncle's collection of collectable books.

I love books, so much, so there is little else I would rather do in this world than to spelunk through a collection this rich.

And Clair? Well, she was smart, funny, and so very easy to be with. It was a delight to spend all those hours behind the counter with her, looking at books, searching for them on the Internet, determining pricing, typing them all into our inventory system.

We talked a lot too. It wasn't quite like the six weeks of practice I did with Paula for "Our Town" but I'm much older and it doesn't take as long to break through my shell.

I found out that she was actually born in Colorado but moved to California when she was a kid. She had studied to be a chef but got burned out on the long hours of running her own restaurant and sold it after her husband died. She was a real estate agent now. She had one son, Charles, and had only been married once.

When things were quiet, our conversations got downright intimate.

"How did your husband die?" I asked one evening. It was late and the store was closed, just the two of us sitting on stools behind the counter, our elbows touching now and then.

Her brow furrowed and she slowly shook her head.

"I'm sorry," I said. "Feel free not to answer. I... I just don't know too many other people my age who have lost their spouse."

She smiled, but it was a dim thing, her blue eyes no longer crystalline but haunted. "It was a rare rainy day in L.A.," she said, taking a deep breath and licking her lips. "Oil builds up on the road and if it's been a while since it rained, the roads get weirdly slick, not that anyone will ever slow down."

"A traffic accident," I offered since it was clear this was hard for her to talk about.

She nodded. "He was in a coma for six days and three hours before he died."

"I'm so sorry," I said.

"Thank you," she said, leaning against me a little, our shoulders touching. "And I'm sorry about Paula. I can't imagine dealing with doctors and procedures and hospitals for that long. The week I spent with Al was more than I could bear."

"But you move on," I said.

She nodded. so I added, "If you are alive, you have to keep living."

She nodded and said, "I like that."

"Paula used to say it all the time," I said. "Especially when things got tough."

Clair straightened up and pulled out another book, a second edition of *The Hobbit*. Evan Michaels didn't just read mysteries.

We were back to business then. This kind of thing happened multiple times. It was like there were two ghosts in the store with us, even when we were alone. My dead wife and her dead husband.

There was an undeniable attraction, but once we started getting closer, the past and its ghosts would insert itself between us.

CHRISTMAS EVE DAY CAME COLD AND BRIGHT AND I found myself, much to my surprise, on a ski slope with the undulating forested land flowing off to the horizon, the sky bright and blue.

After two-and-a-half days, Clair and I got through her uncle's collection of books, made a plan, and put the books up for sale. A few in the bookstore, some on our website, and most on eBay.

If I am being honest, it was the best few days I had had since Paula died. I felt younger than I had in ages and couldn't help but smile as I breathed in the frigid air through my nose.

This morning of skiing was Clair's "thank you" for dealing with the books. I told her it wasn't necessary, but she insisted and Jannie did her part to get me to say yes.

It had been sleds for me up until I was eleven when I discovered skis. It's everything that I love about sledding magnified, but the truth is, it had been before Paula got sick that I had put the skis on.

Clair was next to me, her white pompomed beanie on, the one that kept tickling the memory I couldn't quite retrieve. She had a red down jacket on, red ski pants, and some expensive reflective sunglasses. Her curly red hair was somewhat contained in a ponytail and she had a big smile on her face looking over this land that was so familiar to me.

That moment felt so comfortable. It was like I had known her forever and I couldn't explain why.

"Race ya?" she asked, a smile playing on her lovely lips.

I blinked and stared. Her smile widened showing off her perfect teeth.

"Race ya, Billy?" she asked, using the name I used to have and it all clicked into focus. Finally.

"Clair..." I began. "Clair Thompson?"

She didn't answer but laughed and launched herself down the

slope. "Clair Thompson!" I shouted, the two words filled with more delight than all the words I had said in the last two years combined.

I suddenly felt like a kid again and the connection I had with this woman finally made sense. I launched myself down the slope after her with abandon.

Clair and I had the best day of skiing ever. We spent the whole morning racing down the steepest, trickiest runs. She was an excellent skier, but so was I despite the hiatus, my body remembering the glory of the icy wind in my face, the swoosh of the skis against the snow, the epic inspiring views.

We ended our beautiful morning of competition the same way we he had when we were kids, with each of us having the same number of wins and big smiles on our faces. How could it be any different?

"Best day of skiing ever?" Clair asked.

We were back in front of the bookstore with Clair's Prius loaded and ready to go. She wanted to be back in Los Angeles for Christmas.

Things were busy with last-minute shoppers out in force all over our quaint, historic, red-bricked downtown, enough snow still present to make the whole scene snow globe worthy. The wrought iron street lamps were wrapped in colorful oversized red and green ribbons and several different Christmas songs floated on the breeze to us. It was all quite perfect.

"The best," I said. "I feel like a new man. How long have you known?"

"I figured it out yesterday," she said. "All that time in the bookstore and I finally noticed your old sled up on the wall."

"Why didn't you say anything?" I asked.

"I... I..." She looked away. Clair was not a shy woman, so I was confused. "I wanted to see if you figured it out. Do you get that?"

And I didn't get it.

Why was it important to her for me to figure it out? Shouldn't solving the mysterious connection between us be something to share and celebrate?

That day on Sledder's Hill had meant something to me and I would have been nothing but excited if she had told me.

And then a thought crept into my mind, one that made the day colder and the sun dimmer. What if that day didn't mean much to her? What if she didn't tell me directly for that very reason?

"I don't understand," I said, feeling the few words fall flat and the Christmas cheer around me look suddenly dull.

She looked away and bit her lip and said, "Just thought it would be fun if you figured it out too, but then time ran out." She ended in a weak shrug.

I knew that wasn't it, but I felt this pull to be in the bookstore. April was there and I hadn't seen my daughter in six months and I missed her. The awaiting Major Christmas Eve Feast needed attending to.

At that moment, I blamed my restlessness on that, but I was clearly fooling myself. While I longed for connection and partnership it scared the absolute hell out of me. I'm not a kid anymore. I realized that saying "hello" to love meant that someday you will say "good-bye" to it. This wasn't some theoretical concept in my brain. I had done it and it was terrible.

"I should get moving," Clair said, her eyes darting to the windows of the bookstore and back.

"Okay…" I said, feeling just as awkward as I had when I was eight and she was nine after our day of epic sledding.

And then she was hugging me. Tight. And I hugged back and I felt a little like the Grinch when his heart grew several sizes and I didn't care anymore why she didn't tell me when she figured out our connection.

I stood there struggling to find words to go with my feelings, but then she was in her car and driving away.

APRIL MAJOR'S HAIR WAS PIXIE SHORT AND BLOND, BOTH rather large changes since I saw her last, but I would recognize her anywhere. She has so much of her mother in her, not just her adorable upturned nose and hazel eyes, but in the way she talks and sees the world. So much so that it often takes my breath away.

She was readying for the upcoming event with the obligatory ugly Christmas sweater on. It was Christmas red with a bright green Christmas tree with lights that blinked.

She was at the back of the store fussing over the potted fir tree, applying a few more ornaments.

"Daddy!" she shouted when she saw me, running across the store and hugging me so fiercely.

She didn't take her mother's illness well, but after Paula died we had taken turns pulling each other out of the pit of despair. I like to think that our closeness is one of the gifts of that terrible event.

I hugged her back and told her I loved her and that I was so glad to see her.

"Where's Clair?" April asked. "Jannie was sure you'd invite her for tonight. I want to meet this mysterious woman from your past. Jannie says the last few days have been like having the old you back."

I was looking at my twenty-five-year-old daughter but it was almost like I was seeing her mother. Paula could be shockingly practical about things.

One night when it was quite clear that the end was near, Paula said, "Don't be afraid to love again."

"There's only you for me," I had said.

She'd shaken her head, her sallow complexion and the hospital bed that had taken over our small living room speaking volumes. "You are a man who thrives in partnership. Don't be afraid to love again."

"I... Uhhh..." I stammered while my daughter stared at me.

"Mr. Major chickened out," Jannie said from behind me. "Red is so into you, all you have to do is take a chance."

But saying hello to love meant saying goodbye. Could I bear to say goodbye to another partner? What if it didn't work out? What if it did? Could I bear to live the rest of my life alone?

"Where is she, Dad?" April asked.

"She... she left," I said, suddenly longing to see her crystalline blue eyes again. "She's on her way back to California."

"Well then go get her," my sweet daughter said. Her round face sparking another memory, really a series of memories. Paula adored rom-coms. She was quite clear that sometimes you just have to have a happy ending and nothing else will do. There is often a point in those movies where someone, usually the man, would act dense or stupid, would turn away from love that was right in front of him and my Paula would yell at the TV, saying something like, "Go after her dummy! Kiss her already!"

"But..." I stammered, the only word I could get out.

"Mom talked to me about this," April said, her voice pitched low so only I could hear her. "Before... You know... She made me promise that if you found a spark that I would do everything in my power to see that it took hold. So William Major, you either go after this woman or I'm going to do it for you."

I swear that April was channeling her mother with that last sentence. Paula only used my given name when she really wanted to get my attention.

I didn't hesitate. I ran out of Major Books looking to see if the spark could be nurtured into a flame, knowing full well that saying hello to love means someday saying goodbye, but also knowing that a single day with love in your life is worth many, many days without it.

WHEN I RAN OUT OF MAJOR BOOKS, I ENVISIONED HAVING to run to my car, which was parked several blocks away where I wouldn't have to pay for parking, getting on the highway, and driving like a maniac east until I found Clair's car.

The cold air hit me like a slap because I left without my coat, but there was no way I was going back.

Instead of a high-speed chase, I got half a block away and found Clair Smith purposefully striding towards me with her jaw set and her cheeks flushed red.

"Look," she said before I could get a word out. "I want to make one thing clear. I wanted you to remember that day on Sledder's Hill on your own because in all my years I have never experienced that easy a connection with another human being.

"I have never forgotten that day and I was worried that you had. I was worried it didn't mean the same thing to you.

"But I get it. It's complicated. We aren't young. We live in different states. We have baggage. We have the trauma of having lost love before, but I think that love is—"

Her monologue came to an abrupt halt and she was staring at me. I think it was because of the silly grin on my face.

"What?!" she demanded.

"I feel the same way," I said as a shiver passed through me. Maybe from the cold, maybe from the moment, maybe from both. Mariah Carey's "All I Want for Christmas is You" was playing and a few lazy snowflakes started falling.

"You do?" she asked.

"Yes," I said. "I'm sorry I couldn't put together why you were so familiar, but I felt it. Believe me, I felt it. And I have to tell you I'm scared to feel again. So scared. But maybe there was a reason we had that amazing day almost fifty years ago. Maybe...."

I couldn't continue. I didn't have the words. While I love to read, I am no poet.

"Maybe what?" she asked taking a step closer to me.

"Maybe I should kiss you now," I said, feeling my cheeks flush red.

"Maybe I should kiss *you*," she said. "Wanna race and see who kisses who first?"

And then there was no more talking, no more need for words as we let our lips express what words could not.

THE MAJOR CHRISTMAS EVE FEAST WAS AMAZING. THERE were fifteen of us crowded into the central aisle of the bookstore with our decked-out live Christmas tree standing as sentinel over the proceedings. The table was a smorgasbord of delightful food and even better company.

Clair fit in like she was one of the gang, and I was happier than I had been in years.

Clair and I were sitting together in the middle of the table with Jannie at the head of one end of the table and April at the head of the other. At one point after our bellies were full and several glasses of wine had been drunk, I looked down at April and I swear it was Paula looking back at me.

Clair had just kissed me on the cheek and given me a side-hug that made me feel young again. I have no idea where the spark will lead but I am dedicated to nurturing it to the best of my ability.

April's eyes locked with mine and she smiled and gave me an approving nod, and it felt like it was Paula, like one of the ghosts that had been between Clair and I had given me her blessing.

I will always love Paula. Always. We had our "perfect" marriage where we always loved each other, always liked each other, and always worked on our relationship.

But maybe, just maybe, there was another "perfect" relationship waiting for me. One that had started nearly fifty years ago when two kids had the best day of sledding ever.

. . .

ROBERT J. MCCARTER IS THE AUTHOR OF MORE THAN
*fifteen novels and over one hundred and fifty short stories. He is a
regular contributor to* Pulphouse Fiction Magazine *and his short
fiction has also appeared in* The Saturday Evening Post, Andromeda
Spaceways Inflight Magazine, Everyday Fiction, *and numerous
anthologies.*

*Robert writes in a variety of genres from contemporary fantasy to
science fiction and just about everything in between. His diverse background—including a career in software engineering, growing up on a
ranch riding horses, and acting—colors the stories he tells.*

*He lives in the mountains of Arizona with his amazing wife and
his ridiculously adorable dogs. Find out more at https://robertjmc
carter.com/*

About this story, Robert says:

*"My first thought for this story was to write a second-chance
romance between two older people. Love is love, of course, but I think
there are some fascinating differences that come with age. Age brings
more experience, and those experiences can get in the way of and also
facilitate finding a real connection. Being a bit older myself these days,
I like to think the results of those extra years as 'experience' or 'character'
rather than 'baggage.'*

*"The sledding aspect of this story was inspired by my own love of
real sleds and the very steep hills I raced down as a child in a lovely
mountain town very much like the one in this story, a town I still call
home."*